To Jennifer —

[handwritten inscription]

SERVANT

THE CHRONICLES OF SERVITUDE BOOK ONE

J. S. BAILEY

[signature] J Bailey
7/27/2019

OPEN WINDOW

Livonia, Michigan

SERVANT

Published by Open Window
an imprint of BHC Press

Library of Congress Control Number:
2017938467

ISBN-13: 978-1-946848-08-6
ISBN-10: 1-946848-08-5

Visit the author at:
www.jsbaileywrites.com &
www.bhcpress.com

Also available in eBook and audio

Book design by Blue Harvest Creative
www.blueharvestcreative.com

ALSO BY J.S. BAILEY

NOVELS
Rage's Echo
The Land Beyond the Portal
Sacrifice
The Chronicles of Servitude, Book Two
Surrender
The Chronicles of Servitude, Book Three

NOVELLAS
Solitude
A Chronicles of Servitude Story

SHORT STORY COLLECTIONS
Ordinary Souls

MULTI-AUTHOR ANTHOLOGIES
Through the Portal
Call of the Warrior
In Creeps the Night
A Winter's Romance
The Whispered Tales of Graves Grove
Tales by the Tree

This story is for Nathan. He knows why.

There are different kinds of gifts, but the same Spirit distributes them. There are different kinds of service, but the same Lord. There are different kinds of working, but in all of them and in everyone it is the same God at work.

Now to each one the manifestation of the Spirit is given for the common good. To one there is given through the Spirit a message of wisdom, to another a message of knowledge by means of the same Spirit, to another faith by the same Spirit, to another gifts of healing by that one Spirit, to another miraculous powers, to another prophecy, to another distinguishing between spirits, to another speaking in different kinds of tongues, and to still another the interpretation of tongues. All these are the work of one and the same Spirit, and he distributes them to each one, just as he determines.

—1 Corinthians 12:4-11, New International Version

"Then I asked, 'Who are you, Lord?'
"'I am Jesus, whom you are persecuting,' the Lord replied. 'Now get up and stand on your feet. I have appeared to you to appoint you as a servant and as a witness of what you have seen and will see of me. I will rescue you from your own people and from the Gentiles. I am sending you to them to open their eyes and turn them from darkness to light, and from the power of Satan to God, so that they may receive forgiveness of sins and a place among those who are sanctified by faith in me.'

—Acts 26:15-18, New International Version

1

GRAHAM WILLARD had a decision to make.

He stared out his bedroom window at the rain falling upon the yard and surrounding woods. The moon peeked through a gap in the storm clouds, illuminating the pair of rain-washed automobiles parked in front of the detached garage at the bottom of the hill. The man tried to remember if he'd left his Grand Marquis unlocked and hoped that he had. It would enable a speedier getaway.

He drew back from the window and dragged in a deep breath. Not so long ago, making a decision such as this would have taken him no longer than a second. If asked the same question he was now asking himself, he would have responded with a resounding "No!" and gone about his business as if nothing improper had been suggested.

But the seed of an idea had taken root in his mind, planted by an invisible hand that came from nowhere. It arrived during breakfast on a sunny morning that dawned after a long week of rain, when the grass outside the dining room window was so speckled with dew that it looked like tiny pieces of the sun had fallen from the sky and come to rest among the blades. He could remember it quite clearly: he'd asked the young man to bring him more sugar for his coffee, and when the lad's back was turned he suddenly imagined himself lifting a gun and firing it into the back of his skull.

At first he'd waved the idea away as he would a pesky insect, dismissing it as the fantasy of an aging mind. He would never do it. The young man was his friend. He loved him much in the way that a grandfather would cherish his grandchildren.

But the pesky insect would not go away. The seed planted itself and began to grow.

His heart continued to pound. Yes, maybe he could do it. His friend would not suspect a thing until it was too late. But if the young man's heart could be changed . . .

That was it. He would give the young man a choice. If he chose wrong, he would die.

With a trembling hand, the old man picked up the gun that lay on his bedside table and made his way toward the door.

———— ✦ ————

THE WALL clock ticked away the time like a beating heart. Most people would be wrapped in the mantle of dreams at this hour, but Randy Bellison found comfort in sitting at his desk in the finished basement-slash-office as he read through the New Testament as part of his quest to pick out a decent passage for his and Lupe Sanchez's as-of-yet unscheduled wedding. The verse would have to be unique, as was their relationship. Forget Corinthians. 1 Peter 4:8 sounded like a worthier candidate.

And above all things have fervent love for one another, for love will cover a multitude of sins.

Behind and above him, the basement door opened and closed and was followed by the sound of soft footsteps. Maybe Graham Willard thought he'd fallen asleep down here and didn't want to wake him up. Graham could be a night owl too, but unlike Randy, the older man was pushing seventy-four. He was lucky to have lived that long. Many in their profession hadn't seen thirty, or even twenty-five.

Randy continued reading while Graham's unmistakable shuffle crept up behind him. What was he doing, trying to scare him? Randy wouldn't offer him the pleasure, so he kept his gaze fixed on the Bible in front of him and pretended to have lost his hearing.

A minute passed. Then another. He could hear the old man breathing a few feet behind him.

Randy turned another page even though he hadn't read anything since Graham came down the stairs. Keep up the illusion of ignorance. It would drive Graham bonkers.

Graham finally cleared his throat. "Randy." Years of smoking had blessed Graham with a gravelly voice, but tonight it held a hoarse note that made it sound like he'd been crying.

Randy heaved a melodramatic sigh and swiveled the chair around to face his mentor. "What—"

The question died on his lips. Sweat dampened Graham's gray hair and forehead, and the armpits of his baggy white t-shirt bore additional signs of excessive perspiration. He held a gun in front of him, with the barrel pointed at Randy's head.

Randy felt the hair on his scalp stand on end. "What's going on?"

Thin red blood vessels traced their way through the sclera of Graham's eyes. "Hold up your hands."

At first Randy wondered if this was another of Graham's jokes. For all he knew, the weapon could have been a harmless replica. "What if I don't?"

"Then I'll blow your head off."

The harsh tone of Graham's voice told Randy that this was no joke.

Randy put up his hands, wondering if all the neurons in Graham's seventy-four-year-old brain had started firing the wrong way. "You know what'll happen if I die before finding someone to replace me."

Graham smiled, revealing two rows of nicotine-stained teeth. "If you step down, I won't shoot you."

For a few seconds the only sound in the basement was the ceaseless ticking of the clock. Randy's mind raced to find the root of Graham's intentions. Stepping down without a replacement would have the same repercussions as if he died without one. Why would Graham even suggest such a thing? How could he?

Randy silently cursed his failure to find someone else. He'd set his sights on a couple of people in the past few years but after some consideration he'd decided that neither would fit the job. Lupe suggested on a daily basis that he hurry and find a replacement—they couldn't marry until he did since his current duties would not permit him to devote himself entirely to her. And as much as Randy longed to finally wed her, he wasn't about to settle by replacing himself with the wrong man.

Graham still hadn't lowered the gun. His eyes no longer looked like wells of anguish. They were cold. Like daggers.

"Can you at least tell me what's going on?" Randy asked, trying not to look at the weapon too closely so he wouldn't lose his nerve. He hadn't even known Graham owned one.

Graham ignored him. "What's it going to be?" He coughed into the crook of one arm and then looked back to him, waiting with a confidence he hadn't shown when he first came down the stairs.

The answer was simple, even though Randy knew that by giving it he would die. "I'm not going to step down. I don't break my promises."

Suddenly Graham's brow furrowed as if he had briefly forgotten where he was. The look passed in an instant, and his eyes turned cold again. He lowered the gun to the height of Randy's chest. "Too bad. I didn't want to have to do this."

Pain seared through Randy's right shoulder before his brain could register the fact that Graham had fired the gun. Randy's vision doubled and a high-pitched ringing began to sound in his ears. "That wasn't my head," he hissed through clenched teeth, longing to scream but knowing it would further weaken him. Warmth spread down both his back and front—a sure indication that the bullet had passed all the way through his flesh.

"You'll die slower this way," Graham said, a note of indecision entering his voice. He lifted the gun, winced, and fired it again.

Something went numb somewhere in Randy's head, though that wasn't where the second bullet hit him. He slid out of the chair, ears continuing to ring from the sound of the shots. Graham's running footsteps ascended the stairs a million miles away, and the basement vanished in sudden darkness as the overhead lights winked out. A minute later he heard the engine of Graham's Grand Marquis cough and turn over out in the driveway.

Randy tried to pull himself to his feet but collapsed to the floor, gasping. The thought that he would be dead within minutes excited part of him because at last he would be in full communion with his Maker, never to suffer again. Yet the world he left behind would be thrown into turmoil at his passing, and he couldn't bear to let that happen when so many of his loved ones would have to endure it.

The carpet felt scratchy against his face. *I should ask Lupe to go out and buy a throw rug to cover up the big bloody stain,* he thought idly as dizziness filled his head. Only a few more minutes now and it would be over.

Even as his pulse slowed, his heart broke for Lupe. Her faith was not strong. She had been through so much already, and he knew that his death could very well break her.

Father, he prayed, not sure if he said it aloud or only in his head, *if it be your will, take me. But if not, I'd appreciate it if you gave me a hand—not for my benefit, but for all those who will suffer if I die.*

The image of Lupe's face wavered before him for a moment before dissolving into darkness. A jolt of energy entered his body in answer to his plea, and the pain lessened enough to allow him to focus on getting to a phone. He pulled himself onto his knees, and with the aid of his left arm, crawled in the direction of the staircase.

<hr />

EIGHT HUNDRED miles away, an anxious teenager sat in his apartment with a road atlas open on his lap. It was high time he moved on from the place he'd called home for the past eleven months because it wasn't home to him, not really. Unable to make up his mind on where to go next, he'd resorted to pulling the atlas out of his shelf and leaving his destination entirely up to fate.

He closed his eyes, riffled back and forth blindly through the pages, and stabbed a finger at one that felt right to him.

He cracked open one lid and found himself looking at a map of a state he had never been to. He leaned closer and made note of the town to which his finger pointed.

Autumn Ridge, Oregon. Sounded like a nice place.

He reached for a suitcase and started packing it.

2

ONE YEAR LATER

MANY BOYS he knew dreamed of being firemen and astronauts when they grew up, but deep down, Bobby Roland had always wanted to be a superhero.

The plan was simple. He would have a secret lair and identity (unassuming musician) and devote the rest of his time to helping those in need. He would help old ladies cross the street. He would scare off bank robbers with his self-taught karate moves. He would be adored by the public and lauded a champion of the people in the newspapers, which would fly off the stands and be read by citizens the world over.

He had even come up with a name for himself: Rescue Man. Because that's what he would do. Rescue people in whatever way necessary to ensure their protection.

Ah, the follies of childhood. If only he had known.

Bobby steered his way home through the driving rain, trying his best not to let his anger blind him to the perils of the wet road.

The condemning words repeated themselves in his mind like a broken record. *You're fired. You're fired. You're fired.*

Part of him wanted to cry. Part of him wanted to smash his fist into something soft and warm, preferably his former manager's face. But he'd just stood there, numb, and listened to the man's words like a truant schoolboy receiving a scolding from his principal.

Within his veins, however, his blood began to boil. He had only been doing the right thing. Rescue Man would have done the same, but Rescue Man did not exist.

He pulled into the driveway of his one-story rental bungalow at 10:17 pm. Funny how he'd only left for work half an hour before. Now he would be up all night with nothing to do but seethe.

A glow shined though the living room curtains. His roommate, Caleb Young, liked to stay up late studying. Bobby wondered how he would take the news.

He put the car in park and killed the engine. Caleb was generally a calm guy, but that didn't mean he would gladly pay all of the rent until Bobby had the luck to find more work. At least Bobby's frugal lifestyle had enabled him to put some cash away in savings. He could only hope it would last.

He dashed up the walk through the rain. Turned the key in the knob. Tried to take breaths to calm his simmering nerves, and swung the door open.

Caleb occupied his usual spot on the end of the squashed second-hand couch, his nose in a book called *Quantum Mechanics*. He claimed to be studying for a degree in liberal arts, but judging from the variety of tomes Bobby had seen him poring over during the months they'd known each other, the guy had to be taking every single course the college had to offer.

Caleb peered at him over the top of the book, his thick glasses magnifying his eyes so he looked like some kind of brown-haired insect. His expression seemed to ask, *Well?*

Bobby hesitated in the living room. Should he talk to Caleb now? No, he needed to meditate first. That's what you did when you were angry. Relax first, rant later. It might not feel as good initially, but in the end it was better than yelling and cursing.

He went into his bedroom and shut the door.

The room exuded stillness, just the way he liked it. He kept his few belongings in their proper places: band posters on the walls, papers in the filing cabinet, CDs and movies in the shelf beside his dresser. You could move around the country easier when you didn't have as much junk to haul. Clean easier, too.

He picked up a lighter and lit the unscented jar candle he kept on his nightstand, then got up and turned out the light. The flame of the burning wick spluttered and then grew longer and still.

Bobby sat down Indian-style on top of the bedclothes and stared at the flame for a long time. His hands, previously clenched into fists, began to loosen. His chest didn't feel as tight. Was he still angry with his boss's unfair treatment? Yes. Did he still feel like giving the man a black eye? Maybe a little.

Eventually he flopped onto his back and stared at the ceiling. "I suck at life," he muttered. His twenty-year span of existence had been one big failure. He had no friends, he had no girl, and now he didn't even have a job.

Only somewhere deep inside, he knew that this new bump in the road was no failure on his part. Failure resulted from poor decisions, and he didn't doubt that the one he'd made last night was the right one.

God, please don't let Caleb be angry with me when I tell him, he prayed. *Please make him understand.*

Out in the living room, the floor creaked and footsteps padded up to Bobby's door. Caleb said, "You all right?"

"I haven't figured that out yet," Bobby said, pulling himself back into sitting position.

The door swung open, and light from beyond filled the front end of the bedroom. "What are you doing in here, holding a séance?" Caleb stepped into the room but stayed near the doorway.

"Yeah, I was trying to contact the spirit of my old job. You can turn the light on."

Caleb did, and when Bobby faced him he could see a knowing glint in his roommate's eyes. "You got canned."

"Yeah."

"Sorry about that."

For some reason, Caleb's lack of anger made Bobby feel even guiltier than if the guy had started screaming obscenities in his face. "I'm the one who's sorry. I know you don't make much at the book-store, and—"

Caleb lifted a hand. "It's okay. These things happen." His relaxed attitude made it seem as though he'd anticipated the news and already come to accept it.

Bobby hadn't expected it at all. If anything, he'd expected praise for what he'd done. Just showed what he knew.

He jumped to his feet, feeling a sudden need to pace. His blood began simmering again. "How is it okay? I do the best I can to get by. I work my tail end off so we can pay the rent, and then BOOM! I'm out of a job!" He marched out of the room and over to the refrigerator in their small kitchen. He grabbed a Sprite out of the door just to have something to do. He wished it were gin.

Caleb had followed Bobby out of the bedroom and watched him without comment. Some days Bobby wondered if his room-mate was some kind of robot. The only time he'd ever seen Caleb display emotion was when they saw a story on the news about a young girl who had been brutally raped, stabbed, and left to die along the side of a nearby hiking trail.

Bobby remembered fear slicing through him as Caleb's face turned red and the can of root beer from which Caleb had been drinking crumpled like foil in his fist. "I'm glad I'm not in law enforcement," he'd said in a dark tone that made Bobby think that a very different Caleb Young lived inside the geeky college student. "Because if I caught him, I'd kill him just like he killed her."

Later on, Bobby had found the smashed can and marveled at how tightly Caleb had crushed it. He'd tried it out himself by trying to crush an empty Sprite can but only succeeded in cutting his palm when the metal split.

"It won't hurt you to lighten up a little," Caleb said, returning Bobby to the present. "You know it isn't the end of the world."

Bobby took a long swig of Sprite. "Tomorrow's another day, right?"

"You've just read my mind."

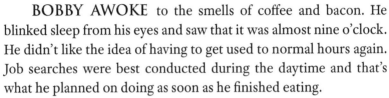

BOBBY AWOKE to the smells of coffee and bacon. He blinked sleep from his eyes and saw that it was almost nine o'clock. He didn't like the idea of having to get used to normal hours again. Job searches were best conducted during the daytime and that's what he planned on doing as soon as he finished eating.

Hopefully his new job would be at night, too. Something about being awake while the rest of the country lay asleep in their beds calmed him and gave him time to think.

Except when men with guns came to the restaurant.

He pulled on a shirt and went to the kitchen, where Caleb sat at the center island reading a newspaper spread out before him. A plate of bacon and eggs and a mug of coffee sat at Bobby's place. He sat down and murmured a quick thanks before taking a long draw of coffee.

"You might want to reheat that," Caleb said, nodding at the plate. "I didn't know when you'd be up."

Bobby plucked a crisp piece of bacon from the neat little stack Caleb had made and popped it in his mouth. "It's good enough for me. What's with the paper?"

Caleb lifted an eyebrow. "You lose your job, you see me looking at the wanted ads, and you can't figure out what I'm doing?"

Bobby chewed up the rest of the bacon in silence, not having an intelligent response to that.

Caleb's eyes lit up. "Here's one. Check it out." He circled a block of text with a pen and slid the paper across the tabletop.

Bobby scooted his plate aside and leaned forward. "St. Paul's Church is currently accepting applications for a maintenance position," he read. "Must be at least 18 and have reliable transportation." It told him to contact someone named Randy at the provided number.

Caleb watched him with great attentiveness. "Are you going to call him?"

"It's a *church*," Bobby said. Though he believed in God in the same way he believed the sun would rise in the morning, he didn't particularly enjoy visiting God's house for reasons he preferred not to contemplate at the moment.

"It's a job."

"I'm not a janitor."

Caleb crossed his arms.

"Fine," Bobby said to appease his roommate. "I'll call the guy and see if they're still looking for someone."

"Now that's the spirit, *hermano*," Caleb said as a crooked grin crossed his face. "That is the *spirit*."

ST. PAUL'S Church sat in an unfamiliar part of town along a street lined with massive trees. McDonald's cups and Subway wrappers collected in the gutters and a broken mailbox lay prone on a cracked sidewalk four blocks before he reached the church.

Bobby wondered if the houses along the stretch came with barred windows and giant dogs named Spike to keep the local riffraff out.

It was almost eight o'clock. Why Randy, the man whose number he'd called, had chosen this time of evening for Bobby to come in for an interview was beyond him, but Bobby didn't dare complain.

He whipped the car into the church lot with a squeal of tires and pulled into a space as close to the front steps and wheelchair ramp as possible, wishing he had a policeman's nightstick with him in case any trouble arose. The only other vehicle in the lot was a nondescript blue Ford sitting about twelve spaces to his left and two rows back from the church. Clearly Randy had no fears about thugs attacking him for his wallet. Maybe the guy was seven feet tall and a bodybuilder.

Bobby, not even half the size of a bodybuilder, stepped gingerly out of the car and dashed up the cement steps. Randy had told him he'd leave the door unlocked, and Bobby was grateful that Randy had kept that promise.

A cluster of rosy lights hanging from the ceiling lit the church entryway. A long table pushed against one wall held an array of pamphlets, and a large mural next to the entrance of the inner sanctuary portrayed a lifelike depiction of a robed man on horseback with an arm thrown across his face as a dazzling light shined down from above. The Conversion of Saul, if Bobby guessed correctly. Along with the Resurrection accounts, it was one of his favorite stories from the Bible.

"You like that?"

The voice made Bobby jump, and he turned.

The man he assumed to be Randy stood about six feet away. The guy looked about thirty and wore a black t-shirt emblazoned with a skull and roses and black boot-cut jeans. He had disheveled coffee-colored hair and bags under his eyes that gave him the appearance of not having slept well in years. Though he had well-muscled arms, he stood under six feet in height and didn't look capable of snapping anyone in half.

Bobby quickly regained his composure. "Yeah. You're Randy?"

The man nodded. "The one and only." He stepped forward and held out a callused hand. "And I presume you're either Bobby Roland or a lost soul seeking spiritual guidance." He winked, and Bobby felt himself relax.

They shook hands and then Randy checked his watch, which not surprisingly was also black. "And you're right on time, too. Come on back and let's get this started."

Bobby followed him down a side hallway and through a door into a small office cluttered with a mahogany desk sitting perpendicular to the door, three chairs, a computer, and a bookshelf so full that tomes were stacked multiple rows deep on each shelf.

Randy took a seat behind the desk. Bobby sat in one of the chairs across from him.

The chair groaned when Randy leaned back to get more comfortable. Bobby remained sitting ramrod straight, hoping his posture would help inspire the confidence he didn't feel.

The man studied him with hazel eyes. "So, Bobby, tell me why you're interested in this job."

Bobby took a deep breath. "Because I don't have one." That wasn't quite the way he'd wanted it to come out, and he cursed himself for not having rehearsed every last detail of this interview. "And I've got bills to pay."

"Makes sense. What's your employment history?"

"I worked at Gold Star Chili for two years when I was a teenager. That was back in Cincinnati. I grew up there."

Randy nodded. "I thought I detected some out-of-towner in your voice. Anything else?"

Bobby paused to check his mental resume, figuring that the few gigs he'd played in on the weekends here and there would bear no significance to this maintenance job. "I worked at a Burger King for about a week in New York. Hated the city so much that I got out of there in a heartbeat."

"Don't like crowds?"

"It wasn't that. The guy who lived in the apartment next to mine was murdered in the parking garage. Three gunshot wounds to the chest. I had nightmares about it."

Randy absently rubbed his right shoulder. "I can see why you left, and I'm very sorry to hear about your neighbor. That must have been terrible." The man cracked a sympathetic grin. "I bet you thought you'd go to the big city to carve out a new life for yourself and didn't realize you'd bitten off more than you could chew. Am I right?"

Boy, was this guy good at reading people. "That would be an affirmative."

"So what else have you got?"

"I lived in Utah for awhile. Nice scenery. I worked at a music store."

"And now you're here in the great State of Oregon."

"And now I'm here," Bobby agreed.

During the following seconds of silence, something like a flung pebble tapped against the office window, giving Bobby a start. He narrowed his eyes as he studied the closed blinds. Just what had done that?

"How long have you been here?" Randy asked, paying the sound no heed.

"Just over a year."

"And you haven't had a job this whole time? I wouldn't have pegged you for someone who's been living in a box."

Tap. The sound came again, further piquing Bobby's curiosity. "I wouldn't say I haven't had a job. My employment was terminated last night."

Randy's eyebrows rose. "You were fired?"

"Terminated sounds more sophisticated."

"No, it sounds more Schwarzenegger." He shook his head. "What happened?"

Bobby's pulse quickened. This interview would be over practically before it began. "I don't want to talk about it."

"I'm not willing to hire someone who has something to hide."

Tap. What the heck was out there? "Let's just say I violated company policy. I didn't hurt anyone and I didn't break the law, and if we could just forget about all that now, it would be great." In truth, Bobby didn't want to discuss what happened at the restaurant because he'd start ranting about the man who fired him and might say something that would make him look less desirable for this new job.

Randy rested his chin in one hand and continued to dissect Bobby with his stare. "Are you sure you didn't do anything illegal?"

"Not unless it's against the law to save someone's life."

This seemed to catch the man off guard. "What?"

"Forget about it. It's over."

"Fine, be that way. But since you obviously have no desire to sate my curiosity, could you at least tell me where you worked?"

Tap. This time it sounded like an object the size of a walnut hit the glass, and Bobby saw Randy flick an irritated gaze in the direction of the window, which if open would have given them a view of the parking lot.

"What is that?" Bobby asked.

Randy returned his gaze to Bobby. "Intimidation."

"What?"

Tap. "Ignore it."

"It sounds like someone's throwing rocks at the window."

Randy shrugged. "Rocks, sticks, whatever else they can find. I'm used to it."

"Who's 'they'?" *Tap.* "Thugs?"

Randy surprised him by letting out a chuckle. "Sure. Thugs." But if Bobby wasn't mistaken, the man's face had lost some of its color.

Tap.

Bobby stood up and went to the window to peer through the slats of the blinds, even though a voice in his head screamed at him to sit back down and finish the interview before Randy decided that Bobby shouldn't have the job after all. All he saw through the pane of glass was his and Randy's cars bathed in the yellow glow of the streetlights.

As he let the slats snap back into place, three louder taps sounded on the pane in quick succession like very large, very solid raindrops.

He yanked the slats apart again. Where could they be hiding? There was no way anyone could—

"Bobby, please sit down," Randy said in a quieter tone. "You're not going to see anything."

"But—"

"What is the name of the place that terminated your employment?"

Bobby clenched his teeth and returned to the chair. "It's called Arnie's Stop-N-Eat. They're open twenty-four hours a day so they get a lot of truckers and people who work the graveyard shift."

Tap-tap-tap. "I know the place. Over on Seventh, right?"

"Right." *Tap-tap-tap-tap.* "Don't your thugs ever get tired of that?"

"I said you need to ignore it."

"Why should I?" Bobby realized he'd been raising his voice, and his cheeks flushed.

Randy heaved a drawn-out sigh. "Do you know what poltergeist activity is?"

Bobby almost snorted. What kind of churchgoer would believe in that kind of thing, even if he was wearing a shirt bedecked with a grinning skull? "Sure. Angry ghosts throw your stuff around and make a mess of the place. You're saying that's who the thugs are?"

"Sort of, but not really. But it's probably best if you think of them like that."

Suddenly Bobby wasn't so sure he needed this particular job. "Uh, yeah. Is there a way to make them stop?"

"Praying hard about it tends to keep them at bay for awhile. They're like a bunch of bratty kids. You don't have anything to worry about though, since it's me they're after. As soon as I'm gone everything will be just peachy around here."

"What do you mean? I thought you might be the pastor." Albeit a very modern, unorthodox one.

The man grinned, his eyes shining with mirth. "Me, a pastor? I'd feel sorry for the congregation. I'm the maintenance guy, and will be until I hire a new one."

"Shouldn't the priest or pastor be in charge of that?"

Randy shrugged. "Father Preston and I have an understanding. He trusts me to make the right decisions that pertain to my job." He smiled. "For example, yesterday I decided not to hire an individual who showed up for his interview in flannel pajama bottoms."

Bobby looked down at himself to make sure he still looked presentable. He'd been smart to wear a button-down shirt and a tie with his khakis. He'd even used the iron on them before heading out.

Randy must have read his mind. "Don't worry, you're in good shape as long as you know how to push a vacuum and clean toilets and remember to show up when you're supposed to. Come on, I'll show you around and give you the gist of the place. You like it, come back tomorrow and I'll give you a key and your list of duties. You'll be on church payroll in no time."

As they rose from their respective chairs, it occurred to Bobby that the tapping sounds had finally ceased.

3

IT DIDN'T take long for Randy to give Bobby the grand tour, and soon they headed back to the parking lot, Bobby feeling immensely better than he had upon arrival. It was too bad that he and Randy wouldn't be working together. Something about the guy's jovial nature put him more at ease than he'd felt since that long-ago day when he'd found his neighbor's dead body lying on the parking garage pavement between a Smart Car and a Geo Metro.

"What made you decide to quit?" Bobby asked as Randy turned the key in the outer lock and jiggled the wooden double doors to test them. A light rain that started falling within the last fifteen minutes sent eddies of water across the parking lot and down a grate embedded midway between their cars.

Randy pocketed the key. "I need some time off to think about what I'm going to do with the years left in me. Strange as it may seem, employment isn't the true meaning of life."

"You're retiring?"

"In a way, yes, but hopefully not forever."

The statement startled him. "Wow. I thought you were only in your thirties."

"Actually, I'm only twenty-six. Big surprise, huh?" A shadow seemed to pass over Randy's eyes, but it vanished in an instant. "I'll see you tomorrow night at seven."

Bobby let the matter drop. "I guess I'll see you then."

Randy dipped his head. "Farewell, young Roland, until we meet again."

Bobby remained standing beneath the overhang as he watched Randy retreat to his car. It occurred to him that the man had been somewhat guarded about himself. What had Bobby learned about him during the interview? Not much, except for the facts that Randy was some sort of poltergeist magnet and something had caused him to age prematurely.

Randy's figure grew smaller as he drew closer to the blue Ford. Bobby wondered what thoughts passed through the man's head. Was he sad to be leaving his job or would quitting come as a relief?

Bobby had been too focused on his own side of the interview to even ask. Not that it would have been his business.

Bobby loosened his tie and took one step toward his car when his breath caught in his throat and the too-familiar tidal wave of terror crashed over him and left him gasping for air.

The man kept walking, oblivious to any danger.

Those about to meet their end generally were.

"Randy," Bobby said, but it came out barely above a whisper.

Randy had nearly reached the car, key in hand.

"Randy?"

He was going to open the door.

Bobby broke free from his unwanted paralysis and barreled at the man, knowing that if Randy so much as got inside the car, he would die.

"Randy!"

Randy turned his head at the last second, but Bobby was coming at him too quickly for him to get out of the way in time. Bobby's momentum enabled him to shove Randy over even though he weighed a deal less than the man, and both of them went sprawling to the ground, Randy on his side and Bobby on top of him.

Bobby was vaguely aware of a cell phone skittering out of a pocket and into a puddle. He dragged in a breath. "Randy, you can't—"

Randy threw Bobby off of him before he could finish his warning, his face far more livid than the situation should have warranted. Bobby let out a yelp as a well-toned bicep caught him around the neck and nearly crushed his windpipe.

What was going on?

Bobby struggled to break free from his grip, but Randy had him pinned against his chest, and now something cold and sharp pressed into the tender skin of Bobby's neck just below where Randy had hold of him.

Bobby could feel the man's breath on his ear when he spoke. "Who sent you? Was it Graham?"

Bobby's mind buzzed like a hive of trapped bees. He'd only meant to save the man from certain death, and now he was about a millimeter away from having his throat slit. "I think there's been a misunderstanding."

"Who sent you?" Randy repeated, his voice as cold as an Arctic lake.

"Nobody sent me! My roommate found your job listing in the paper, and—"

"What's his name?"

Bobby's heart tried to beat a hole through his chest. "My roommate? Caleb Young. College kid. Wears huge glasses." And could crush a pop can into the size of an atom with his bare hands. "He only found the listing this morning, so I—"

"If nobody sent you to attack me, then may I ask why you felt the need to bowl me over?"

"Only if you let me go. If I try anything, go ahead and stab me."

Randy let him go.

They stared at each other.

A new light had been kindled in Randy's eyes. His six-inch blade, clenched in his right fist, looked sharp enough to filet a bear. He slid it back into a sheath hidden under the length of his t-shirt.

Suddenly the skull on Randy's shirt appeared all too fitting.

Bobby took a deep breath, well aware that they were both being soaked to the skin. "If you get into that car, you'll die."

"How do you know that?"

Bobby's thoughts went to Tyree, his neighbor in New York. They'd only known each other for a few days but had discovered a mutual interest in guitars, so a fast bond had formed between them.

They had been sitting in Tyree's apartment strumming out tunes when the premonition came to him.

"Hey, Tyree, I don't think you should go out tonight."

"Why not?"

Undefined images of blood and death had filled Bobby's head. "It's dangerous out there."

Tyree laughed. "It's New York, bro. What isn't dangerous about it?"

Bobby found Tyree dead between the cars the very next morning. Tyree's face had been frozen in an expression of surprise and his pockets had been turned out.

Killed for a bit of cash. A casualty of greed.

"I just know," Bobby said, feeling sick at the memory.

A look of impatience crossed Randy's face. "Can you also divine the future from tea leaves? I'd like to get home and into some dry clothes."

"I'm telling you, if you get into that car, it's going to blow up or something."

"Did you plant a bomb in it?"

"No."

"Did you see someone plant a bomb in it?"

"No."

"Then what do I have to worry about?"

Bobby decided to use Randy's bizarre behavior to his advantage. "You clearly think someone is after you or you wouldn't have tried to kill me."

A muscle twitched in Randy's cheek. "A man has to protect himself." He stepped past Bobby and jammed his key into the slot on the door.

Bobby felt the blood drain from his face. "Please don't."

Randy threw him an annoyed glance and pulled the door open.

Bobby couldn't believe it. The man's stubbornness was going to kill him. And just like with Tyree, Bobby could do nothing to stop it short of wrestling the knife away from him and slashing his tires.

"Wait a minute," Bobby said as an idea dawned on him. "Don't start the car yet. I'll be right back."

Please don't let him start the car, he prayed as he dashed across the parking lot to his own vehicle. He got the door open and flipped open the glove box. There. A flashlight. Just what he needed to prove to Randy he was right.

He hurried back over to the Ford, where Randy sat in the driver's seat drumming his fingers on the wheel. He'd left the door open.

"What are you doing?" Randy asked. Some of the sharpness had left his voice, and he eyed the flashlight with interest.

"Checking something." Bobby got down on the ground and squeezed himself under the car, wishing he had one of those flat, wheeled jobs mechanics used while they repaired the undersides of vehicles.

His memory conjured an image of a sweating, overweight man gasping for breath at a kitchen table.

He banished the memory into the back of his mind. He had no time for that now.

Water running across the blacktop soaked into his clothes as he shined the light up into all the nooks and crannies under the car. What exactly did a car bomb look like? Did people even put them down here, or did bombs go under the hood with the engine?

All he knew was that nothing looked out of place to him. Which didn't mean much since he'd never paid attention when his father tried to teach him Cars 101.

He was about to crawl out from under the vehicle and have Randy pop the hood when something that wasn't rain dripped on his head.

Bobby scooted a few inches to the side and shined the light on the spot from which the drip had originated.

"Uh, Randy?" he called. "I think I found your problem."

4

LUPE SANCHEZ tried not to give much thought to Graham Willard once Randy left the hospital after that fateful night last year. Thinking about Graham at all made a cold weight settle upon her heart, and since she wanted to be strong for Randy while he mended she'd done her best to banish the old man's face from her mind.

Graham had dropped off the face of the earth after he'd left Randy for dead. His face appeared on news broadcasts for weeks. His bank accounts and credit card showed no activity. An all-points bulletin had been issued for his Grand Marquis, which later turned up at a used car lot sixty miles away. The lot owner explained that the man who sold the car to him for $500 cash looked "nothing like the guy on TV" so he hadn't suspected a thing.

That brought the investigation to a dead end. Graham had not purchased a new vehicle at that lot so it was anyone's guess as to what he drove now. Police went to other car lots with photographs of the old man in addition to the sketch that had been created from the description provided by the dealer. No one had seen him. If he'd gone to another dealership, he must have worn a disguise and used a different name.

Follow-ups of all recent vehicle purchases came up with nothing. None of Graham's kin had heard from him, either. Randy said he hoped the man had crawled away somewhere and died because it would have been better if he'd never been born.

Lupe hadn't been able to help but agree with him.

But then, just as life began its gradual return to normal, Graham came back

The encounter took place in the Walmart parking lot over on Skyline Avenue. Lupe had just finished loading groceries into her trunk and was wheeling the empty cart over to the nearest corral when a man stepped out of a nearby vehicle into her path.

At first she didn't recognize him. The man had black hair and brown eyes and wore a Portland Pilots t-shirt. Since Graham had gray hair, blue eyes, and staunchly supported the Oregon Ducks, she made no connection with the man standing before her and the one who had very nearly murdered her soon-to-be husband.

"Excuse me," she said, trying to push her way around him.

The man smiled. "Don't you know who I am?"

Her heart froze at the sound of his voice.

She let go of the cart and started to run back to her car, but the man's hand shot out and gripped her wrist. "We need to have a chat," he said, pulling her toward an unfamiliar slate-gray Nissan.

Lupe wished she could feign ignorance of the English language like she'd done on other occasions when she wanted to avoid conversation with certain people, but Graham knew her far too well to fall for that trick. "I'll scream," she said, glancing around to see if anyone stood within earshot.

Graham's smile broadened. "I'll shoot."

This was so wrong. Graham had been an honorary grandfather to them all, and if Lupe hadn't known about what he'd done to Randy, she would have thought this was some kind of sick joke.

"What will killing me accomplish?" she asked in a low voice.

"Not much, I'm afraid."

"If I get in your car, will you kill me?"

"I already told you we need to have a chat. I can't talk to you if you're dead."

Lupe had no idea what the man had in mind, and she wasn't sure she wanted to know, either. "Will you kill me after we have this chat?"

"Only if you try to pull something stupid. You get in the car, we talk, and then you go free. Make sense?"

"What's going to stop me from going to the police?"

The man chuckled. "That would fall under the category of pulling something stupid. Now get in the car."

Twenty minutes later when Graham finished their one-sided chat, Lupe wished she had just asked him to shoot her on the spot instead.

Now, months later, Lupe sat on her living room couch trembling so badly she thought she would burst while waiting for the phone call that would come before the night reached its end. She'd tried hard to thwart Graham but had no way of knowing if her partial defiance would work.

She considered killing herself if her plan failed. She had pills. She had knives. It wouldn't be hard to do.

But she also had faith, weak as it may have been at times. It had been years since the terrible nights of sitting in a warm bathtub with a razor in one hand while she examined the dark blue threads of vein pulsing beneath her skin. She had been so close to doing it one night. The tip of the razor had barely pierced her flesh when an unexpected voice inside her mind clearly said, "Wait."

So wait she did. With tears in her eyes, she wiped up the single bead of blood and threw the razor blade in the garbage.

The next day was a Sunday, and for the first time since coming to Oregon she went to church. When the service concluded, the young, dark-haired man sitting to her left turned and in flawless Spanish said, "Are you new here? I don't recognize you." His smile could have melted a glacier. It certainly melted her heart.

She'd nodded. "I'm Lupe," she said, feeling a blush warm her cheeks. She didn't notice any Latinos in the congregation aside from herself, and the sound of her native tongue made her feel even more out of place.

The man stuck out a hand. "And I'm Randy Bellison. It's nice to meet you."

"*Gracias.* It's nice to meet you, too. But how did you know I speak Spanish?"

"Easy: I knew it in my heart."

They had chatted for awhile longer after church let out, and then Randy offered to take her to lunch that day since he didn't have any plans and the weather was so nice. Though nervous about it, Lupe agreed for the sole reason that nobody had ever asked her to a restaurant before, and she wanted to know what it was like.

They'd sat out on the restaurant's patio beneath a giant umbrella as they dined on authentic Chinese cuisine. At first they'd talked about simple things like their jobs and what they enjoyed doing in their free time (Lupe liked to crochet and Randy often spent time with friends or in prayer), and after awhile Lupe brought up some of the happier things that had happened to her in Mexico, which surprised her since she rarely spoke of her old life. In turn, Randy told her how he'd had a troubled childhood and finally found peace when he turned such cares over to God.

It soon became a ritual for them to sit together in church and then go to lunch. At first Lupe simply considered Randy a new friend whose company she enjoyed, but as weeks passed she found herself wishing they could stay together longer each Sunday. She would think of Randy often throughout the day and eventually started calling him to chat whenever she wanted to hear his voice.

She noticed an odd thing, though. Sometimes he would not pick up his phone, and when he returned her calls, he would sound unimaginably exhausted.

It would not be until their relationship deepened further that she would learn the reason why.

In the present, Lupe checked the time. It felt like an eternity since the last time she'd looked at the clock but in reality it had only been a handful of minutes.

She closed her eyes and prayed. *Padre, keep watch over your child Randy. Protect him from all harm and the hand of evil. Send your angels to guard and guide him, and never let your Spirit leave him.*

She had done a terrible thing, but she did it anyway. And why? Because while she had often sought to end her life and left it open as an option, she feared dying—especially at the hands of the one who controlled her.

I am a terrible person. Padre, don't let him die.

Her cell phone let out a shrill ring that nearly stopped her heart.

She answered it with a shaking hand. "Hello?"

5

RANDY TRIED to be calm while the kid in the tie rummaged around underneath his car, but being calm did not always come easy to him, especially after what happened last year. Sure, on an ordinary day he'd feel as composed as he ever had been, though every once in awhile certain events would trigger his fears and he'd end up doing something rash. Only last month he'd been taking trash to one of the bins at the church when a car backfired out on the street, and the next thing he knew he was dashing for cover as if he were under attack.

It wasn't something he cared to admit. He'd always been the self-possessed sort of guy who kept his head during crises.

Not so much anymore. He had Graham Willard and his gun to thank for that.

If Bobby hadn't been sent by Graham to harm him (if knocking him into a wet parking lot could even be remotely classified as such), then what in the world was going on?

Father, a little advice here would be awesome.

The Voice within him sounded amused. *Be patient.*

Bobby said something, but Randy couldn't tell what it was over the sound of the falling rain. He hopped out of the car and joined Bobby beneath it. It wasn't like his clothes would get any wetter at this point. "What did you say?"

"Look at this." Bobby's flashlight illuminated a piece of severed tubing that dripped something onto the wet pavement.

Randy felt the breath leave his lungs. "That's not a bomb," he said, though if he'd driven away without heeding Bobby's warning, the effects would have been just about as disastrous for him.

Bobby shook his head and glanced at Randy with fear in his eyes. "No. I don't know much about this kind of thing, but I think it's one of your brake lines."

That's what Randy thought, too, and it made his stomach squirm. You cut the brake lines, you lose the brake fluid; you lose the brake fluid, you lose the brakes. Not exactly a death sentence but close enough.

"Let me take a closer look at that."

Bobby handed him the flashlight and moved aside. Randy prodded the severed line with one finger. It looked like it had been snipped with wire cutters. "How did you really know about this?"

The kid didn't immediately reply. Randy glanced over at him and saw that tears had welled up in his eyes.

"Look," Randy said, feeling a shred of guilt at having pulled the knife on him. "I'm not mad at you. Did someone tip you off and you're afraid to tell me about it?"

"No." Bobby cleared his throat. "Nobody tipped me off. Sometimes I just know things, okay? You're a church guy. I figure it's God who told me you'd be meeting him at the Pearly Gates if I didn't jump in and save you."

Now that was an interesting thought. "In any case, it looks like I'm safe now," Randy said as he wriggled his way out from under the car. He patted his pocket for his cell phone so he could call a tow truck and discovered it had vanished. He made a quick scan of the area and found it lying screen-side down on the ground four feet away. He picked it up, shook droplets from its screen, and tried to dial Lupe's number just to see if it worked.

It didn't.

Bobby joined him in the growing downpour a moment later. "Sorry about that," he said, eyeing the lifeless phone. "Here, use mine. Are you going to file a police report? There could be vandals in the area doing this to other people's cars."

Randy shook his head. It would be one thing if this was the work of ordinary vandals out to wreak havoc upon the neighborhood, but his gut told him this was Graham Willard's doing. The church had no outdoor security cameras and a tall row of shrubs lined one side of the lot, so the culprit might not have been seen. The police would have nothing to go on other than Randy's own suspicions. Besides, how would he explain his knowledge of the severed line? He hadn't driven the car anywhere to know something was wrong with it, and he hadn't seen the leaking brake fluid since it had mingled with the water on the pavement. "Nope," he said. "I just need the tow truck."

Before he dialed 411 for information about sending over a wrecker, he called Lupe to let her know what had happened. Hearing her voice eased some of the tension in his chest. It was strange, though. When she answered the phone, it sounded like she was crying.

AFTER CHECKING his own brake lines to make sure the vandal hadn't struck twice, Bobby sat in his Nissan and watched Randy's defunct Ford get loaded onto a flatbed and secured into place. He'd considered leaving but thought better of it since Randy would need someone to take him home.

Bobby's heart fluttered more frantically than a caged bird and he had to take slow breaths to prevent his vision from going gray. Running across a parking lot didn't top the list of things he often did. Rarer still did he find it necessary to tackle someone who exceeded him in both strength and weight. But if he hadn't . . . if he'd hesitated for only one moment . . .

A knock sounded on the passenger side window, which Bobby then rolled down. "Were you waiting for me?" Randy asked.

"I thought you'd need a ride."

"Thanks. I appreciate that."

Bobby disengaged the locks, and a very wet, very forlorn Randy climbed into the seat beside him. "I'll direct you," Randy said. "It's not far."

They spent the next few minutes in silence save for the occasional "Turn here" that came from Bobby's passenger. Every minute or so Randy would twist around and glance out the rear windshield as if he were concerned about being followed.

Bobby wanted to ask the man a thousand different questions, but he suspected that Randy would either be elusive or refuse to answer altogether.

At last Randy directed him to turn left down a long, gravel lane about a mile north of the Autumn Ridge town limits. Trees pressed close on both sides so Bobby couldn't see the house that lay at the end. The car jolted as he failed to avoid inches-deep potholes that seemed to comprise most of the lane. Mud sprayed onto the hood and windows, but if the weather kept up like this, it would be washed off again in no time.

"I think you need to get a new load of gravel," Bobby commented as they struck another pothole that sounded like it nearly busted an axle.

Randy shrugged. "Sorry. I don't want it to look like anyone lives here."

The statement added yet another question to the long list that had already formed in Bobby's mind. Randy seemed less and less a janitor and more like a fugitive.

His mind replayed the image of Randy sliding his knife back into its leather sheath.

He hoped he wasn't unknowingly abetting a criminal.

They pulled up in front of a ramshackle house begging for a bulldozer to come put it out of its misery. The concrete porch had more cracks than a California fault line, all the windows hid behind nailed-on plywood, and white paint peeled away from the siding like skin after a bad sunburn.

Randy must have been reading the look on Bobby's face. "Don't judge," he said. "I got it cheap. The bank was practically giving it away."

"I haven't the slightest idea why."

Randy pierced him with a long gaze and then smiled. "Come on inside. I'll fix you something to eat."

———◆———

BOBBY IMAGINED confronting a horde of rats and garbage when they stepped through the door, so his surprise couldn't have been greater when he saw that unlike the house's façade, the inside was clean, organized, and smelled of fresh paint.

"Wow," Bobby said when Randy flipped on the light. Most of the furniture looked like cheap IKEA finds that would have been named TAYBULL and CHAYURR or something along those lines. The walls were a vibrant coral color, and a large print of Our Lady of Guadalupe dominated the one to Bobby's left. A crucifix hung over an open archway leading to a kitchen that had white cabinets, aqua countertops, and a coral-and-aqua checkerboard floor.

"Lupe helped decorate," Randy explained. "She's my fiancée."

Bobby looked back at the painting. "Lupe? Like Guadalupe?" He pointed at the piece of art, which depicted the Virgin Mary standing atop a crescent moon with her hands pressed together in prayer.

"It's her namesake, but don't ever call her Guadalupe to her face or she might try to sucker punch you." Randy kicked off his Doc Martens and went into the kitchen. Bobby followed for lack of anything better to do. "Now if you'll excuse me, I need to put on some dry clothes before I catch my death. You want me to bring you a fresh shirt and pants?"

He had to be kidding. Bobby barely weighed 145 on a bad day, and Randy weighed at least forty pounds more than that. "Thanks," he said, "but I'll pass."

"Suit yourself—or not." Randy disappeared through a second archway at the other end of the kitchen, leaving Bobby alone.

Bobby sank into a metal chair that had a vinyl cushion the same color as the countertops. This was crazy. Being the quiet type, he'd barely spoken to anyone other than Caleb Young and his coworkers at the restaurant since coming to this state a year ago, and here he was loafing around in the kitchen of a man he'd only met in the past hour—a man who, by the look of it, may or may not be a serial killer.

Below him, a creaking sound put his senses on alert. Did this place have a basement? He thought he'd heard Randy go up a set of stairs when he left the kitchen, not down. Maybe sound just traveled funny in this house. Yeah, that was it. This place had to be fifty or sixty years old. Houses like this made all kinds of spooky noises. He should know; he'd grown up in one.

He shifted his weight in the chair and checked the time on his phone. Five minutes to nine.

Below him, a toilet flushed.

Ten seconds later, someone else did the same on the floor above him.

So two people lived in the house. Big deal. Except the lights had been off when they'd arrived, and no other cars occupied the driveway.

"I'm back." Randy emerged from the darkness beyond the archway, this time wearing a plain red shirt and blue jeans. "Are you all right?"

Bobby stuffed his phone back into his pocket. "Who said anything is wrong?"

Randy glided over to the refrigerator and pulled a pizza out of the freezer. "Your face did. You may not be aware of this, but you're not very good at hiding your thoughts."

"You pulled a knife on me back there!"

Randy's face sobered. "I'm sorry about that. Truly." He put the pizza on a tray and shoved it in the oven. "If it makes you feel better, it wasn't anything personal. An old friend almost killed me last year, so I've been a little more cautious lately. When you knocked me over, I assumed the worst."

A little more cautious. Ha. "Was it that Graham person you mentioned?"

Randy turned away for a minute and busied himself at the sink. "Yes."

"What did he do to you?"

"Why do you want to know so badly?" Randy turned back from the sink and folded his arms, wearing a dark expression that sent goosebumps racing down Bobby's spine.

"Just making conversation, I guess." Bobby swallowed. He shouldn't have agreed to come inside. He should have just gone home to pick around on his guitar like he'd do any other time he wasn't working. At least around Caleb he usually didn't feel like a guy walking across a minefield.

"Conversation is fine," Randy said. "Just not conversation about that. I just . . ." He shook his head. "Sorry. Graham was a good friend who, for reasons unknown to me, thought my life should end. I don't have an explanation for it."

"I'm sorry to hear that."

Randy pulled two glass tumblers out of a dish strainer, filled them from the tap, and plunked them down on the table.

Creeeaaak. Bobby stiffened. That sound again from below. "Do you have a basement?"

"Why do you ask?"

Then a muffled sound like a sneeze came through the floorboards. Sweat began to bead on Bobby's brow. "Is somebody down there?"

"Is somebody down where?"

"Never mind." Bobby pushed back from the table and stood up. Randy Bellison was a creep, plain and simple, and Bobby had always done his best to avoid that type of person. "Thanks for the offer of dinner, but to be honest, I ate before I came to the interview."

"That's too bad."

No, really, it's just fine.

Bobby made his way to the door as fast as he could without actually running, and Randy followed him. "I'll see you at seven tomorrow night."

Bobby pulled the door open. "Yeah. Uh, thanks for letting me have the job."

A genuine smile brightened Randy's features. "That was nothing. Thank you for saving my life."

Bobby had no fitting response to that, so he just nodded and left and prayed that Randy wouldn't come after him.

As he drove home, he thanked the heavens that he and Randy wouldn't be working together at the church. Bobby's life was creepy enough already.

6

WHEN THE oven timer went off, Randy got out two paper plates and divided the hot pizza between them, then poured a third tumbler of water—this one plastic—and carried it and one of the plates downstairs, saying a silent prayer for the wellbeing of the person staying with him.

She'd been here for days already. Too many by his count.

He couldn't let her go free until he was finished with her.

The entrance to the basement lay a short distance down the unlit hallway. Bobby wouldn't have been able to see it or the faint light that spilled from under the closed door from where he'd sat in the kitchen, but the soft sounds of his guest moving around would have been a dead giveaway of her presence.

It had probably been a mistake to have let Bobby inside in the first place, but he couldn't just send his unlikely savior away without offering him the courtesy of food and drink.

Randy reached the bottom of the stairs and stepped out into the refurbished space that had been a bare concrete room when he moved in seven months ago. He and his friend Phil Mason had furnished it with plush furniture and a bathroom and walled off the half that contained the furnace, water heater, and washer and dryer. A burgundy couch in the center of the open space was heaped with red and gold throw pillows, as were the matching armchairs. He and Phil had covered up the drab cement floor with deep red wall-to-wall carpet that felt as soft as goose down beneath one's feet.

His guests would never complain of discomfort.

A midnight-blue comforter and pillows covered the bed in the corner. On it a pale, slender figure sat upright with her legs dangling over the edge. Her hair, which had been a tangled mess of blond mats when she first came to him, had since been brushed out but now looked disheveled as if she had only recently awakened.

She watched him with dark eyes. "Who was that?" she asked in a quiet voice.

"A visitor." He set the plate and tumbler on the polished coffee table in the center of the room.

"For me?" The plaintive note of hope in her voice nearly rent his soul in two.

"No," he said, "not for you. I didn't even tell him you're here. Now come and eat."

She rose gingerly and crossed the room on bare feet. A bead of sweat rolled down Randy's brow when she drew near to where he stood.

She sat down on the couch and continued to stare at him. Her manner was both innocent and sinister, and the combination spooked him. He knew very little about her except for her name: Trish. She looked about eighteen. Maybe twenty. No more than that, for sure.

"Go on," he said, making certain his voice remained firm. "Eat it."

Her gaze seemed to bore a tunnel into his soul, and he knew that the thing living within her was reading him. "Why should I?" That same soft voice, though with a slightly harder edge to it.

He took a deep breath. *Father, help me remain patient.* "Trish, we've been over this before. You need to eat so you can be strong. We can't have you wasting away like this."

She had been a wisp of a woman to begin with, but now she looked even thinner. It crossed his mind that she might be purging herself of food every time he left her following a meal. It might do her well if he stayed down here to watch her for a greater length of time each day just to make sure she didn't.

Trish's eyes welled up with tears. "I don't want to live anymore. It's terrible. They say awful things to me." She shuddered. "Did you know our time is drawing near?"

He didn't know exactly what she meant, but he nodded anyway. "Our time is always drawing near. That's why we need to repent of our sins now before it's too late."

"I can't repent! Randy, if only you knew the things I've done to people! To poor girls like me." Her expression softened with a suddenness that startled him, and the soul-reading gaze returned to her face. "Look at you, Randy. You think you're such a holy man, but you're no different from anyone else." Her lip curled. "You think you're better than I am! You think you can keep me here!"

"You came here of your own accord," he reminded her. They had been through this before, as well. She had shown up at church in hysterics, and since Father Preston had been out visiting a sick parishioner that day, Randy was the only one around to offer her any solace.

Her problem became apparent to him even before she spoke.

His heart had broken with the knowledge that yet another soul lived under such oppression, even after he had helped rescue so many already. But there would always be others no matter how many he saved. He could only keep their numbers in check, and pray.

And Graham had wanted him to step down from it all.

Randy quickly banished all thoughts of his would-be murderer. The feelings he had for the man were anything but holy, and he had no desire for Trish's tormentor to use those thoughts against him.

"Trish," he said in the gentlest voice he could muster, "please eat. Have faith, and you'll come through this just fine."

She glared at him.

"Your pizza's getting cold."

She told him to put the pizza in a place where no pizza ever deserved to go.

He sighed.

This was going to be a long night.

———◆———

GRAHAM WILLARD had the television on as he nursed a Bloody Mary he had concocted himself. He felt younger than he had in decades, and every nerve ending in his body buzzed with anticipation as he watched the news reports for word of the accident he'd thought about day and night since he'd planned it.

He'd thought he might feel a sudden shift in the atmosphere when it happened, but there was no guarantee such a thing would occur. Randy's death would likely have all the fanfare of a snuffed candle, though the newfound darkness that would ensue would be decidedly more terrifying than that.

Such was the price he would pay for his freedom.

Right now the news anchor yammered on about a robbery at that god-awful Arnie's Stop-N-Eat place a couple nights ago. Graham had been there twice before deciding the manager was too conceited to deserve anyone's hard-earned cash. Served him right he'd been robbed.

Graham yawned and checked the time. Maybe Randy hadn't left yet. He'd always kept an unusual schedule, so depending on when he'd shown up, it could be hours before he got done washing toilets and dusting hymnals and whatever else he did in that confounded church he attended.

The next segment covered an upcoming Founders Day parade and festival. Then a discussion about a proposed tax levy, and after that, a recap of a 5k race that had been held at Dennison Park earlier in the day. The traffic report stated that all roads and Interstate

5 were clear, except for a disabled semi that had been sitting on the shoulder of Highway 98 for the past hour.

Graham's patience began to wear thin. He clicked the television off and set his glass aside. It had been a mistake to leave Randy immediately after shooting him last year because the man had survived. Heck, it had been a mistake to not shoot him straight through the brain or heart. And the thing was, he didn't even know why he hadn't. A momentary lapse in judgment?

He wouldn't be making mistakes like those anymore. You live and you learn.

If Graham left the house right now, he might have the chance to watch the debacle himself if it hadn't happened already. That way he would know without a doubt that Randy had died.

He tested his sobriety by walking in what approximated a straight line across the floor. He wobbled a little and had to grab onto the arm of a chair to steady himself, but it would be good enough. If asked by an officer, Graham could blame his unsteadiness on his age.

He put on his shoes and drove the twenty-odd miles to St. Paul's, not once topping the speed limit or crossing the yellow lines in the center of the road.

He turned into the church parking lot.

A crumpled potato chip bag skittered across the pavement. Some leaves that had blown out of the trees were plastered to the ground like green papier-mâché. A cat loitered near the overflowing recycle bin tucked into the lot's northwest corner by the road.

Other than that, the lot was empty.

Graham gripped the wheel so tightly the joints in his fingers practically screamed their objection at him.

He made a big looping turn and sped back out onto the wet street. It was high time he paid somebody a visit.

AS HE drove to the apartment, Graham thought about the other plan he had put into motion. It had been intended as a joke, but Graham knew he'd be the only one laughing.

However, Graham had grown impatient with that plan. As far as he knew, the joke had not yet played out. Killing Randy by disabling his car would cut the joke short, but sometimes you had to sacrifice your fun for the sake of convenience. He couldn't keep putting off the boy's murder. Graham was seventy-five years old now, and though the quality of his health exceeded that of other men his age (or so his doctor said), it wasn't unheard of for an unexpected stroke or heart attack to strike a man down.

He would have liked to see Randy's reaction to the joke—and maybe he still would if Graham was able to salvage it.

Graham hobbled up to the door when he arrived at the apartment, playing the part of decrepit grandfather for the benefit of anyone who may have been watching.

He rang the bell.

Footsteps crossed the floor inside. The occupant hesitated at the door, probably looking at him through the peephole.

"I strongly suggest you let me in," he said.

The lock disengaged with a click and the door swung open.

He strode inside and allowed the door to latch behind him.

The woman cowered before him like an animal about to be slaughtered. "You told me you did it."

Her face went as white as chalk. "I did do it. I'd swear it on all the Bibles in the world."

"I don't think it's your place to go swearing on the word of God."

"Graham, you have to believe me!"

"How can I believe you when Randy's car is neither where he left it nor wrecked anywhere? If you'd cut the lines like I'd said, he should have crashed into the Winslow building at the bottom of the hill on Pike Street."

"I would never lie to you. If he didn't crash, then perhaps God was with him."

Graham's patience was wearing thinner than a sheet of ice in the sun. "Prove it."

"Prove what?"

"That you would never lie to me."

"How do I do that?"

Graham strode past his reluctant accomplice and planted himself on the couch. He patted the cushion beside him. "Sit down," he said, "and I'll tell you."

She obeyed without question or comment.

"I want you to tell him what you did."

The objection was immediate. "But you said if I told him—"

"I know what I said then. But this is now. I want you to tell him everything you know, but you will *not* tell him that I told you to do it. You should act the part of the terrified lover who had no other choice but to obey me."

"You haven't given me any other choice!"

"There's always a choice, Lupe." Graham smiled. Miss Sanchez was such an easy mark. He wasn't sure what Randy had ever seen in her aside from her pretty looks.

When he left the apartment, his foul mood had lifted. He would have to set a new plan into motion, but at least he still had the chance to observe the punch line of his joke.

7

BOBBY WAS barely more than a boy again. His father had the hood of his 1978 Chevy Nova popped open and pointed to what looked to Bobby like nothing more than a tangle of tubing.

"Now what did I say this one is?" His father, Ken, had a twinkle in his eye. He wore an ancient, grease-smeared University of Cincinnati t-shirt that had more holes in it than a piece of Swiss cheese. As usual, his paunch of a gut stuck over the top of his grimy blue jeans. His keg, he called it, though he was more likely to drink Pepsi than beer.

Bobby had been wearing a clean black Muse t-shirt and tan cargo pants. Small details, but ones he remembered well.

"Uh . . ." Bobby had strained to recall the name of the particular component his father indicated. So many parts and things were jammed up under a car's hood, and Bobby would have found it more interesting to watch paint dry on a wall than to memorize their names. "The catalytic converter?"

Ken Roland threw his head back and laughed. "Son, you never will learn, will you? Catalytic converter's part of the exhaust system. C'mon, I'll show you."

Bobby obliged his father by poking his head under the old car. Ken joined him and pointed at a gray container-looking thing that had pipes coming out of it. "Now that's the catalytic converter. EPA says we've gotta have 'em so we don't ruin the ozone layer, or some garbage like that." He chuckled again. "Not that you care, right?"

But Bobby didn't know what he cared about. He was only fourteen. He played around a lot on his electric guitar. He liked to cook with his stepmother. Sometimes he and his younger half-brother Jonas would kick a soccer ball around the yard, but only for short periods of time because Bobby easily became short of breath.

He cared about those things a lot more than hot rods, no offense to his father.

Bobby just shrugged. "Uh, sure." He stood back up and walked back around to the hood, but Ken didn't follow. "Dad?"

His father's voice sounded strained when he next spoke. "Come 'ere and help me up, Bobby. I don't feel so good all the sudden . . . I think I need a drink."

Bobby didn't think much of it. The gleaming sun baked everything below it to a crisp, so it was natural for someone like his father to be sensitive to the effects of the heat. He went around to the back of the Nova, where his father struggled to stand. Ken held out a hand and Bobby took it, helping his father to his feet.

"Thanks," Ken said, rubbing his chest and grimacing. "Don't know what's come over me. Guess it's too hot out here. Let's go in and get some lemonade, huh?"

"Sure." Bobby led the way and held the door open for his father out of courtesy, and once the man was inside Bobby ran to the refrigerator and grabbed out the pitcher of lemonade his stepmother had made that morning before taking Jonas to the dentist. He got two glasses out of the cabinet and filled them nearly to the brim. "Here you go."

Ken lowered his bulk into one of the dining room chairs. "Thank you, sir." He swallowed the entire drink in a single gulp and set the glass aside. "Sweet Jesus, I don't feel good." His gray shirt had turned an even deeper gray from the sweat pouring out of him in rivulets.

That's when Bobby had the first inkling that he should be concerned. It had been a few years since he quit Scouts, but he could remember having to watch a first-aid video in order to earn one of his merit badges. In addition to teaching the boys ways to patch up cuts and scrapes, the video had also taught them what signs would indicate that a person was having a stroke, seizure, or heart attack.

Bobby's gut began to squirm. He didn't want to alarm his father, but if he didn't push the man for details . . .

Ken's expression changed to one of worry. His thinning hair was so wet it looked like he'd just climbed out of the shower. "Are you all right?"

Bobby shook his head. "Dad, is your left arm hurting at all?"

"A little, but I was moving those boxes around yesterday. Remember?"

Panic seized Bobby like a fist. How could the man be in such denial about his health? "No, Dad, I—I'm going to call 911."

His father's face paled. "What? Why?" He started wheezing like he couldn't get a decent breath. "Jesus, you don't think—"

Bobby ignored him as he sprinted toward the telephone and dialed the three numbers he'd hoped to never use.

A faint voice came on the line. "This is 911, what is your emergency?"

As Bobby opened his mouth to speak, Ken slumped out of the chair onto the white linoleum floor.

BOBBY AWOKE screaming.

At least he thought he did. The scream might have just been in his mind, though his throat felt raw as if he'd just been bellowing at the heavens with all his might.

Something tickled his face and he slapped at it like it was a marauding spider in search of his mouth. Instead of spider guts, his hand came away damp with tears.

He closed his eyes in the hope of returning to slumber and dreaming about something far less nightmarish like bikini-clad babes on a beach, but his pulse hammered away at such a rapid pace he knew it would be hours before he could sufficiently calm himself.

He could feel every pulsation, every quiver of his heart. That fragile organ. The one that would eventually wear itself out and cease to beat.

It made sense to have dreamed about that final day of childhood. He'd crawled under Randy's car earlier that evening, just like he'd done with that stinking Nova minutes before his father died.

Bobby rolled over and shivered. He wanted to think neither about Randy nor his father. The former was a creep and the latter was pushing daises, and for all Bobby cared, he could forget that either had ever existed and move on with his life, whatever that meant.

Yawning, he decided he must not have screamed after all. If he had, his roommate probably would have come bounding in with a 12-gauge shotgun or an Uzi. Not that Caleb owned such things, but after seeing what he'd done to the pop can, nothing would have surprised him.

Just as his tired mind began to wander off on some other tangent, something ticked against the window to the left of his bed. A bug, probably, or something kicked up by the wind. Funny though. It kind of reminded him of that crazy sound he kept hearing earlier when—

Tap. Tap-tap-tap.

Bobby's muscles froze. It was the same sound he'd heard in the church office. And what had Randy said? That whatever caused it was like a poltergeist. The sounds wouldn't bother Bobby when Randy left his job at the church because Randy was the one whom the unnamed thugs were after. But now Bobby had associated with the man, and the beings—whatever they were—had followed him.

Tap-tap. Tap.

Of course Bobby was being silly. Poltergeists did not exist, and he certainly didn't believe in ghosts. Randy had simply freaked him out with some kind of sound-throwing trick back at the church. Maybe the tapping hadn't been on the window at all and was really something Randy himself was doing under the desk. Or had it been a recording? It was even possible that Randy owned a secondary vehicle and had followed Bobby home at a distance just to torment him further. Bobby could see no motive for such actions, but crazy people didn't follow the same logic that others did.

Bobby held his breath and continued listening for any indication that a solid, flesh-and-blood human stood outside the window. Aside from the tapping, all he heard was the soft sighing of wind in the trees.

He waited five minutes before tiptoeing out of bed and peering through a gap in the drapes. The moon lit up the night with a pale milky glow, though the wind made patchy clouds scud across the sky at a fast clip that alternately dimmed and brightened the orb. The brief periods of brightness weren't enough. If someone lurked in the yard, he couldn't see them.

Tap. The sound, louder this time, originated from a more distant point. The creep had chosen another window and upgraded to small boulders instead of pebbles.

"That's it." Bobby jammed his bare feet into gym shoes and pulled on a sweatshirt. If he didn't stop the guy, he would break a window and then Bobby's landlord would jack up the rent to astronomic proportions if he didn't throw Bobby out for associating with the wrong crowd.

Bobby owned no weapons. He did have a fireplace poker hanging in a stand by the hearth out in the living room. He had no intention of using it, but it might strike fear into the creep's heart and make him run away.

He crept out of his bedroom, slowly lifted the poker out of the stand so it wouldn't make a clanging noise that would rouse Caleb, and undid the deadbolt on the back door.

The porch light had burnt out some months before and neither of the house's occupants had bothered replacing it, much to Bobby's current regret. The moon disappeared behind a bank of fast-moving clouds again. He could have brought out a flashlight, but stealth might be in his favor if he could catch the guy by surprise.

He made sure the door wouldn't lock behind him and stepped onto the small cement slab where they kept the tiny charcoal grill they'd used maybe twice all summer. His eyes already adjusted to the darkness since he hadn't turned on any lights during his short flight from the bedroom to here. He took quick inventory of the yard. Garbage cans. Stunted bushes. Chain-link fence. The creep didn't have many places to hide. Though it was possible he'd heard Bobby and dashed around to the side of the house to hunker down behind the giant pine tree that took up a good portion of the side yard.

Anything was possible.

Well, almost anything.

He was about to step off the slab when something whizzed by his head and bounced off the lid of the grill before clattering to the ground.

He wanted to whirl around and see what it had been, but if he turned his back, the creep might sneak up behind him and conk him on the head. He squinted. What direction had the thing come from? He didn't see—

Clunk. Another something landed at his feet. Keeping his gaze trained on the yard, Bobby stooped and found the object with his hand. He picked it up and held it in front of his face.

The moon emerged briefly from behind the mantle of clouds.

He held a crushed can of Dr Pepper. Not nearly as crushed as it would have been had it been in Caleb's grip when that news bit about the murdered girl had been on television, but crushed nonetheless.

Bobby remembered part of his exchange with Randy earlier in the evening.

It sounds like someone's throwing rocks at the window.

Rocks, sticks, whatever else they can find. I'm used to it.

The Dr Pepper can had previously resided in one of the garbage cans along the back fence ten yards away, or more specifically, the "recycle" can sitting next to the one reserved for regular waste. Though Bobby didn't see how a grown man could remain concealed behind the bins while launching such an assault, that's where he had to be.

Bobby squared his shoulders to make himself appear braver and marched across the damp grass, wielding the poker like a baseball bat. He stopped five feet away from the cans and cleared his throat. Maybe he could be diplomatic about this. "I know you're back there, and if you don't want me to bash a hole in your head, you'll come out with your hands up." It sounded cheesy, but he didn't have time to think of a more elaborate threat.

He waited. Nothing moved. Maybe the guy was holding his breath.

"Hello?" He took another tentative step forward. The lid of one can rested on the ground beside it. A few other crushed cans lay scattered in the grass. "I've got a fireplace poker."

Nothing.

"Do you know what a person can do with a fireplace poker?"

He hoped none of his neighbors would hear him and think he'd flipped his lid.

He continued anyway. "You don't?" His voice shook. "Well, I'll tell you. There's this guy back home, you see. Lived with a crazy mama. She tried to kill him, but he killed her first with one of these things. He gives talks now. Stuff about forgiveness and moving on and things like that." Now he was just rambling like a nutcase. "Do you want me to do that to you? Kill you with a poker like you're a crazy mama?"

He thought he heard a faint snicker somewhere in the night, but it might have just been the wind rustling through the grass and trees.

Somehow the silence behind the garbage cans seemed far louder than all the nighttime sounds surrounding him. Gripping the poker in one hand, he dragged the recycle can aside with the other.

Nobody was there.

Behind him, something else ticked at the side of the house. Bobby broke into a run, turned his foot in a hole dug by some animal, almost lost his grip on the poker as pain spiked through his ankle, and continued toward the giant pine. The creep could have gathered up cans in a bag and chosen the tree as his new launching point.

He circled the tree three times before deciding that nobody hid there, either. Then he edged his way along the back wall of the house, inspecting the ground. On top of the grass lay one additional pop can and a far greater number of rocks of varying sizes, the smallest of which looked an awful lot like the ones in the driveway.

He dashed around to the front of the house and looked up and down the street. No fleeing figures in sight. Most of the windows in the two rows of cookie-cutter bungalows were as black as the sky. Three street lamps illuminated sodden yards that looked almost identical to his own, save for the occasional shrub or birdbath that set the residences apart from one another.

If the creep wasn't out here, did that mean he lingered in the yard? Just how well could a person hide on a quarter-acre lot?

"Bobby?"

He whirled around even though he knew the voice, and instinct made him come within about two inches of clobbering Caleb Young in the head with the poker. His roommate simultaneously ducked and snatched it out of his hand.

They stood there staring at each other in silence for a moment or two, Bobby's heart racing at what felt like seven hundred miles an hour. Could Caleb have been the creep? No, Caleb was too level-headed for that. Besides, Bobby hadn't told him about what happened at the church. That he would mimic the tapping sounds he knew nothing about would have been a coincidence too huge for Bobby to believe.

Caleb kept his gaze fixed on Bobby and passed the poker back to him. His glasses sat crooked on his face as if he'd jammed them on in haste. "You okay?"

"Somebody's out here," he panted. He did a visual sweep of the street again in case the creep had waited to sneak away when Bobby was distracted, but the road remained vacant.

"Are you sure? The only person I see is you."

"I wasn't the one throwing rocks and junk at the house. Come on, maybe you can help me find him."

Without asking any of the questions that likely sat on the tip of Caleb's tongue, he nodded. "I'll get a flashlight."

Caleb turned on his heel and disappeared through the front door.

He reemerged a minute later. "I lied," he said. "I got two flashlights."

Bobby took one and clicked it on. Caleb did the same.

"Alright," Caleb said. "Now what?"

Bobby started in the direction of the back yard. "We find him."

Two beams of light swept the ground as the pair rounded the side of the house. A number of indentations had flattened the grass where Bobby circled the pine tree, but other than that, there existed no sign that anyone else had spent the evening slogging around the yard.

Bobby shined his light on a scattering of rocks in the grass. "See that?"

Caleb approached the back wall of the house and kicked at a stone the size of a golf ball. "Interesting."

"Interesting is right. Do you have any idea how someone could have done this without leaving any footprints in this muck? I've just about got mud up to my ankles."

"Maybe they don't have feet."

Bobby could almost feel his blood pressure rising like mercury in a thermometer. "How can you just joke around when some weirdo's out here trying to vandalize our house?"

Caleb lowered the arm holding the flashlight so the beam only illuminated a small circle of grass. "Did they hurt you?"

"No."

"Did they break anything?"

"No, but they would have if I hadn't come out here. Can you imagine what Dave would've done if the guy broke a window?"

Caleb shrugged. "He would have known it wasn't our fault."

Bobby tucked the poker under one arm and dragged a hand through his short, dark brown hair. "I think whoever was here is gone now. Let's go in."

"Sounds good to me."

They went in through the rear door, clicking off the flashlights as they passed over the threshold. Bobby replaced the poker in its stand and turned around to discover that Caleb was drilling him with an expectant stare.

"Do you believe in poltergeists?" Bobby blurted.

A muscle twitched in the corner of Caleb's mouth. "Do you?"

Bobby sank onto the couch after removing his muddy shoes by the door and put his head into his hands. "I don't know. You read all that quantum physics stuff. Do you think poltergeist activity can be explained by science?"

"Sure. Powerful electromagnetic fields can move objects around. Makes it look like invisible people are picking things up. Why?"

Bobby shook his head. "This is crazy." He briefly recounted the tapping on the church window during the interview and Randy's request to ignore it.

"Are you suggesting that an electromagnetic field that tossed rocks around at the church followed you home and started tossing them at our windows?" Amusement glistened in Caleb's eyes.

Bobby's face heated up. "Do you think it's possible?"

Caleb finally took a seat in the recliner opposite him. "This is a strange and mysterious universe. Anything could be possible."

"But what do you *think*? Could it have been some freak energy field doing all this? Because I don't believe in ghosts."

Caleb leaned back in the chair and closed his eyes. "It could have been that."

Bobby waited. "Or?"

"Or it could have been spirits." His eyes opened. "Randy was smart in telling you to ignore it. You'll make yourself go nuts if you don't."

Bobby couldn't believe he was hearing this. "I'm already going nuts!"

Caleb raised an eyebrow. "You didn't need to tell me that. You're the one who woke me up talking up a storm with a pair of garbage cans. I was watching you out the back window, you know."

Great. "And you're the one telling me there might be invisible spirits outside? You're nuttier than I am!"

The insult didn't faze him. "Bobby, I went nuts eons ago." Caleb stood up and stretched. "Now I've got to get some sleep. My first exam of the quarter's in two days and I've barely studied."

BOBBY WENT back to his room and sat on the edge of the bed. It was almost midnight now. Sleep would no doubt continue to elude him, especially since he wasn't used to keeping these hours in the first place.

Bad dreams and phantom prowlers didn't help.

He thought about picking up his guitar and plucking away at it in the hope of finding a new song to write down, but his nerves were stretched as taut as the strings that made the sweet sounds he loved to hear. His pulse had finally slowed to a more tolerable rate, though he could still feel his heart pounding behind his ribs like a prisoner demanding freedom.

Tap.

Oh no.

Tap-tap-tap.

The phantom prowler had returned.

Bobby clenched his hands into fists, longing to rush to the window to catch a glimpse of him or her but knowing he would see nothing if he did. So Caleb thought spirits were responsible for this? Maybe he was right. For all Bobby knew, Randy performed occult rituals in his free time and had therefore acquired an entourage of unsavory souls that cried out for human flesh.

He stood up. As much as he detested the idea of paying the man's house another visit, he had to go talk to Randy. Man to man, face to face. If Randy really was into the occult, there might be some way for him to call off his invisible brethren and leave Bobby alone for good.

8

LUPE SANCHEZ didn't know what to do.

Her prayers had been answered and Randy survived. She should have been overjoyed. And maybe she would be if Graham hadn't barged in and demanded that she tell Randy she'd been in contact with him now for months.

How would she tell Randy without making him hate her? In fear, she had betrayed him. He didn't deserve to be with someone who would willingly place his life in danger. If Randy died, how much evil would roam free?

She knew one thing for certain: if Randy had died tonight causing the world to burn, it would have all been her fault.

She lay on her back in the bathtub staring at the textured ceiling, hoping against hope that it would come crashing down and drive her into the grave she'd dug for herself so long ago.

And to think she had prayed to her Maker only hours before!

God must hate her. She was a pitiful creature, the spawn of two strangers who tumbled about in the lacy sheets of a cheap Nogales motel room. She had grown up begging for food and eventually turned to the profession that had been her genesis so she would never have to starve again.

But they had beaten her. Scratched her. Choked her until she was nearly blue in the face.

And, worst of all, they had impregnated her more times than she cared to admit because many refused to wear the one thing that would have protected them all. *Inconvenient*, they said. Pregnancy was her problem, not theirs.

It had hurt then, but it hurt even more now. Back then she knew she had about as much worth as a worn-out rag. Now she pretended to be the holy woman she wasn't. She was nothing more than a monster wearing saints' clothes. An imposter.

Nothing she could do would ever fix that.

Randy was insane for wanting to marry her, but perhaps God had made him insane. Randy knew almost everything about her. He knew about the little ones who never had the chance to be named. He knew about the terrible nights and the razor blades. And he accepted it like a big, dumb oaf whose heart was ten times bigger than it should be!

Lupe gripped her abdomen as tears leaked down her face. She didn't want to die, but she had to before she made things even worse for Randy and the rest of the world. It was the only way to make things right.

As she lay there, she decided what she would do. It might not work, but it was worth a try.

When preparing her bath, Lupe had filled the tub until the water was over a foot deep. The bubbles she'd added came up to the rim of the tub when she'd eased herself into the water. Relaxing. If only she could pass away in comfort like this instead of agony.

She closed her eyes and exhaled every last bit of air in her lungs. "I love you, Randy," she mouthed. And then, even though she didn't believe he would, she prayed, *Padre, please forgive me.*

Lupe Sanchez let her head slip below the level of the water and took a deep breath.

THE RAIN fell again after a brief lull as Bobby navigated the streets back to Randy's home. He felt even more awake now than when he sat in bed, and wave after wave of irrational thought crashed against the shore of his mind.

If Randy couldn't help him, he didn't know what he'd do. He couldn't let the poltergeists hound him forever. Maybe he could even leave and return to Cincinnati, or more specifically, the small river town that lay twenty-odd miles east of the city he claimed as his home: Eleanor, population 2,000.

Yes. Go home. He could do that. His stepmother and Jonas would welcome him with open arms. They would probably even throw a party for him to celebrate the return of the prodigal son, though he hadn't a clue who else would come. It didn't matter, though. He loved the two remaining members of his family and missed them with an intensity he hadn't even realized until now. If the party consisted of just the three of them, that would be okay.

He blinked a few times. What was the matter with him? Of course he missed his family, but this was his life now. A few spooky noises in the night couldn't make him pack up and go crawling home like a college dropout who'd squandered all of his money on booze.

Not that he could legally buy any yet, anyway. He wouldn't be twenty-one until November.

He continued driving, keeping an eye out for the correct turnoff.

It could have been the weather; it could have been the fact that he'd been chasing spirits in the dark. Either way, an undefined sense of dread began to gnaw at Bobby's bones like sharp-toothed rats.

Randy Bellison's driveway came up so suddenly Bobby almost missed it.

He turned.

———◆———

"IN THE name of Jesus Christ, the son of God and savior of those who have fallen and seek forgiveness for their transgressions, be gone from her!"

Trish's eyes blazed. She had been unable to hold still for a single moment since Randy began this evening's session, and he'd had to resort to restraining her with thin strips of cloth he'd long ago commissioned for this very purpose. He'd felt ugly inside as he'd tied her struggling hands behind her back and bound her ankles and midsection to the chair he'd brought down from the kitchen, but he couldn't allow her to harm herself.

Or him.

She swore at him, saying words that would have shamed a ship full of sailors. Sweat seeped from every pore of her body. Her face turned red and feverish. She looked like she would have fared better in a hospital bed than here.

Though the Spirit filled him as always, Randy could feel his own strength waning. Ever since he'd almost bled to death at Graham Willard's hand, he'd been unable to sustain the energy he'd once had in situations like these. Months of physical therapy and exercise had been unable to bring it all back.

Despite that, he kept his composure. On a previous day he had gotten the woman's tormentor to admit its existence—a sign of progress he found encouraging. Any display of weakness could send both him and Trish careening back to square one, and his attempts to get the tormentor to open back up would be immeasurably more difficult than before.

"Jesus Christ suffered and died so that this child might have life!" He said the words with such conviction that tears filled his eyes. "In his name, leave her and never torment this child again!"

Trish let out a hair-raising wail. "Get him out of here!"

Randy let out a small breath of relief at this apparent progress. "Yes, Trish! We *can* get him out of here! Be strong, and pray that your father delivers you from this oppression!"

She pinched her eyes shut as if unable to bear the sight of Randy's face. "We thought he was gone for good! We don't need him! We don't want him!"

She started to rise with the chair still attached to her tiny body, but Randy forced it back to the floor with his hand. Her enigmatic words were likely intended to confuse him. After all, who would cause the tormentor so much revulsion other than God himself?

He wasn't going to fall for it.

———◆———

NOBODY RESPONDED to Bobby's light rapping on the door. He waited, shivering, for the temperature had dropped a few degrees since he'd prowled around his yard not so long before. Raindrops hissed through the thick growth of trees surrounding the decrepit dwelling. Since plywood covered the windows, he had no way of knowing if Randy was still awake.

He knocked again, harder this time; just not too hard because he didn't want the house to collapse on itself like a pile of sticks. Randy was nuts for keeping the outside of his home in this condition.

And Bobby was nuts for having returned.

When neither Randy nor anyone else came to the door, Bobby tried the knob. Locked, of course. Randy claimed that someone was after him. If Bobby had been in his shoes, he'd make sure the entrances were bolted at all times, too.

He raised his hand to knock a third time when a faint female scream issued from beyond the walls.

The sense of dread that accompanied him in the car slammed back into him at full force, and all thoughts of the can-throwing poltergeists were instantly forgotten.

Fact one: A woman inside the house was being injured or even killed.

Fact two: If Bobby acted now, he might be able to save her.

Fact three: He would have to plow his way through Randy first. Bring it on.

He started to swing his foot back so he could kick at the door with all his might, but the sound of that would put Randy on full alert if the knocking hadn't already done so. There might be another way in. An unblocked window, maybe, or a back door.

Bobby hurried around the right-hand side of the house. Boards covered those windows, too. Kind of freaky, if you asked him. But what was that? There. A screen door, sans plywood.

It swung open with a screech so loud that Bobby was sure it hadn't been used since the days of Moses. The interior door was set with nine square panes of glass so dirty he couldn't see through them.

Randy had locked this door, too.

It looked like Bobby had no choice but to make some noise. Even though he knew it would hurt, he brought his fist back and punched the pane closest to the doorknob as hard as he could.

The glass remained intact. He punched it again. This time his knuckle split open, sending a spike of pain through his hand. His eyes watered but he couldn't worry about that now. Act first, patch wounds later. At least that's what heroes did in the movies.

Wishing he'd had the foresight to bring a hammer, Bobby propped the screen door open, drew back a short distance, and ran at the door with his elbow jutting out like a miniature battering ram.

All he received for his efforts was a crunching sound that was more likely bone than glass. He forced bile back down his throat and blinked so his vision would clear. If he maintained this course of action, he would have one giant body-sized bruise when he got up in the morning, and he still wouldn't have gotten into the house.

The scream from within repeated itself, only from this new vantage point Bobby could tell it was a shout of words rather than a shriek of agony. What was the woman saying? Was she begging for mercy?

He didn't want to think about what Randy might be doing to her. He had to think about how he might gain easy entry.

Suddenly it came to him.

His memory flashed back to a day roughly four years before when Bobby was a scrawny teenager of sixteen. His stepmother, Charlotte, left town to visit relatives, and Bobby chose to stay home since he still worked at Gold Star Chili and didn't want to take a vacation.

"If you get locked out of the house," Charlotte said before leaving, "there's a spare key underneath the flowerpot."

"What if I lose it?" Bobby had asked, holding back a grin.

She'd given him her best scolding look. "Then you'll be spending the next week camping out on the porch and using the birdbath as a toilet."

In the present, Bobby scanned the ground for a place where one might hide an extra key. His late grandfather had stashed his spare key inside a watering can he'd weighted down with a rock, and an aunt had hidden hers under a cement rabbit that guarded her flowerbed.

He couldn't see any pots or lawn animals (they probably would have made the house look occupied), but there was an old mat on the ground where he could wipe his feet.

He threw the mat aside and patted the small concrete slab on which it had lain. His hand touched a cool metal object, and he closed his fingers around it.

Randy needed to jack up his security if he wanted to continue hiding from whoever was after him.

As he slid the key into the lock on the doorknob, Bobby had the sudden fear that the key actually belonged to a shed or barn or even Randy's Ford, but after a few jiggles the knob yielded and he swung the door inward.

He felt as though he was about to enter a dank cavern where a fire-breathing dragon lay in wait for its next meal, and he had the wild idea that he wouldn't survive the night all in one piece. Fear made him hesitate on the threshold. Yes, he could very well die here. Only his concern for Randy's prisoner kept him moving forward. Better to perish saving another than to run away allowing her to die instead.

Bobby went into stealth mode the moment he set foot in the hallway. Light came from the coral and aqua kitchen to his left. The air still smelled faintly of pizza, and it was no wonder why: a plate of it sat on the table even though hours had passed since Randy put the pizza in the oven.

He paused on the threshold between the hallway and kitchen to listen. Then: "You're wasting your time!"

The voice dripped with vitriol, and something about its timbre made legions of goosebumps spread over Bobby's skin.

He ducked back into the hallway. A door on the left remained somewhat ajar. Light from the gap spilled across the carpet.

With a shaking hand, he pulled the door the rest of the way open. A flight of stairs leading downward ended at blood-red carpet where a human-shaped shadow splayed across the floor.

Bobby placed a foot on the first step, fully aware that he was weak and unarmed. *God be with me,* he prayed. If he acted fast, he might be able to knock Randy over again and pull the guy's own knife on him.

Before he could take another step, Randy spoke. "In the name of the judge of the living and the dead; in the name of our creator God the Father and his son, Jesus Christ; and the Holy Spirit who fills my veins; depart from this child! Christ has defeated you! Return to that pit to which you have been damned!"

Bobby stared at Randy's shadow. This had to be a joke. But Bobby couldn't hear anyone laughing. His desire to rush down there and save whoever Randy had imprisoned vanished on the spot.

The female voice spoke again. "Maybe we don't want him gone after all. Look how he stands there in terror, not understanding what he hears!"

Bobby's blood turned to ice water. From his position at the top of the stairs he couldn't see anyone, so it wasn't possible for them to see him, either.

"You will not distract me with false claims!" Randy bellowed in a voice entirely unlike the one he had used while conversing with Bobby at the church. "You will remain silent!"

The woman let out a snicker. "Listen to the blind man as he jabbers!"

"Silence! In the name of Jesus Christ—"

The step on which Bobby stood creaked beneath his weight.

He could have cut up the ensuing stillness with a knife and spread it over toast.

"Who's there?" Randy called, a new note of anger coloring his voice. "Speak!"

Bobby opened his mouth. "I . . ."

Randy appeared at the bottom of the steps, glowering like one with murder on his mind. His expression turned to one of disbelief when he and Bobby made eye contact. "What are you doing here?" Randy asked, his eyes round. "Do you have any idea what you've done?"

Bobby didn't, but he had the feeling that whatever it was wasn't good. "They followed me," he blurted. "I needed to talk to you. I thought you could make them go away." Tears sprang into his eyes. "You've got to help me! Please!"

"Bobby, I'm not even going to ask how you got in, but this is a really bad time for you to be here."

Bobby dragged in a breath. "You can't make me leave. Not until you tell me how to get rid of them."

With a pained expression, Randy glanced over his shoulder at whoever accompanied him. "If you could wait just a—"

A sharp yelp cut him off, and Randy broke into a run in the direction from which he'd come.

Bobby followed.

The rest of the basement came into view as he descended the remaining stairs. Most of the décor was done in reds and golds, except for a sleeping area consisting of calming shades of blue.

Randy rushed to untie a young woman who had been lashed to a kitchen chair. Her head listed to one side, and her watery blue eyes gazed unseeingly at the carpet.

Bobby felt his jaw drop. "What did you *do*?"

Randy ignored him. As soon as the woman was free, he laid her limp form on the floor, tilted her head back, and began to administer CPR.

"Is there . . . should I . . ." Bobby licked his dry lips, suddenly overcome with the sensation that he was a distant observer viewing this scene from afar. Detachment. Classic sign of shock. "Do you want me to call an ambulance?"

Randy shook his head as he pushed on the woman's breast-bone. He breathed into her mouth but she remained still. He repeated the process. No movement, no sign of life. After minutes that seemed like an hour, Randy placed his fingers on her wrist, and his expression twisted into one of unquenchable grief.

Bobby knew then that the woman was gone.

9

RANDY ATTEMPTED CPR for five more minutes, then shook Trish's shoulders as if to throttle the life back into her. "Please don't do this to me," he kept saying. "Please don't do this to me."

Bobby opened his mouth and closed it. He didn't know what to say or do.

Randy sat back on his heels and dragged a hand across his sweaty forehead, looking lost.

"Who was she?" Bobby asked dumbly.

Randy cleared his throat, his gaze lingering on the dead woman's face. "Her name was Trish. She needed help. This wasn't what it looked like, I can promise you that."

Good to know. "Did you . . ." Bobby took a deep breath in order to force the words out. "Kidnap her?"

Randy gave his head a listless shake. "She came here of her own will when I told her she could be freed of what afflicted her. She told her family she was checking into rehab and wouldn't be able to be reached for several days."

"Rehab."

"Yes."

Judging from what Bobby had heard from the top of the stairs, Randy specialized in the most unorthodox form of rehab imaginable. "It sounded like you were performing an exorcism," he said, knowing how ridiculous the words sounded in his mouth. Priests performed exorcisms. Maintenance men mopped floors.

Randy stood without answering and continued to stare at the motionless woman. He ran a hand through his hair. "I don't know what I'm going to do. It's never ended like this before."

Bobby gaped at him. "What do you mean, you don't know what you're going to do? You're going to call the cops and tell them a woman died in here!" A wave of nausea swept through his gut. He hadn't been in the presence of a dead body since he found his neighbor's corpse in New York, and though this scene wasn't nearly as gruesome, it still made him sick.

"No, I'm not."

Randy's response surprised him. "No? Then what do you plan on doing?"

"I already said I don't know."

"This is crazy!" The superhero part of him rebelled against his failure to rescue the woman, though he perceived that more to this situation existed than met the eye. "You said she's got a family. Don't you think they should know what happened to her?"

"I didn't say I was going to take her to the river and dump her." Tears spilled unchecked from Randy's eyes. "Oh, God, why would you let this happen? I was helping her!"

His words made Bobby's mind flash back to last night when he'd shown up for his shift at the Stop-N-Eat.

"You're fired," his boss had said.

Bobby's breath had left his lungs like he'd been punched. "What?"

"You are no longer employed by this establishment."

"But why? Is it because of last night?"

His boss gave him a cold stare. "You left the restaurant unattended."

Bobby had tried to explain. "The robbers could have killed Chrissy and me if we hadn't run. There weren't any customers in here. I swear!"

"You both left the premises while clocked in. You know this violates company protocol; you were informed of this when we hired you."

"What, you mean Chrissy's fired, too? It was my idea, don't punish her for it! I wanted to save her life!"

"Miss Evans should have known better, just like you."

Though Bobby harbored no romantic feelings toward his female coworker, he felt it was his duty to protect her. As soon as the men came up to the counter demanding that he relinquish the contents of the cash register to them, he wadded up a hefty stack of bills and threw it at them before grabbing Chrissy by the wrist and fleeing with her through the kitchen and out the back door. They'd hidden behind the dumpsters at the neighboring Burger King while Bobby phoned the authorities.

By the time the police arrived with sirens blaring, the armed men had vanished.

In theory, the robbers should have been appeased by their gift of stolen cash. But Bobby had watched enough of the news over the years to know that innocent employees were often gunned down even after giving in to the robbers' demands.

Bobby wanted to take no chances. Besides, he had already known that something bad would happen that night, much in the way he had known that Randy would have died had he left the church in his own car. Bobby informed Chrissy when he clocked in that she should be on full alert in case something terrible should go down and had already formulated his escape route.

He had done his best to help Chrissy but gotten them both fired as a result. Because of that he could sort of understand Randy's pain, even if he didn't fully understand what the man had been trying to do for Trish.

"What do you think happened to her?" Bobby asked.

Randy shrugged. "Heart attack? Aneurysm? I'm no medic, that's Phil's job. Of course my job was to free her. Guess it worked because they're gone now, aren't they? Oh, man. I should call Phil and see if he knows what to do. Let me see your phone."

10

AFTER RANDY called the man he referred to as "Phil," they went upstairs, leaving the deceased where she lay. Bobby felt an odd compulsion to stay with Trish so she wouldn't be alone, but Randy assured him it wasn't necessary. Bobby insisted they leave the basement light on. The thought of a body lying still in the dark gave him the creeps.

As they emerged into the hallway, Randy stopped short, eyeing the open side door that Bobby forgot to close in his haste. "You broke in."

Since Bobby hadn't damaged anything during his entrance other than his aching knuckle and elbow, he didn't see how it could be considered such. "I didn't break in. I found the key under the mat. Which if you ask me was a really dumb place to hide it."

Randy twisted the lock on the knob and gently shut the door. "I didn't have anywhere better to put it. Why did you come?"

"I had to get in somehow. I heard someone screaming."

"Not all the way from your house. Where's the key now?"

Bobby patted the pockets of his shorts. "I think I left it in the knob."

Randy let out a terse breath, opened the door, and jerked the key out of the doorknob. They went into the kitchen, neither of them saying a word. Because what could be said at a time like this? Bobby itched to call the authorities—it was his civic duty, he supposed—but he couldn't risk having Randy come at him with a knife again.

Bobby lowered himself into a chair, and Randy did the same, eyeing the cold pizza sitting before him with something like remorse.

"I wish you'd chosen some other time to show up," Randy said.

"Look." Bobby placed his hands on the table. He needed to be frank with the man. "If I hadn't been so desperate, I wouldn't be here, okay? So at least hear me out."

Randy lifted his head. "I'm not sure I understand."

Bobby took slow breaths to regulate his erratic pulse. "You know how something kept tapping on the window down at St. Paul's?"

Randy's eyes narrowed. "What about it?"

"It started happening at my house. Same sound as at the church. I went outside with a flashlight and found rocks and crap lying in the grass."

"And nobody was there?" Randy's face became ashen.

"Right." Bobby's heart began to hammer again so he tried to calm himself by picturing waves caressing a shoreline—one of his self-taught relaxation techniques. "I don't know what kind of voodoo you're involved with, but I want you to call whatever it is off of me because I haven't done anything to deserve being harassed like that."

Randy stared blankly at him for a moment. "You think what I do is voodoo?"

"Yes!" Bobby thought back to Joel Fontenot, a friend he'd had for a few years during grade school who had grown up in the Louisiana bayous. Joel loved to fascinate the class with tales of monsters and evil spirits that had supposedly been true accounts of things that happened to his family, though Bobby suspected Joel had invented most of it. "I mean, I don't know. I've heard that people who mess with the occult accidentally open themselves up to demons." Not that exorcising evil spirits in the name of Christ seemed like it would be a standard voodoo practice, but someone could always pervert a Christian rite into something unholy.

"Oh, boy." Randy paused as if formulating his thoughts. "If you can believe me, Bobby, I've never once practiced witchcraft, voodoo, or whatever else you're thinking of. Just because a higher power works through me doesn't mean it's evil."

"Whatever decided to bombard my house certainly wasn't good."

"And you're absolutely right. Do you remember what I told you to do about it?"

"You said to ignore it, but that obviously doesn't help you any since they were having a blast bugging us at the church anyway."

Randy stiffened. "They're not always there, you know. And there's something else I said to do, too, if you'll remember."

Bobby was too worked up about the evening's many events to recall every single word of their conversation at St. Paul's. "If you could jog my memory a little, it would be great."

A sudden knock on the front door made Bobby jump. "That would be Phil," Randy explained, not bothering to do as Bobby requested. He got up, went to the door, held his eye to the peep-hole, and pulled it open.

Bobby watched as a skinny man easily half a foot shorter than himself stepped into the living room. He looked to be in his late thirties, had a dishwater-blond buzz cut and glasses, and wore flannel pajama bottoms, a pair of old Vans slip-ons, and an Oregon Ducks t-shirt: the typical attire of one who has been forced from bed on short notice.

A black zippered tote bag hung over his shoulder. Bobby wondered what was in it.

"Whose car is that?" Bobby heard Phil ask once Randy closed and bolted the door behind him.

"You'll meet him in a second."

"I take it he's the one I'm here to see?"

"Not exactly."

Phil's eyes narrowed in suspicion when Randy led him into the kitchen. "Then what's going on? Ashley's been sick and I don't want to leave Allison alone with her for long."

"I'm getting to that. First of all, this is Bobby Roland, the kid I just hired to take my place at St. Paul's. Bobby, this is Phil Mason, an old friend of mine."

Bobby dipped his head. "Hi."

Phil didn't return the gesture. "I don't understand."

"Long story," Randy said before Bobby had the chance to answer. His hazel eyes glistened. "We have a problem downstairs."

Phil's expression darkened, and his grip tightened around the straps of the tote bag. "Should this be discussed in present company?"

Randy gave a slow nod. "He's already been clued in to some things, so it won't make any difference at this point if he hears anything else."

"Clued in?" Phil raised his eyebrows at Bobby as if demanding an answer. Bobby gave him his best I-have-no-idea-what's-going-on look, which seemed to satisfy the man for the time being.

Randy led the way out of the kitchen and into the basement. Bobby brought up the rear, a large part of him wishing he'd chosen to stay in bed.

Phil brought a hand to his mouth when he laid eyes upon the deceased. "What in God's name happened?"

"She just died." Randy's voice became choked with emotion. "She was fine one moment and like this the next."

Phil approached the woman with so much caution that Bobby thought he was afraid she'd leap up and come after him. "I doubt she was fine. How long ago did it happen?"

"I called you as soon as I knew she was gone. I tried giving her CPR for almost ten minutes."

"Why didn't you have your buddy here call me the moment she collapsed?"

"I was preoccupied."

Phil knelt down beside her and placed his hand on Trish's forehead. "Hmm." He unzipped his bag, pulled out a stethoscope, and held the end against her chest for a minute or so before setting it aside.

His lips began to move in silent prayer.

A lump of emotion rose in Bobby's throat but he quickly swallowed it. He couldn't cry. He didn't even know the girl.

But he did know that she had a family, and that she'd been so desperate to be cured of what afflicted her that she went home with a stranger and entrusted her life to him. She'd had hope. And what did it give her? An untimely death in Randy Bellison's basement.

He snapped back to attention. Phil had concluded his prayer and was speaking with Randy.

"If I'd still been the Servant, I might have been able to save her," he said in a low voice. "If there'd been any life left in her, she would be up doing cartwheels right now."

"Your ability has waned that much? You never told me."

Color rose in Phil's cheeks. "Why do you think I didn't patch you up after you were shot? I couldn't even cure Ashley of her stomach virus. It's been too long since then."

"Six years is long?" In contrast, Randy's face was a shade grayer than before. "I wish you'd told me about this. We might have been able to do something about it."

Phil gave his head a shake. "No, we couldn't have. I don't even have a tenth of the abilities I used to. I feel dried up inside. Like I'm already getting old."

Bobby cleared his throat, feeling much like he'd just arrived on a planet where the citizens were real-life Rescue Men, minus the capes and spandex tights. "Uh, guys?"

They stared at him, looking as haggard as men who had gone a week without sleep.

"I really think you should call the cops about this." Heck, the cops had even shown up when he'd called 911 about his father's heart attack, and there hadn't been anything suspicious about it.

Randy shook his head. "They'll wonder what she was doing here in the first place."

"You could tell them she was rooming here," Phil said. "Maybe she was a runaway and you offered her refuge."

"She already told her family she was going to rehab. The stories won't match up."

"So she was lying to her family. That's true enough, isn't it?"

"No." Randy gave his head another shake. "I don't want to bring any attention to myself. I'd end up on the news again, and then what would stop Graham from showing up on my porch with another gun?"

"I understand your concern," Phil said, "but real estate information is a matter of public record. All he would have to do is enter your name in a search engine to find you."

"This is Graham we're talking about here. He doesn't know how to turn a computer on, much less run an Internet search."

Phil gave him a grim smirk. "He didn't own a gun either, remember?"

Randy scowled at him and rubbed his shoulder.

"And he could always follow you home from work."

"I'm aware of that."

"I have an idea," Bobby said, even though it would in all probability be met with staunch opposition.

Two heads swiveled his way in unison.

"You could anonymously drop her off at a funeral home."

"A funeral home." Randy's tone was dubious.

"Yeah, at the back door, maybe."

"That wouldn't be suspicious at all," Phil mused. "They'd only have to start an investigation as to how she ended up there."

"Maybe she was a drifter."

Phil crossed his arms. "Someone finds the body of a young white female on their back porch; the cops are going to pull security footage from every building in a block's radius to see who the geniuses were who dropped her off." He blew out a sigh between pursed lips. "Randy, I know this isn't any of my business, but did you know her personally?"

"No, and she only ever told me her first name: Trish."

"Was she carrying any ID?"

Randy's face lit up. "I didn't think about that. She brought a purse and a little suitcase with her. I think she stuffed them under the bed."

Both men turned and stared at the unmade bed in the corner, but neither seemed to have the desire to rummage around in the personal belongings of a dead woman. In the shadows beneath the bed, Bobby could make out the rectangular shape of the suitcase and a smaller item that was probably her purse.

He might as well put himself to good use since neither Randy nor Phil seemed to be jumping up to get anything done. "I'll get them," he said, and crossed the room in eight long strides. He got down on his hands and knees on the soft carpet and reached under the bed.

"But what if you leave finger—"

His hand closed around the handle of the purse. "Prints? Too late now."

Bobby carried it and the suitcase back to the coffee table and plopped the latter down at the end furthest away from Trish's body.

Randy and Phil watched in silence as Bobby turned the purse upside down and dumped its contents onto the table. Keys, leather wallet, lip balm, loose pennies, a tiny stapler emblazoned with the logo of the college Caleb Young attended. This woman had traveled light.

He unzipped the wallet.

"Are you sure you want to do that?" Phil asked.

He shrugged. "It beats standing around doing nothing while you two continue your little debate."

Bobby felt his heart break when he saw Trish's bright-eyed expression in her driver's license photo. Nobody of such cheer should have been capable of spouting the hate-filled words he'd heard upon entering the house. "Her name is Patricia Louise Gunson," he said.

Neither Randy nor Phil showed any hint of recognition in their eyes.

"She's nineteen."

Phil said a word that Bobby didn't think should be spoken by someone who had just been praying, and he turned away from them.

"Where does she live?" Randy asked.

"Her address says Portland." The city lay nearly two hundred miles north of Autumn Ridge, so Bobby guessed she'd recently been living elsewhere. He held up the stapler. "Maybe she's a student at Autumn Ridge Community College. I could ask my roommate if he knows her."

"Don't do that. It would look suspicious."

That was true enough. Once it was made known to the public that Miss Gunson had died, Caleb might phone a tip to the police if he remembered that Bobby asked about her before anyone knew she'd passed.

If Caleb didn't crush him to a pulp first.

Bobby set the contents of the purse aside and moved on to the suitcase. He unzipped it with care, revealing a few rumpled outfits crammed inside without regard to order. He lifted them out, tried not to blush when he saw an assortment of flowery undergarments, and deciding he'd rather not put his hands on every single thing Patricia Louise Gunson had packed for her stay in Randy's basement, dumped the remaining contents out just as he'd done with the purse.

The only item of note was a day planner with a black cover. He flipped through the pages. Most of them were blank.

He tossed the planner back into the suitcase.

"Well?" Phil asked.

"I still don't know what you're going to do with her." Bobby had hoped that something in Trish's effects would help him think of something, but he remained at a loss. "All I can say is call the police and tell them what happened. Maybe some of them will believe she was here for an exorcism."

Randy and Phil exchanged solemn glances. "Some things aren't meant to be shared with law enforcement," Randy said.

Bobby couldn't believe his stubbornness. "A girl is *dead*! I think that overrides anything about keeping secrets from the cops. Besides, priests don't keep secrets about that stuff, do they?"

"I'm not a priest."

"Okay. So what?" Bobby crossed his arms. Not doing something about Trish went against everything he'd ever stood for. "Are you just going to bury her somewhere and hope nobody ever notices she's gone? Is that what you want to do?" His voice verged on the edge of hysteria, and he realized his eyes had filled with more tears he didn't remember shedding. "She'll end up being one of those cold cases they talk about on TV." The Patricia Gunson Story, they'd call it. Young college girl following her dreams vanishes without a trace.

Randy rubbed his chin. "I should call Father Preston. Maybe he'll—"

A shrill ringtone cut him off. Phil glanced dumbly at the pocket in his pajama pants for a moment before withdrawing an old flip phone. He glanced at the screen, furrowed his brow, and answered it. "Hello?"

Bobby could hear snatches of a frantic female voice on the other end of the line. Phil's face paled and a crease appeared in his forehead. "Uh-huh." A pause. "I don't know; his phone must be dead. Believe it or not, I'm at his house right now. Here he is." He held out the phone to Randy.

Randy took the phone from him but did not immediately hold it to his ear. "Phil, what is it?"

The blond man's face was troubled. "It's Lupe," he said. "She says she just tried to kill herself."

11

RANDY WISHED he'd had the time to deal with Trish before Lupe called. It pained him to leave her body alone and unattended in his basement, but right now the troubles of the living far outweighed those of the dead.

Bobby Roland, God bless him, drove Randy to Lupe's apartment so Phil could go home and be with his sick daughter. Right now the kid was sitting out in his car so Randy and Lupe would be able to talk in private.

Lupe sat sideways on the couch with her knees drawn to her chest. Her eyelids were swollen and she kept dabbing at them with the sleeve of her violet pajama shirt. She had been abnormally reticent since he'd come in the door, and nothing he'd said so far had gotten her to open up.

"Lupe, you need to tell me what's going on."

She shook her head, her hair still damp from her bath. On the phone, she told him she'd sucked in bath water with every intention of drowning herself, but it had burned her lungs so badly she'd risen out of the tub like a flailing fish and spewed it all back up onto the bathroom rug.

She had neglected to tell him why she'd attempted such a thing.

He took her left hand in his palm and covered it with his other. Her skin gave off a slight warmth that fought off some of the iciness in his fingers. "Lupe."

She lifted her head and met his gaze. The brown eyes that could light up with joy on a sunny day were twin pools of sorrow. "What?"

"It isn't fair of me to spend so much time away from you. I knew when we started going to our Sunday lunches that I wouldn't be able to be with you as often as I liked. I should have waited."

Lupe frowned. "What do you mean, waited?"

"I should have had a replacement lined up before I asked you to lunch that first day."

A faint smile. "You couldn't have known that would have led to this."

Randy forced down a knot that had formed in his throat. His mind filled with memories: Lupe walking hand in hand with him along the wooded trails behind the home in which he'd once lived; the two of them snuggled next to each other in the grass staring up at the night sky to find constellations and wondering if light years away a couple on another world was doing the same and staring straight back at them; a young woman with a troubled face sitting beside him in the church pew, looking as though she didn't have a friend in the world.

The moment he'd first laid eyes upon her, he'd had the sense that she, like him, had once been a victim of mankind's penchant for selfishness, though he couldn't quite put his finger on why he'd thought this. Perhaps it had been the haunted look in her eyes as she stared at the crucifix hanging above the altar, or maybe even the way she'd clasped her hands tightly together in front of her as if desperately trying to hold herself together.

Randy knew all too well the feeling of having no one in which to confide. He'd asked Lupe to lunch that day in the hope that his company would help cheer her up—and maybe, in time, he would open himself up to her and tell her it was possible to overcome that which had hurt her. He'd wanted her to know he would be her friend, if only she was willing to befriend him.

He'd had no idea that such a friendship would blossom into something far greater.

Randy squeezed her hand and pulled her closer to him. She leaned her head against his shoulder and sniffled.

He could feel her shaking.

"Does this have to do with the way things used to be?" he asked, remembering how she'd sobbed in his arms as she told him about the men she'd had no other choice but to lie with as a young teen.

She immediately jerked away from him, her eyes full of fear. "No. No. I can't."

"Lupe, I love you. If it's about that, tell me. You know I'm not going to judge you."

She cast her gaze downward. "I know, Randy. But I—I betrayed you. It was supposed to look like an accident. I didn't want you to think . . ."

Betrayed? Randy knew that Lupe had not truly intended to kill herself this evening. If so, she would have chosen some other means of ending her life. Something must have made her depressed, and she'd inhaled the water in the peak of despair.

Betrayed . . .

Randy felt cold inside as he regarded her. "What did you do?"

"Your car. I didn't want to. I really didn't." Tears streamed down her tan cheeks.

"You mean you cut the brake line on my car?"

She gave a frantic nod. "He said he'd kill me if I didn't. He even had a gun, and he showed me the bullets inside so I'd know it was loaded." She hugged her arms to her chest. "And he—he said he would kill me if I told you anything. So now I'm going to die anyway."

Randy's mind went numb. How could the sweet girl to whom he'd given his heart have become involved in such a thing? "I could have died."

"You didn't, though. God answered my prayers."

Randy did his best to suppress a wave of anger even though every cell in his body yearned to jump up and find the monster who'd given Lupe such orders. "You mean to tell me someone forced you to vandalize my car?"

"Yes! But he told me to cut all of the brake lines, and I only cut one because I thought it wouldn't be as bad that way. But that boy you talked about on the phone, he must have seen me do it and that's why he warned you not to drive away."

Randy had briefed her on what happened at the church when he'd called her earlier in the evening, leaving out the part about Bobby's supposed premonition because he still wasn't sure what to make of that. "Who told you to do it?" he asked, even though there was only one logical answer to that question.

"Who do you think?"

Randy immediately pictured a stooped old man pointing a gun at his chest, and his hand immediately went to his shoulder to rub the place where the bullets had entered him. "Why didn't Graham do it himself?" Or, for that matter, why didn't the old creep try to kill him face to face again? Forcing Lupe to carry out his bidding was the epitome of cowardice.

"I don't know. Maybe he was afraid of being caught in the act. Better me than him, right? But he comes here sometimes. Other times he makes me go there."

Randy's anger started to rise again. Just how long had Lupe been in contact with Graham? "Where does he make you go?"

"I don't know where it is. I meet him at the park or here, and he has someone blindfold me so I don't get to see where we go."

Randy felt his stomach turn. Graham had placed his own twist on the Servant safe house system that had been used for centuries. Once a victim was sufficiently rid of an afflicting spirit, he or she would be sent to a safe house to receive counseling and to be nursed back to health. In order to protect the location of the safe house, the victim would be willingly blindfolded during transportation, though more recently Phil would drive them to the safe house in a work van that lacked rear windows.

After Graham attempted to kill him last year, Randy instructed Phil Mason to find a new safe house and not tell any other former Servant its location just in case another traitor dwelled in their midst.

"Can you describe the place?" he asked. Maybe if she could provide enough details, he would be able to figure out where Graham had taken her so he could confront the man there himself.

She shrugged. "It's a house. It has two floors and a basement, I think."

"What about the outside?"

"I've never seen it. When they—he—takes the blindfold off, we're usually in the kitchen or living room."

"You said someone else puts the blindfold on."

"Yes, but he isn't there when Graham takes me into the house. I think he stays in the car."

"Do you know who it is?"

"How should I know? I've never seen him, either." She paused to wipe her eyes. "Most of the times I've been there, the drapes have been closed. But one day I peeked through them when Graham wasn't looking. I saw the mountains. Lots of trees. I'm not sure how far away from here it is."

Her description of the outdoor scenery could have fit any number of locations in the area. "How long does it take you to get there?"

"Sometimes thirty minutes, sometimes an hour. I think maybe they take different routes so I can't guess where they're taking me. But it's always the same place. The walls in the living room are dark purple so it sucks all the light out of the room. The furniture is plain. There's a TV and some books on a shelf. There's even a crucifix on the wall." She shivered.

The latter touch sounded just like the Graham he'd thought he'd known—not the one who had shot him. "And what is it you do when you're there?"

Her expression darkened. "Mostly we talk. He asks me about my childhood and tells me about his like he's trying to be my friend. Did you know that when he was a boy, his dog was running around the yard with his shoe in his mouth like it was a toy? He said it ran right out into the street and got hit by a car, and it died still hanging onto the shoe. He said he went and burned the pair because he couldn't bring himself to put them on again."

Randy shook his head. He had never heard that tale, and he wondered why Graham would have bothered to share it with her.

"What else?" he asked.

"Sometimes he talks about his wife and daughters. He'll mention that drug store he used to run. He'll talk about people he knew years ago who died before I was born and some friend named Nate he met at a nursing home. Normal things, you know? Only I know he isn't doing it to be my friend. There's something else he isn't telling me, like there's this huge gap in the middle of everything else where he hid all the ugliness inside him."

Her words chilled him. Graham couldn't have hidden the blackness for that long. He had been a Servant, too. God never would have chosen him to do his will if he had harbored evil in his soul.

Judas, a voice whispered inside his head.

Well, there was that. But if Graham, like Judas, had fallen away from God after previously being devoted to him, when had it happened? And why?

Randy had wondered those things for the past year, and he suspected he would never learn the answer to either of those questions.

"Has he ever laid a hand on you?" he asked, praying to God Graham hadn't.

She shook her head. "No, but he will now that I've told you this. And then he'll kill you."

Randy stood up, feeling the urge to take action but not knowing which action to take. Graham had mentally violated the woman he loved. Who knew what else they had talked about in the house with the purple walls? He could be slowly poisoning her soul, causing her to sink back into the depths of despair from which Randy had fought so hard to rescue her.

And he knew very well why Graham had chosen to do so: he knew it would hurt Randy more than a physical wound ever could.

Every vein in his body burned with a righteous rage. Feeling somewhat hypocritical, he said, "I'm going to call the police. Maybe they can arrest Graham the next time he comes to pick you up."

Lupe's face turned gray. "He said he would kill both of us if I did that."

"You said he'll kill us anyway. And if you want to live so badly, why did you inhale all that water in the bathtub?"

"I—I don't want Graham to kill me."

His voice broke. "But you can kill yourself?"

Her expression tightened. She made no reply.

Randy understood now. Lupe feared dying perhaps more than anything else, but if it was going to happen she would prefer to do it herself rather than suffer at the hands of another who might torture her first. "Promise me you'll never do that again. Okay?"

"Okay," she whispered.

"We're going to get through this together. I don't know how, but we will." He paused. "And how is Graham going to know the police have been called?"

She shrugged and drew her knees closer to her chest. "I don't know. I'm afraid. I'm just afraid."

Randy couldn't blame her because fear had settled into his heart, too.

———◆———

DESPITE THE fact that Bobby had long ago grown accustomed to nocturnal hours, the stressful events of the evening were taking their toll on him. At first he leaned his head back and closed his eyes to pass the time while Randy consoled his girlfriend, but before he knew it, he was slouched over the center cup holders onto the passenger seat using his hands as a pillow and the darkness as a blanket.

Tired as he was, his mind wouldn't shut off. He kept thinking about things. Bad things. Like the girl named Trish. And the woman named Lupe who'd tried to kill herself.

Randy may have claimed to be a man of God, but he seemed more and more like a herald of death.

Bobby swallowed and wondered what that might mean for him.

Then again, people tended to die around Bobby, too. Like his father and Tyree.

For a few minutes he entertained the idea that this might all be a dream and he'd wake up back in Kansas (or, in his case, Ohio) and everything would be back to normal.

His father would make fun of him right now if he could see him. *Son,* he'd say, *you've done gone and made a fool of yourself. Running around in the dark like that—what's gotten into you? And what did I tell you about never trusting a man who says he's involved with spirits?*

Ken Roland had been a practical man. He worked. He ate. He drank. And whenever Bobby showed a greater interest in his guitar than in physical labor, he would catch Ken shaking his head as if loving music was something to be ashamed of.

His stepmother had supported him, though. Even paid for all his lessons. But technically she wasn't his stepmother anymore. She was simply the woman who had married his father and raised him as her own and then became his legal guardian when Ken passed away.

Simply. Ha. Charlotte Roland was the only mother he had, even though she'd never bothered to adopt him.

Loneliness tugged at his heart like a fish on a hook. He hadn't visited his family once during the past two years because thoughts of them took a backseat to this new life outside of Ohio.

Again, the notion that he should pack his bags and return to his hometown flashed through his mind. *Go home,* an inner voice whispered. *Go home.*

The basement bedroom at the Rolands' house was probably still unused unless Jonas had occupied it subsequent to Bobby's departure. It wouldn't matter. He could show up on their doorstep and be settled in within five minutes.

A car door slammed close by and the patter of footsteps crossed the apartment's parking lot. How much longer would Randy be in there? Not that Bobby needed to be anywhere in the morning, but he had about as much desire to camp out here in his car as he did of sleeping on a park bench.

He sat up and stared at the distant door of the unit Randy had disappeared through. The light still glowed behind drawn curtains. He hoped everything was okay in there. Randy had told him he'd be back, but it grew so late he considered asking if Randy would be willing to stay there until morning.

But Bobby wasn't going to be the guy to interrupt their conversation.

Or anything else that might be going on in there, for that matter.

Ever the gentleman, he waited for Randy to emerge.

Seconds turned into long minutes. It had to be two o'clock by now. Tomorrow he would be cleaning a church at this time of night. By himself. In a seedy part of town. Where people cut brake lines on cars and unseen beings tapped on the windows.

As if on cue, a small object bounced off the windshield and rolled down the hood. Fear seized his heart for a second before he realized it was only an acorn that had fallen from one of the tree limbs hanging above the car.

The night became still once more. He waited.

A length of time passed. He shifted positions and gazed out the window again. The apartment lights were still on.

He sighed.

A speck of orange light inside the car to his left caught his eye as he went to lie down again. He squinted. It looked like the burning tip of a cigarette, but aside from that he couldn't see anything other than vague shadows within the vehicle.

It would seem Bobby was not the only one waiting for something in the dim parking lot, and since he hadn't heard anyone enter or exit the other vehicle since he arrived, the smoker must have lurked behind dark windows for the entire duration of Bobby's wait.

Creepy.

He continued to watch the cigarette. Intuition told him the person smoking it was a man. What was he doing here? Casing the joint? Waiting for someone to meet him? Or was he just out here to smoke?

Bobby held his finger over the automatic lock button, knowing he was probably overreacting. But he wasn't in the best shape. Kids in school had made fun of him, calling him Knobby Bobby and Skinny Ninny and things like that, generally before he got slammed face first into a locker. If this guy wanted to break into his car and steal his wallet, Bobby wouldn't be able to stop him without getting broken himself.

He pushed the button. The sound of the locks engaging was as loud as a car backfiring in the quiet air.

The cigarette went out.

Bobby stopped breathing. Two eyes that he couldn't see were likely staring in his direction.

"Randy," he whispered, "it would be great if you could get out of there so I can leave."

He supposed he could leave the car himself and take refuge inside the girlfriend's apartment, but it would be rude to barge in on such a scene. The woman had tried to *kill* herself. She had to be messed up on something. Drugs, maybe. Normal, healthy people didn't want to die. They wanted to—

The voice of reason spoke inside his head. *Get out of the car. Now.*

Bobby didn't need to be told twice. He scrambled across to the passenger seat, made sure he had his keys and wallet, and dove out the door.

The temperature of the night air had dropped into the upper forties. He shivered as he raced between and around other parked cars and resisted the urge to glance back the way he'd come.

He rapped on the apartment door he'd seen Randy enter earlier. *Please don't let them be angry.*

He heard movement inside. After several moments, the door swung open, and a haggard-looking Randy greeted him. "Come in."

Bobby stepped into a tidy living room decorated in shades of orange and hot pink. A single lamp burned on an end table. Randy sat down on a couch where a slender Hispanic woman dressed in violet pajamas lay on her side. Randy began running his fingers through her hair.

"Lock the door, please," Randy said in a quiet voice.

Bobby did as instructed and shoved his hands into his pockets. "Look, I'm sorry I—"

Randy held up a hand. "I'm the one who's sorry for keeping you so long. I was about to tell you to go on home."

"I'm not going home yet," Bobby said. "There's someone outside in the car next to mine. I've been out there for what, more than an hour? I noticed him smoking a cigarette, and nobody got into the car after I parked, so that means he's been out there the whole time."

Randy's face became grim. "Could you see what he looked like?"

"No. It was too dark. I didn't get a good look at the car, either." Bobby went to the window facing the parking lot and held an eye to the gap between the slats of the blinds, but the glare from the lamp prevented him from seeing if the man had left the vehicle.

Lupe sat up and blinked sleep from her eyes. She had long, dark hair that was almost black, and it came down nearly to her waist. She bore no signs of self-injury that Bobby could see. "What's going on?" she asked in a slight Mexican accent, looking from Randy to Bobby and shoving a strand of hair behind one ear.

"Bobby says someone's been waiting out in a car the whole time we've been here."

Lupe looked at Bobby and frowned. "Man or woman?"

"Man, I think."

"Was he doing anything?"

"I don't know. But what kind of creep sits in his car all night?"

Lupe gave Randy a worried glance. "What if it's him?"

Randy stood up. "That's what I'd like to find out."

She seized him by the arm. "No! I won't let you go out there if it's really him."

Bobby wondered if the "him" she referred to was the person Randy had mentioned when he had a knife pressed against Bobby's throat back at the church. "It's either go and check it out or wait here until he leaves," Bobby said. "And I don't think you two would like it very much if I spent the rest of the night sleeping on your couch."

Randy pondered this for a moment. "Lupe, where's your flashlight?"

She went to the end table and pulled the drawer open. "Here. If you're going, I'll go with you."

Randy clicked the flashlight on and checked the peephole, then opened the door. "Fine. Both of you stay behind me."

Randy didn't make the best human shield since he was neither tall nor wide enough to effectively conceal the two of them, but Bobby was still thankful he wouldn't be the first one out the door.

They stepped out onto the concrete walkway leading past the row of units. Lampposts spaced every so many yards along the walk lit the apartment building's façade. Bobby thought they should have installed lighting at the back of the lot, too. It had probably been some kind of budgeting issue. Who cared if you couldn't see anything when you parked back there at night? If you couldn't see the weirdoes, maybe they couldn't see you, either.

Randy swept the yellow beam across the lot toward Bobby's Nissan. "Is it the car on the left or the right?"

"If we're facing it, it's on the right." Bobby squinted. Randy had the beam pointed at the car's windshield. A male figure sat motionless behind the steering wheel.

The car was a newer make of Chevy, maybe a Cruze. Bobby tried to make out the plate number. "One, four, nine . . ."

The Chevy's engine roared to life and two high-powered headlights pierced the darkness as effectively as twin suns. The rest of the license plate number vanished in the glare.

Randy broke into a run and Bobby almost followed, but the smoker's car squealed out of the parking space, nearly grazed the back end of a parked sedan, and sped out onto the street without stopping.

"Did you see the rest of the plate?" Bobby asked as he tried to blink the afterimage of the headlight beams from his eyes.

Randy shook his head. "I was focusing more on who was driving that thing. Lupe, have you seen that car around here before?"

"Not that I remember." Lupe stepped off the edge of the sidewalk into the parking lot and stared in the direction of the road. "Who was it? Did you see?"

"No," Randy said, defeated.

12

BOBBY ROLLED out of bed at eleven in the morning, surprisingly well-rested after the night's hectic events. He did some stretches for a few minutes and then threw open the curtains to see that the garbage cans still sat in disarray along the back fence and assorted pop cans lay here and there in the grass like poorly-concealed Easter eggs.

Looked like he'd be doing some yard work once he'd gotten a bite to eat. What fun.

He lumbered out of the bedroom. "I'm up," he said. "Fix me anything good to eat?"

Silence greeted him, and he did not smell any food.

"Caleb?" He did a quick scan of the house, most of which could be seen from where he stood. Caleb did not occupy the kitchen, living room, utility room, or bathroom, leaving few other places for his roommate to hide.

Apprehension put him on edge. Caleb sometimes went out to grab fresh bagels from the shop down the street, but he always asked Bobby if he wanted anything before he left.

It seemed unlikely that Caleb would still be asleep at this hour.

Bobby knocked on Caleb's bedroom door anyway. It swung open at his touch.

His stomach flipped when he saw inside the room.

He blinked.

Pale blue walls met bare, tan carpet. The science posters Caleb taped to the walls were gone. The closet stood open and empty.

Dizziness nearly overcame him as he tried to process the scene. Caleb could not have gotten all of his things, furniture included, out of the house in a single night without help and without waking him. And hadn't his car been in the driveway when Bobby got home? He would have noticed it missing.

Caleb's bedroom window gave Bobby an ample view of their driveway and the sole Nissan that occupied it.

Bobby raced back into the living room. Caleb's usual mound of schoolwork was nowhere to be seen. No books, no papers, not even a pen or a paperclip. The piece of junk mail Caleb liked to use as a bookmark sat neatly next to the lamp on the end table.

As far as Bobby could see, the only sign that Caleb Young had ever existed was the squashed place at the end of the couch where he sat each evening, but it might have been that way when they'd bought it secondhand.

This was nuts.

I've entered The Twilight Zone, Bobby thought. Now he just needed Rod Serling to show up and start narrating his life.

It was possible, however unlikely, that something came up requiring Caleb to leave. Bobby had been exhausted when he got home. He might have overlooked Caleb's missing vehicle, or he could have slept through Caleb's departure.

He had one way to find out.

He dialed Caleb's cell phone number. Held his breath. Waited.

A robotic voice informed him that the call could not be completed as dialed.

He punched in Caleb's number a second time and got the same result.

Rats.

His only other option was to call the bookstore where Caleb worked. Bobby knew the campus's main number since he'd seen it on some of the papers Caleb usually left lying around.

After connecting with the campus operator, he was patched through to the bookstore.

A female voice—human this time—came on the line. "Campus Books and More. This is Cassidy speaking. How may I help you?"

"Um, hi. Is Caleb there?"

"I'm sorry, who?"

"Caleb Young. He works there."

A pause. "Sorry, but you must have the wrong location. Which store were you trying to reach?"

"The one at Autumn Ridge Community College."

"I've worked here two years, and I don't know anyone named Caleb."

"He's got brown hair and glasses," Bobby said. "Wears a lot of polo shirts. Looks like a geek. You're sure you don't know him?"

"I'm very sorry, but no. I wish I could have been of more help."

A rash idea occurred to him. "Actually, maybe you can. Does Trish Gunson work there?"

"Trish?" Genuine surprise colored the woman's voice. "No, why?"

"I wondered if I could get ahold of her." He hoped God would forgive him for the tasteless lie. "I haven't seen her in a few weeks and wondered if she was okay."

"Oh, you know, Trish is Trish. She's been sick a lot lately. Started acting real odd awhile back, too, but she won't talk about what's bothering her." Then came a longer pause. "Wait. If you knew Trish, you'd know she doesn't work here."

"Uh . . . I don't know her that well. She's in some of my classes."

"I don't think she's taking any summer classes this year. What's your name?"

"Nobody," he said and disconnected the phone.

He sat down on the non-squashed end of the couch. Caleb had been lying to him the whole time he'd claimed to be working at the college bookstore. Where could he have gotten the money to pay his half of the rent, and where did he go each day when he claimed to be at work and school? Did he sell drugs for a living and have a deal go sour? That might explain why he left with such abruptness.

He shook his head. Caleb couldn't have been a dealer. The guy was too friendly and unassuming, characteristics which Bobby supposed might throw suspicion away from someone who dealt in illegal substances.

Bobby returned to his roommate's bedroom to think. He looked at the floor again. Such nice carpet. Countless drink stains speckled the carpet in Bobby's room, but the carpet in here was as pristine as if it had only just been installed. There weren't even any flattened indentations where Caleb's bed, dresser, and desk had sat. Bobby squatted on the floor and ran his hand across the carpet fibers. This didn't make sense. A heavy object sitting in one place for only a day or two would leave a mark once it was moved, and Caleb's furniture had sat in this room for an entire year.

Even if Caleb had run the vacuum before leaving (which in turn would have jolted Bobby from his slumber), it would not have eliminated the marks entirely.

His head began to spin. Something had to be horribly wrong with Bobby's perception of reality. Had he been so lonely when he first came to Oregon that his mind fabricated a friend for him?

He thought of the times he and Caleb went to the bagel shop together. The cashier interacted with Caleb just as he had with Bobby, but that might just mean Bobby imagined that, too.

And what if he imagined every single thing that happened last night? What if he never really arrived in Oregon? Had he truly lived in Salt Lake City for eleven months? Had he ever set foot in New York?

Bobby realized he'd developed the shakes.

He recalled with clarity the day he chose to come here. He'd been sitting in his Utah apartment brainstorming the next leg of his journey of seeing the world but was unable to make up his mind on where to go. There were so many places to visit, but he would have to live to be ten thousand years old to get to them all. Should he go to California? Colorado? Alaska? Arizona? He'd picked up his Rand McNally road atlas, closed his eyes, shuffled through the pages, and jabbed his finger at one at random.

He'd opened his eyes to find his fingernail bisecting the name of Autumn Ridge, Oregon: a town he had never heard of in a state to which he had never given more than a passing thought.

A week later he arrived in the small city and started looking for a place to live. When another week went by in which he couldn't find an apartment that fit his qualifications, he'd placed an ad online asking for a roommate who would be willing to rent a house with him. Caleb phoned him two days later, introducing himself as a college student who would gladly split the cost of a house.

Surely nobody could imagine so many specific details.

Yet he had apparently hallucinated the entire existence of Caleb Young. That, or the guy had been a ghost.

Or was playing a brilliant practical joke on him. What could Caleb have done, installed new carpet during the night?

He stood up. He would have to put this out of his mind before he went mad.

He wanted to tell Randy what the girl on the phone said about Trish. Thing was, the guy's phone would be stuffed in a bag of rice right now after its altercation with a puddle last night. Randy had used Bobby's phone to call his friend Phil. Phil might know how Bobby could get ahold of Randy with a different number.

He found a number he didn't recognize on the list of outgoing calls. Selected it. Hit the call button.

Six rings later, Phil Mason's recorded voice said, "This is Phil. I can't come to the phone right now. You know the drill."

Beep.

Bobby opened his mouth. "Uh, this is Bobby Roland. We met last night at Randy's place. I really need to talk to him right now, but I think his phone might still be dead. Do you know how I can get ahold of him? Thanks."

He disconnected and tried Randy's number in case his phone had been resurrected overnight. It went to voicemail without ringing.

The phone rang in his hand as soon as he hung up. Phil Mason was calling him back.

"Hello?"

"Bobby?"

"That's me. Is Randy with you?"

"Not at the moment. What's this about?"

"A certain thing that happened at his house last night." These days one never knew who might be listening in. Mention a dead body in a basement over the telephone, and you could have a SWAT team banging your door down within ten minutes.

"Ah." This was followed by something else, but a burst of static made it impossible to make out Phil's words.

"What was that? Sorry, you're cutting in and out."

Something garbled. Then, "—me at the library parking lot in fifteen minutes. You know where it is?"

"What?"

"The library. Over on Twelfth Avenue."

Bobby often went there to borrow CDs. "I know where it is. I just couldn't hear the first part of what you said."

"Meet me there. Fifteen minutes. I drive a burgundy Taurus that's probably older than you are. You can't miss it."

The line went dead.

Bobby hesitated. Did he really want to get involved with these people? Not particularly, but it looked like the only way he'd be able to tell Randy what he'd learned was to meet up with Phil.

A meeting like that wouldn't take long—no more than a few minutes. He could be back home to continue figuring out what happened to Caleb in no time.

Bobby threw on a clean pair of jeans and a navy blue t-shirt, tucking his phone and wallet into his pockets. He ran a comb through his hair, checked himself in the bathroom mirror, decided that waiting another day to shave was fine by him, and stepped out into the strangely cloudless day.

Lunchtime traffic clogged the streets, making him about five minutes late for the rendezvous. The library parking lot was so packed Bobby had to park almost at the far corner of the lot out by the road.

Which coincidentally was right next to the only burgundy car in sight.

Bobby backed into the space and killed the engine. Phil's car sat to the left of him. The man tapped away at his phone but laid it down when Bobby waved to get his attention.

Phil beckoned to him with one finger.

"Sorry I'm late," Bobby said when he climbed into the Taurus's passenger seat. The black zippered tote bag Phil carried last night sat on the floor at his feet. "Traffic was killer."

"Don't worry; you're fine."

"Is your daughter feeling better this morning?"

A faint smile lit up Phil's features. "Thankfully, yes." Then he folded his arms and stared straight through the windshield at the row of cars in front of them. "Who are you, really?"

The question caught Bobby off guard. "Bobby Roland. I already told you."

"You're going to have to be more specific."

"Robert Jackson Roland?"

"I don't care what your name is. I want to know who you are."

"I don't follow."

Phil threw him a brief glance. "It isn't that hard to figure out. I need to know who you are as a person so I can decide whether or not we can trust you."

"We?"

"Just answer the question."

Bobby still didn't know what the man wanted to hear. "I'm from Cincinnati," he said.

"They have good chili, I've heard. Go on."

"I play the electric guitar."

"Professionally?"

Bobby shook his head. "I wish."

"What else?"

"I like to travel. That's how I ended up here. Growing up we didn't go many places. Mostly Kentucky and Michigan. As soon as

I turned eighteen I left home so I can see as much of the world as possible before I die. You don't get to see much of creation when you don't go anywhere, you know?"

Phil nodded. "You're a man of faith, then?"

"Sure."

"Are you a man of good character?"

This interview was getting stranger by the second. "I don't know. I've never stolen anything and I've never killed anyone, if that's what you mean."

"Have you ever lied?"

Bobby thought about his phone call to the campus bookstore. "Yes, I have. Now can we talk about why I'm here?"

Fatigue lined Phil's pale face. "I understand you only met Randy last night."

"That's right. I needed a new job and my roommate—" Bobby's chest tightened—"found the maintenance listing and thought I should give it a try."

"Then you understand why I find it strange that you would end up at Randy's house after midnight, only a handful of hours after meeting him for the first time."

"It's a long story."

"Most are."

"It's complicated, too." Bobby started drumming his fingers on the armrest as he waited for Phil to get to the point.

"This is a complicated situation," Phil said. "You understand why we can't trust just anyone who walks into our lives the way you just did."

"Sure I do. Randy's been trying to hide from a friend who tried to kill him."

"Graham Willard." Phil sighed. "He shot Randy twice in the shoulder and left him for dead. Don't you remember hearing his name on the news?"

"I must have missed it." Bobby could see why Randy had acted so paranoid when he'd tackled him in the church lot. "That's awful."

"What's more awful is who Graham was to him. He let Randy live in his house for free for five years. Randy grew up in foster care, so Graham was like his adoptive grandfather. With the way they acted around each other, you'd think they were two peas in a pod."

"Until last year."

Phil dipped his head.

"What would make Graham snap like that?"

The blond man shrugged, and they both fell silent.

"About why I called you," Bobby said when it was apparent Phil had no desire to continue the previous discussion. "I found out some things about Trish."

Phil nodded, all business once more. "Hold that thought. Randy needs to hear this more than I do. But first let me see your phone."

Bobby didn't know why Phil would need it, but he slid it out of his pocket and handed it over.

"How old is this?" Phil asked as he flipped it open and examined the screen.

"About four years. I never saw a reason to upgrade."

"So there's no GPS on here."

"Nope."

Phil returned the phone and held up a black paisley bandanna that had been lying on the seat beside him. "I know this is going to make you uncomfortable, but we have to do this in order to maintain absolute secrecy."

Bobby blinked. Phil held the bandanna out for him to take. "What do you want me to do with it?"

"First," Phil said, "you need to get down on the floor in the back seat. Then you'll tie this over your eyes so you can't see anything, and then I'll put a blanket over you so any passersby won't know you're there."

His pulse quickened. Phil was going to kidnap him!

Bobby grabbed the door handle, but Phil said, "Wait."

"Only if you tell me why you feel the need to tie me up."

"I won't be tying you up. *You* will be covering your eyes so you can't see where we're going."

"And where's that?"

"It's called a safe house. If you know where it is, it might not be safe anymore. Normally I'd just stick you in the back of our van, but unfortunately the transmission in it went out last week and I'm still waiting for it to be fixed."

"I don't want to do it."

"Then you don't get to talk to Randy, because that's where I took him this morning after picking him up from Lupe's apartment. If you don't want to see him, then get out and go home. I was going to have lunch at home with my wife and daughter and already told them I won't be able to because something came up— that *something* being you."

"You're going to steal my keys and wallet."

Phil rolled his eyes. "Just get in the back seat. You still have your phone. If I so much as make a move to take your things, you have my permission to call the cops on me. Deal?"

"Deal," Bobby sighed.

13

GRAHAM WILLARD was a busy man. That's what other people couldn't understand. To them he was just another seventy-five-year old retiree who'd spent four decades running the Trustworthy Drug Store in Hillsdale before selling it to some foreigners. His years were waning. He should be put away in a retirement home so he could dawdle away the time playing checkers with deaf World War II veterans old enough to be his parents and widowed housewives whose children found it too much trouble to take care of them.

His daughter Kimberly had hinted at the idea of selling the house. "Daddy," she'd say, "don't you think it's time to move into a group home? That house is so big with only you and that boy living in it, and you know he's old enough to get a place of his own."

One of her main concerns was his difficulty in climbing and descending the stairs. Kimberly just knew he'd fall and break his hip one of these days, or maybe his neck if he were extra unlucky. And she would just die if she showed up one day when Randy wasn't home and found her old daddy sprawled at the bottom of the staircase like a broken doll.

Kimberly didn't know Graham's infirmity was all an elaborate act that made him grin inside like a mischievous schoolboy. Graham was almost as fit as he had been twenty years ago, in part because he exercised in secret almost every day, shunned red meat, and took the proper dietary supplements to ensure he received all the nutrients his aging body required.

His only vice other than the Bloody Marys were the cigarettes. If he ever found the willpower to quit, he'd probably feel as young as fifty again. Maybe younger.

When Graham botched Randy's murder, he severed all contact with Kimberly so she wouldn't turn him in. Even though Graham loved his daughter, he did not miss her. He did miss Stephanie, the estranged one he hadn't heard from since she left home at the age of eighteen. But not Kimberly. She was too nosy. Maybe she had suspected something all along and wanted to uncover the truth for herself, but Graham would never let anything slip.

"How do you feel today?" he asked the woman seated with him at his dining room table. Her skin was sallow, her head wrapped in a pink bandanna in such a way it reminded him of a turban. She could have been a fortune teller if she'd worn a shawl and gold hoop earrings, though if she truly had the ability to predict the future she would have run from him the moment they met.

Her thin lips twisted into a smile. "I feel at peace. No matter what happens to me, everything will be okay." She paused to sip at the hot tea Graham had set in front of her. "Jim, have you ever wondered what it's like to die?"

Graham smiled when she used the false name he'd given her. "Every day of my life."

"Don't you find that unusual?"

"Not at all. It's a healthy thing to ponder one's own mortality. Those who think they're immortal in this flesh are the unusual ones."

To his surprise, the woman laughed. "I just can't stop thinking about it. Will I even feel myself dying, or will I simply be here one moment and there the next without any awareness of a transition?" She took another drink and shivered. Her mug was nearly half empty.

Graham shrugged. "And there's always the possibility of a purgatory, you know that? How does that make you feel?"

She lifted a hairless eyebrow. "You Catholics will never make sense to me. If there's a purgatory, we're living in it right this second. God knows life is hard enough as it is."

"Whoever said I'm Catholic?" Graham took a long draw from his own tea and licked his lips in an effort to subconsciously tell the woman she needed to hurry with her drink. He was eager to get started.

"It was just . . . a thought." She blinked, shook her head, and drank again. "Goodness, I feel like I need a nap."

"Or maybe your time is just coming sooner than you expected." Graham loved the part when they finally caught on, and at that point it was always too late for them to do anything about it.

She started to laugh, but her face froze in an awkward expression somewhere between a smile and a frown. "Did you put—"

Graham stood up, rounded the table, and caught her under the arms just as she started to slump out of the chair. She weighed about as much as a bag of leaves. He hoisted her limp form into his arms and carried her down the squeaking stairs to the basement, where the operating table awaited its use. He had repeated this ritual so many times he barely gave it any thought. Find a potential victim, either at a homeless shelter or elsewhere. Get to know them. If they had close friends and family, dump them and find somebody else. If not, gain their trust. Invite them over. Give them a drink and words of reassurance.

Then let the experiment begin.

This woman called herself Mary, which Graham found humorous because of the drink in which he so loved to indulge. He laid her out straight on the table and buckled the leather straps across her body so she would be unable to escape when she awoke.

He did not feel guilty about killing her. She had stage three lung cancer and would not last long anyway. He was merely doing her a service by ending her suffering sooner than she anticipated.

The pink bandanna slid off her head and onto the plastic-covered cushion that ran the length of the table to provide the woman as much comfort as possible while she passed, revealing a scalp as smooth and white as a bird's egg. Graham gently secured it back into place so Mary wouldn't feel ashamed he'd seen what the cancer-killing drugs did to her body. He believed in helping people maintain their dignity as they died—as long as their name wasn't Randy Bellison.

Next Graham selected a thick rubber band from amid the clutter on his workbench and tied it around Mary's right arm just above the elbow. The veins in the lower part of her arm popped up blue and cordlike.

Graham's only regret about the procedure he had so often repeated was that he had not yet found a way to deaden their pain. Novocain might have worked, but he wasn't about to go raiding a dentist's office and risk being arrested for breaking and entering. He had lived under the radar for so long that he knew which risks to avoid. Selecting his victims and transporting them to this house was dangerous enough in itself.

The attempt on Randy's life had been the rashest decision Graham ever made. He hadn't been thinking clearly then. In retrospect, he could have staged Randy's murder to look like an accident in order to throw suspicion away from himself, but instead he'd placed himself directly into the spotlight by choosing a gun he wasn't used to using as the murder weapon and then fleeing like a fool.

Mary's eyes fluttered open like startled moths, jarring him from his reverie. Her gaze darted from the rafters to the workbench to Graham himself. Though he didn't think it possible, her face grew paler.

He approached her side wearing a sympathetic smile. "Don't be afraid, Mary. Everything is going to be okay."

The look in her eyes told him she believed otherwise.

"Don't you have anything to say?"

Her head shook almost imperceptibly from side to side.

Graham waited. This Mary was an interesting one. Some of them had wailed and screamed and tried to flail their way out of their predicament, but here was a woman already resigned to her fate.

"I need you to talk to me," he said. "Will you do that? It's very important that you do."

She drew in a ragged breath. "What do you need me to talk about?"

"What it's like. I need you to talk for as long as you can. Tell me everything you see while it's happening." He held up the razor-sharp knife, and the pupils in Mary's eyes contracted into black pinpricks. "I sharpened this earlier today, so you might only feel a slight sting. I'm sorry if it hurts more than that. I don't want to cause you an unnecessary amount of pain."

A tremor took hold of Mary's body. "Why are you doing this?"

Not wishing to delay any longer, Graham pressed the tip of the knife into the vein visible in the crook of her arm and slid it downward to her wrist. The blade passed through her paper-thin skin with the ease of a hot knife through butter. "Because I have to know."

Tears welled up in both of her eyes, but she didn't cry out, even though he could tell the cut had caused her a great deal of discomfort. "If you want to know what it's like to die, then why don't you kill yourself instead?"

He didn't answer her. Blood left her cancer-ridden body at such a pace it already pooled on the plastic cover and soaked into the woman's clothing. Some had splashed on Graham's shirt. He would burn it after he'd cleaned up everything else. "Tell me what you see," he urged her. "Is there a tunnel of light? Do you see loved ones? Angels?" *The face of God himself?*

She let out a whimper. Her eyes closed and her lips began to move in silent prayer.

Graham's pulse thudded in his eardrums. Soon. Soon! This one had to talk. So many of them didn't. Some spouted words that would have gotten his mouth washed out with soap had he uttered them as a boy. One claimed to see a field full of purple cows wearing halos. Yet another spoke of long-dead friends Graham cared nothing about.

His hope rested on Mary. And if not Mary, then whichever one came after her, or the one who came after that.

Crimson dripped onto the ground and ran in a snaking line toward the drain set in the smooth floor. The smell made his stomach churn. "Tell me what you see!"

Her words were muffled by a choked sob.

Graham leaned closer to her. "What?"

"Can't you see him?"

"See who?"

"He's watching you."

Graham whipped his head to one side, half expecting to see someone else in the room with them, but all he saw was shelving on which he stored additional cloths and household cleaners. "Who's watching?" he asked. "What does he look like?"

The air smelled like that in a slaughterhouse. Thick. Cloying.

To avoid getting sick, Graham started breathing through his mouth, even though it increased his likelihood of tasting the scent that lingered in the air.

"He's watching you," she whispered.

Her eyes closed. They did not open again.

14

RIDING ON the floor behind the front row of seats in Phil Mason's car was every bit as uncomfortable as Bobby had anticipated, partly because every muscle in his body was tensed and ready to spring and partly because half a dozen first aid kits he'd shoved aside kept sliding around with each turn the car made.

His imagination conjured a dozen terrifying scenarios. Phil was going to tie him to a table in the "safe house" and harvest his organs to sell on the black market. Phil was going to lock him in a room and hold him for ransom. Phil was going to take him to a secluded mountain valley, tie his hands behind his back, and shoot him execution style before burying his bleeding body in a mass grave with other hapless victims.

You could never be disappointed when you always expected the worst.

At least Bobby still had his phone.

He had tried to determine their course when they left the library. Phil swung a right—north—out of the parking lot, traveled in that direction for several minutes in between stops at traffic lights, and turned right again. After that their route became more difficult to track. The road curved, lifted, dipped. A few different times Bobby had the sensation they were backtracking, and now by the whine of the transmission and tilt of the car, he knew they were headed uphill.

His empty stomach clenched into knots. They crested the rise, stayed level for a brief distance, and coasted downward to the left. Rose again. Dipped. Rose again. Dipped. If Bobby had taken the time to eat, the contents of his stomach would now be all over the floor.

At last the car slowed and turned right onto a gravel lane that jolted him more than he would have liked. "You all right back there?" Phil called over the sound of the radio.

The blindfold was making Bobby's head itch. "Can I sit up?"

"Not yet. We're almost there."

"Almost there" took nearly five more minutes, placing their travel time at more than three quarters of an hour. The car rolled to a stop. Bobby sat up and pulled off the blindfold as the fleece blanket that covered him slid to the floor.

They had parked in front of a two-story house with cream-colored siding and blue trim that sat on a wide lawn. Wooded hills covered in conifers rose up on all sides behind it. The gravel driveway disappeared from view as it rounded the bottom of a hill a quarter-mile away in the direction from which they'd come. From his position Bobby could see neither the road nor any other houses.

The music cut out when Phil shut off the engine. "You can gawk at the scenery later," he said, glancing in the rearview mirror before picking up his zippered bag. "Follow me."

Bobby hesitated before stepping out of the car, his nerves still taut as wires. Was there any imminent danger here? He sensed none of the urgency he'd felt prior to the discovery of Randy's severed brake line or the restaurant robbery. Surely if his own demise were to happen within the walls of this supposed sanctuary, he'd at least have some inkling of it ahead of time so he might be able to defend himself against an unexpected attack.

He would proceed with caution anyway. A little vigilance never hurt anyone.

Following Phil to the porch, he drank in the sights despite Phil's admonition not to. The sky was the color of a robin's egg—a stark contrast to the rainclouds that blanketed the heavens the day before. The sun hung almost directly overhead, making it impossible to judge east from west.

Two young women tossing a yellow Frisbee on the front lawn stopped and eyed the pair in silence as they neared the house. Bobby lifted a hand to wave at them. One continued to stare, but her friend glanced away with the shyness of a wild deer.

"Residents," Phil said in a low voice. "Don't pay them any mind."

Phil pulled open the door, and Bobby followed him inside. "What kind of residents?" Bobby asked once the door latched behind them. A safe house was supposed to be where people could hide from whatever entities threatened them, but the term "residents" made Bobby think of psychiatric patients.

Like ones who imagined the existence of their roommates.

Sweat beaded up on Bobby's brow. He wiped it away with the back of his hand.

"The kind that doesn't concern you," Phil said. To their left, a carpeted flight of stairs rose to the second floor and a doorway to the left of that opened into a spacious living room containing a bunch of plaid furniture and a piano. To their right was a dining area, and beyond it lay a kitchen.

"Randy?" Phil called. "Mr. Roland says he has something to tell us."

Randy stood in the kitchen with his back to them, gazing out a window that comprised a large portion of the wall. He didn't turn when they entered the room. "I hope he brings good news. I could use some."

"You can ask him yourself. Bobby, you're welcome to grab a bite to eat. It looks like there's plenty left over." Phil set his bag down and gestured at a tray of sandwiches cut into triangles sitting on the marble-topped island in the center of the room.

"Thanks." Bobby took a seat at one of the barstools lining the island on two sides and selected two halves of a roast beef sandwich from among the triangles, though he was hungry enough to eat triple that.

The room was quiet save for the sound of Phil rummaging through a cabinet. Bobby wished someone would speak.

"So are you guys FBI, or something?" he asked, knowing full well they were not. If he pressed them for answers, they might let something slip.

Phil, who had been in the middle of setting a glass of ice water in front of Bobby, raised his eyebrows. "What gave you that idea?"

"You have a safe house. The FBI has safe houses. I didn't think it would hurt to ask."

"I did think about joining the FBI back when I was a kid," Phil said as he took the stool next to Bobby. "But then I saw *The Silence of the Lambs* and decided I would rather be a nurse."

Randy turned. His lips formed a thin smile. "So, Bobby, what brings you here this fine morning? You can't have missed me."

Bobby had to finish chewing before he could speak, knowing they would think he was insane.

"It started this morning when I got up," he said. "My roommate was gone."

At that moment the front door squeaked open and closed, and two female voices traveled across the entryway and up the stairs.

Bobby paused, not wanting to be overheard.

"Go on," Randy said, looking intrigued. "If you keep your voice down, they won't hear you."

Bobby's mind quickly retraced the first few moments of his morning. "He didn't just leave. He vanished. All of his things, too." He explained how Caleb's missing furniture hadn't even left marks on the floor and how his phone had been disconnected. "So then I called the bookstore where he works, and the girl on the phone said nobody by his name has ever worked there. Explain that."

A strange light had been kindled in Randy's hazel eyes. "What's your roommate's name again?"

"Caleb Young. I've known him for a year, so I know he's not the type to just pack up and disappear." Especially not when Caleb mentioned the need to study for an exam only half a day before. "You're going to think this is nuts, but I'm afraid I might have imagined he existed."

Phil put a hand over his mouth and started coughing.

Heat washed over Bobby's face.

"If you don't mind my asking," Randy said, "what does this have to do with anything that happened last night?"

"Caleb said he worked at the campus bookstore at Autumn Ridge Community College. We knew Trish probably went there since the stapler in her purse had the college logo on it, so I asked the woman on the phone if she knew her. She did."

Phil's face became ashen. "We said not to do that."

"I know what you said. But I was cool about it. I pretended to be a concerned classmate wondering why Trish hasn't been in class."

"Because people call bookstores all the time to find out about missing classmates, especially when it's the middle of July and most of the students have the summer off."

His words made Bobby feel stupid. "I didn't know what else to do!"

Randy, who seemed to be taking this news much better than his friend, sighed. "I'm sure you didn't. Now what did she say about Trish?"

Bobby strained to remember her exact words. "She said Trish had been acting odd for awhile. And she'd been sick. I know it isn't much, but I thought you should know."

"I suppose every little bit helps," Randy said, "but what you described is typical for someone with her condition. Erratic behavior is usually one of the first signs that someone has been possessed by—"

Phil cut him off. "Loose lips, much?"

"It's a little too late for me to worry about guarding my words." Randy directed his attention to Bobby. "Did she say what was wrong with Trish? If it was something subtle I might have missed it. The combined strain of illness and possession might have been too much for her body to handle."

Bobby wished Randy had heeded Phil's advice. This talk of possession was giving him the creeps. "No. Like I said, that was it."

"That's too bad." Randy fell silent for several moments. "Tell me more about your roommate."

"How does that even pertain to the situation?" Phil interjected before Bobby could respond. "There's a corpse lying in your basement, and if you don't do anything about it soon you're going to have a rather unfortunate mess on your hands."

"I'll get to that in a minute. Bobby, what was Caleb like?"

Bobby found himself agreeing with Phil. "I don't think that's as important as getting Trish out of your house."

"She'll be gone in due time. Was Caleb friendly?"

Bobby let out a terse breath. "Yeah. He's quiet. Reads a lot. Weird stuff, too, like quantum physics and string theory. He says he's getting a liberal arts degree. He's helpful, too. Likes to shop for groceries. He found Randy's job listing in the paper for me."

"I like Caleb better already," Randy commented with a smile. "Where do you think he got his money?"

"I don't know. He never mentioned anything about a family giving him any. He never mentioned a family, period."

"Drugs?"

It was as if Randy had read his mind from earlier in the day. "I wondered that too. Only I never found any lying around, and he never smelled like them."

"A dealer would be careful."

"I can't see him doing that, though."

"So no drugs, then."

"I guess not."

"Maybe he has wealthy parents and didn't want to admit it," Phil suggested, throwing a glance at the clock on the wall.

It was a nice theory, but it still didn't work. "That doesn't explain why there weren't marks on the rug where his furniture had been. If I'd gone into his room and seen the places where his dresser and bed sat for the past year, I'd think he skipped out on me."

"Let's switch topics for just a second," Randy said. "What would you have done if this had been a normal day?"

Again, Bobby couldn't see what this had to do with anything. "You mean what would I have done if I got up and Caleb was there like always?"

"Yes."

"That's easy. I would have eaten breakfast, played around on my guitar for awhile, maybe gone for a walk. And then I would have gone to meet you at the church to start my new job. Then I would have done whatever I needed to do—mop floors and stuff—and then I would have gone home and gone to bed."

"What about the next day?"

Bobby shrugged. "The same, I guess."

"Don't you ever hang out with anyone?"

"No. Only with Caleb."

"That's got to be lonely."

He supposed it was. More lonely than he had ever realized if Caleb had been a figment of his imagination.

Randy continued. "But instead of going about your mundane life, Caleb's disappearance inadvertently led you back to me and Grouchy here."

"Yeah. I guess. Though I would have preferred to talk to you on the phone."

Randy cleared his throat. "I understand that. Now about Trish. Phil, before you picked me up from Lupe's apartment, I called Father Preston for advice, and if you hadn't been so eager to go home for lunch and be rid of me, I would have had the chance to tell you all about it."

"You should have called him last night."

"I would have, if something quite a bit more important hadn't come up." A shadow passed over Randy's face. "I said I'd meet him at my house at two o'clock and that I'll call the police then. He said I'll have his full support, and he'll gladly be a character witness in a trial if things come to that."

Bobby gaped at him. "Trial? But you didn't do anything to her!"

"I did plenty. I took her into my home and into my care, and as a result, she died." He drew a heavy sigh. "Father Preston says I need to be fully honest with the authorities and cooperate with them as best as I can."

"I pray you'll use some discretion in your honesty," Phil said in a dark tone.

"Would you expect any less from me?"

"I'm just concerned. I thought last year's fiasco was going to be the end of us." Phil looked at the clock again. "We'd better leave now so we can get there in time."

Bobby stood up, alarm bells ringing in his head. If Phil's Taurus was the only available vehicle, that meant they would have to take Bobby with them when they left. "Wait a minute. I don't want to have anything to do with this."

"You already have something to do with this," Phil said. "That's why you're here, right?"

"I didn't know that coming here was going to get me involved in a police investigation!" Talking to the cops after the robbery had been bad enough. They asked him so many questions that he'd begun to harbor doubts about his recollection of events. By the end of the interrogation, he'd felt nearly as guilty as if he had committed the crime himself.

He could only imagine what sort of questions this investigation would entail.

Mr. Roland, what were the circumstances of your arrival in Mr. Bellison's basement?

Well, you see, officer, I heard screaming inside the house and I thought someone was being hurt so I found the key under the mat and let myself in.

I see. And why were you on the premises in the first place?

Because a ghost was throwing rocks at my house, and I thought Randy could make it go away.

Bobby's mouth had gone dry. "What am I supposed to do?"

Randy was already heading toward the door. "A: You can come with us. B: You can stay here."

Neither prospect appealed to him. "What about C: You take me home right now?"

"I don't think we'll have time," Randy said. "Besides, if you stay here and we end up needing you anyway, we'll know exactly where you can be found."

Bobby followed them to the door. Since Option C wasn't an option at all, he would have to pick B since it didn't involve police officers and cars with flashing lights. "What am I supposed to do while you're gone?"

Randy shrugged. "What you would have done if this had been an ordinary day at home. Absolutely nothing."

"But—"

"I really don't think this is a good idea," Phil interjected as his eyes flicked to the ceiling.

You can say that again, Bobby thought.

Randy clearly wasn't convinced. "Make yourself comfortable. We'll be back as soon as we can."

"DO YOU really think it's wise leaving him there?" Phil asked as he tightened the bandanna over Randy's eyes. It was strange that the skinny kid had latched onto Randy the way he had. No matter which way Phil looked at it, he could make no sense of the matter.

"Wise? No. Necessary for the time being? Yes." Randy crouched down on the floor of the back seat and gathered the fleece blanket around himself. Phil thought Randy's decision not to learn the location of the new safe house was extreme to say the least, though he did understand the reasoning behind it. If Graham, a righteous man, could turn on the One he had served, then what would prevent Randy from doing the same?

Phil had faith that Randy would never turn, but he took precautions anyway just to make Randy happy.

He started the engine, and the car lurched as he put it into gear. He cast a long look at the house before letting off the brake. "How can you know he won't try to hurt Carly and . . . what's her name?"

"Joanna."

"Right." Phil didn't ordinarily know the names of those who had been sent to the safe house to recover since it wasn't his business. "I don't know why you trust him."

"He hasn't given me a reason not to. After all, he saved my life."

Phil sighed. He hoped talking to the police wouldn't take long but knew it would. Carly was smart enough to call for help if the Roland kid tried to hurt either of them, but the problem was she didn't know the safe house's address. Didn't it take awhile to trace a cell phone's whereabouts?

He gnashed his teeth together and tapped on the accelerator. If they ended up at the police station for too long, Phil would call one of the others and tell them where the safe house was so they could go there and make sure everything was okay with Bobby and the girls. It would defeat the purpose of keeping the location a secret, but sometimes you had to do things you didn't want to in order to protect the innocent.

"And why does he keep hanging around you?" Phil asked. "Graham could have sent him to catch you unawares."

"I thought that at first, but I don't think so now."

"Why, then? He barely knows you."

Phil heard Randy shift positions on the floor behind him. "I don't know that he'd ever admit it to anyone, but he seems to have a messiah complex. Whenever someone appears to need help, he's there to help them."

"It could be a ruse."

"Yes, it could be. But it could also be that he really does want to help us solve the issue with Trish. Plus it seems like he's kind of lonely. Maybe he just wants a friend."

"Hmph." Phil didn't buy it. As he turned out of the long lane toward Autumn Ridge, he vowed to stay close to Randy's side for the next few days to see if the Roland kid tried to pull something. If he didn't, good for Bobby. If he did . . .

"Are you at least scared about what's going to happen in regard to Trish?" Phil asked in order to change the subject. "Because it seems to me you're taking this surprisingly well."

"Worrying isn't going to expand my life expectancy. I've been through worse."

"Always the optimist."

"I try to be."

They both fell silent. Phil focused his attention to the two-lane road before him, praying to God Randy was right about the visitor at the safe house and praying even harder that Randy wouldn't go to jail.

15

BOBBY WATCHED from the front window as the old Taurus grew smaller and eventually disappeared as it rounded the bend in the driveway. Pangs of loneliness made him hungrier for companionship than he had been for food.

The feeling unnerved him. Bobby had been a loner for as long as he could remember, largely because few people had ever given him notice other than his father and doting stepmother. And Jonas. Bobby cracked a slight grin. He and Jonas were about as alike as fire and water. Jonas, the athletic one who played three different sports. Bobby, the skinny one who fainted in the sun.

He wondered what had changed and why.

He sat down at one of the eight chairs surrounding the dining room table which, by the smell of it, had recently been polished. Randy was right. Bobby would be doing nothing right now if he were at home, especially since Caleb had gone away to parts unknown. But what would he do here?

Already feeling the edginess of one locked in a cage, Bobby rose and went to the living room at the other end of the house. The piano he'd seen from the entryway was a black baby grand that bore not even a speck of dust. Bookshelves lined two of the walls, overflowing with tomes bearing titles like *Daily Devotions* and *The Ten Commandments: Covenant of Love*. White doilies covered the end tables on either side of the plaid couch. A stack of *Guideposts* sat on the coffee table beside a vase full of fake roses.

The room contained no television and no computer. Nothing electronic that he could see unless he counted the clock on the wall.

Bobby ran his hands through his hair. Randy and Phil hadn't been gone five minutes and he was already going stir-crazy.

He sat down on the piano bench and stared at the keys. His stepmother loved to play the piano and had encouraged Bobby to play, too, once upon a time. She'd taught him the basics herself: which note was which, the difference between sharps and flats, common major and minor scales, and so on. He had even appeased her by studying under a retired concert pianist for three years before he'd opted for professional guitar lessons instead. The guitar presented a greater challenge to him. It hurt his fingers more, too. But the beautiful sounds he was able to conjure forth from the instrument made all the pain, calluses, and practice worth it.

Too bad Phil didn't stock his safe house with a greater array of musical instruments than this. Bobby hadn't played the piano in years.

His hand and elbow still ached from trying to burst into Randy's house the night before. Ignoring the dull pain, he placed his hands on the keys and closed his eyes, willing himself to remember something, anything, if only to alleviate his boredom for a little while.

Nothing came to mind. At least nothing that had to do with music. His thoughts kept circling back to ones of the lifeless girl lying on the floor in Randy's basement. Gone from the world so young, not much younger than Bobby himself. What had been her life's purpose? Did it make any difference that she had ever lived at all?

He had to quit dwelling on it before depression rendered him miserable.

Bobby opened his eyes. His left thumb rested on the first D below Middle C, sparking something in his memory. A piece had begun on that note: one he'd known well but stored away in the archives of his mind like an old memento that no longer meant anything.

He gave the key a tentative tap. His foot found the pedal, and then his right hand gravitated toward an inverted D chord.

Without giving the music any conscious thought, he began to play, slowly at first but then faster as his hands recalled the melody.

The notes washed over him as he traveled back in time to a year which he had forgotten, and he could hear an audience of parents and grandparents clapping, and his no-nonsense father was there, too, clapping with the rest of them even though the man found music as pointless as sending rockets to the moon.

And later, his piano teacher's voice: "I'm so sorry you've decided to quit, Bobby. I thought you were going to go all the way with this."

"It's just not for me," he'd said. "This isn't what I'm meant to do."

"And what *are* you meant to do?"

Bobby had been as baffled then as he was now. "I don't know."

There was the sad truth.

What is your life's purpose? Will it make any difference that you ever lived at all?

He ended the piece without even remembering its name.

The unexpected sound of sniffling behind him nearly sent his pulse through the ceiling.

He whirled.

The two young women had left the upstairs room and now stood no more than six feet away from him. One had tears in her eyes. The other gaped at him like he'd just been dropped off by a flying saucer.

"Hi." Bobby stood up, feeling heat wash over him not for the first time that hour.

"That was beautiful," the first girl murmured as she wiped a tear from her cheek. She looked to be about nineteen, but unlike the late Trish, she had mousy brown hair tied back in a ponytail and wore a yellow summer dress. "That's the song they always play in weddings, isn't it?"

Then Bobby remembered. The piece was a simplified version of Pachelbel's Canon in D Major. A cousin of his had asked him to play it during the entrance procession at their wedding but he had declined, citing nerves and lack of experience as his excuse.

"Yeah, it is," he said. He held out a hand. "I'm Bobby."

She gave him a soft smile. "I'm Joanna. And this here is Carly." Her hand was surprisingly warm when he took it. Smooth, too.

He let go as quickly as he could before he made an idiot of himself.

Joanna's auburn-haired friend scrutinized him with a green-eyed gaze. "You're not one of Randy's," she said. "If you were, he would have called Roger in before you got here."

Bobby didn't dare ask who Roger was. If he acted like he knew more than he did, this girl might impart some knowledge to him that he didn't currently possess. "No, I'm not," he said, hoping he sounded more confident than he thought he did. "Randy's just letting me stay here for a little while. Getting a feel for the place, I guess."

A crease formed between Carly's eyebrows. "But why would he leave here without you? Shouldn't you be with him at all times if that's the case?"

Evidently Randy had not informed her of Trish's death. Maybe she didn't even know about the girl. "Something came up. He said he'll be back as soon as he can, but I don't know how long that will be."

She nodded. "Poor Randy. It seems like too many things are coming up for him lately, and not in a good way." Her face brightened. "Except for you, I guess. He's been looking for a replacement for a long time."

Replacement? Bobby felt his insides turn to ice. Somehow he doubted she meant the maintenance job at the church.

He continued to play along, even though every cell in his body screamed at him to ask her what she meant. "I know. I guess last year was really hard on him."

"You can't even imagine." Carly glanced to her friend. "Joanna, if you don't mind, I'd like to talk to Bobby alone for a little while."

Joanna dipped her head. "That's okay. I'll be up in my room." She turned and disappeared up the stairs leading out of the entryway.

Carly took a seat on the couch and placed her hands on her knees. Though she wore no makeup, her short khaki pants and orange sleeveless blouse made her look like the kind of nice girl he'd want to ask out if he ever worked up the courage to do so, not the street walker type that other guys seemed to be into these days. "Sit down," she said.

Bobby obeyed, opting for the matching plaid recliner instead of the uncomfortable piano bench.

"What all has Randy told you?"

Bobby's mind raced to come up with a quick response. "He performs exorcisms. Allegedly."

"Allegedly." She laughed and tucked a stray wisp of auburn hair behind her ear. "Priests perform exorcisms. Randy drives out demons."

To hear something so remarkable stated so bluntly made Bobby want to laugh, though he did a good job at keeping a straight face. "Isn't that the same thing?"

"The end result is the same, but the methods are somewhat different. He should have told you that."

"He must have forgotten."

"Typical." She rolled her eyes. "Okay. I've obviously never performed one myself, so forgive me if I'm a little shaky on the details. In a traditional exorcism, the possessed has to first be examined by medical professionals to make sure he or she isn't actually suffering from a condition like schizophrenia or epilepsy. A thorough analysis of the patient can take months. Plus, the priest who'll perform the exorcism has to get permission to do so from his bishop."

That surprised him. "What for? If someone really is in that condition, wouldn't it make sense to get the job done as soon as possible?"

She shrugged. "Thoroughness takes time. From what I understand, not any priest can be an exorcist. He has to be of good character and be right with God, or the exorcism won't work. He has to have unfailing faith. He has to *believe* he'll be able to cleanse the possessed through the power of Christ, and not through any power of his own. Not many can do it."

Bobby found himself nodding. "So what makes Randy different?"

Carly's expression faltered. "You should know that. That's why you're here, isn't it?"

He just stared at her. His lies had pushed him into a corner from which he wouldn't be able to easily escape.

"You're not Randy's replacement at all."

"No," he said. "I'm not."

"Then what are you doing here?"

"Waiting for him to get back so I can go home, that's what. Did Phil make you and Joanna hunker down in the back of his car on your way here, too?"

She stiffened. "As a matter of fact, we were taken here in the back of a windowless van."

"Why?"

"To protect the security of the safe house. Only Phil and his wife know where we are."

"You mean Randy doesn't even know?"

"He wouldn't let Phil tell him."

Phil must have carted a blindfolded Randy here earlier in the morning, probably because Randy didn't want to go back to a house that had a dead body in it. "What in the world are you people hiding from?"

She folded her arms. "Hiding isn't the point. It's for protection."

"I don't get it."

"Is there anything you do get?"

Anger flared up inside him at the sound of her annoyed tone and he clenched his hands into fists. "No, because nobody seems to think it's necessary to explain anything to me."

"How can I explain anything to you when I don't even know who you are?"

Not that again. "Listen. The past twenty-four hours have been crazy. I nearly had my throat slit in a parking lot, I've been hounded by poltergeists, my roommate ran away, and I got stuffed in the back of a car so I could be dumped off here and left completely in the dark about who you people are." He glanced around the room until his gaze rested on a crucifix hanging over the doorway. "You're some kind of religious cult, aren't you? And Randy thinks he's the son of God who can cast out demons with the wave of a hand."

Her green-eyed glare could have brought a pot of water to boil. "I'd be careful about what you say."

"Why? Am I right? Does Randy have some kind of messiah complex?"

"Bobby, please keep your voice down. You're going to upset Joanna."

Bobby didn't currently care who he upset, but he lowered his voice anyway. "Is she part of your little cult, too?"

Carly's face turned the approximate color of a beet, no longer looking like the friendly girl next door. "Joanna is a very troubled young woman who's staying here to recuperate. That's what we do here. Once the possessed have been cleansed, they're sent to stay here with me, Roger, or Beverly to receive prayerful counseling and companionship until they're ready to reenter society."

Joanna had been possessed? He tried but failed to reconcile her tear-streaked face with Trish's unearthly screams. "How did she get that way?"

"How does anybody 'get' that way? You must be as clueless as they come."

Bobby ignored the jab. "And how can you be a counselor? You've got to be younger than I am."

"And how old is that?"

"Twenty."

She laughed. "Sometimes the experience that comes with age arrives a little sooner for some people. But not for you, apparently."

"You don't sound like somebody who should be counseling people."

"I bet when Jesus got mad and started flipping tables in the temple people didn't think he sounded much like their savior, either."

"So you've got a messiah complex, too?"

"I do not!"

"You just compared yourself to Jesus."

"It was an analogy."

"You're giving me a headache."

Carly stood up, her eyes blazing. "And you're a jerk."

She stormed from the room. Bobby wanted to follow her but tact told him to stay put. This was like the old days all over again. The days of not being able to keep his mouth shut and getting a black eye as a result. Oh, his stepmother had loved him, good little child that he was, but she didn't know what he did to his peers while out of her sight.

Bobby had finally learned that he couldn't expect to get his way by yelling at people—the very reason he'd developed his self-meditation technique of envisioning ocean waves caressing a beach. Relaxing in such a way defused his anger before he did something he would later regret.

Today's stress pushed all thoughts of meditation from his mind. Instead of gaining Carly's trust so she would open up, he had just formed a gulf between them that would grow even wider if he didn't try to make amends as soon as possible.

He counted off fifteen seconds, took a deep breath, and left the living room.

Carly stood in the kitchen sipping an ice water. Red spots of indignation still colored her cheeks, and when he entered the room she eyed him as she would a cockroach.

His words seemed terribly insufficient even before he said them. "I'm sorry."

She set the glass down and wiped a bead of water from her lips. "That's it?"

"What else do you want me to say?" He sat down on the same stool he'd used before and stared at the marble tabletop so he wouldn't have to look her in the eye, hoping the act of submission would make her soften up a bit.

"I don't know; 'Forgive me for acting like a toddler' might be more appropriate."

"Forgive me for acting like a toddler. You don't know what I've been going through these last couple of days."

She gave a curt nod as if accepting his statement. "But you just told me. Runaway roommate, near-death in a parking lot, poltergeists. Fun stuff."

He lifted his head. "I didn't know you were listening."

"I always listen." She sat down on the other side of the island and leveled her gaze at him. "And I remember everything, too. Which is why it'll serve you well to choose your words wisely around me. If I run into you sixty years from now, I'll always remember you as the one who accused me and Randy of having messiah complexes." A smile tugged at the corner of her mouth. "Which is actually pretty funny when you think about it. Who almost slit your throat?"

"Randy." A phantom tingle ran across Bobby's neck where Randy had pressed his blade against it. "It was a minor misunderstanding."

Carly's face became a mask of concern. "But why would he— on second thought, I don't want to know."

"Does it bother you that Phil took me here after that?"

"I suppose he has his reasons." Her expression became more relaxed. "And I guess if Randy and Phil trust you to be here, I can, too."

"Then you're not mad at me anymore?"

"Oh, I'm still mad at you. I'm just trying to be nice."

"Uh, thanks." He swallowed. "I think."

The sound of Joanna moving around upstairs made them both give an involuntary glance at the ceiling.

"So, do you live here?" Bobby asked, recalling Phil's statement that both Carly and Joanna were residents of the safe house.

"Only when we have a female in residence, and only when she's roughly my age, which in our case means any woman under the age of thirty-five."

He stared at her, unable to detect a single facial crease or gray hair that would indicate the first signs of aging. "You're not thirty-five."

"I didn't say I was now, did I?" It was almost as if she were daring him to ask her age. He wouldn't give her the pleasure. "Sometimes we have two guests here at the same time so we have to share space with Roger or his wife."

"And she counsels the older women?"

She nodded. "We don't require her service very often. Most of the residents are young."

"Why?"

"Easy pickings, I guess."

"For demons, you mean."

"Yes."

"You get that this all seems kind of crazy to me."

"What can I say? Life is a crazy thing."

"But this?" He spread his arms wide. "This is like something from a movie. *The Exorcist*, or something."

"This has been going on for a lot longer than there have been movies. And I've never seen *The Exorcist*."

"Me neither."

"Then what's your point?"

"My point is this doesn't seem like something that could be real." But as soon as he said it, he heard in his mind the ticking at his windows and saw the pop cans flying at him in the back yard without anyone having thrown them.

Okay, so maybe it did seem real, but he didn't want it to.

Carly smiled. "Quiz time," she said.

"What?"

"I'm going to ask you some questions."

"Why?"

She ignored his query. "Do you believe that God created the universe and everything in it?"

He tried to set aside his frustration with her and thought of the roses that his stepmother liked to grow and the way each bloom started out as a small, closed thing before unfurling its petals into a crimson blossom. He thought of the day Jonas entered the world and remembered his unspoken fascination at seeing a human being who bore the likeness of his stepmother and father yet at the same time was totally different and separate.

He thought of the day his father died on the kitchen floor.

"Yes," he said.

Carly gave him an odd look, and he wondered if his thoughts had been displayed as plainly on his face as they had been in his mind. "And do you believe that God created angels to serve him?"

"Yes."

"And do you believe that they, just like us, have the free will to choose between good and evil?"

"I guess so."

"Then why is it hard for you to believe that some formerly angelic beings chose the darker path and now seek to destroy everything good and holy?"

It was a good question, and Bobby wasn't sure how to answer—maybe because his mind rebelled at the knowledge that something so vile could happen and be allowed to happen, or maybe because believing that evil spirits could oppress humans in such a manner was too traumatic for his mind to handle. "Because it scares me," he said, and that was true enough.

She looked him right in the eye, all traces of anger and irritation gone. "That's the most honest thing I've heard come out of your mouth."

"It is?"

She just smiled.

16

AS GRAHAM wrapped the corpse in sheets, he did another visual sweep of the basement work area. *He's watching you,* she'd said. Maybe she had only been trying to scare him. He couldn't fall for such pranks. Having spent five years driving out the blackest of spirits from their suffering victims, he knew all too well what it was like to be in the presence of one of the fallen. An evil spirit would give itself away by its aura, black and pulsating like a living void in his mind.

He had lost the ability to detect evil spirits when he'd passed the mantle of Servitude on to his successor. He supposed that a demon could have paid the basement a visit while he worked, but he didn't think so.

Later, after he finished cleaning up, he would review the recording of the killing taken by the camera hidden up in the corner and transcribe their conversation into his journal, and then he would compare it with the many others he'd accumulated over the years in order to find a pattern.

With each transcription he included a brief biography of the victim. Name, age, physical description, personality, and religious background were of greatest importance, but if the individual had any remarkable quirks or health problems, he made note of those, too. For example, the one who had seen the purple cows with her dying eyes claimed to be Lutheran and grew up in Indiana Amish country. Mary, on the other hand, attended a nondenominational church and had knitted scarves and mittens for the poor before her health declined. It was all very interesting. Useless, maybe, but interesting nonetheless.

Having set the cocoon-like body off to one side of the room, Graham went to the washbasin and filled a five-gallon bucket nearly to the brim. As he prepared to slosh it on the floor to wash the blood down the drain, the telephone upstairs began to ring.

He paused and stared at the ceiling. "I'm busy," he said, and tipped the bucket over. His caller would have to wait.

The ringing ceased as the water mingled with the congealing liquid and formed a whirlpool as both dissipated into the drain. He filled the bucket again. Dumped it on the floor. The drain gurgled, and the sump pump kicked on as it delivered the evidence to a place where no soul living or dead would ever find it. Once he finished he would scrub the floor with bleach to help eliminate the smell and stains.

He took a few moments to catch his breath, and the phone started ringing again. What was going on? He could count the number of people in possession of that number on fewer fingers than he had on his hand, but he couldn't guess why any of them would be calling him now.

Again, the ringing fell silent. Graham checked his shoes to make sure he wouldn't track blood on the living room carpet and, satisfied that at least that part of him was clean, went upstairs.

He had left his cell phone—the prepaid kind that couldn't be traced back to him—sitting on the kitchen counter. It rang in his hand when he picked it up, and the number on the screen gave him a start. He accepted the call with his thumb. "What is it?"

His contact sounded breathless. "It happened like you said it would."

Graham closed his eyes and willed himself to remain calm. "Are you sure?"

"Positive."

"How positive?"

"I have eyes, and I can see."

"You're there?"

"How else would I have known for certain?"

Graham gripped the phone so hard his hand hurt. "What do you think you're doing? Get out of there!"

"I plan on it." A pause. "But don't you think it's interesting?"

"Interesting that nothing has been done about it yet? I knew it would be like this. Now get out before someone shows up."

"I told you, I will. But I have an idea. I thought I should run it past you first before I did anything."

Graham thought about the nasty job he had yet to complete downstairs. If he put it off much longer, it would become even nastier. "Make it fast. I'm in the middle of something."

"I understand. Now what if we . . ." The contact proceeded to explain the idea as well as its details. It was a grand idea. How had Graham not thought of it himself?

By the time Graham hung up five minutes later, he was smiling. The joke he'd started had a new punch line.

———◆———

RANDY PULLED off the blindfold when Phil announced they were about to turn into his driveway. He brushed his hands through his hair so it wouldn't look suspiciously disheveled to the officers to whom they would be speaking. "How do I look?"

Phil glanced in the mirror. "Like a dead man. Did you get any sleep?"

"No." He'd dozed off a few times at Lupe's apartment but the scattered minutes of sleep could hardly be counted as such. The only things keeping him going at the moment were about four cups of coffee. When the caffeine wore off, he would crash worse than a falling jetliner.

Oh, Lupe. I should have told you about Trish. He'd wanted so badly to bring it up that morning, but Lupe's mood had improved from the night before and he didn't want to say anything that would put a damper on it.

But he would have to tell her. Soon. And he didn't have a clue how he would say it.

He saw that a tan car had already parked in the driveway when they drew up to the house. A man sat in the driver's seat talking on a cell phone and was jotting down something in a notebook that lay open on the dashboard.

"Looks like Father Preston got a head start on us," Randy said. He prayed that the priest would lend him some credibility when facing the authorities. His presence certainly shouldn't hurt.

Randy got out his house key and let himself and Phil into the living room, leaving the front door open so Father Preston wouldn't feel the need to knock when he got off the phone.

Phil put his hands in his pockets and looked uncertain. "Do you want me to look around and make sure nothing looks incriminating?"

Randy shook his head. "You know they're going to go over this place with a fine-tooth comb no matter what. It's probably standard procedure."

His friend's face grew long. "I don't want you go to prison."

"St. Paul was in prison."

"Stop that."

"Stop what?"

"Acting like this is a joke. Suppose something really goes wrong. Say you're convicted of involuntary manslaughter or worse. What are we going to do?"

"We're going to take it one step at a time. That's the only way to get through any crisis."

"I'm talking about *you*. The Servant. You can't do your job if you're locked up."

"The Lord works in mysterious ways, dear Philip. You should know." Randy gave him what he hoped was a reassuring smile even though his insides tangled themselves into knots. "Whatever happens to me is what was meant to be."

Phil opened his mouth to reply, but Father Preston's arrival at the door cut him off. "Sorry about that," the priest said, hesitating in the doorway with the closed notebook clutched in his hand. "Parish business. Mind if I come in?"

"That's why the door's open." Randy walked up to the man and shook his other hand in greeting. The priest had dressed in the traditional black slacks and shirt with a Roman collar, probably so he'd leave a better impression on the police when they arrived. "Thanks for coming."

"Not a problem." Father Preston stepped inside and nodded at Phil. His graying hair had been parted in a neat line off to one side, and it was damp with sweat. "Afternoon, Phil. I wish I could say it was good."

Phil dipped his head. "And the same to you."

Father Preston tucked the notebook under his arm and clasped his hands in front of him. He had one of those faces that always seemed to analyze everything. His gaze flicked from Randy and Phil toward the kitchen, to the contents of the living room, and back again as if assessing every last detail of the place. Randy wondered if he was looking for where they'd left Trish. "You both understand this isn't a situation I'm fully used to," the priest said.

Randy pitied him. From what he'd learned from talking to Father Preston over various lunches and from books he'd read on the subject, he knew that the vast majority of clergymen wanted nothing to do with exorcisms. It terrified them as much as it would anyone who believed such evil existed in the world. And what better way to quell their terror than by turning a blind eye to the very source of it?

He said, "I understand. But if it makes you feel better, the afflicting spirit is gone. It left when she died."

Father Preston let out a long breath. "I'm glad to hear it." He straightened his shoulders. "Before we call anyone, I'd like to see the deceased. Have you moved her?"

"No, but I did touch her while administering CPR. I hope that won't be a problem."

"It shouldn't be." Father Preston's face took on the countenance of stone. "Please lead the way."

Randy led him through the kitchen and into the back hallway, with Phil bringing up the rear. "We converted the basement into the safe room," he explained, but now that a death had occurred there, the name seemed morbidly ironic. "It's more comfortable than the meeting room at church."

"I'm sure it is."

Randy opened the basement door and flicked on the light. He didn't know how long it would take for a corpse to smell, but he covered his nose with the collar of his shirt just in case decomposition had already set in. "It happened right down—"

He froze three steps from the bottom and let his shirt slip off his face.

The floor in front of the couch accommodated no corpse. The body of Patricia Louise Gunson was gone.

"What's the matter?" Phil asked.

Randy swallowed and finished his descent, not bothering to answer. There had to be an explanation for this. Maybe in his shock the previous evening he'd mistaken the location of the body. He could have laid Trish on the other side of the couch where he couldn't see her from the bottom of the steps.

He walked up to the burgundy couch and peered over the back. No Trish.

His pulse thumped in his ears. *Father, help me. Please tell me what happened to her.*

The reply was less than satisfying. *Open your eyes.*

They are open.

Then use them to see.

Behind him, Phil and Father Preston spoke in agitated tones. "She was right here!" Phil said, gesturing at the floor beside the chair to which the young woman had been tied.

Father Preston's pale blue eyes were wide. "You're absolutely sure she passed away?"

"She wasn't breathing and had no pulse," Randy said, feeling so lightheaded all of a sudden that he sat down in one of the more comfortable chairs. "It doesn't take a genius to do the math."

A shadow fell over the priest's face. "Yes, but it does take a physician. What if the possession caused her to go into a deep coma?"

Phil's expression oozed skepticism. "Nonsense. Don't forget I'm a registered nurse. I couldn't even find her pulse with a stethoscope. Unless she somehow came back, which I doubt."

Open your eyes. Randy found himself staring at the coffee table in front of him, or rather the empty place where Bobby had gone through Trish's things last night. "Her purse and suitcase are gone," he said, which bothered him because he had known without a doubt that Trish had indeed died—and dead people had no need of luggage.

"Did you move them anywhere before you went to see Lupe last night?" Phil asked.

Randy shook his head. "I left everything as it was. Someone's been in here."

"Unless she was really alive and decided to bail on you," said Father Preston.

"She wasn't alive."

Phil put his hands on his hips and stared in the direction of the sleeping area where Trish spent her last few nights. "I don't know, Randy. You've got to admit his theory works better than yours, as much as I don't like it. Who could have come in here and taken her away? The only people who know about Trish are here."

"You're forgetting someone."

"Bobby?" Phil gave a nervous laugh. "The person you trust oh so much? To be honest, he doesn't look strong enough to have moved her on his own."

Randy's jaw clenched. Could Phil have been right about Bobby after all? He didn't want to believe that the kid who'd saved his life could do something so vile, but there were few alternative explanations for Trish's disappearance. And if Bobby told the truth about his disappearing roommate, then he didn't even have an alibi for the hours between two in the morning and noon when Phil had taken him to the safe house.

"Who's Bobby?" the priest asked, his interest piqued. "How did he know about Trish?"

Randy had no desire to go into detail about how Bobby had snuck into the house the night before. "To make a very long story short," he said, "Bobby is the new hire for the maintenance job, and he accidentally walked in on the procedure. That's when Trish collapsed and died."

Father Preston closed his eyes as if in deep thought. "Why didn't you bring him back here so he could be questioned with the two of you?"

"The death wasn't his fault. He didn't want to be involved."

"Don't you find that suspicious?"

Randy wasn't about to accept that Bobby had anything to do with this. "Heck, Father, *I* don't want to be involved! Bobby's just a kid who ended up in the wrong place at the wrong time."

Now Father Preston was the skeptical one. "If you really believe that Trish's body was abducted, then I would talk to him. He may have told someone else about the young lady's demise, and *that* individual took it upon himself to retrieve the corpse."

This theory didn't sit right with Randy at all, but he said, "Fine. I'll talk to him about it as soon as I can."

An awkward silence settled over them. Randy suddenly wished that Trish had never come in that day at the church; that he had never seen her and sensed the blackness feeding on her thoughts and on her soul. That he had never promised her that he could help her be free.

His vision blurred for a few seconds. *Trish, wherever you are, please forgive me.*

"What are we going to do in the meantime?" Phil asked, glancing back and forth between Randy and the priest as if waiting for either of them to initiate some form of action.

Father Preston straightened his collar. "I can keep an eye out for Trish at the church in case she's alive and decides to return there."

"How will you know what she looks like?"

He gave Phil a piercing stare. "Randy and I spoke at length on the phone this morning. If his description of the girl is accurate, I believe I know exactly what she looks like. I've seen a girl fitting her description at Mass a few different times. She sat toward the front but wouldn't take communion, so I assumed she wasn't Catholic." He looked to Randy. "Was she Catholic?"

Randy had no idea, as the subject never came up during the painful conversations he'd had with the young woman. "I'm not sure. I actually don't know much about her at all."

"Shouldn't God have given you better insight than that?"

Randy's muscles tensed. "You make it sound like I should have all the answers."

The priest gave him a hard look, and Randy didn't like it. "You told me his Spirit flows in your veins."

Phil muttered "Uh-oh" and turned away from them both.

Randy tried to keep his tone civil. Father Preston, also a servant of God in his own way, couldn't imagine what it was like to be in his position. "That may be, but I am not God. He just enables me to see the evil that walks among us."

"You didn't see the evil in your old mentor."

"Graham wasn't possessed. What he did was of his own choosing."

"But you didn't see it coming."

"Clairvoyance is not my spiritual gift, Father, nor am I a prophet. I've been chosen to help free the afflicted and encourage them to devote their lives to Christ. I can't read minds and I can't predict the future with any more certainty than you can. I'm simply a humble servant like you."

Father Preston gave a slow nod. "I thought your abilities extended beyond that."

"You give me too much credit."

Silence engulfed them until Phil broke it a second time. "Okay. Father, you're going to keep an eye out for Trish at church, but we should check the woods around here first. If you're right about her being alive, she's going to be a danger to herself and anyone she meets in her present condition."

"It's a shame she can't be reported as a missing person," Father Preston said. "It would help to have her face posted all over town."

Not if she's dead like I know she is. Randy nodded in agreement anyway. "I guess we should go outside and start looking."

"That's the best idea I've heard since we got here," Phil said as he started up the stairs.

Randy stood and let Father Preston go in front of him, and when the priest and Phil reached the top of the steps, he said, "Go ahead and start without me. I'll be with you in a minute."

"We'll start in the back," Phil said. "If you don't see us when you come outside, give us a holler."

The sound of their footsteps moved toward the door that Bobby entered the night before and faded as they left the house.

Randy turned from the stairs and looked over the basement once more in search of an explanation. Bodies did not rise from the dead, nor did they dissolve into nothingness overnight like a puff of smoke.

"Trish," he whispered, "you've got to give me a hand here. God says I need to open my eyes. Can you tell me what I'm supposed to be looking at?"

The bed in the corner was just as messy as it had been last night since neither he nor Trish had been available to straighten the covers and fluff the pillows. The throw pillows on the couch sat in their usual places. The matching armchairs were undisturbed. The chair he had tied Trish to had not been moved. The cloth bindings—

Wait a minute.

He stepped closer to the strips of cloth that lay on the vinyl seat of the kitchen chair and picked one up. Both edges were frayed from when he had created the strips from cutting up an old sheet. They weren't the best bindings in the world, but he'd had no desire to inflict additional suffering upon the possessed by tying them to a chair with rope.

He wished he didn't have to tie them at all. It gave him the sick sense that he was the tormentor and they the prey, but it had to be done because sometimes the afflicted became violent.

He brought the cloth close to his face, gripped it tighter in his hand, and closed his eyes. His mind replayed the scene of Trish suddenly listing to one side in the chair. He had untied her as quickly as he could and laid her on the carpet between the couch and the coffee table so he could try to revive her.

The cloth strips had fallen on the floor. He'd had no need to pick them up.

He opened his eyes and set the strip back on the chair with the others.

As he started up the stairs to join Phil and Father Preston outside in what would be the most fruitless search in which he had ever participated, a rather disturbing thought filled his head.

If a stranger had come to take Trish's body, he or she would have needed to break in since Randy had not returned the spare key to the mat outside.

Someone who knew him well could have simply made a copy of his key.

17

RANDY FOUND Phil and Father Preston standing beside the house, where footprints in the muddy grass indicated that someone with a man's stature had slipped and staggered while walking from the driveway to the side door.

"These aren't a woman's footprints," Phil said as he pointed to a particularly prominent one sunk about a quarter of an inch into the flattened grass. "Unless Trish was wearing a man's shoes when she left."

Father Preston had his hands folded in front of him and was doing a poor job of masking a troubled face. He remained silent.

Randy came up beside them. "Any progress?"

"Only if this counts."

Randy bent over to examine one of the prints. He held his foot next to it, noting the print was slightly smaller than those his own shoes made. He would have to take note of Bobby's shoe size when they returned to the safe house. "There isn't anything else?"

"No. We checked around back and didn't see a thing."

Randy wasn't surprised. "Then that settles it. Trish must have had enough of her own wits about her that she followed the driveway back out to the road." He spoke only for the priest's benefit and hoped his tone didn't ring overly false. Fibbing wasn't something he preferred to do.

Father Preston nodded. "Then it looks like my job here is finished."

And that was that.

As soon as the priest left, Randy went to the bathroom medicine cabinet and swallowed three extra-strength Tylenol to quell the headache forming behind his eyes.

Phil appeared in the open bathroom doorway, hands in his pockets. "You alright?"

Randy wiped the sweat off his face with a damp cloth and eyed his reflection. A sleep-deprived stranger stared back at him with bloodshot eyes. "Yep. Let's get back to the safe house and take Bobby home."

He turned toward the bathroom door but Phil made no motion to leave. Phil had always looked young for his age, but right now every one of his thirty-eight years and then some were etched in lines upon his face.

Sometimes he forgot that Phil often shared the weight of the crosses Randy carried.

"Just stay here and get some sleep while I go get him," Phil said. "There's nothing else you can do today."

It sounded like a wonderful idea, but he couldn't do that just yet. "No. I need to talk to Bobby. I don't think he really snuck in here after we left last night, but maybe he knows something else about Trish that we don't."

———————◆———————

AS HE lay on the floor behind the front row of seats in Phil's car, Randy fell into a light doze and dreamed about the day when Phil passed the mantle of Servitude on to him.

It was a dream he had often, and it never failed to fill him with peace.

He had been twenty then and eager to serve his Maker, but like all entering the fold for the first time, he didn't quite know what to expect. He had been overcome with a terror that he couldn't put into words even though Phil and the others assured him that all would be well.

He remembered trembling. He remembered praying and wondering if it all might be a cruel joke intended to torment him just when he was finally getting his life together.

They had been alone in Phil's house and all the blinds had been drawn. They wore ordinary clothes. No candles and no incense perfumed the air.

"We don't do big ceremonies," Phil had said. "I've never been fond of pomp, anyway."

Randy sat cross-legged on the floor. Phil stood before him, wearing an expression that seemed to convey both sadness and great joy. "Do you, Randy, accept this mantle and all that is associated with it?"

And Randy had said, "I do."

"And do you vow to serve God the Father, Jesus Christ his son, and the Holy Spirit no matter the cost?"

Randy bowed his head. "Yes."

Then, as if a great spotlight suddenly shined upon him, his soul lit up with the dazzling brightness of ten thousand suns, and he knew without a doubt this was no joke.

"We're here," the Phil of the present said, and Randy sat up with a groan.

———◆———

JOANNA'S LAUGHTER brought a grin to Bobby's face. "Just think of what everyone is going to say when I get home and show them I finally learned how to play 'Twinkle Twinkle Little Star'!" She plunked out the tune again with her right index finger and smiled as if she'd just won a million dollars. "Maybe someday I'll even learn how to play it with more than one finger."

Bobby couldn't help but feel her enthusiasm. After he and Carly made amends, Joanna came downstairs to grab a drink, and since she'd been so emotional about his botched rendering of Pachelbel's Canon (and since there was absolutely nothing else in the house that he could do), he'd offered to show her how to play some things if she was interested.

"I don't know," she'd said. "The only instrument I've ever played is a kazoo."

"The piano's a piece of cake," he said. "I guarantee you'll have learned something by dinnertime."

That had been two hours ago. She sat down on his right at the piano bench, and he'd instinctively scooted as far to the left as he could without falling on the floor. Touching other people did not figure among his favorite things to do. Sitting hip to hip with a member of the opposite sex was even worse because he wasn't used to being around women his age and he had the uncanny ability to always make an absolute fool of himself.

Fortunately Joanna didn't seem to notice his discomfort—and Bobby became so engrossed in showing her how to play that he'd nearly forgotten about Randy and Phil's prolonged absence.

Carly watched them for awhile from her place on the couch, but finally she left them, saying she needed to think about supper.

The latter word gave Bobby a jolt, and he'd whirled around to see the clock. It was after three. Either Carly planned to prepare a feast, or she'd just wanted to leave the two of them alone.

It wasn't his job to understand the minds of women.

"That was great," Bobby said when Joanna finished the song. "What did I tell you?"

Her cheeks turned pink. "You're just saying that."

"Fine. It's great for your first day."

"That's better."

"You've really never played the piano before?" Nearly everyone he'd known growing up had a piano in their house, though sometimes the instrument only served as a shelf on which the owners would sit their family photos. But what child wouldn't be fascinated by the row of shiny black and white keys and prod at them to see what they would do?

She shrugged. "My grandparents had one, but when I was little they'd yell at me every time I'd touch it. Like I could break it with my bitty little fingers."

"That's mean."

Her shoulders slumped, and Bobby suddenly had the impression that Joanna's excitement at learning the song masked a much deeper, aching sadness. "Yeah. They'd yell at me about other things, too. They raised me until I was eight and my mom got out of prison. She's clean now, though, my mom. She and I get along fairly well. I mean, we did for awhile."

"Um, that's good." What was he supposed to say to someone who had been in Joanna's situation? "I'm sorry you had to go through that."

"It's okay." She stood up and smoothed out the skirt of her summer dress. "Do you want to go outside? I hate being cooped up. Gives me cabin fever."

"Sure." Bobby could use a breath of fresh air, himself. "Where to?"

"The front porch. Didn't you see the chairs out there when you first came in?"

He hadn't because he had been too busy watching Joanna and Carly tossing the Frisbee, but he wasn't going to tell her that. "I must have missed them. Let's go."

Joanna led the way out of the room. "Carly, we'll be out on the porch," she called into the kitchen.

Carly lifted her gaze from a recipe book she'd propped open on the island and gave them a knowing smile. "Have fun."

A gust of wind rippled Bobby's clothes when they stepped out onto the porch. Four wrought-iron chairs with cushions were lined up facing the driveway, and a barrel covered with a square piece of painted plywood served as a table.

Bobby sank into one of the chairs and Joanna took the one to his right. They sat in silence for a minute or two. Inside, the piano had given them something to talk about, but out here, there were only the trees and the sky.

"You're quiet," she finally said, glancing his way.

His face flushed, and he cursed himself for it. The majority of men his age had dated before (and gone much further than that, besides), and here he was acting like an awkward schoolboy who didn't know the first thing about talking to a woman. "I don't have much to say."

"People lie when they say that. They have plenty to say but they're just afraid to say it."

"Is that it?"

"I'm positive. So just say whatever you want."

Bobby locked his eyes on the point where the driveway vanished around the bottom of the hill. Talking didn't appear on his list of favorite activities, either, but he decided that doing so might help cheer her up. "How did you meet Randy?"

"Oh." Her voice faltered a bit. "I don't know if you want to know that."

He glanced over at her and saw that a frown had etched itself on her doe-like face. "I don't want to upset you. I just want to understand what happened. I want to know why Randy does what he does and how he finds the people to do it to."

A shadow crossed over her face. "I'm not so sure I understand, myself. Randy got *it* to speak when . . ." She shook her head and cleared her throat. "Sorry. I'll try to start at the beginning so I don't confuse you. I'm only twenty, so I haven't been out of school for very long. My senior year of high school I started hanging out with some people my mom didn't like. They were into drugs, and I tried them too because I thought if I did they'd think I was cool. It sounds so stupid now. I thought a lot of stupid things."

She paused and stared down at her slender white hands. She wore a cheap silver ring with a heart-shaped pink jewel on one finger—the kind you could get out of the machine at the grocery store for a quarter.

"My friends were into the occult," she continued, her face becoming increasingly pained. "They acted like it was a game. One of them was the son of a pastor, and it was his way of spiting his parents. They'd try to cast spells and hold séances, which I'm not even sure I believe in. The things we saw and heard were probably caused by the drugs.

"Finally I overdosed and had to be rushed to the hospital. If my mom hadn't been home I probably would have died. After I got better I realized I needed to dump my friends before their lifestyle killed me. Once I was clean I never went back to them. I got a job at a grocery store and got my grades back up just in time for me to graduate."

She paused to draw in a breath. "Are you bored yet?"

Bobby shook his head, his eyes wide. "Not even close."

She gave a shy smile. "About a month after graduation, I started getting really moody. These thoughts kept popping into my head out of nowhere. 'Joanna, you're no good,' they'd say. Or, 'Joanna, face it. You were so much better off with them because at least you could feel like you belonged.' And then the images started coming. I could be sitting at home eating a bowl of cereal and all of a sudden I'd have this vivid image of picking up the spoon and jabbing it into my mom's eye. And a voice would say, 'Do it!' and I knew that I would *never* do something so horrible because who in their right mind would ever try to kill their mother? And with a spoon! And I'd have horrible nightmares where I'd walk into a daycare and pour gasoline everywhere and light a match, and I would laugh and laugh as the kids burned, and I was burning too, but I couldn't stop laughing."

She stopped again. This time tears glistened in her eyes. "You can't imagine how vivid it all was. I could see those things more clearly than I can see you sitting next to me."

Bobby felt his head nod. "I think I can."

"No. You really can't. Not unless you've been there, too."

He had nothing to say about that.

She went on. "It got so bad I couldn't leave the house or even my bedroom. I quit my job. I barely ate. I told my mom to stay away from me because even though I knew I'd never try to hurt her, something inside of me wanted to do it really badly. This voice kept saying that everything bad that had happened in my life was her fault since she'd been in jail for so many years, and that if she died, my life would become so much better. It kept telling me that if Mom was gone, all the bad thoughts and nightmares would go away, too."

"But you resisted it."

"Yes!" Her cheeks flushed. "But the more I did, the worse it got. I didn't know it could get any worse because it was so bad already. I would see things that weren't there. Visions, you know. Only instead of staying in my head I could see them like they were happening right in front of me. Mom thought there might be something wrong in my head so she had me tested again and again only they couldn't find one single thing in my brain that was out of whack. Then she started talking about taking me to a shrink and I flipped out. Because I knew I wasn't crazy. I knew that whatever was wrong with me was something evil and that no therapy could fix it. I started wondering if fooling around with the occult had opened me up to something wicked."

"So you knew you were possessed?"

"What else could it have been? The doctors said I was fine but anyone who took a good look at me knew I wasn't. Some people even said I was faking the whole thing just to get attention, but Bobby, there's no way I could have faked what I saw and felt. No way at all."

Though tears still gave her eyes a glassy sheen and her face remained as pale as cream, Joanna had slumped back in the chair and breathed slower, as if reciting her ordeal to a stranger had given her some measure of relief. "Do you believe anything I've just told you?"

"Of course I do." She would have no reason to lie to him, and she bore none of the telltale nervous signs of one inventing a story on the spot. "So what led you to Randy?"

"Oh, you'll love this." She rubbed her eyes and blinked away tears. "I went nuts one night about two weeks ago. I hurt so bad I started breaking everything I could get my hands on to try to dull the pain. Plates. Picture frames. Lamps. Mom was screaming and got my stepdad to pin me down before I killed somebody. He flipped me onto my stomach on my bed and was tying something around my wrists so I would stop, and all the sudden I heard something smash against the wall. Then everything got really quiet."

Bobby's pulse quickened. He had a good idea of where this was going. "What was it?"

"A glass angel figurine. My aunt gave it to me when I was a baby. I didn't know it then, but later I heard Mom say it flew off my dresser all by itself and exploded against the wall."

"That's crazy."

"Crazy, yes, but it hurt me so much when I found out what happened. My aunt died when I was a little girl. That angel was the only thing I had that she gave me, and the whole thing ended up in the trash. But I'm getting off topic. Mom and Bruce, my stepdad, sort of guessed what was wrong with me as soon as the angel jumped off the dresser. I heard them talking out in the hallway—they'd left me in my room, but at that point I'd mostly calmed down anyway—and then they led me out to the car and drove me to the nearest Catholic church. We're Methodists, but they thought a priest might know more about that kind of thing than our pastor does."

"And the priest referred you to Randy."

She nodded. "I met Randy that same night. He went off and talked with my parents and the priest for awhile, and then he came in to talk to me by myself, and he agreed that he'd do his best to set me free so long as I was willing. And I guess the rest is history."

"How long have you been here at the safe house?"

"About a week and a half. Carly and Randy both say in another few days I can go home."

The wind bent the blades of grass on the lawn in front of them, and further away, it rustled the treetops making it sound like the whole world whispered. It was peaceful out here. Bobby could see why Phil had chosen this location for a safe house. Anyone who had been through the same hell Joanna experienced could come here and finally believe it possible to live in peace again. "But where did the demon come from?" he asked. "Was it from the things you did with your friends?"

Joanna took several moments to answer. "That's what I thought. But when Randy finally got them to speak, they said they'd been with me from the day I was born and had only been waiting until the time was right to torment me."

Bobby thought of the tapping at his windows and the ones at the church, and he felt cold. "Why would they do that? Wait so long, I mean?"

"I don't know. Randy never got them to say. But they're gone now, and that's the important thing. But I'm still scared. Because they could come back if I'm not 'vigilant,' as Randy said. I've been praying a lot more than I used to. Praying that I'll never have to go through any of that again."

"I'm sorry all those things happened to you." Hearing about Joanna's problems made his own seem terribly insignificant. Who cared that he'd been wrongly fired by a boss who cared more about money than the wellbeing of his employees and lost his roommate in the span of a couple days? At least he was still in control of his wits.

"Ah. Well. It's okay. One good thing came out of it, though."

"What's that?"

"It restored my faith in the human race. I was such a cynic before. Randy didn't know me from Adam but despite that he risked his own life to save mine." She sighed. "You probably think I'm a chatterbox spilling my guts like this."

Actually, Bobby had become so engrossed in her story he'd barely given any thought to the fact that she'd done ninety-nine percent of the talking. "No."

"I don't know a thing about you."

He laughed as he thought about his simple existence of waking up and eating and breathing. "There isn't much to say."

"Sure there is! Besides, it evens things up. I tell you my life story, you tell me yours." She grinned. "Come on. It's got to be all kittens and butterflies compared to mine."

He couldn't help but smile. "Fine. My name is Bobby, I'm also twenty years old, I'm from Ohio, and I like music."

"That's it?" She looked disappointed. "There's got to be more than that."

"I'm addicted to Sprite and eat too many bagels."

She poked him in the ribs, making him jump. "Oh yeah? Where do you put them?"

"I—"

He broke off. Phil's burgundy car had just come into view and was drawing closer to the house. Bobby had the sudden sense that something had gone terribly wrong during the men's absence. Had Randy been arrested? No, of course not. Randy was in the car, too. His head popped up from behind the seats as the car came to a stop.

Joanna remained oblivious to Bobby's thoughts. She stood. "They're back! Come on, we should help Carly get dinner ready for everyone."

Bobby let her go into the house ahead of him. Intuition told him he needed to stay put.

Besides, Joanna's story had made him lose his appetite.

18

FATHER PRESTON James left Randy Bellison's house in a brooding mood. Randy had been hiding something from him, and he didn't like it one bit. Father Preston understood that the Servants and their comrades had to keep a low profile in order to protect themselves from the rest of the world. But to hide something from *him*? What had he ever done that would make Randy feel he couldn't be trusted?

He hadn't told a soul about the Servants, not even his fellow priests even though the temptation to share something so fascinating had burned like a wildfire on some occasions. He had prayed, though. Prayed that he wouldn't be a fool and let something like that slip from his tongue in front of those who would tell someone else in turn. There were some who craved miracles in this world. They would stop at nothing to try to witness them for themselves— including exploiting a selfless young man who only wanted to serve God by casting out spirits in His name.

There *was* one other person who knew about the Servants, though Father Preston hadn't been the one to inform him of their existence.

Father Preston turned into the driveway, snatched up his notebook and pen from the passenger seat in case he would need them, and barged into the house without knocking. Though he was a man of God, right now he felt more like a father about to berate a wayward son. "Tony?" he called out. "Are you in here?"

A suspicious silence answered him. Father Preston set his things down on the coffee table. His manners were too refined to go ransacking the house in search of the man. Tony would emerge sooner or later. Father Preston could wait.

More seconds ticked by. "Tony?"

The man still didn't answer. Father Preston heaved an agitated sigh.

Just as he was about to call the man's name again, the sound of the back door opening and closing carried through the house. The clomping of footsteps fell heavy on the floorboards, and he heard a sneeze.

The man who entered the front room a moment later halted at the sight of Father Preston. His face blanched, and Father Preston tried to keep a stern expression as the younger man rushed to regain his composure. "I didn't know you'd be dropping by today," Tony said. "Would you like me to get you anything?"

"An explanation might be in order."

Creases formed in Tony's forehead. "Explanation?"

This was no time to beat around the bush. "What were you doing there?"

"What was I doing where?"

Father Preston glared at him, and Tony seemed to deflate. "You may not have noticed me, but I passed you on the road about a mile before I got to Mr. Bellison's house. You told me you would be visiting your brother this afternoon, and correct me if I'm wrong, but you wouldn't have headed that direction to get there."

"I had to come back to get something."

"If that's the case, why are you still here?"

Tony said nothing.

Father Preston took that as a sign he should continue. "There's mud on your shoes."

The younger man glanced down at his feet. "I was just out in the back."

"And you were also at Randy Bellison's house. That's the only reason you would have been out that way this afternoon. You must have overhead my telephone conversation this morning and knew where I was going, and you took it upon yourself to beat me there."

"Why would I do that?"

"I don't know, Tony. You tell me."

The men stared at each other for several long moments, neither of them saying anything.

"An item was missing from his house," Father Preston said when it became clear Tony had no desire to speak. "Would you know anything about that?"

"Should I?"

Father Preston crossed his arms. "If I call your brother, will he say you planned on meeting him today, or will he have no idea what I'm talking about?"

Again, no answer. Time to try a new tactic.

"I had to cover for you," he said. "I tried to convince Randy that the item left of its own accord, but he doesn't believe that any more than I do. I told him I would keep an eye out for the item in case it turned up. Do you think it will be doing that anytime soon? Because if not, I'll have to report you to the police."

Muscles began to move in Tony's jaw. Father Preston's heart gave a flutter of triumph. Yes! He had finally broken through to the man's conscience, and now he would confess.

Tony said, "It's not what you think."

***

WHEN RANDY and Phil came up to the safe house porch, neither man looked as though he were in the brightest of moods.

"What happened?" Bobby asked in a low voice after making sure Joanna had closed the door behind her. "What did the cops say?"

Randy's face was grim. "Nothing. We didn't call them."

Even though Bobby should have felt relieved that Randy wouldn't be hauled off to prison today, the words made a weight form in his stomach. "Why not?"

Phil's tired eyes probed Bobby's face. "Did you go back to Randy's house at any point after you left him with Lupe?"

The question took him aback. "Why would I have gone back there?"

The men exchanged a glance he didn't like. "You're absolutely sure?" Phil asked.

Bobby's irritation began to rise again. "What, you think I forgot what I did last night? I went straight home, got in bed, and didn't get up until eleven this morning. If you don't believe me, ask Caleb." The last words slipped from his mouth before he could stop them, and his face flushed. "Or not."

"So you *could* have gone there," Phil said, his tone now accusing.

Bobby's mind started to whirl. What was wrong with these people? Was it because he'd used Randy's key to get in last night? Did they think he used the key again?

Then it hit him. "Something's missing," he said. "And you think I took it."

Phil's expression twisted into a devilish smile that seemed to say, *Aha!*

Bobby glanced back and forth between him and Randy, silently pleading for one of them to explain. "I don't understand. What's missing?"

Suddenly, as if several puzzle pieces in his mind snapped into place, their problem became clear to him. *Trish.*

The weight in his stomach began to squirm like an eel, and he hoped he wouldn't be sick. "Trish is gone?" he asked, though he knew it had to be the truth. Why else would they have not phoned the authorities? If the body had been taken, they would have nothing to show for their claim that a woman died in the house.

"Not just Trish," Phil said. "All of her things, too."

"And," Randy said, "someone took the time to tidy up."

Bobby sank back into the wrought-iron chair. Their implied accusation was like a knife in the heart, and it shocked him too much to elicit his anger. "What makes you think I did it?"

"Look," Randy said, lifting a hand. "*I* believe you're innocent. Phil, however, is being realistic."

"How is that realistic? I would *never*—"

"You had the ability to do it," Phil butted in.

"But I didn't! What would I even do with a dead body?" Several gruesome images appeared in his mind, and he banished them as quickly as he could. Sure, other people might find various uses for a female corpse, but Bobby wasn't one of them.

Phil just shrugged.

Bobby turned to Randy instead. "You've got to believe me."

"Chill out. I already said I do."

The front door swung open, and Carly appeared in the doorway looking flustered. "Are you three ever going to get in here?" she asked. "Joanna and I are looking for volunteers to help us get dinner ready."

"I'll help out," Bobby said, jumping at the opportunity to end the conversation. "What do you need me to do?"

———◆———

"SO WHAT'S the occasion?" Randy asked as he piled a slab of lasagna onto his plate. He'd taken a nap out on the couch while Bobby helped the girls cook and Phil made some phone calls outside where no one would overhear, but he still looked terrible.

"It's time to eat," Bobby said, snatching up the best-looking piece of garlic bread. His appetite had returned at the first scent of cooking food. "That's enough of an occasion for me."

Randy shook his head as his eyes traveled over the creamed peas, cooked carrots, and tray of cinnamon rolls that Bobby hadn't yet gotten to.

"I was just going to make lasagna," Carly said, "but Bobby said we had to eat our vegetables, too." She turned to Bobby and winked, and he felt his face turn red all over again. "Besides, you've welcomed him into the fold. That's a call for celebration if I ever saw one."

It became so quiet Bobby thought someone had hit a mute button.

Phil's expression turned to stone. "Just who welcomed him?"

Carly filled her plate without looking at him. She hurried from the kitchen and took a seat at the dining room table, her cheeks flushed pink.

Randy, Bobby, and Phil followed her and took their respective chairs while Joanna scooped food onto her plate.

"Carly?"

She lifted her head and stared at Phil. "What?"

"Who welcomed Bobby into the fold?"

She glanced back down at her plate. "I just assumed . . . I thought . . ."

"You thought *what*?" Phil snapped, startling all of them, Bobby included.

Carly stabbed at a carrot and raised it to her mouth. "I guess I got a little confused."

"You're not the only one," Joanna said softly as she slipped into a chair at the end of the table, her doe-like eyes wide.

Randy glanced at Joanna. "Maybe this shouldn't be discussed in present company."

"It's a little too late for that." Phil continued to drill Carly with a stare. "Carly, would you please answer the question?"

She swallowed and glanced to Randy. "You guys left Bobby here for a reason, right?"

Startled, Bobby lowered his fork. Reason?

"I brought him here," Phil said, "because he wanted to discuss something with Randy, whose phone was dead."

"Then he didn't know anything about the Servants beforehand?"

Phil's eyebrows shot up. "Not very much. What all did Miss Jovingo tell you, Bobby?"

"Jovingo?" The sudden tension in the room made it difficult for Bobby to think. "Who's that?"

"Me," Carly said, her voice small.

Oh. Right.

"It's my fault," Bobby said, hoping that Carly wouldn't be punished for imparting certain information to him. "She thought I was going to be some kind of replacement for Randy, and I sort of played along."

"Why would you do that?"

Bobby didn't attempt to keep the sarcasm out of his voice. "Gee, I can't imagine. Maybe I was tired of being left in the dark and figured if I pretended like I was a replacement, she'd tell me things so I wouldn't be in the dark anymore."

"So you lied to her."

"Basically."

Phil's lip curled. "We have no place for liars here."

Bobby started to object, but Randy lifted a hand. "Phil, what do you call what we did back at my house with Father Preston?"

Phil snatched up his fork and sliced a corner off of his lasagna. "We were doing what needed to be done."

"Exactly. And Carly, I would have told you if Bobby was to be my replacement."

"That's what I thought, but then I wondered if you'd sent him here to help out in a different way. You know, like me. When he said he didn't know what made you different from other exorcists, I thought you just hadn't had the time to fill him in yet." A tear glistened in the corner of her eye, and Bobby had the sudden mental image of himself leaning over and wiping it away.

He quickly composed himself.

The room became quiet.

Joanna pushed her chair back and stood up. "I'll be right back," she said. "Bathroom."

She slunk up the stairs, throwing a nervous glance over her shoulder, and a door clicked shut moments later.

Randy let out a sigh. "You'll have to forgive Phil," he said to both Carly and Bobby. "We've had a very long and stressful day, and Carly, I'd love to tell you about it, but that'll have to wait until we can discuss it somewhere else."

"I wasn't aware that I need to be forgiven," Phil said with a scowl. He popped another piece of lasagna into his mouth, his jaw clenching and unclenching as he chewed.

Carly lifted her eyes to Randy. "So if Bobby isn't your replacement and he isn't here to help us, who is he?"

"I'm afraid you'll have to ask him that."

"I am Randy's replacement," Bobby said. "At the church."

"And that's it?"

"That's it," Randy said.

Without warning, Bobby was struck with that now-familiar urge to flee. *Go home. You don't need these people. Charlotte and Jonas miss you. Go to them. Go home. Go home.*

Shaking, he stood up and pushed in his chair.

"What are you doing?" Randy asked with a note of surprise in his voice.

"I need to leave," Bobby said, even though most of his food remained untouched.

Randy checked his black wristwatch and frowned. "What for? We don't have to be at St. Paul's for awhile yet."

"I'm causing too much trouble by being here," he blurted. "If I leave, everything will go back to normal and you all can be happy again."

"Come on, Phil's just being cautious!"

Bobby hardly heard what Randy was saying. He started toward the entryway, feeling the walls closing in upon him. Randy reached out to stop him but Bobby shook him off. "Leave me alone. I'm going home."

———◆———

A TINY voice screamed at him inside his head. *What are you doing? Get back in there with those nice people and finish your supper!*

Bobby strode down the gravel driveway, hands clenched tightly at his sides. He didn't want to go back to Ohio. He had to go back to Ohio. He wanted to get to know Randy and Phil and Carly better. He had to get away from them before something awful happened.

Shameful tears flowed down his cheeks. God, what was happening to him? He felt like a sheet of paper held in two separate hands that wanted to tear him into pieces.

When he reached the end of the driveway, he would either thumb a ride or walk all the way back to Autumn Ridge, whichever came easier. So what if leaving without a blindfold made him learn the location of the safe house? It wasn't like he'd tell anyone about it. With Caleb gone, the only person he could talk to was himself.

The crunch of gravel behind him made him turn. Randy was following him at a fast clip. "Bobby, wait up!"

The part of Bobby that wanted to stay halted at the sight of the man, but the other part—the one that knew that getting out of there as fast as possible was the only real option he had—rapidly overcame his hesitation and made him break into a run, never mind that he was as out of shape as an unwound paper clip and would probably faint if he kept at it for long.

Bobby huffed and wheezed and nearly turned an ankle as his foot lost traction in the gravel, and he started to think he was actually covering some ground when bright spots that began to dance in his vision forced him to a stop.

His vision went gray the moment he bent over and put his hands on his knees so he could draw deeper breaths.

Something warm touched his shoulder. A faraway voice said, "Come back inside. Running away isn't going to solve anything."

Bobby tried to reply but he wasn't sure if the words made it out of his mouth or not.

"What?"

"I'll die if I stay." Which, of course, was absurd, but right now it made more sense than anything else.

"What makes you think that? Are you okay?"

Bobby shook his head both as an answer and to dispel the grayness. A sliver of driveway emerged from the shadows, and the more he caught his breath the faster the rest of the grayness vanished.

"Sorry. I get dizzy spells." He blinked and straightened. "I used to pass out a lot in gym class."

Concern etched lines into Randy's face. "Why?"

"Bad heart, I guess." He didn't know why he was telling Randy this when he'd never even mentioned it to Caleb. "But I've got to go. Bye."

His legs started to carry him away again but this time Randy seized him by the arm and didn't let go. Bobby's chest grew tight as if he were being squeezed to death in the grip of a giant fist.

"Bobby," Randy said, his tone firm. "You're not going to die if you stay with us. In fact, you're probably safer with us than with anyone else."

"A crazy guy tried to kill you. Do you really expect me to feel safe?"

"Graham doesn't know where we are, and he doesn't even know you exist, so I don't see why you're so worried."

"I'm not worried. I'm afraid."

A faint smile formed on Randy's face. "Don't be. Now I know I frightened you yesterday, and I apologize for that, and I know you're upset about Phil. But try to understand that as long as you're with us, you're with friends."

"I don't even know why I'm with you. God knows we've got nothing in common."

"I'm afraid you were 'with us' in part the moment you walked in on Trish's exorcism. And we have more in common than you think." Randy let go of him and let his arms fall to his sides.

Bobby rubbed his chest, unsure of what to say.

They stood like that for a minute or two. The trees near the house whispered a wordless chorus, and a mild calm came over Bobby once more.

Randy gave a sudden nod as if replying to someone Bobby hadn't been able to hear. "I don't know about you," he said, "but I'm going to go finish that dinner you threw together."

With that, he turned and retreated to the house, leaving Bobby where he stood.

He stared at the man's dwindling figure. Randy was neither stupid nor deaf. He had to know Bobby wasn't following him.

A sea of conflicting thoughts churned in his mind. He looked at the house. Turned. Looked at the place where the driveway vanished around the base of a hill. Took one step in that direction and stopped.

A door slammed behind him as Randy reentered the house.

What should he do? Go home? What would he do there? Sit around reminiscing about his childhood dreams of becoming a superhero and lamenting the fact he'd grown up to be anything but that?

A terrible longing welled up inside him. As a kid he'd dreamed of actively helping strangers in need, but had he ever taken the time to actually do such a thing? No! Sure, he'd saved people he knew whenever a premonition told him they needed saving, but other than that he'd been too caught up with music and his odd jobs and his journey of seeing as much of America as he could. It seemed the only person he'd ever done anything for was one Robert Jackson Roland, and he didn't even deserve it.

Rescue Man would be ashamed.

He thought about the story Joanna recounted to him. She'd joined a group of drug addicts so she could become part of something, and as a result she'd ended up in a hospital to have the lethal dosage of drugs pumped out of her body. But that didn't mean all human company could bring about harm. People joined churches. They joined Scouts and sports teams and book clubs. Men and women joined together in their mutual attraction for each other and called it love. It didn't matter what the uniting factor was. People did not wish to be alone because alone, they were nothing.

Bobby let out a sigh, and the wind riffled his hair in response. "I'm only staying with them because I don't have anywhere else to go," he said, though he wasn't sure to whom he spoke. "You hear that?"

Yes, the whispering trees seemed to tell him.

It was as good a confirmation as any.

19

LUPE SANCHEZ went to work as usual, though the voice of reason tried to convince her she would be better off staying in bed after her emotional breakdown last night. Randy had even suggested she call in sick, but she had rent to pay and a wedding to save up for. The days of getting paid for staying in bed were over.

When she first came to Oregon, she found work in the kitchens of Mexican restaurants (the easiest jobs she'd been able to find). They didn't pay much, so when she and Randy began dating she got a job as a server at The Manor House, a high-end restaurant that served seafood to the town's wealthier citizens. She had been working there for almost five years now and had no intention of quitting.

Today, however, she could hardly focus on her work. Early in her shift Randy had sent her a text via Phil's phone that she'd discreetly answered when no one was looking: *"The best thing in life to hold onto is each other."* Will call you when I can. Love, Randy.

The message made her smile and respond in kind but it wasn't enough to take her mind off of Graham. Twice she brought people the wrong food, and at one point she accidentally knocked over a glass of water onto a couple's tablecloth. She apologized profusely while another server helped her clean up, and though the couple assured her everything was okay because accidents happen to everyone sooner or later, she still had a hard time not bursting into tears. Not once in her years of employment had she been this inept. She was losing her grip on herself, and she didn't know how much longer she would be able to hold herself together in public.

When the couple had been given a new tablecloth and their plates returned to their respective places, Lupe excused herself and went into the restroom to blow her nose and regain her composure.

What a disaster. Her nerves were unraveling like threads in an old rag, and she knew she would be reprimanded or fired if she made another mistake before the end of her shift.

She had justified coming into work by saying it would be better to stay around people than to be alone at the apartment while Graham and his accomplice were still at large, but every time someone new sat at one of her tables, her suspicions kicked in. At least one person worked with Graham. It had likely been the faceless person sitting out in the parking lot last night watching her apartment. He would have reported to Graham that Randy and another man had shown up at her place at that late hour, and Graham's suspicions would have been aroused.

Graham knew where she worked. He could send his buddy or accomplice or whatever you wanted to call him to the restaurant to harass her. If only she knew what the man looked like so she could protect herself!

Taking calming breaths, she left the bathroom and went back onto the floor. Well-dressed diners of all ages sat around talking and laughing and cutting into their beer-battered fish and popping butterfly shrimp into their mouths as if they hadn't a care in the world. Could one of them be spying on her? What if she was attacked in the parking lot when she left to go home?

At least she'd done as Graham asked. She'd told Randy what Graham had instructed her to impart to him, and then some. Sharing the details of what Graham liked to discuss with her might not have been part of his instructions, and the overwhelming fear that he would find out and become enraged nearly made her ill.

The fact that none of the diners paid her special attention didn't alleviate her fears.

She passed a table where a gray-haired gentleman was pulling a strand of white meat out of a crab leg, and she tensed up even though he looked nothing like Graham. At another table, a thirty-ish man in a business suit spoke heatedly into a cell phone about errors he'd found in a profit and loss statement. He flicked his gaze her way when she walked by but didn't pause in his conversation. Could he be Graham's accomplice? He could have been speaking into the phone for show just to throw her off his trail.

She shook her head. She was seeing ghosts where they didn't exist.

Her shift lasted from eleven in the morning to five. When she finally clocked out and gathered her things, she found she was reluctant to leave. Graham could have had his accomplice cut the brake lines on her car for the sheer joy of it. It would have been bold to do such a thing in broad daylight, but Graham was a bold person.

If only Lupe had the courage to share that trait with him.

Trying not to appear timid, she left the restaurant through the employee exit and made her way over to her white Prius, which nestled safely between her manager's Lexus and a coworker's Altima. She did a visual sweep of that side of the lot before unlocking her car door, eyeing nothing amiss behind the dozen-odd windshields gleaming in the sun. If someone watched her, she couldn't see him.

Satisfied she was in no immediate danger, she climbed behind the wheel and started the ignition. She eased backward out of the parking space without trouble, then shifted into drive and tapped experimentally on the brakes a few times before leaving the lot. Yes. Good. Very, very good. Nobody had tried to sabotage her Prius after all.

She drove two blocks before noticing the slip of paper tucked beneath her left wiper blade.

Her heart leapt into her throat. On any other day she would have thought it was a flyer for an upcoming event.

This was not one of those days.

Lupe turned into the nearest gas station and pulled to the edge of the lot, leaving the engine running as she opened the door and snatched the index card-sized paper out from between the blade and the windshield. Blocky handwriting that she didn't recognize spelled out her name.

She unfolded it and read.

I want to help you. Do you want to be helped? Yes, I think you do. I know what's been going on, or at least some of it. If you'd like to find out more, meet me at 9:00 tonight in the parking lot at St. Paul's. I promise I won't hurt you.

P.S. Don't tell anyone about this unless you want to get us both killed.

She read the note twice, but despite the sender's reassurance that he or she meant no harm, a chill went up her spine. The note bore no signature. Was this a trick? The words were vague enough to have meant any number of things, and if it weren't for the mention of her church and name she would have thought the note had been intended for someone else and placed on her windshield by mistake.

Did she want to be helped? More than anything! To finally be free from Graham's twisted schemes . . .

She pulled her phone out of her purse so she could call Randy and ask his opinion of the matter, but the note expressly forbade her from doing so. She gritted her teeth. She couldn't keep isolating herself like this. It had felt so good telling Randy she'd been in contact with Graham all these long months even though Graham had commanded her to do it, and it would feel even better telling him about the note.

But of course! Randy would be at St. Paul's tonight with the kid he'd just hired, so if anything were to go wrong, he would be there to protect her.

Feeling somewhat relieved, she pulled back out into traffic. Today was a different day from yesterday. She wouldn't let herself sink as low as she had last night. Randy had said they would get through this together, and that gave her hope. She would take charge of her life once more, and if that meant defying the rules of the old man who had threatened her, then so be it.

She kicked off her shoes as soon as she stepped through her apartment door. Standing for six hours every day could really take its toll on a girl's feet. Maybe after she had a bite to eat she could go soak in the tub and—

A creaking noise in the direction of the kitchen made her freeze and lose her train of thought, and before the signal from her brain reached her legs telling them to run, Graham Willard stepped into view.

His hands hung limply at his sides as if to imply he didn't intend to harm her. "It's about time," he said, his gaze cool as he stared at her.

"I—I get off work at five," she stammered, wondering how in the name of heaven he'd gotten in here without breaking down the door.

"That was twenty minutes ago."

"I had to stop at a gas station." No need to tell him she hadn't gotten any gas.

He took a few steps closer to her. "Do you have plans for this evening?"

Her heart thudded against her ribs. She couldn't tell him about the instructions in the note. He would start asking too many questions and find out that she planned on being disloyal to him.

"No," she said, and hoped her face didn't betray her.

"Is Randy coming over?"

She shook her head. "He just hired someone to replace him up at St. Paul's and I think he'll be . . . how do you say it? Showing him the ropes tonight."

This seemed to pique the old man's interest. "Why's he quitting?"

She just shrugged. Graham didn't need to know how she'd been begging Randy to find a replacement for well over a year. If she'd been a more cynical woman she would have thought Randy was stringing her along all this time, but he'd at least agreed to quit his job so he could focus more of his energy on looking for a new Servant.

"You don't know why your fiancé is quitting his job," Graham said. "Is there anything you do know?"

She straightened her shoulders. "I know you're here for something and have yet to tell me what it is."

A faint smile played across his features. "Good call. I want to show you something."

"What?"

"It isn't here. You'll have to come with me."

Be brave, Lupe, said a tiny voice in her head. *Be bold!*

"I don't want to come with you."

"You don't have a choice."

Suddenly an idea occurred to her. Graham had been conniving with both her and Randy, but what would stop her from doing the same to him? She would have to be subtle, though, or he would catch on too easily. Maybe he would catch on anyway.

She cast her gaze to the floor in an expression of defeat. "When are we going?"

Graham glanced at the clock. "Now's as good a time as any. Go ahead and change into more comfortable clothes if you'd like. I'll wait here."

———◆———

LUPE DIDN'T like how Graham was acting. His politeness was likely meant to disarm her, but for what purpose?

She thought of the olden days as she rode blindfolded in the back of his car, now comfortably dressed in a purple hooded sweatshirt and black sweats—it may have been hot outside, but since she didn't know how long they would be gone this evening she thought it wise to wear an extra layer.

When Randy first introduced Lupe to his "family," she'd thought Graham was sweet. He didn't talk a mile a minute about the war and taxes and lying congressman like Randy's other "grandfather" Frank Jovingo did. Graham would smile and nod and only speak his opinion when directly asked, and he loved to prank people and throw the blame on Randy or Frank. In all, a good-natured man whose manners and sense of humor could have charmed a woman of any age.

And now this. Graham's decision to turn on Randy couldn't have been spur of the moment. It had to have been festering inside of him for years—maybe even since before she and Randy met.

Finally the car came to a stop. Graham got out first and led her by hand to the door. Lupe had taken this to mean that no other houses were in sight because any neighbor spotting a man leading a blindfolded woman over his doorstep would have called the police in an instant.

There seemed to be an extra spring in Graham's step. "You can take it off now," he said when he closed the front door.

She obeyed and handed the blindfold to him. "Where is your friend?"

He provided her with a blank stare. "Friend?"

"You know. The one who's always with you. The one who ties the blindfold over my eyes."

"He's busy at the moment. But that's okay. This secret is only for you."

Her stomach squirmed. "What secret would you want to show *me*?"

"You'll find out in a minute. It's downstairs." His eyes gleamed with boyish excitement. "I'd like to know what you think about it."

Sweat broke out on her forehead. Anything that made the old man this happy couldn't be good, and why he wanted to let her in on his secret was beyond her. "Okay."

"First I want to ask you some things," he said.

She waited for him to continue.

"How hard do you think it is for one person to live as two?"

Her head shook. This was one of those rare instances when she truly didn't comprehend something spoken in English. "I don't understand."

"Then let me rephrase. Do you think it's difficult for someone to act like two completely different people and never have anyone notice?"

She wasn't sure where this was going. "Yes, I think it would be."

His smile grew broader. "That's where you're wrong. No one ever knew, did they?"

Ah. He was talking about himself. "But we *do* know."

"Only because I was a fool. If I'd been smart about it I would have staged Randy's murder as a homicide that occurred during a break-in. Oh, his death would have been unfortunate indeed, and to think the feeble old man living upstairs was too slow and afraid to fend off the burglars!"

If she'd had a full stomach, Lupe would have thrown up. "The police aren't stupid. They would have found out it was you sooner or later."

He shrugged. "It doesn't matter now anyway. But as I was saying, two people can only exist together inside a person for so long before one dominates the other. It's taken me some time to truly understand what that means."

"So you admit that you used to be a good man. Or at least partly good."

He lifted an eyebrow. "Two people live inside each and every one of us. Look at you, Lupe. I know what you used to be. A whore. How many men did you lie with? A thousand? Ten thousand? And now you've turned your life around to wait on snobs who drive Porsches and live in million-dollar homes while little children in *Meh-hee-co* go barefoot and have nothing to eat. Have you really changed inside, or is it only your circumstances that have changed? If you lost your job tomorrow would you go running to the first pimp who would have you?"

Her face burned at hearing her life summarized in those terms. "I would never do that again. Not if my life depended on it."

"And what about all those little babies of yours?"

Tears welled up in her eyes, and the part of her that had wanted to die last night was rapidly reawakening. "Graham, please. I don't want to talk about this anymore. Just show me what you want to show me and take me home."

"All in good time. But how many were there, Lupe? Four? Five?" *Please deliver me from this man.* "Six."

"*Six* little babies dead and gone. How terrible, my child. How terrible."

Her hand flew out and slapped him across the face, and he staggered back, stunned. "How *dare* you talk to me like this!" she shrieked. "If you knew the hell I've lived through for all these years . . . The first times I had it done I was too stupid to know any better. My mother told me it was nothing, not a baby, not alive. But I know now. And if God condemns me for what I've done, I deserve it. You think I haven't changed? I've spent years trying to be as good a woman as possible so that maybe God will change his mind about what to do with me."

Graham massaged his cheek where she'd hit him. "What is good, Lupe? And what is bad?"

She spat on the floor at his feet. "You're old enough to know the answer to that."

He gave a thoughtful nod despite her blatant rudeness. "Very well. Now walk ahead of me."

Padre, forgive me for everything I've ever done, she prayed as he directed her to turn right down a hallway and open the first door they came to. Maybe the secret he wanted to show her was her own deathbed, and she'd just spent the remaining minutes of her life feeling miserable about herself.

"Going down," he said as he flicked on the light behind her. "And mind your head at the bottom of the steps; the ceiling is a bit low."

She took the steps one at a time just to spite him and ducked to avoid banging her head. The walls of the stairwell were all cement blocks, and the stairs creaked as if they were about to collapse from rot.

The first thing Lupe noted in Graham's basement was the quantity of stuff stacked on shelves along three walls. Someone who had lived there only briefly wouldn't have had the time to accumulate so many things. Buckets, old cans, tools, boards thick and thin, stacks of cloths—Graham must have had this place for years without anyone knowing about it.

The second thing she noticed was the body lying on a table in the center of the room.

She brought her hands to her mouth as if they expected to stifle a squeal, but no sound came out. The pale-skinned dead woman before her wore bloodstained clothes and a head scarf, and the floor had a wet look about it like it had just been scrubbed—and it probably had since the air smelled of bleach.

Graham glided over to the table like an excited child about to show off a new gizmo he'd received for his birthday. "This is Mary," he said. "Take a good look at her."

Lupe closed her eyes and shook her head.

"Can you guess how she died?"

"You killed her."

"Open your eyes and come here."

She opened her eyes but remained rooted to the spot. Graham took hold of the woman's right arm and turned it so she could see the inner part, where a gash ran from the crook down to the woman's wrist.

No blood spotted her skin. Graham must have wiped her up after killing her, though Lupe couldn't guess why he would have taken the time to perform such a useless task.

"I said, come *here*," he snapped, manners suddenly gone.

"I can see well enough from where I am."

"The knife I used on her is still down here."

Heeding the implied threat, she stepped up to the table and covered her nose.

Graham smiled. "Very good. Now touch her."

She gaped at him. This wasn't at all what she had expected. "What?"

"Touch her. I want you to feel her skin."

The very thought made her recoil. "Why?"

"Just do it."

"I won't."

Graham walked over to a workbench, where he plucked up a knife.

Lupe felt her blood run cold.

He rejoined her at the table. "Now do what I said."

She took a deep breath through her mouth, and very gingerly prodded the woman's arm with her index finger. The skin felt cold and papery.

She jerked her arm back as quickly as she could.

"We're all going to end up like this someday," Graham said, satisfied for the moment. "Our spirits here one moment and in the great beyond the next. I've always wondered what the transition is like. For years I've asked them about it but I can never get a clear answer."

Her heart skipped a beat. "What do you mean, 'they'? How many have there been?"

He smiled. "Far more than six."

"You mean to say . . ." She swallowed. "You kill people just so you can learn what it's like to die?"

"Mary was dying anyway." He gestured at the table. "Cancer. I granted her release from her pain. Some would call it mercy."

"What about the other ones? Did they have cancer too?"

"Some did."

"And why didn't you do this with Randy when you shot him? Wouldn't you want to know what it was like for the Servant to die?"

He didn't answer. "I was going to bury Mary this evening but decided you could be a part of it, too. I cleaned her up as best as I could so you wouldn't be as upset looking at her."

Lupe found herself hoping this was some nightmare from which she would soon awaken. "I don't understand why you wanted me to see this."

"It's simple. I wanted to show you how we're alike."

"I'm nothing like you."

He shrugged. "If you think that, let me to put you to the test. How much do you love Randy?"

The question took her by surprise. "More than anything. If it weren't for him, I don't know where I would be today." Probably a worse place than in a basement standing next to a madman and a corpse, if such a place existed.

"Would you do anything for him?"

"Within reason."

"Would you die for him?"

She was sure she was diving headlong into some kind of trap. "Yes."

"Then hold out your arm."

She didn't move.

"Hold it out!"

This was it, then. He had been planning to kill her after all.

He grabbed her wrist and yanked it to draw her arm away from her chest, and with his other hand he pulled up her sweatshirt sleeve and gently pressed the tip of the knife against her skin. "You have a choice," he said in his gravelly tone. "If you agree to die right now, I'll never have anything to do with Randy again. I'll leave the state and start over somewhere else with whatever time I have left. He can forget I ever existed."

She could hear her pulse in her ears when she spoke. "I don't believe you."

"No?" Graham lifted an eyebrow. "And why is that?"

"If you kill me, you'll just go after him anyway."

"If I kill you, he'll be as good as dead."

The knife drew a bead of blood, and Lupe winced. Graham's tight grip on her wrist was making her hand go numb. "You aren't making any sense. We know the only reason you tried to kill Randy is because you want the world to be without a Servant again. You want us all to suffer the same as your parents' and grandparents' generations did."

The old man's face flushed. "That's pure speculation. War may have broken out the same year Hans Mueller died without a succes-

182 | J.S. BAILEY

sor, but it does nothing to explain the second war or all the others that came after that."

Lupe, who had been mostly unschooled in her youth, didn't know enough about world history to argue, but she pressed onward to keep delaying him from cutting her open. "I've heard all of you talk about how evil will run wild if there is no Servant. You have to believe that. You were one yourself."

"Evil is already running wild. Or have you not turned on a television recently? But we've gotten off topic." He smiled. "You still haven't made your choice."

"I don't want to choose anything."

"If you don't make a decision, I'll make one for you and then you'll both be dead."

Lupe was smart enough to know that if she followed Graham's rules and sacrificed her life, she and Randy would both be dead anyway. Graham was not a man to uphold promises. "I will not let you kill me today," she said.

"Then you've given me permission to murder your lover."

Tears welled up in her eyes anew as she struggled to regain control of her emotions. "I didn't say that."

"But you understood the conditions that I laid out for you. By choosing to live, you've condemned Randy to death. I also know that you plan on running back to him to warn him about me, which is why you'll be staying here until he dies."

Her heart plummeted and the room began to sway. She had been a fool to think she could outsmart him. "They'll miss me at work," she said, trying not to let her fear show through. "Someone will come looking for me and report me missing when they find out my car is at home and I'm not."

He smiled. "Tomorrow morning I'll let you use a phone to call in sick."

"The police will be able to trace it."

"Not this phone."

She silently cursed herself for not having smuggled her own cell phone to this house. (He always forbade her to bring a purse.)

She could have stuffed it in her bra and he never would have known. "So I'm your prisoner."

"If that's what you'd like to call it." He fell silent as he directed his gaze to Mary's corpse. He seemed deep in thought. "You said Randy is hiring a replacement."

"At the church, yes."

"Why would Randy be the one doing the hiring? He's not in charge of such things."

"I . . . I don't know. I didn't think to ask about it."

"Do you know who he hired?"

Lupe pictured the skinny kid who had briefly visited her apartment last night. "Someone named Bobby. I don't know him. I'd never seen him before."

"But you have seen him."

"Yes. He drove Randy to my apartment last night."

"Presumably because his car was out of order."

"Yes, but I told you I didn't tell him about the brakes."

"Then who did, I wonder? Randy is no psychic."

Lupe folded her arms. "Maybe *God* told him he shouldn't drive home. Did you ever think about that?"

Graham's face darkened. "Let's go upstairs. You can stay in the guest room while I take care of Mary's body."

20

NOBODY COMMENTED on Bobby's silent return to the dinner table. The sounds of clinking silverware and glasses made his mind flash back to the family gatherings the Rolands had during his childhood before his paternal grandparents died. How long ago had that been now? Ten years? It felt like a hundred.

The gatherings had been fun. Some of his cousins were close to his age, and after dinner concluded they played with action figures and Legos and had a grand old time. It had been the Golden Age of childhood, he supposed. When the only real things he had to worry about were who got to play with Darth Vader and whose Lego ship would be blown up first. There was laughter all around and few arguments, except for when Bobby's conservative father would get into debates with his liberal brother-in-law and the rest of the family would leave the room to have some peace.

Following the deaths of Bobby's grandparents and father, the gatherings ceased. He stopped seeing his cousins. He wasn't even sure what they looked like anymore.

Until now, he hadn't even realized he missed them.

The gathering here at the safe house bore little similarity to those he remembered, but that was okay. Here in Oregon he would turn over a new leaf. He was no longer the boy who had dreams of wearing a cape and leaping tall buildings in a single bound. He was just Bobby Roland—whatever that meant.

He slid into his place at the table and scooted his chair closer to his plate, pleased to find that the food had not gone cold.

Conversation gradually resumed while he ate.

"We'll have to feed you more often, Bobby," Carly said as he cleaned his plate some time later. "Right, Randy?"

Randy dabbed a napkin at his lips and nodded. "Only next time we should all meet over at the Jovingos' place instead of here, for obvious reasons."

Bobby pushed his empty plate back from the table, certain his stomach was about to split at the seams. "You mean Carly's family?"

She smiled at him, and he saw a dimple form in her cheek. "You bet. Everyone says I inherited my culinary skills from my mother." She patted her flat stomach. "I also inherited her high metabolism."

"In other words, nobody ever starves under their roof," Phil added, still studying Bobby with calculating eyes. Bobby was surprised he'd spoken to him.

Before Bobby could say anything else, Joanna's face became long. "Will I be invited to their house, too?"

Randy shook his head. "I'm afraid not. Once you're home we'll only be meeting once or twice a year. We've discussed this already, remember?"

She gave a halfhearted shrug. "That didn't mean you weren't going to let me visit whenever I like. You saved my life. Doesn't that mean anything?"

Randy took her by the hand, and Bobby felt an awkward lump rise in his throat. "It means everything, Joanna. But it's necessary for us to remain apart so I can help other people too. Okay?"

She stabbed at a cut-up chunk of lasagna. "Whatever," she said, and popped it into her mouth.

Bobby checked the time and saw it was already six o'clock. How had the past couple of hours gone by so quickly? "Uh, Randy? Shouldn't we be getting to work soon? Last night you said we should meet at seven."

"That was before certain circumstances changed, but I agree. Of course this all depends on whether or not our chauffeur is ready to go."

Phil stood up and smoothed out his slacks, looking resigned. "I've been ready to go since yesterday. At this rate Allison is going to think I've left her."

Even though Carly assured him that she and Joanna would be able to take care of cleaning up the kitchen, Bobby felt a shred of guilt at leaving the whole mess for them to take care of. "You're sure you don't want us to stay a little longer to help out?"

Carly waved her hand in dismissal. "Go on, get to work. We're big girls here, right Joanna? We can take care of ourselves."

But Joanna had become sullen and didn't answer, and as they were leaving Bobby saw tears in her eyes once more.

———◆———

WHEN BOBBY made it home to change into different clothes, he was at first startled by the lack of Caleb's car in the driveway, but then the truth returned to him like a knife in the heart.

Bobby went into his room and put on a frayed pair of jeans and a shirt that had acquired a few holes in the last couple years, trying not to think about the empty bedroom next to his. Though Caleb wasn't one to make much noise, the bungalow's silence seemed to shout at him: *Alone! Alone!*

Well, he wouldn't be alone for long.

Bobby arrived at St. Paul's just over an hour after he and Randy had first agreed to meet, and as he climbed out of the car, he saw that Randy's Ford was back from the shop and parked close to where he'd seen it the other night.

A sense of unease gripped him. Whoever cut Randy's brake line might come back, only this time they might make a sport out of vandalizing Bobby's car, too.

He would just have to be careful when he left in case his premonitions didn't warn him about the danger. Check the lines, do circuits of the lot a few times, and if all seemed well, he would drive home. But only then.

Bobby found Randy dozing at the desk in the cluttered office. He jerked his head up when Bobby rapped on the door frame. "I'm glad you came back," Randy said through a yawn.

Bobby sat down in the chair. "Running away is for sissies."

"You didn't seem to think that awhile ago."

"I changed my mind. I really need this job."

Randy slid some papers across the top of the desk. "Good. I'll need you to fill these out to the best of your knowledge. For taxes, you know. I'm sure you've been through this rigmarole before."

Bobby had. As he began to fill in his name, Social Security number, and other information on the forms, he said, "Are you upset with Carly?"

The question seemed to take Randy by surprise. "Why would I be upset with her?"

"She spilled the beans about the whole driving-out-demons thing. Phil seemed mad enough about it."

At first Randy didn't say anything, and when Bobby looked up, he saw that a hint of sorrow had entered his eyes.

Bobby laid the pen down even though most of the form remained blank. "What is it?"

Randy leaned back in his chair and diverted his gaze to the windows. No tapping sounded from beyond them. "I know I'm going to sound like a broken record, but try not to let Phil bother you."

"He doesn't like me."

Randy shook his head. "He doesn't know if he *can* like you since you just showed up out of the blue. Phil is a guarded kind of guy. He won't just befriend anyone he meets. He has to get to know someone well enough to determine whether or not he or she can be trusted."

"He could run a background check on me if he's worried I'm a crook. I've got nothing to hide."

Randy laughed. "I'm sure you don't. But don't feel bad about him. He treated me the same when we first met."

"You're kidding."

"Nope. Though I admit he wasn't quite as open about his distrust. Many things have changed since then." He paused. "Many, many things."

Bobby glanced back down at the incomplete employment forms. He was in no hurry to finish them because as soon as he was done Randy would leave and he'd be alone all over again. "Can I ask you something slightly off topic?"

"It depends."

Bobby continued, praying that Randy wouldn't object to what he was about to ask. "Why do you need to be replaced? I don't mean here at the church. I mean for the other thing. You know."

Randy sighed. "How deep do you want to get into this?"

"How deep am I now?"

"About three inches."

"Out of what?"

"A whole lot more inches than that."

Well *that* was helpful. "Why do you need to be replaced?" Bobby repeated.

"Do you promise you'll never tell another living soul anything about what I'm going to tell you?"

"Sure."

Randy's hazel-eyed gaze bored into his with such intensity that Bobby wanted to look away but found he could not. "Good," Randy said. "I trust you to uphold that. I wouldn't like to be in your place if you broke that promise."

Bobby felt sweat break out on his forehead. "I won't break it. If you can't trust me, you can't trust anyone."

"I hope so." Randy folded his hands together. "It's necessary for me to find a replacement for lots of reasons, the first and foremost being that Lupe and I aren't permitted to be married until I pass what we call the mantle of Servitude on to someone else."

"Servitude?" Bobby had heard them mention the word "servant" at various times, though none of them had elaborated on what that meant.

"Yes. That's what we call our service to God."

It all sounded so strange. But it couldn't be strange. The Bible practically overflowed with stories of ordinary people who spent their lives serving God. Bobby had just never considered the driving out of spirits to be a part of that.

"Go on," he said.

So Randy did. "Being the Servant is a gift. A special union, you might call it. Those who take on the mantle are granted special abilities that help them cast out spirits, and they have a greater awareness of God's presence."

"What do you mean?"

"Stand up, and I'll demonstrate."

Bobby rose, uncertain, and Randy pointed at the hallway floor just outside the office door.

"Go stand there," he said.

Bobby resisted the temptation to ask what Randy was doing. He took up his position and stared into the office.

Randy stood just a few feet inside the doorway. "Okay. How far apart would you say we are?"

Bobby made a quick mental estimation. "Maybe seven feet?"

"Seven feet. Good. Now stay where you are." Randy closed the door between them but left a one-inch gap between the door and the frame so they could still hear each other. "Now how far apart are we?"

"If you didn't move, it's still seven feet."

"Can you see me?"

"No."

"But you still know I'm here."

Understanding slowly dawned on him. "So you're saying if you're this Servant person, a door that separates us from God is opened?"

190 | J.S. BAILEY

Randy swung the door back open and gestured for Bobby to resume his seat. "Yes. But the door isn't really there. We just think it is."

"Okay." Bobby sat on the edge of the chair while Randy returned to his side of the desk. "That makes sense, I think. What does this have to do with marrying Lupe?"

"I was getting to that. When I marry Lupe, I won't be able to devote time to my duties as a Servant, which is why someone else needs to take over for me. That's the way it's always been. You could say it's a little bit like the priesthood."

"But priests aren't ever allowed to marry."

"That's why I said 'a little bit.' I may be able to spend time with Lupe now but I can't give myself fully to her until someone else becomes the Servant."

"I guess that sort of makes sense. What happens to you when you aren't the Servant anymore?"

Randy wore a wistful smile. "God's Holy Spirit will no longer flow within me the same way it does now, and I'll no longer be able to cast out evil spirits in his name, which brings me to the second reason why I need to find someone else to bear the mantle. Do you think it's easy doing what I do?"

Bobby squirmed a bit in his seat. "I guess not."

"The physical and emotional tolls are astronomical. Not to mention mental. They say things to you, things that cut deep if you're not prepared for them. They know every sinful thing you've ever done and they hound you about it to distract you from your task. It's exhausting. I have to work out as often as I can and practice mental control so they can't ruin me, and even though the Spirit gives me strength, I'm still human. I'm worn out. Some days when I look in the mirror I swear I can see through myself like I'm evaporating."

It all sounded terrible to Bobby, but at the same time he was intrigued. This was more than he had ever hoped for the man to explain. "How long have you been doing it?"

"Six years. Since I was twenty like you. Most only stick with it for four or five if they aren't killed first."

A shiver passed over Bobby. "Why would someone try to kill people like you? Wouldn't casting out demons be a good thing?"

Randy stretched the collar of his t-shirt down to where Bobby could see the upper part of his chest below his shoulder, where two circular scars stood two inches apart from each other. "I don't know, why *would* somebody try to kill me?" he asked, letting his shirt slide back into place. "Because there are people who hate the work we do, as well as the One who chose us. It's almost funny. You can feed and clothe the poor and offer a helping hand to those in need, and few will bat an eye. But if you suggest that people should repent and turn their lives to Christ, that's when things get ugly. You'd think they wouldn't care. But they do. Boy, do they."

"But if you had died then, you wouldn't have had someone to replace you. Right?"

Randy's expression grew solemn once more. "It's always been advised to choose a replacement soon after being chosen just in case of an early death—I've just never come across anyone I feel is suitable for the position. If a Servant dies without having chosen a successor, then it's thought that evil will reign unchecked until the first male child born after the Servant's death is located by the Servant's surviving predecessors and the mantle is passed to him at the age of eighteen. I'm not sure why that is, but it's what tradition tells us, and I don't see any reason to doubt it. Are you going to finish filling out your form?"

"Oh." That task had already slipped from his mind thanks to Randy's words. Bobby looked back down at the papers and scribbled in the last bits of information they asked for. "Well, good luck finding your replacement. How do you find one, anyway?"

"It's different for everyone. Phil found me right here at church. I didn't know him well back then. One day he stopped me when church let out and asked if I wanted to come to lunch with him and his friends who, as it turned out, were Carly's parents, Graham Willard, an old fart named Frank, and a few others who are part of our circle. Great people. Most of them, anyway. We met again and again and eventually Phil let on to what he did, and I agreed to accept the mantle of Servitude so he could marry his longtime girlfriend, Allison. They have a little girl now. She's a cute kid."

"You did this just for them?"

"Not just for them, but for all of those whom I might be able to save from suffering."

"That sounds noble, I guess." Bobby scanned the papers to make sure he hadn't missed anything and handed them back to Randy. "Were you scared?"

"A little. I didn't know what would happen, but I just trusted God, and well, here I am, six years later. You should trust God, too. I think it will serve you well." Randy stood and pulled a set of keys out of his pocket. "Here, this is yours." He tossed it to Bobby, who caught it in his fist. "The big one unlocks all the outer doors, the medium one is for the meeting room and office doors, and the smaller one unlocks the janitor's closet. Please don't lose any of them."

Bobby committed which key was which to memory and slipped them into the pocket of his jeans. "You're leaving already?" He had hoped to at least get to talk to Randy for awhile longer, in part because being in the large building by himself sounded about as appealing as spending the night in a graveyard.

"If I don't get some sleep soon, I'm going to be a dead man." He yawned as if to give credence to his statement. "Oh. I almost forgot." Randy picked up a white binder lying at the edge of the desk and handed it to Bobby. "You don't need to look at this whole thing tonight, but be sure you know the basics. There's also some emergency contact numbers in there in case you ever need them."

Bobby flipped the binder open. The first page listed the table of contents for a manual outlining his duties and other things he should know now that he was an employee of the church. "Thanks. Is this mine, too?"

"Only for the duration of your employment. Keep it safe, because I'm not sure our secretary would enjoy having to type up a new one." Randy snapped his fingers. "You know, there's something else, too. You'll need to have a background check done, but I'm sure you're not worried about that." Randy held out his hand,

and Bobby shook it. "Good luck. If you need anything, call my cell phone. Those bags of rice work miracles."

"That's good. And thanks."

Randy gave a halfhearted salute and walked out the door without further ado. His heavy footsteps receded down the hallway before they were cut short by the opening and closing of the wooden double doors.

Bobby heaved a sigh and opened the binder again. He didn't think it would tell him what to do if evil entities started throwing rocks at him while on the job.

He could only hope that whatever followed him home last night would not return.

21

BOBBY SET the binder on the desk, made a mental note to take it with him when he went home, and made his way to the janitor's closet three doors down the hallway. St. Paul's was laid out differently from the church to which his father and Charlotte took him as a child. Colorful stained glass windows that opened to the outside lined that sanctuary. Here, hallways leading to meeting rooms and assorted offices boxed the sanctuary in on all four sides like it was an enclave.

Or a crypt.

Last night when Randy gave him the grand tour of the place, Bobby saw that the only way natural light could enter the sanctuary was through six clear glass skylights in the peaked ceiling. "If you're ever going to climb up on the roof and clean the windows," Randy had said, "make sure it's bright enough out so you can see what the heck you're doing. Father Preston won't like it if he has to scrape what's left of you off the ground."

Since washing the windows wasn't an option tonight, Bobby would start cleaning in the office and work his way clockwise around the building.

It was best to get started.

He unlocked the closet and flicked the light on. Shelves upon shelves of cleaning supplies stared back at him: Windex, Clorox, paper towels, rags. A sad mop leaned against the wall next to a broom missing some of its bristles. If he remembered later, he would buy the church a new one.

He ignored these and reached for a box of garbage bags. Emptying the trash was as good a place to start as any.

While he moved from room to room gathering up overflowing wastebasket liners and stuffing them into a Hefty bag he dragged along behind him, he found himself thinking about Joanna and her yellow summer dress and the way tears had glistened in her eyelashes, and how Trish had just died in her chair without apparent cause far before her time should have come.

Joanna and Trish. Two troubled women who had both needed help and turned to the same person to receive it.

Funny, how Bobby had turned to Randy for help in a way, too. The man did more than Rescue Man could have ever dreamed of doing.

Bobby decided he didn't want to think about Rescue Man anymore. It was kid stuff. Done. The past. The end.

The next hour saw Bobby dusting shelves, vacuuming carpet, disinfecting doorknobs, and straightening papers that had been left behind on desks. Such dull, tedious work.

He couldn't complain.

"And I thought it would be creepy working here," he said out loud as he lugged yet another full garbage bag to the dumpsters outside. "Just shows what I know."

He went back in and was about to consult the binder again when the flash of headlights—accompanied by the low rumble of an engine—shined through the slats in the office blinds.

He checked the time. Nine o'clock. Who would be here this late in the day? Had Randy forgotten something and come back to get it?

Doubtful. Randy could have just called him.

Bobby switched off the office light and peered through the blinds. Mere yards away from the window sat an idling car of indeterminate make and color.

Seconds ticked by.

The headlights winked out and the engine fell silent. Bobby could hear his pulse in his ears. It was the person who'd vandalized Randy's brakes. He knew it. He just knew it.

The car's interior light came on. A man he didn't recognize stepped out into the night and set off toward the church entrance.

Which Bobby had left unlocked.

Fear made him hold his breath. He waited for the sound of the doors opening but heard nothing other than the occasional pop and creak of the building settling down for the night.

Another minute passed. Bobby looked through the slats again and was surprised to see that the man had returned to his vehicle. The dome light glowed again. The man seemed to be checking his watch.

So he was meeting someone here and they were late. Bobby still didn't think he could trust the man. Phil Mason must have been rubbing off on him.

Bobby forced his nerves to unwind themselves, but he feared that if he got busy doing something else, the man would enter the church, sneak up behind him, and scare him to death.

Or worse.

He would have to do the logical thing and lock the door.

"God, don't let him come in here," Bobby said as he headed toward the entrance. "Make him stay away."

Whether God was listening or not from beyond the nonexistent door that sat between them, Bobby didn't know.

But then a car door slammed.

The man was coming back.

Bobby froze midway between the office and front doors, knowing he wouldn't get to them in time. It took him half a second to decide he would rather hide than face whoever was about to come through the door.

He turned and made a mad dash toward the open janitor's closet. He slammed the door behind him, let out a mild curse when he discovered he couldn't lock it from the inside, and sank to the floor amid the clutter.

He left the light off so it wouldn't spill out through the crack under the door.

His heart continued to pound.

Far away down the hall came the telltale squeak of the wooden doors opening and swinging shut.

Footsteps echoed on the tile floor. "Hello?"

Bobby didn't dare call out a reply.

The man spoke again in a voice fraught with anxiety. "Is anybody here?" The footsteps moved into the sanctuary for a minute and back out again, stopping in the area close to the first office. "Father Preston? Mr. Bellison? Are you here?"

For a second Bobby wondered if the man might be the one who'd tried to kill Randy but decided otherwise. Graham was an old man, and this man's voice bore none of the telltale rasp indicative of advanced years. If Bobby had to guess, he'd have said the speaker was in his thirties or forties.

That didn't mean the man could be trusted.

The footsteps continued his way once again. "I know somebody's in here."

Well, duh. Unless cars drove themselves and church lights were left on all night to illuminate ghosts.

Bobby could only hope the guy wouldn't look in the closet. "Hello?"

Now the man stood just outside the closet door. *Please don't come in.*

"Mr. Bellison," the man said, "if you're in here, we need to talk."

Since Bobby was not Mr. Bellison, he felt no need to reply.

Bobby shifted an arm so he could scratch his nose and accidentally knocked into something he couldn't see, which then fell to the floor with a loud *thunk*.

And though every cell of his body dreaded it, the closet door swung open with a squeal.

The man standing in the doorway wore black sunglasses, a black jacket, and black pants. "You're not Mr. Bellison," he said, a note of surprise in his voice.

Bobby stood. "I guess not." He heard a tremor in his voice and hated himself for it.

A crease formed in the man's forehead and he backed up a few steps into the hallway. "What are you doing here?"

"Working."

"You don't work here."

Bobby felt his confidence begin to build. "I do now. Randy hired me to replace him."

Brown eyebrows arched over the top of the sunglasses. "I wasn't aware he'd intended to quit."

"And I wasn't aware that people go sneaking around churches this late at night."

A smirk. "I'm not the one hiding in a closet." The man straightened his sunglasses. "Step on out so I can see you better."

"Maybe if you take those glasses off, you will."

The man's manner became terse. "Look. I don't have a lot of time. I was supposed to meet someone here and she hasn't showed."

"She?" Bobby stepped forward into the closet doorway.

"Yes, a woman in her twenties. She has to have gotten the message, and I know she wouldn't refuse to come."

Well there's your problem. "Maybe her phone died and she couldn't get to her voicemail."

He shook his head. "It was the written variety." He clasped his hands together and glanced in the direction of the entrance. "I'm hoping the note wasn't stolen. This is very important."

The man's agitation seemed genuine. "I could keep a look out for her," Bobby said. "Something might have held her up."

"That's what I'm afraid of." The man stared down at his feet, deep in thought. Then, "I can't stay any longer. If she shows up, can you tell her she missed me? Here." He pulled a tiny notepad and pen out of his jacket pocket and scrawled out a phone number. "You can give this to her. If she still doesn't show, throw it away or burn it."

Bobby took the paper without looking at it and stuffed it into his jeans. "What's her name? So I know it's her, I mean."

"Do I need to tell you that? At this hour, she'll be the only person looking to meet someone here."

That made sense. "And what's your name?"

The man hesitated. "You can tell her my name is Paul."

"Is it?"

His face became impassive. "Also," he continued, "if anyone aside from her shows up asking about me, pretend I was never here. You didn't see anyone, not even a man named Paul. Do you understand?"

This situation was becoming stranger by the minute. "Sure. I never saw you."

"Thank you." The man who wasn't Paul moved a few paces toward the entrance and stopped. "I mean it. Even if someone threatens to hurt you, you've got to remain silent."

Bobby opened his mouth to ask him why in the world someone would torture a mere janitor to obtain information about the black-clad man, but he was off in a flash. Seconds later the outer doors opened and closed, and not long after that Bobby heard the thump of a car door slamming shut.

A whirlwind of thoughts spun through Bobby's head.

One: Paul knew Randy.

Two: Randy was being targeted by Graham Willard.

Three: Paul was being targeted by persons unknown who might resort to harming an innocent bystander in order to obtain information.

Could Graham and Paul somehow be connected?

He prayed Paul was wrong in his fear and nobody except for the woman would arrive at the church this evening. Luckily, the sense of foreboding he generally felt before the occurrence of unpleasant events remained as silent as the church building itself. Paul meant him no harm, and if other men did, they would not show themselves tonight.

Not for the first time, he'd worked himself up for nothing.

As Bobby started back toward the office where he'd left the binder, it occurred to him that he hadn't heard the engine of Paul's car as he had when the man arrived. To sate his curiosity, he looked out the window for what felt like the thousandth time and saw that the light in the man's car had not yet clicked off. Paul—or whatever his name was—sat half-turned as he stared out toward the empty street.

Bobby dared not move. Even though it was none of his business, he had to see who the man desired to meet.

No one came for as long as Bobby watched. Five minutes later, Paul backed the car out of the space and made toward the exit.

Bobby let the blinds snap shut. Curiosity burned inside of him like an unquenchable fire. The man couldn't just leave without telling Bobby more.

Hardly giving thought to his actions, Bobby raced down the hallway, out through the main doors, and into the parking lot, fortunately not succumbing to another dizzy spell. Paul's car turned right onto the street just as Bobby threw his car door open and hopped inside.

His tires squealed as he tore off in Paul's direction, but now three other cars accompanied his on the road. Which one was Paul's? There. The darker sedan up ahead looked like a potential candidate.

Paul traveled at the posted speed limit, and Bobby pushed the pedal a little harder so he could catch up to the man at a pace that wouldn't alarm him. He stopped two cars behind him at a traffic light and eased back a bit when traffic got moving again.

After ten minutes of tailing the man at a distance through residential streets, Bobby's quarry pulled into the driveway of a small white two-story house along a less-populated street on the far edge of town. Bobby turned around three driveways up, cruised past Paul's house again, and committed the number on the mailbox to memory: 2128.

Tomorrow he could do additional detective work and try to figure out who owned the place. In the meantime, he had to get back to work before someone learned that the new janitor had run off leaving the building easy pickings for burglars.

He returned to the church. Bobby checked all of the rooms to make sure no undesirables had crawled in during his absence, and soon it became clear that St. Paul's remained as vacant as it had been when he left.

He continued cleaning where he'd left off. And though from time to time a faint tapping noise in a far corner of the church he couldn't pinpoint made him think that some other entity kept him company, he saw no one else for the rest of the night.

22

MORNING DAWNED all too soon, and Bobby found himself rolling out of bed at the ungodly hour of nine o'clock. He'd returned home at two and tossed and turned half the night as images of Randy, Caleb, Joanna, and Trish fought for dominance in his semiconscious brain; and when he finally did fall asleep, he'd dreamed he was ransacking the bungalow from top to bottom while he searched for something that he never found.

He left the room after dressing and stuck his head through Caleb's doorway. Empty. Like he'd expected any different.

He went into the kitchen and pulled a stale bagel out of the breadbox, and when he went to the refrigerator to get out the cream cheese, a plain white envelope stuck to the door with a guitar-shaped magnet caught his eye.

All thoughts of breakfast were immediately forgotten.

He tugged the envelope out from under the magnet and stared dumbly at it for a few seconds. It had not been sealed. He lifted up the flap and removed a folded piece of notebook paper.

Tucked between the folds was a check for $1,000.

The note read:

Bobby,

I'm sorry I can't stick around. I wish I could explain but it isn't my place to do so. I hope this check will help cover the cost of rent for a little while. Your friend, Caleb.

The check came from Caleb's bank account, and the signature was his. Even though the letter explained nothing, Bobby felt some of the weight lift from his chest. Caleb did exist! And he still cared enough to help Bobby with the rent as usual. Something personal must have come up that required Caleb to leave town.

"But how did you get out of here without me hearing it?" Bobby asked the room.

It was a mystery he had no way of solving, and perhaps it was best left that way.

Bobby could solve one mystery. The man at the church lived at 2128 Maple Road—Bobby had paid close attention to the signs so he wouldn't have to retrace his steps today just to learn the name of the street. An Internet search might inform him of the man's identity.

Sacrificing the cream cheese for the sake of haste, Bobby ate his bagel, washed it down with orange juice, and fired up his old laptop that sat on a table in the corner of the living room like a forgotten friend.

He pulled up Google and typed the man's address into the search bar. The search returned links for sites listing estimated property value, but none mentioned anything about who lived there.

He leaned back in the swivel chair and folded his arms. The fact that Paul felt threatened bothered Bobby more than anything else about last night's encounter. Just what sort of meeting was supposed to have taken place between him and the nameless woman?

Spies, said the voice in his head, but he disregarded that idea the moment he thought of it. This was Autumn Ridge, Oregon; not Washington, DC or London.

What, then?

204 | J.S. BAILEY

Remembering the piece of paper Paul handed him, he went to his bedroom and withdrew the slip from the jeans he tossed on the floor when he'd returned home.

The note was short. Paul had written down a local phone number and the request to "Ask for Paul."

By asking for the false name, Paul would have known the woman spoke with Bobby and received the paper from him. Too bad she'd never arrived so Bobby could deliver it.

Bobby stood up, unable to continue his detective work on the computer. He had the whole day ahead of him with little to do other than practice guitar solos on the Fender Stratocaster that had been his one constant companion on his journey from Ohio to New York to Utah to here.

He put on his shoes and pocketed his wallet. Guitar practice could wait.

First he went to the bank and deposited the check Caleb gave him.

Next he drove to 2128 Maple Road. The white house sat at a slight distance from its neighbors, its driveway unoccupied.

Bobby occupied it, killed the engine, and got out.

The lawn in front of the house had recently been trimmed and the mulched flowerbed running along the front wall and porch was populated with bushes and decorative grass. The white siding on the house gleamed in the morning sun, and the welcome mat at the edge of the porch looked as though it had never been touched by human feet.

Despite the fact that nobody appeared to be home, Bobby boldly went to the porch and pushed the doorbell.

He stepped back to wait and looked back out toward the road. The green rectangle of the Autumn Ridge corporation limit sign sat on metal posts about a tenth of a mile away. A few cars passed. Some birds swooped through the air and alighted in a treetop.

Bobby pushed the doorbell again. Still no one came to greet him.

He walked back to the car, not knowing what he had hoped to accomplish by coming here. If Paul had been home, he would have accused Bobby of being a stalker. He might have even thought that Bobby was in alliance with whatever person who sought to hurt him.

Maybe Randy would know more about the man.

As Bobby drove back into town, he dialed Randy's number.

Randy answered on the fifth ring. "Hello?"

Other voices spoke in the background but Bobby couldn't make out the words. "Randy?" he said. "It's me."

Bobby sensed that something was amiss when Randy next spoke. "Oh. Hey, kid." Then, "Can you two quiet down? I'm on the phone."

"Who's there?" Bobby asked. "Are you at home?"

"Yes. Bobby, I hate to cut you short, but this is a bad time to talk."

"Why? What happened?"

"Long story. I'll call you back as soon as I can, okay?"

"Okay. Bye."

Bobby disconnected and gazed unseeingly at the traffic in front of him. Could this be about Trish again? Maybe her body had been found! Or maybe not, and the continued absence of it weighed heavily on Randy's mind.

Bobby mulled over his options. A: He could go home, practice his songs, and go to work in the evening as planned. B: He could try to be a useful, helpful human being who thought of others before himself.

He chose Option B.

One car he didn't recognize was leaving when Bobby arrived at Randy's artificially-junked home. He had to pull his car so far to the right on the lane so the other car could pass that branches and brambles screeched against his passenger-side windows. The driver—an overweight man with salt and pepper hair—raised his eyebrows at him, and in response Bobby gave the man a sheepish wave.

Bobby pulled up to the house and parked next to Phil Mason's Taurus. He went to the porch and was about to knock when the door flew open. Today Randy wore a black skull t-shirt, black jeans with a chain connecting a belt loop to the left pocket, and an unbecoming scowl.

"I said I'd call you back," Randy said. Stubble peppered his chin and his hair looked as shaggy as Bobby had ever seen it.

Bobby took an involuntary step backward. "I thought you might need me for something."

"What would make you think that? I didn't even tell you what's going on."

Clean-cut Phil appeared beside Randy in the doorway. "This kid keeps turning up like a bad penny," he said with a frown.

Bobby's face flushed. He had to prove to Phil there was no reason to distrust him. "Look. I thought this might be about Trish, and I thought maybe I could be useful for once in my life and come out here to be with you guys."

Randy's expression softened. "I appreciate your concern, but this isn't exactly about what you're thinking."

"Should I leave?"

Randy sighed. "No. Come on in. There's coffee in the kitchen if you want it."

Bobby followed the two men inside. "I'm sorry if it seems like I'm intruding," he said, joining Randy at the kitchen table while Phil busied himself at the coffee maker. "I'm not trying to be a pest."

To his surprise, Randy's face cracked into a grin and he laughed. "You, a pest? You're more like a stray dog."

Bobby didn't know if that was supposed to be an insult or a compliment.

Phil placed a mug of hot coffee on the table in front of Bobby despite the fact he hadn't asked for one—an odd gesture from someone who supposedly didn't like him. Bobby sipped at the steaming drink and waited for someone to do or say something, but both Randy and Phil seemed to be waiting for Bobby to initiate the conversation.

Here went nothing. "Something odd happened at the church last night."

"If it was more unexplained noises," Randy said, "you know I told you to ignore it."

"It wasn't that. Do you know if people like to meet there?"

The question seemed to take Randy by surprise. "Of course. There's a bereavement group, scouts, a writer's group, a book club, the worship commission, planning committees . . . There's a meeting of some kind or another four or five nights a week, and sometimes more than one a night. Most of them are cleared out by the time I get there."

"No, I don't mean that. A man showed up looking for someone he was supposed to meet in the parking lot. He acted kind of strange, and it bothered me."

Randy's brow furrowed. "Was he looking for the priest?"

Bobby shook his head. "He told me he was meeting a woman in her twenties. He said he couldn't wait much longer, and that if she showed up later, to give her this." Bobby pulled the paper with the phone number out of his pocket and passed it to Randy, who scrutinized it like one trying to solve a cipher. "He said his name was Paul, only it really wasn't. Like an alias, I guess."

Randy handed the paper back to him. "This is a bit unusual, but what does it have to do with us?"

"He knows who you are and said something about needing to talk to you. When he came inside, he was calling for you and Father Peter, or Perry, or something."

"The priest there is Father Preston," Phil said with a flicker of interest in his eyes.

"Yeah, that was it." More of Paul's words from last night came back to him. "Only he called you Mr. Bellison, so I'm guessing he isn't someone who knows you well."

Randy rubbed at his chin. "Many people know me by name and know I was employed by the church. I still don't see why this sent you running back here."

"I'm not finished yet." Bobby cleared his throat. "Paul said if anyone other than the woman showed up asking about him, I should pretend I never saw him even if they tried to torture it out of me. I didn't think it was normal for a guy dressed up all in black like some kind of agent to show up at a church saying things like that."

Phil's eyes grew wide, but Randy remained calm. "When you say 'agent,' what exactly do you mean?"

"He had on sunglasses and dark clothes." Bobby paused to sip at the coffee for a few moments. "I don't think he was actually an agent. He just seemed like he was trying to disguise himself. He acted like someone was after him, which makes me wonder if someone was after the woman he was supposed to meet, too. She never showed up."

"I can see why you wanted to come see me," Randy murmured. He propped his elbows on the table and rested his chin on his hands. "Did he have any identifying marks you can remember?"

Bobby racked his memory for anything about the man that would set him apart from others but came up with nothing. "He had short brown hair, was of average height and build, and drove a dark-colored car. I kind of followed him when he left. He lives on the east side of town."

Randy gaped at him. "You left the church unattended to go tail someone? What if he'd caught you?"

Bobby hadn't expected Randy to respond favorably to that news. "Nothing happened, okay? But the guy lives at 2128 Maple Road, or at least that's the place he stopped at. I thought that knowing where he was staying might help us."

Phil gave a thin smile. "You're starting to become far more interesting than a bad penny."

"He's going to be a *fired* bad penny if Father Preston ever catches wind of what he did." Then to Bobby Randy said, "Did you at least lock the doors when you went out?"

Bobby's face flushed. "I didn't have time. If I'd let him get too far ahead, I wouldn't have been able to follow him."

"What did you hope to accomplish by doing this?" Phil asked.

"I don't know. It just seemed like the right thing to do." And now that he was telling Randy and Phil about it, his actions made even less sense to him than they had when he'd actually committed them. "If it makes you feel better, I checked the whole building when I got back to make sure no one snuck in."

Randy leaned back in his chair. "What you did may have been dumb, but I'd be a liar if I said I wouldn't have been tempted to do the same thing. I still wouldn't do anything like that again because Father Preston has the unfortunate tendency to learn every single thing that is said or done under that church's roof."

"But it wasn't under its roof," Bobby said. "It was outside on the road."

A muscle twitched in Randy's cheek. "Which makes it even worse."

"So you don't know anyone who lives at that house?"

Randy glanced toward the ceiling as he ruminated. "Maple Road, you said? A few parishioners live out that way, but I don't see why any of them would be engaging in some kind of illicit meeting on church property."

"Paul never said it was illicit. And I didn't get any bad vibes from him. Not horrible ones, anyway."

"No offense," Phil said, "but I wouldn't hold much stock in personal feelings for someone you'd never met before."

Speak for yourself. "You don't understand." Bobby knew they wouldn't believe him, but he couldn't keep his premonitions a secret any longer now that Randy had let him in on secrets of his own. "I can sense things other people can't. That's how I knew something was wrong with Randy's car the other night."

Creases formed in Phil's forehead. "You're clairvoyant?"

Bobby cringed at the term, which conjured images of old women bending over crystal balls telling the future to people who were too stupid to know they were being ripped off. "No. Nothing like that. I don't read palms and I don't conjure spirits. I just get these strong premonitions sometimes. It's like a fire starts burning inside me and I know I have to be on full alert for whatever is about to happen."

"This has happened before?"

"Lots of times."

"Tell us about it."

Bobby took a deep breath. Of course it would all come to this sooner or later. If they thought he was some kind of monster, then so be it. "I had this neighbor in New York—I already told Randy about this. His name was Tyree. I told him not to go out one night because I knew he'd be hurt if he did. He brushed me off like it was nothing, and I found him shot to death in the parking garage the next day." A knot rose in his throat and he banished the painful images to the back of his mind before he became misty-eyed and made a fool of himself.

Phil nodded, looking surprisingly sympathetic. "I'm sorry to hear that."

Bobby cleared his throat again. "That's okay. But it really got to me. I knew Tyree died because I hadn't been firm enough with him. If I could have convinced him that he was about to die, maybe he would have listened to me. He might still be here today."

"I don't advise you to linger over the things that might have been," Randy said. "You'll make yourself sick with regret. How old was Tyree?"

"About forty. I'd only just moved in so we didn't know each other well. I think he just took me for a dumb, scared kid from the country and that's why he didn't believe what I said."

"That's too bad."

"Not all of my premonitions have turned out that way, though," Bobby said, changing the subject as quickly as possible. "When I was in high school my brother Jonas wanted me to take him to see some new superhero movie, and I said it would be more fun if we stayed home and had a cookout instead. I had this gut feeling we would've died if we'd driven anywhere that night. Later on my step-mom turned on the TV and there was breaking news footage of a fatal accident that happened between our house and the theater. If we'd gone, we would have been in the accident, too."

"So these premonitions don't tell you the future," Phil said. "They just warn you that harm is imminent."

"Right."

"Have you always had them?"

"Not always, no. The first one I can remember happened right after my dad died. It was so sudden. His death, I mean. And I was there when it happened. It messed me up really bad for awhile." He could feel his eyes brimming with tears again as he saw his father drinking that final glass of lemonade in their kitchen.

"Do you think the shock of his death somehow opened you up to a higher power that enabled you to foresee unpleasant situations?" Phil asked.

Bobby had often wondered the same thing but never thought about it in those exact words. "It's possible. The first premonition I had was maybe two weeks after he died. I knew I had to go outside all the sudden, and when I stepped out the door I saw our neighbors' two-year-old walking out into the street. She got their door open while her mom was taking a nap."

"How long ago did your father pass away?" Randy asked.

"It's been six years. I was fourteen."

"And not once in those first fourteen years did you have premonitions of any kind," Phil said. All traces of skepticism had vanished from his voice.

"Not that I can remember."

The three of them were silent for several moments as Randy and Phil digested what he told them. Finally Randy said, "I'd like to know more about this gift of yours. It reminds me of the gift of Prophecy, with some obvious differences."

Bobby shrugged. "That's really all there is to say. And I wouldn't call it a gift."

"Yet it's already saved multiple lives, my own included. If that isn't a gift, then I don't know what is."

"If it were a gift, I wouldn't feel like wetting my pants every time it happens."

Phil snorted. "You have so much to learn. Randy told me you know some things about the mantle of Servitude, which I admit concerns me since you aren't one of our number and have no apparent desire to join us in that respect. But do you think the gift of being able to cast out evil spirits is warm and cozy? We use the gifts we're given because they're meant to be used in service to God and to others, not because they make us feel good."

Having the power to expel demons didn't sound much like a gift either, but Bobby wasn't going to argue about it. "It would be nicer if it felt good," he said.

"If that were the case, we'd be tempted to use our gifts for our own personal gain, which isn't something that Servants are permitted to do." Phil glanced to Randy. "It is okay to be talking about this, right?"

Randy dipped his head. "No secrets between friends, new ones included."

"That's news to me," Bobby said. "And if you aren't keeping secrets anymore, why haven't you told me why this was a bad time for me to show up?"

Randy's expression darkened. "Our friend Roger was just here discussing our options with us. He thinks we should conduct a search of all the former Servants' homes to see if any of them have stashed Trish's body away. I understand his reasoning, but still. We have to trust each other. And that isn't my definition of trust."

"How many former Servants are there?"

"Of the ones still living and in contact with us? Five. There's Frank, Graham, Roger, Frank the Second who some of us call Frankie, and Phil."

"What if Graham's the one who took her?"

"He doesn't know where this house is. I bought it after he tried to kill me."

Bobby couldn't believe Randy would be so naïve. "Anyone could find out where you live. He knows where you worked, right? He could have followed you home one night to see where you've been staying."

Randy shook his head. "I thought about that many times, which is why I always made sure I wasn't being followed. I'm more cautious than you make me out to be."

"He could have looked up real estate records and found you."

"And he could have hidden a tracking device on my car and followed me that way," Randy said, his voice suddenly laced with sarcasm. "I don't think this is Graham's doing." But then his expression faltered. "I mean, if he knew I was here, he could have come in and killed me any time he wanted. Why would he come in and take a body when I'm his intended victim?"

No one had an answer to that.

"What I want to know," Bobby said, "is why someone who acted like your friend shot you and left you for dead. Maybe if you can figure that out, you can figure out why he would do everything else."

"I think," Randy said, "we would need a real clairvoyant to find the answer to that."

23

LUPE AWOKE staring at a mint green wall. Here and there chips had fallen out of it to reveal an older sky-blue paint beneath it.

A tiny black ant crawled in a zigzagging line up to a windowsill and disappeared into a crack where the caulking hadn't been properly smoothed over.

The walls in Lupe's bedroom were a cheery peach in color. She was not at home.

She jolted upright and forced herself back against the headboard, as if leaning against the wall would offer her any additional protection from the monster that dwelled in the house with her.

Graham had said such terrible things to her yesterday, and then to top it all off he'd locked her in this room so he could go off by himself and bury that poor woman he'd killed.

A cruel voice inside her head wondered if he had dug a grave for Randy as well.

She had to give Graham a little bit of credit. The bedroom where he'd imprisoned her had an attached bathroom, though she'd been unable to find any towels or shampoo; and the bar of soap perched on the edge of the tub had a shriveled look as if it had sat there unused for years.

She climbed out of the bed (who all had slept here over the years, and had they been prisoners, too?) and went to the window. Last night she had tried in vain to see if any neighbors were in view, but from that vantage point all she could see were trees and the green lawn below.

That didn't mean there weren't homes lurking just out of sight down the road. When dusk fell and the sounds of Graham traipsing around on the ground floor had ceased, she'd flicked the bedroom light on and off in the SOS pattern in the hope that someone driving by would notice the blinking in the window and come to her aid, but if anyone had seen it, their suspicions hadn't been aroused.

She'd tried to open the window. It wouldn't budge. She'd looked for something heavy so she could smash out the glass and climb down the outer wall to safety, but the room was sparsely furnished and the only thing that would have been remotely solid enough to do the job was the bedside lamp.

If she'd tried to break the window with the lamp, she would have only smashed the latter to smithereens, and the sound of it would have sent Graham storming to her room with a gun in hand.

Right now, however, she wanted to determine the position of the sun in the sky. She would have to be at work before long, and Graham had said he'd give her a phone so she could call in sick.

Then he would go out to kill Randy, but where and by what method, Lupe did not know.

Tears welled up in her eyes. Even though it had not been her intent, she had betrayed the only man who had ever loved her. Again.

She glanced back at the wall, where another ant climbed its way to the crack beneath the windowsill. If only she could shrink down to their size and follow them, she could get out of this confounded house. But if she did find a way out, what would she do? Hitchhike her way back to town and pray that whoever picked her up wasn't a worse creep than Graham? At least the old man hadn't physically harmed her.

Yet.

She sat down on the edge of the bed and crossed her arms. Surprisingly, her stomach growled—she hadn't thought she could ever be hungry in this place. Last night when Graham had heated up a bowl of Campbell's soup for her, she'd barely eaten half of it before her stomach could take no more.

Her reluctance to eat had stemmed in part from the fact that she didn't know if Graham had laced her food with poison or not. He'd promised he wouldn't hurt her, but the promises of a murderer were worth next to nothing.

Judging by the light in the sky, the time was midmorning. Where was Graham? He couldn't have just left her here to starve. A small part of her hoped he would forget to have her call the restaurant. Her worried coworkers would then contact Randy, though neither he nor any members of law enforcement would know where to find her.

Minutes ticked by at the pace of a snail. She had to eat something soon or she would start to feel faint.

It occurred to her that Graham might have died. The days of his youth had expired before Lupe's birth, and carrying the deceased woman's body outside for burial had to have been a strain on his aging heart.

If he really was dead, he wouldn't mind if she knocked out the window.

She would have to check first.

Lupe rapped on the bedroom door. "Graham?" she called. "Are you out there or not?"

At first this was met with silence, but then came the sound of someone stirring on the floor below. Floor beams creaked and footsteps ascended the carpeted flight of stairs and stopped on the other side of the door.

"What do you want?" came Graham's gravelly voice, the mock politeness of yesterday wholly absent.

"Two things: breakfast and my phone call."

Graham did not reply. His footsteps receded to the ground floor, and Lupe could hear him rummaging around in the kitchen. She didn't know if he was going to bring breakfast to her room or if he would allow her to dine below like last night.

When Graham returned a minute later, she expected him to pass her a granola bar or something similar, but instead when he unlatched the door and swung it inward, the only thing in his hand was a gun.

She opened her mouth to object but he cut her off. "Walk ahead of me down the stairs," he said. "We're going to the kitchen."

Lupe set her mouth in a firm line as she emerged from the room and walked to the stairs. Graham followed a few steps behind, no doubt with the gun aimed at the back of her head. She turned left at the bottom of the stairs and made toward the kitchen only to behold an empty table. No breakfast of any kind had been prepared for her.

She didn't know what to make of that.

"Sit down," Graham said, moving toward the counter and plucking up a small black cell phone.

Lupe did as she was told. "You don't have a landline?"

"Landlines can be traced. What's the number?"

She started to ask why she couldn't dial the number herself, but then it occurred to her that in reality she could have dialed any number she pleased and pretended to talk to her manager. A 911 operator would have thought it odd indeed if she had phoned them saying she would be unable to come in to work.

Deciding it best to cooperate at the moment, she recited the number to him and he entered it into the phone. Graham held the device to his ear, waited, and at last gave a nod as he shoved the phone into her hand.

As soon as she held the phone to her own ear, Graham lifted the gun and pointed it at her.

"—ello?"

Lupe's pulse quickened, and she prayed that her manager would detect the fear in her voice. "Valerie? It's Lupe. I—I can't come in today. I'm sorry about the late notice, but when I woke up I didn't feel so well and I don't want to make anyone else sick. Do you think you can get someone to cover for me?"

Her manager's tone was sympathetic. "No worries, honey! I can ask Shelly or Marge if they can come in instead. I'm sorry you don't feel well."

Lupe muttered a few words of false thanks and ended the call before Valerie started recommending a dozen different home remedies that would ease her discomforts. She didn't want a prolonged phone call to give Graham an excuse to shoot her.

Graham gave a curt nod and put the phone into his pocket. "You're cooperating better than I expected you to."

"Do I have any other choice?"

He didn't answer. Instead, he went to the refrigerator and opened the door. "Juice?"

Lupe sat down at the table. "Yes, please." She kept her gaze fixed on him while he poured her a glass of orange juice and set it on the table. "Thank you." She took one small sip and set the glass aside. "Aren't you going to let me eat?"

The old man grunted and turned to the corner pantry. He brought out a package of cinnamon Pop Tarts and shook it as if he were enticing a dog with a box of biscuits. "Is this fine?"

Lupe hated Pop Tarts, but she wasn't going to be picky, especially when it might be the last meal she had for a long time. "Yes. Thank you."

Graham raised a quizzical eyebrow and tossed a silver packet of the pastries at her. She caught it and tore it open.

"You're up to something," he said as she began to eat. He sat down across from her, still holding the gun; only this time he had the barrel angled toward the table instead of at her.

She gave him a smoldering glare. "Of course I'm up to something. I'm being held captive against my will, and I would love to find a way to escape that won't get me killed."

Graham's wrinkled face cracked into a grin and he laughed until tears sprang into his eyes. "You seem to have regained some spunk, haven't you? As soon as Randy is dead I'll let you out of here, and you can be free to do whatever you like. Go home. Go to work. Cry over his lifeless corpse, for all I care."

Lupe narrowed her eyes as a new idea occurred to her. "I don't think you really want to kill him," she said.

His cheeks darkened. "And why is that?"

"Because you're afraid of him. You're afraid of what will happen when he dies."

"You're sadly mistaken."

"No, I don't think I am." She drilled her gaze into his, praying that some remnant of the Servant Graham had once been would awaken and cast this monster away. "The first time, you couldn't even shoot him right. The second time, you made *me* cut his brake lines because you were too afraid to do it yourself. What will it be this time? Are you going to ask your 'friend' to murder Randy for you?" Even though she could tell she was angering the man, she found herself unable to stop. "You're an old coward. You can kill innocent people like Mary just to satisfy your curiosity, but when it comes to someone you know, your blood runs cold. You make other people do your dirty work when you don't have the guts to do it yourself. You're pathetic. You know what? I wonder what God thinks about all this. You used to be his chosen Servant, and now you're this . . . this old *thing* that should never have been born."

At first Graham just stared at her, a vein throbbing in his temple being the only indication that her words had gotten to him. She imagined a labyrinth of cogs and gears churning somewhere behind his eyes as his brain mulled over what she'd said.

Then he stood up. He came around the side of the table and grabbed her wrist, jerking her to her feet. She snatched up the package of Pop Tarts a split second before he yanked her away.

She didn't try to resist him as he forced her up the stairs into the bedroom that was her prison. She didn't ask him what he was doing when he locked the door from the outside. She didn't beg for him to have mercy on Randy and to spare both of their lives.

Over the next several minutes, the sounds of Graham doing God knew what carried up the stairwell. Clinking, slamming, muttering . . .

Then the front door opened and closed with a bang. An engine started up outside.

Graham was on the move, and Lupe couldn't do a thing to stop him.

24

NEITHER RANDY nor Phil had come to any conclusions in regard to what to do about Trish's missing body and the possibility that Graham Willard had spirited her away, but despite that Bobby found himself relaxing in their company. Randy and Phil were letting Bobby in on things they had no business sharing with him. He almost felt honored. Then again, he hadn't had much choice in the matter. It wasn't his fault he'd witnessed Trish's exorcism and death. Well, maybe it was since he'd barged into Randy's home like a madman, but that was beside the point.

"I get that you think it would violate people's trust by searching all of the Servants' houses," Bobby said to them, "but what if they all willingly let you look around a bit? I mean, if I were one of them, I'd want everyone to know I don't have anything to hide."

Randy gave a thoughtful nod. "True."

Bobby turned to Phil. "What about you?"

Resignation lined Phil's face. "My concern is that I'd have to let Allison know what you were doing ransacking my house."

"She doesn't need to know about this."

"None of them do. It pains me that we've come to this, but if you need to, feel free to ask Allison if I went anywhere that night."

"A house divided against itself cannot stand," Randy quoted. He picked up a mug of coffee and sipped at it while he gazed unseeingly at the table.

Phil adjusted his glasses and folded his arms. "Then let's not consider this a division. Randy, you know I've sworn to do my best to guide and protect you, and may God strike me dead if I ever betray you."

Randy closed his eyes. "You'd better watch what you say."

Phil turned his gaze toward his lap, brooding.

"Wait a minute," Bobby said. "If you have a greater awareness of God—or whatever you told me last night—can't you just ask him where Trish is and who took her?"

Randy shook his head. "Does a teacher tell you the answers, or does he show you the steps you have to take to find them?"

"Have you even *tried* asking him where Trish is?"

"Of course. I know she's close by, though just how close, I don't know. I also know she really did die, contrary to what Father Preston thinks."

"And just who is this Father Preston? What if he's in on this somehow?"

"I take it you haven't met him yet," Phil said. "The man may be a bit standoffish to some people, but he's got a good heart."

Standoffish. Ha. It sounded like Phil and Father Preston might be related. "Does he know about the Servants?"

"Yes," Randy said. "I used to cleanse the possessed in an empty meeting room at the church at night. I had to stop when there were too many close calls from parishioners showing up at inconvenient times and almost walking in on us."

"Does he have a key to this house?"

"Not to my knowledge."

Bobby did a quick mental review of everything Randy had told him about yesterday. "Okay. So you were going to meet Father Preston here so you'd have his support while facing the police. Who got here first: you or him?"

"Father Preston was here when we arrived," Randy said, giving Phil a sidelong glance. "He was sitting in his car waiting for us."

"See," Bobby said, "*he* knew about Trish because you told him. What if he's really a sicko and snuck inside, took her body, and stuffed it into his trunk?"

"Because he's Father Preston," Randy said. "You're making very unkind assumptions about a man you've never met."

Bobby crossed his arms. "I'm just tossing out ideas since you two seem to have run out of them. I say if the guy had the opportunity to do it, then he's the one who did it."

"Your logic would make sense if Father Preston were indeed a 'sicko,'" Phil said as a smirk played about his lips. "He's a good priest. No scandals or anything like that. And he's always been supportive of our cause."

"I don't care what other people think about him. He had the opportunity to take Trish—"

"And the ability to walk through walls, evidently."

Bobby didn't resist the urge to say something snide. "Maybe he has more than two brain cells and guessed that Randy had a key hidden outside just like I did. But as I was saying . . ."

Get out.

Two words, not spoken yet fully understood, interrupted his thoughts; and Bobby felt the room start to sway as his breath left his lungs.

It was happening again, far sooner than he'd hoped.

He jumped up from the table. "We have to get out of here."

Randy's face grew a shade paler. "Why?"

"I don't know. Something bad is coming." He moved toward the front door and halted when neither of his comrades got up to follow. "I'm serious!"

Randy looked torn between staying and leaving, but the look on Phil's face told Bobby he wasn't at all convinced they were in any kind of danger. "If this is some kind of joke—"

"It isn't!" They had to believe him. If he couldn't convince them to leave the house, someone would die. "We've got to move!"

"And where do you propose we 'move' to?"

224 | J.S. BAILEY

"I don't know. Anywhere but here."

"If there's some kind of danger in staying here, we could stay at Lupe's apartment until it passes," Randy said, shaken.

But as soon as the suggestion had been spoken, Bobby knew her place wouldn't be safe, either. "You both can come to my house. It's not that far from here."

Spots of color formed on Phil's white cheeks. "And what would we do then?"

"We can figure that out later. I live at 12 Fir Street. Do you know the road?"

"I think so," Randy said, rising hesitantly from his chair. "Is that one of the streets off of Ridge Avenue?"

"Uh-huh. You two can follow me."

Bobby ran from the house and jumped into his car. He had to take several deep breaths to slow the sudden spike in his pulse, and just as he thought the two Servants would continue ignoring his warning, both of them emerged from the house and climbed into Phil's Taurus, casting suspicious glances his way.

Bobby took that as his cue to leave.

He swung a right out of the long driveway, Phil and Randy close behind. A quarter of a mile later a gray sedan passed him in the opposite lane traveling several miles an hour below the speed limit as if slowing down. Bobby peeked into his rearview mirror to see what it would do.

In the receding distance, he saw the sedan turn into Randy's driveway.

It was all he could do not to slam on his brakes.

Another glance in the mirror showed Randy gesturing wildly with his hands in the Taurus's passenger seat. The Taurus drew back a few car lengths before speeding up again so it was right on Bobby's tail.

If he had to venture a guess, one of them wanted to go back to the house and confront the driver of the gray car.

He was glad they didn't.

As he reentered the more populous part of Autumn Ridge, Bobby kept checking the mirrors to make sure the gray car's driver hadn't caught on and was following them. He almost expected to see it sitting in his driveway, but he arrived home without further incident. Phil pulled up beside him, his lips drawn in a thin line as he stared at Bobby through the window.

He wondered if Phil believed him now and decided he probably did.

"Did you see that car?" Bobby asked them when they met up on the porch.

"The gray one?" Randy narrowed his eyes at Phil. "Boy, did we."

Bobby fumbled with the house key and almost dropped it before fitting it into the lock. They went inside and Bobby double-bolted the door for good measure. Now he would have to play host, a position with which he had little previous experience. "Have a seat. Do you need anything?"

"Some aspirin might be useful," Phil said as he sank into Caleb's old place on the couch, his eyes holding a haunted look. He'd brought his black tote bag with him and set it on the floor.

Yes, he definitely believed.

Randy remained standing and kept glancing toward the door as if he expected someone to come knocking at any second.

"Did you see who was driving it?" Bobby asked him.

It took several moments for Randy to reply. "I only caught a glimpse of him. The man I saw looked thinner than Graham was when I last saw him, but it's possible he's lost some weight."

"What about the face?"

Randy shook his head. "We were past him before I could get a decent look. Besides, he could have changed his appearance in other ways, too. Could be why he's evaded the police for so long."

Phil looked up at them with remorse. "If we'd gone back there we could have ended this once and for all."

"And died in the act," Bobby reminded him.

Randy glanced to Bobby. "Not to change the subject, but a drink sounds really good right now."

"I don't have that kind. I'm not twenty-one."

"Pop, then. Please."

Bobby was grateful to have something to do. "Is Dr Pepper okay? I'm almost out of Sprite."

"It's perfect."

He hurried to the refrigerator and grabbed a can out of the shelf in the door. He returned to the living room, popped the tab, and handed the can to Randy. "I've never had guests here," he blurted. "So sorry if I do something stupid."

"I actually think you're quite smart," Randy said. "By coming to a place Graham doesn't know about, we're staying hidden just that much longer." He sipped at his drink and then froze. "Phil, you need to call Allison and have her take Ashley somewhere else for awhile. I'll call Lupe."

Phil nodded. "Right."

Both men immediately went to separate ends of the small living room to speak with their significant others, and Bobby drifted to the front window and peered out at the street. None of the vehicles that passed the house were gray.

This did not console him. A knot formed in his stomach. If Graham recognized Phil's Taurus and had seen it pulling out of Randy's driveway, he would have turned around and followed them. Just because Bobby hadn't seen the car didn't mean it wasn't nearby.

The fact that they outnumbered Graham three to one didn't give him any relief, either. A single gunman could cut down a good portion of a crowd all by himself. And three people were much smaller than a crowd.

Phil got off the phone and came up to Bobby's side. "I just told my wife to take my daughter to her sister's house up in Portland."

"That's a long drive."

"Which makes it even better."

Bobby felt a brief sense of pride swell inside of him knowing that these people were heeding his words of warning, but fear quickly replaced it. Randy and Phil were relying on *him* now, and Phil was bringing his own family into it.

What if Bobby was wrong? What if he unintentionally led them all into worse danger by removing Randy and Phil from the proverbial frying pan and placing them into the line of fire?

No. He couldn't think like that. He would know if he were wrong. Everyone was safe at his rental bungalow—at least for the time being.

"What did she say when you told her Graham might be back?" he asked.

"She was surprised, but not so surprised." Phil clasped his hands together in front of him. "We've all been waiting for something like this to happen, and a lot of us expected it to be sooner rather than later. It isn't in Graham's nature to give up easily."

"You mean he's done something like this before?"

The man surprised him by chuckling, though the laugh conveyed little humor. "Now that, I can't tell you. Graham owned a drug store for close to forty years and kept it open even during the times when it seemed certain to go under due to competition. He even managed to keep his marriage together when it got rocky. The man just keeps going. We all knew that since he failed to kill Randy once, he would try to do it again. He'll keep at it until he either succeeds or dies."

Bobby understood why Randy had been so paranoid when he'd pushed him over in the church parking lot. "It's hard to believe someone married a guy like that."

"That 'someone' was named Lisa. She passed away while I was the Servant. They were still married at the time."

"She must have been crazy."

Phil smiled at him. "No, just troubled. Graham loved that woman—at least we think he did, because he was always bragging about her and talking about all the good things she did—but Lisa had problems of her own. I don't like speaking ill of the dead, but Lisa was no angel. Graham caught her having an affair twice. It nearly broke his heart, though somehow they were able to salvage their marriage and keep on as always."

"Maybe she knew there was more to him than he let on," Bobby said. He peeked out the window again. No gray car. Good.

Phil dipped his head. "From what I know now, I'm inclined to believe you're right."

Randy joined them, gripping his phone in one hand and the can of Dr Pepper in the other. The lines on his face had deepened. "I called all the others to let them know what's happened, but Lupe won't pick up either phone so I'm hoping she's just in the shower getting ready for work. I left her a message."

"Let's hope she gets it."

"I don't know," Randy said as if in answer to something else. "I called her as soon as I woke up this morning too, and she didn't pick up then, either. I figured she was still in bed."

Bobby had to ask the one thing he dreaded to say. "Do you think Graham could have gotten to her already?"

Randy must have been thinking along the same lines, because his face turned gray. "We should head out there to check on her. That's the first place he'd look for me."

He and Phil both glanced at Bobby as if seeking his approval. Bobby shifted his weight from one foot to the other, not wanting to make a decision that would condemn any of them to an early grave. "I don't know if that's the right thing to do."

"Well, I say it is," Phil said, striding across the room and picking up his tote.

"Wait." Randy's eyes went out of focus for a moment. His shoulders relaxed, and some of the lines vanished from his forehead. "The three of us need to stick together," he said, looking at both of them. "No matter what happens."

"Even me?" Bobby asked, surprised they would want to take him with them.

"You're the one who makes us three, right?"

"I don't want to mess anything up."

Randy cocked his head. "Whatever gave you that idea?"

"I don't know, I mean . . ." Bobby trailed off, not sure what to say. "What use could I possibly be if I went to Lupe's?"

"We were talking about gifts," Randy said. "Do you know what mine is?"

"You drive out demons." Bobby wished he'd hurry up and get to whatever point he was trying to make.

"Yes," he said, "but there's one other ability I've been blessed with since before I became the Servant. I can understand any language I hear. French, Spanish, Swahili, Arabic—anything. I can speak them, too, even though nobody ever taught me. It's a form of the gift of Tongues."

Bobby didn't know what this had to do with anything. "But I've never heard you—"

Randy held up a hand. "And when Phil was the Servant, he could heal wounds and illnesses with a touch and a prayer. That's called the gift of Healing."

"And just so you're clear on this," Phil said, "it isn't only Servants who are blessed with gifts like these. I met a man in Vancouver who could discern spirits, and one of my aunts could pray in angelic tongues."

That was all very nice, and it would have made an interesting discussion some other time when nobody they knew was in danger. "I still don't see the point."

"I'm not surprised," Randy said. "Bobby, you have a gift that forewarns us of danger. I've been told that Martin, Phil's predecessor, had a similar gift; only instead of seeing future dangers he was able to tell people the specific things they needed to do to remove themselves from present hardship. Am I right?"

Phil gave a slow nod. He stepped back from the door and gave them his full attention. "Martin helped many people turn their lives around after they were no longer possessed."

Martin wasn't one of the names Randy had mentioned when listing the former Servants whose homes would be searched for Trish's body. "What happened to him?"

Pain wrote itself across Phil's face. "He went up to Portland to help a single mother he'd cleansed get a job and a place to live. He told her that she and her children would be able to pull themselves out of poverty if she got a job as a secretary at a certain office even though another position she came across would have paid her more. Her ex-husband saw her and Martin together, assumed he was her new boyfriend, and murdered him."

Bobby was sorry he asked. "Did she get the job?"

"Yes. She eventually was promoted, got remarried, and now she and her new husband help run a women's shelter where, consequently, I met my wife Allison."

Bobby's mouth became dry. "I'm not Martin."

"No," Randy said, "but you've been very helpful to us already. I'd like for you to come along, but it's your call."

Bobby hesitated. If he went with the pair, he might cross paths with Graham Willard. If it came to violence, Graham might try to kill him simply for associating with the wrong crowd.

Which was actually the right crowd, but that wouldn't matter, would it?

Like Randy had said, Bobby could decline their offer. He could stay put in the bungalow and mind his own business. Because what was Graham to him? A perfect stranger. Meddling in the affairs of someone he didn't know could only lead to trouble.

But isn't that what you've already been doing?

He silently chided himself. There he was, doing it again: weighing the pros and cons of being a decent person. He wondered what his father would think, and suddenly he was hit with the realization that he had no idea what Ken Roland would have thought of him in this situation. His father had always been something of a self-sufficient man, and though he'd been kind enough to his family, aiding strangers didn't seem like something he would have rushed to do.

After working sixty hours a week for twenty years and fathering two children, Ken Roland had died of a heart attack on the kitchen floor. His wife and children were the only things of worth he'd left behind—his years of labor at the General Electric plant may have paid the bills, but Bobby couldn't see anyone looking back and saying, "Ken Roland—now there was a man who made a difference!"

Going with Randy and Phil to a place where Graham might be was a frightening prospect, but if Bobby's presence helped save Randy's girlfriend, then his moments of fear would have been worth it.

"I'll come," he said, surprised at how light he felt when the words left his mouth. "But I'm scared about what might happen."

"It takes guts to admit that," Randy said. "I can't guarantee this day will end with all of us in one piece, but Phil and I will do our best to make sure you stay safe."

Said the man who'd been unable to protect *himself* from Graham.

Randy continued. "Besides, you haven't had any new premonitions yet, right? We could all be worrying about nothing."

His words made panic edge its way inside of Bobby again, snuffing his temporary courage like a flame in the wind. "I don't get warned about every tragedy that happens. We could all die if we go to Lupe's."

"But nothing has told you that," Randy said.

"Right."

"Then what are you worried about?" He took a swig from the pop can and pocketed his phone. "Let's get going."

25

GRAHAM WAS seething.

He maintained the speed limit as best he could, even though his foot yearned to stomp the accelerator all the way to the floor. The *nerve* of that girl. Who did she think she was to call him a coward? He should have killed her then and there just to have a little peace.

Truth be told, Lupe was nothing more than a pawn. Once he eliminated Randy he would have no further use for her. If only he could decide whether or not to kill her as he had the others.

As he drove to Randy's new home, his mind began to wander. Graham had learned the location of the ramshackle house after asking his grandson Jack (the illegitimate son of Stephanie, the daughter he hadn't seen in more than two decades) to do a real estate search for properties owned by Randall Bellison. He'd nearly laughed with delight when Jack informed him that a small home had been sold to someone by that name only five months after Graham shot Randy. He could even click on a picture and see what the house looked like. Privacy truly did not exist in this day and age when satellites could zoom in far enough to see someone sunbathing naked by their swimming pool and any crook with an Internet connection could find where anyone lived.

He had thanked Jack for his service and offered to pay him if he would stay on to help him in his other pursuits. Jack agreed.

Now here was a boy who could make his grandfather proud.

The young man had shown up on his doorstep in an air of mystery one day claiming to be one of Stephanie's offspring. Startled, Graham had pressed him for information that only the son of Stephanie could know. What color is her hair? What color are her eyes? What kind of food could she never live without? Where is the scar she got when Lisa wrecked the station wagon?

Graham thought he'd catch the boy in a lie, but Jack answered all questions correctly and without hesitation. In his wallet Jack even had a family photo of a younger version of himself, Stephanie, and a red-haired girl that would have been taken a decade earlier. Graham did not believe the photo had been faked—and seeing his Stephanie after so many years, even if in a picture, had brought tears to his eyes.

Jack did bear some resemblance to the Willard clan. He shared Graham's and Stephanie's crystal blue eyes, and like Stephanie Jack had wavy hair that was an indeterminate shade between blond and light brown. "How did you know where to find me?" he'd asked. "I've been in hiding for months."

Jack had grinned at him. "I have my ways, and it's probably best for both of us if you don't know what they are." He had gone on to say he'd been looking for Graham ever since his name appeared in the news—not because he wanted Graham to be arrested, but because he wanted to learn more about the devious man who'd fathered his mother. Jack wanted to learn some "pointers" from Graham, he said. Pointers that might aid him in his own endeavors.

When Graham pressed Jack for information about where he was staying and what he did for a living, Jack slyly changed the subject.

Graham let the matter drop. If Jack felt the need to guard himself, then so be it.

234 | J.S. BAILEY

About a week later Jack asked why Graham had felt the need for Randy to die. They ended up discussing Randy and his kind for hours, and Jack had nodded in sympathetic understanding. He couldn't stand holy people, either. It was no wonder Graham had wanted to get rid of the man.

When Jack discovered the location of Randy's house, he'd asked Graham why they couldn't go and kill him then since Graham wanted to put an end to him so badly, but Graham had stalled. The time wasn't right. Randy's piety had been a poison in Graham's veins those last few months before he'd tried to kill him, and he wanted Randy to suffer for it just like Graham had been made to suffer.

He'd loved Randy once, perhaps even more than he loved Jack now. But someone like Graham couldn't live with Randy forever. It was like living in a vat of acid.

Lupe's words echoed in his mind as he drew closer to his destination. *You're an old coward.*

Was he?

No, of course not. Delaying Randy's murder was done out of necessity, not fear. And the reason he hadn't stayed behind when he shot Randy last year to ask him what he saw as he died was because . . .

Graham blinked. Had he truly been afraid to see his young friend die? Was that why he'd run?

His pulse pounded in his ears. The driveway lay just ahead.

I am not a coward.

He slowed the car and turned.

THEY DECIDED to take Bobby's car because Graham was less likely to recognize it than Phil's Taurus. Bobby found little reassurance in their choice of vehicle since Graham might drive by the bungalow and spot Phil's car in the driveway there. The man could break in and wait for them with a gun in hand, ready to blow away the first person to step through the door.

"Randy," Bobby asked, "do you have any weapons on you?"

Randy patted his hip. "I've got my knife. What about you?"

"There's a knife block on the kitchen counter."

"I was hoping you'd have something a little more substantial than that."

Bobby held his palms up and shrugged. "When would I have ever needed to own something that could kill someone?" Up until a couple of days ago, a crazy old man who packed heat ranked close to alien invasion and asteroid collision in his list of worries. "Is a knife even going to help if he's still got his gun?"

Randy raised an eyebrow. "Would you rather face him empty-handed?"

He resisted the urge to scowl. Bobby went to the knife block, unsheathed one of the medium-sized blades, and slid it into his pocket. He felt so stupid—what if it poked through the lining and stabbed him in the leg? Some hero he would be. As a precaution, he slipped it back out and wrapped it in a dish towel before returning it to the pocket, only now the increased bulk from the towel made his pants bulge on one side.

Even though nothing about the situation was remotely humorous to Bobby, Randy's eyes sparkled with mirth. "And to think when you jumped on me in the parking lot the other night, I thought you'd been paid to be an assassin."

Bobby's face flushed. "I'm a loner, not a fighter."

"I think you mean 'lover,'" Phil said, hanging on to his tote bag as if it were his only friend. Bobby wondered what else other than a stethoscope it contained.

"I meant exactly what I said." Bobby squared his shoulders, feeling much like a mouse who had just armed himself with a toothpick. "Do you want a knife, too? There's plenty for everyone."

Phil declined with the shake of his head. "I'll pass on that."

The pair of Servants—the current and the former—stood side by side, and Bobby gave them a brief appraisal. Randy's shaggy, coffee-colored hair and black attire would make him stick out like a punk in a nursing home, and Phil looked as though he had just left an office, what with his khaki pants and nice polo shirt. Something in Bobby's gut told him they should tone down their appearances just in case Graham passed them on the road. He may not have known Bobby's car, but he would definitely recognize his passengers if he got a good look at them.

"I think you should disguise yourself a bit just in case he sees us."

"How do you propose we do that?" Phil asked.

"Easy. You'll put on some of my clothes."

Phil threw Randy a look of desperation. "We don't have time for this."

"No, no, I like it," Randy said. "I'm just curious as to how I'm going to squeeze into something that fits *him*."

"Don't worry, I'll find something." Bobby hurried into his bedroom and started tearing through his closet. Pants, shirts, more pants. Randy was right. He was much stockier than Bobby. None of Bobby's clothes would fit him.

Knowing that waiting longer might spell certain doom for Lupe, Bobby yanked a Muse shirt off of a hanger for Phil and plucked an old Cincinnati Reds baseball cap off of the closet shelf for Randy. He rushed back into the living room and thrust the items at each of them respectively. "Sorry. I could have found something better if we had more time."

Randy jammed the ball cap over his head without objection. "It works for me. I hate baseball."

Phil took off his glasses and polo and slipped on the Muse shirt. "I still don't see the point of this. Graham would have to be blind not to know who we are."

"I know it's not foolproof. This is just so he doesn't notice you right away in the car. But if you don't think that'll work, you're welcome to hunker down in my back seat like we're going to the safe house. It's up to you."

The pair declined the offer. Bobby wasn't surprised.

So off they drove, keeping their eyes peeled for any sign of the old man. "He has to be living somewhere close," Randy said as he gazed out the passenger window. "But not too close. He has to have a place that's isolated enough for him to come and go without much notice."

"Or he could have altered his looks so much that nobody has recognized him from the pictures the news kept broadcasting last year," Phil said.

Randy folded his arms. "Or both. Bobby, turn here."

"I remember."

The apartment lot was only half full when they arrived. Bobby slowed down and parked close to Lupe's unit. He didn't see the gray sedan anywhere. "Should we wait out here?" he asked.

Randy nodded. "One of us can act as lookout, and the other two of us can stay inside with her. That's her Prius over there."

"I can keep watch," Phil said as he unbuckled. "I'll take the driver's seat so I can take off after him if I need to."

Bobby's insides squirmed like fishing bait in a bucket as he followed Randy to the apartment door. "Has Lupe been doing better since the other night?"

Randy rapped his fist on the door and stepped back, his face grim once more. "Certain unfortunate circumstances have limited my opportunities to talk to her." He knocked again when the door remained unanswered. "Come on, Lupe. Let us in."

Bobby turned and faced the parking lot. Phil sat behind the wheel of Bobby's Nissan with his gaze trained on the parking lot entrance, and the image of "Paul" doing nearly the same thing at the church flitted through Bobby's head, giving him a jolt.

Bobby blinked. Were Phil and Paul the same person? No, of course not. Paul had brown hair, and Phil was a blond. Phil had a deeper voice, too. And if Phil barged into the church like that, he would have called for Randy, not Mr. Bellison.

Behind him, Randy held his cell phone against his ear. "Come on, Lupe," he said. "Tell me you're in there." He let out a huff. "Voicemail again." He dug around in his pocket and withdrew a key ring. "God, if you've let anything happen to her . . ."

Bobby held his breath as Randy unlocked the door and swung it open. *Please let her be okay*, he prayed as he followed Randy into the living room.

The room was still. Furniture, knickknacks, receipts, and stacks of mail showed all the trappings of an ordinary life, yet Bobby had the sense that something here was not ordinary; that something had gone terribly wrong.

The shades in the front room were drawn. Bobby flipped on a light switch so they could see better.

"Lupe?" Randy called out. "Are you in here?"

A purse sat on the coffee table next to a cell phone. Bobby didn't want to think about what that might mean.

He followed Randy down a short hallway into a bedroom that smelled like potpourri. "Lupe?"

The bedclothes lay in disarray, and no one rested beneath them. Bobby only felt a minimal amount of relief. "Where could she have gone?"

A hoarse note colored Randy's voice. "I don't know."

"What should we do?"

Randy didn't answer. Instead he retreated from the bedroom, poked his head into the bathroom, and shook his head. "She might have felt threatened about something and run away."

"Her purse is out in the living room, though."

"Great." Randy made a visible effort of composing himself. "If I'd been with her, this wouldn't have happened."

"We can ask the neighbors if they've seen anything. Do you think they're home?"

Randy's Adam's apple bobbed up and down as he swallowed more of his distress. "Let's find out."

Bobby led the way out of the apartment and waved at Phil, who had fixed his gaze upon the apartment door.

Bobby stepped off the sidewalk and motioned for him to roll down the car window.

"What's going on?" Phil asked. A small gun rested in his lap. He stared out the windshield at Randy, who had walked onward to a neighboring unit with purpose in his step and was now knocking on the door.

"We've had a change of plans. Lupe isn't home."

"And that explains why Randy's decided to visit the neighbors?"

"Let me rephrase that. Lupe is gone, but her things aren't."

"Great." Phil slid the gun into a holster hidden in his waistband and climbed out of the car. "For once," he said, tugging Bobby's Muse shirt down over his belt, "I would like to have a boring day where nothing happens."

They met up with Randy at the neighbor's door, where he was speaking with a middle-aged woman wearing a calico-print dress that reminded Bobby of a shower curtain. "I haven't seen her leave the apartment all day," she said, "but I'm not always spying on my neighbors, you know. Sorry I can't help you."

"Did you see *anything* unusual this morning?" Randy asked, his voice almost pleading. "Even the slightest thing might help."

She squinted at him, and then at Bobby and Phil. "What is this all about? You don't look like police officers to me."

"That's because we're not," Phil said. Bobby noticed a muscle twitching in the man's cheek. "Now if you could answer Randy's question, that would be great."

The woman was only slightly taken aback. "Like I said, I don't think I can help you." She broke off, the light of an inner epiphany shining in her eyes. "You know, there is something strange, but I didn't even think about it until now. Yesterday when I was carrying my groceries up to the door, a man let himself into that apartment like he owned the place. It was around five o'clock, I think. No later than five-thirty."

Randy's eyes grew wide. "He had a key?"

"Of course he did. At least that's what it looked like. And I thought it was a little odd since I don't remember seeing him before, but I figure since he had a key he must have been that girl's father come to help her out with something."

"What did he look like? Do you remember?"

The woman's brow creased as she strained to think. "He had dark hair, but I thought he looked a little too old for that, so it probably came from a box, if you get my meaning. He shuffled a bit, too. I don't remember what he was wearing."

"Can you remember anything else about him?"

She shook her head. "You're lucky I can tell you that." She stared at Randy for a moment, silent. "And you don't know where Miss Sanchez is?"

"No."

"You don't think that man I saw might have something to do with that, do you?"

"We don't know," Randy said, giving Bobby and Phil a side-long glance. "But thanks anyway. You've been very helpful."

She nodded, suddenly looking anxious. "I do hope she's okay," she said. "We may not have talked much, but I always thought Miss Sanchez was a sweet girl."

THE THREE of them gathered in Lupe's living room to discuss their next course of action, Phil having chosen to leave his post in Bobby's car.

"Yesterday," Randy said as he paced the room. "At five o'clock. That was seventeen hours ago!"

Bobby felt bad for him. There was no telling what Lupe had been going through for that length of time. Having nothing else to do at the moment, he sent up a silent prayer for her safety.

"Maybe we should call the police now," Phil suggested, glancing at Bobby, who simply shrugged.

Randy's eyes became surprisingly livid. "And tell them what? That Graham Willard took my fiancée somewhere? They'll think I'm mad."

"For goodness sake, Randy, what's the matter with you?" Phil raised his voice. "This isn't about hiding a body anymore. This is about Lupe. You're just going to let some creep have his way with her because you're too hardheaded to bring the police into this? They'll know what to do about finding her. You don't."

Randy shook his head. "She's been with him before and hasn't been hurt. She says he's been forcing her to meet with him, and he even made her cut the brake line on my car. He doesn't care anything about her. He's just using her to hurt me."

Bobby felt his eyes widen at Randy's admission. "You mean *Lupe's* the vandal?"

He gave a slow nod. "If she'd refused to do it, he would have killed her. She only did what anyone else would have done."

Bobby couldn't believe it. "This is nuts. If I hadn't been there to stop you from getting into that car . . ." His stomach gave another squirm. He liked Graham Willard less and less, and he hadn't even met the guy.

"There's no point in dwelling on what might have happened," Randy said. "What we need to do is figure out how we're going to find where Graham has taken her. *If* he's taken her."

An idea popped into Bobby's head so unexpectedly that he clapped a hand over his mouth so he wouldn't blurt it out. It was a lousy idea. An insane idea.

But as far as he could tell, it was the only one that might work.

"What are you thinking?" Phil asked.

Bobby cleared his throat, feeling the crushing weight of terror squeeze his chest again. "We think we know where Graham is, right?"

"Uh-huh."

"And if he leaves and we follow him back to wherever he's staying, Lupe might be there."

"How do we stop him from noticing us?" Randy asked, his interest piqued.

"Easy. I park in a driveway close to yours, and when Graham leaves, we follow him at a distance. We might even be able to get his license plate number and give it to the police. Assuming you let us call them, of course."

"This is suicide," Phil said.

"It looks like it's our only option," Randy said, his face long.

"If you end up getting yourself killed . . ."

Randy crossed his arms. "I don't plan on dying today."

Bobby started to object. "But my premonition—"

"Didn't tell you that *I* am going to die, right?"

"I don't want me or Phil to be killed, either."

"Better you than me, right?" He winked, though there was no humor in his eyes. He moved toward the door. "Besides, this was your idea. Graham might not stick around for long once he realizes I'm not there. I think it's best we get going."

26

WHEN RANDY'S house came into view at the end of the gravel lane, Graham decided that the younger man was an honest-to-God idiot. The house looked even worse in person than it did in the photograph Jack showed him online, and he suspected that Randy had taken extra measures to make sure the structure appeared to accommodate only mice. What a way to bring down the neighborhood property values. One might think Randy was paranoid. Ha.

Jack, having returned from one of his excursions, had told him the place looked bad. Graham just hadn't guessed it would be in such an advanced state of decay. Even a burglar would shy away from a place like this because nothing of value could possibly be contained within its walls.

"He probably wants to make it look like nobody's home," Jack said.

"Why would he do that?" Graham asked.

"Can't you guess? To throw you off his trail."

"That's the dumbest thing I've ever heard."

244 | J.S. BAILEY

Jack had just shrugged, and they'd left it at that.

Graham parked his car in front of a sagging garage. No other vehicles lay in sight, but if he knew Randy, his Ford was probably concealed behind the half-rotted garage door if already back from the shop.

The familiar bloodlust rose in his veins. His days of sneaking were over. He would boldly charge through the front door and gun the boy down where he stood or slept.

As he made his way up to the house, it occurred to him that none of this might have happened if not for the accident in which he'd been involved as a young man of thirty.

It was curious how one single moment could change every-thing, and oftentimes Graham wondered what his life would be like today if he had taken a different route home that night, or if he'd left the drug store earlier or later than he had.

Graham had never been a violent man. He'd never sought to kill anyone. But while he drove home from work that fateful night, a drunk had staggered into the street right in the path of Graham's car.

There was no way he could have prevented the collision that would so drastically alter his life. He had been cruising along at forty-five and didn't have enough reaction time to stop a safe dis-tance away from the man.

The drunk was run down instantly with an impact that jolted Graham so hard that for one horrifying second his rear end left the driver's seat and he hung suspended in midair.

The car screeched to a halt. Bile forced its way into Graham's throat as he realized he'd very likely just killed a man, though the accident had not been his fault.

He'd rushed out of the vehicle and found the man lying behind his car. Moaning.

He wasn't dead yet, but the extent of his wounds told Graham that he would be soon.

Graham had emptied his stomach onto the shoulder of the road before turning to the man to comfort him in his final moments like any good Christian would have done—after all, his spiritual gift was Ministry. He'd held the man's hand and prayed with him. Told him that no matter what happened, everything would be okay.

To the drunk's ears, it probably sounded like he was raving mad.

The man had flashed the faintest of smiles through his pain, and then after a few brief minutes of drawing in ragged breaths that hurt Graham to hear almost as much as it hurt the man himself, he died.

Graham watched, enraptured by the sudden cessation of life. Questions began to fill his head. What had the man just seen? What did he feel? What was it like?

He'd peered into the man's lifeless eyes, hoping to catch the image of what had been seen in those final moments, but saw only the dull red glow of his car's taillights reflected in the man's pupils.

If only he had thought to ask him what he was experiencing!

Not wanting to face the accusing questions of the police who would find a way to make sure he rotted behind prison bars for the rest of his life, he had taken the man's broken body and buried it far back in the woods on one of his properties. The man carried no identification and looked as though he hadn't bathed in about a decade, so he was likely a drifter. No one would miss him. Lisa wouldn't even suspect a thing since Graham often worked late. Now Graham was off the hook, and life could return to normal.

But it didn't.

Each night, Graham dreamed he was with the man, begging him for the answers he sought about death. Being the Servant had been extraordinary—the closest thing to heaven he would ever be able to find on earth, because he had felt God with him at his side more strongly than he could feel his human companions whenever they were with him.

It was not that way with all of the Servants. They could all sense God, yes, but many experienced severe attacks of anxiety after prolonged contact with the evil spirits they drove out of people.

Graham counted himself lucky to have never felt the latter.

His awareness of the divine had diminished into nothing the moment he'd passed the mantle of Servitude on to his successor, a tiny man named Alex who'd gotten married the year before

246 | J.S. BAILEY

Graham's accident and moved out east to be near his wife's family after passing the mantle to a brawny ex-football player named
Aaron Carpenter.

Graham had never worked up the courage to ask Alex if he'd
felt depleted, too. It nearly devastated him when Alex took his place.
When the Spirit left him it felt as though he was no longer whole.

Graham had to find out if being in heaven was remotely the
same as being the Servant. Would he be whole again in heaven?
Would he be in communion with God once more, or would God
overlook him to focus his attention on the other millions of souls
who had passed on ahead of him?

He had to ask. He had to know. But the drifter was dead, and
the dead tell no tales to those who speak to them.

It soon became an obsession to learn more about the process
of death. He *had* to know what happened. Not knowing caused him
more anxiety than the possibility that heaven might not be so heav-
enly after all.

The only way to have his questions answered was to find
another dying person and ask them about it.

In the present, Graham smiled. If only he'd known who he
would become. If only he'd known to what lengths he would go to
learn the answers to his questions.

He had no guilt about those he had killed in his pursuit of
knowledge. They were all dying anyway because every human
being is born dying. He was merely speeding up the process—and
since they all would go to heaven when they breathed their last, he
was sure they would thank him.

He arrived on Randy's porch and tried the knob. Locked, of
course. But no matter. He was Graham Willard. A locked door
couldn't stop him.

He withdrew a key ring from his pocket and let himself into
the house.

It took several seconds for his eyes to register the fact that
the interior of the home did not match its outside appearance.
The place was immaculate. Cheap but clean furniture. Painting of

Our Lady of Guadalupe on the wall. Nice. Very, very nice. External appearances could indeed deceive.

Graham waited on the threshold for several seconds. The house remained silent.

He resisted the urge to call out to the man as he took slow steps across the floor, which creaked beneath his feet like unoiled hinges on a door. He passed through what was probably supposed to be a 1950's-style kitchen. Beyond it lay a hallway running left to right. Right led to an outer side door, and left led to three additional doors and a flight of stairs.

The interior doors opened to a basement, bathroom, and empty bedroom. After an in-depth inspection of each (especially the basement, which greatly intrigued him), he ascended to the second floor, which consisted only of an upper landing and an additional bedroom and attached bath that appeared to be, like its first-floor counterpart, vacant.

The bedroom was more sparsely furnished than a monk's cell. A royal blue bedspread with matching pillowcases covered the queen-sized bed, and a rectangular crocheted doily he recognized as Lupe Sanchez's handiwork lay draped across the dresser.

That was it. Even the closet contained only a cheap suit and a pair of dress shoes, which Graham couldn't recall Randy having worn on any occasion.

It occurred to him that Randy would have bought the suit to wear at his and Lupe's wedding.

The wedding that would not happen if Graham had his way.

He stood there, agitation welling up inside of him like magma. Where could Randy be? He couldn't just turn invisible. Though maybe he really wasn't home. Randy could be gone all day, and then he would see Graham's car the moment he returned. Nothing would stop him from calling the police and blocking the driveway, and despite Graham's overall good health, he didn't think he'd be able to successfully evade law enforcement on foot.

He silently cursed Lupe. She had made him angry and forced him to leave in haste, and as a result he hadn't thought this through with a clear head.

He should go home and have another long chat with her. Yes, he would do that. It only served her right.

On his way back through the kitchen, Graham noticed that the coffee maker sitting on the counter was switched on.

Interesting.

He stepped up to it and touched a finger to the partly-full carafe. He jerked his hand back in surprise when it burnt him, rubbing his fingertip against his thumb to stifle the pain.

How long could the pot have been like this?

He turned and stared at the kitchen table. On it sat three mugs of coffee containing varying levels of the beverage. A fourth mug sat upside down in the sink.

A faint buzzing began to sound in his skull. If Randy had guests, they would have finished their coffee before they left, so something must have made them get up and leave in such a hurry that they couldn't waste any time downing the rest of their drinks and switching off the pot.

He walked into the living room in search of clues that might indicate why everyone had left so quickly, but Randy kept the place too tidy.

Graham could make no sense of it. They couldn't have known ahead of time that Graham was coming unless Lupe had smuggled her cell phone into Graham's house and called to warn them.

No. That didn't make sense, either. If that had been the case, Lupe would have phoned the authorities last night while Graham slept.

So no phone, then. But what? What could have caused Randy and his guests to flee?

Graham closed his eyes and willed himself to think. Four coffee cups. No cars. Could it be mere coincidence that they had all abandoned ship right before Graham's arrival? It made him think of the case of the *Mary Celeste*, the vessel discovered adrift and abandoned in the Atlantic Ocean with the missing crew members' belongings and provisions still in place as if the men had been drinking and dining one moment before ceasing to exist.

Only this was different. Randy and his guests were not lost at sea. They had gone into hiding.

Graham would start by searching the woods surrounding the house. And if he still couldn't find them, he would go back inside to see what he'd missed.

LUPE HAD cried for awhile after Graham left, but she forced herself to stop when she realized that weeping wouldn't remedy her situation.

Nor would killing herself. She understood that now. In the past she'd thought she wanted to die, but in reality she simply feared living.

She supposed she had Graham himself to thank for her new-found self-preservation. Telling Randy about her meetings with Graham had taken an enormous weight off of her chest, and even better, Randy didn't hate her for obeying Graham's order to van-dalize his car. That's what she had feared the most: losing the only human being who had ever cared about her.

And she wasn't about to lose him now, either. He would encourage her to be strong, so strong she would be.

She stood with her back to the bedroom door in order to bet-ter assess the situation. A: The bedclothes could be cut into strips (with what?) and made into a rope so she could lower herself from the window to the ground outside. B: The window would first need to be smashed. C: She would have to firmly tie the makeshift rope to one of the bedposts. D: In order to smash the window, she would need to use the lamp because there wasn't anything else available for her to use unless she took the bed apart with tools she didn't have and broke the window with one of the posts.

Was nothing ever easy?

The lamp base consisted of cheap metal colored to look like brass. If she put enough force behind it, it might cause the glass to shatter anyway.

In order to minimize the mess, she removed the shade and unscrewed the bulb, setting them off to the side. *Padre, let this work.*

She gripped the lamp in her fist, brought her arm back, and bashed the base against the glass as hard as she could.

The metal bent upon impact but had no effect on the glass.

She gnashed her teeth and tried it again. The glass remained intact in open defiance of her intent.

She sank to the floor, trying not to let her tears flow anew. So she couldn't break the glass. Big deal.

Lupe stared at the bent-up lamp base. The felt-coated bottom cover had popped off, exposing its wiry guts.

She closed her eyes and leaned back against the bed.

Maybe things were meant to come to this. She was a sinner, far worse than many. Some people spoke of karma. You do horrible things, horrible things happen to you in return.

Thing was, Lupe held great remorse for the things she'd done. She had cried herself to sleep at night begging God for mercy more times than she could count. That had to mean something.

Be free.

Yes, she wanted to do that. Be free from sin *and* this house. She could only do the former through the grace of God. She would have to do the latter on her own.

She lifted her gaze and stared at the door. For the first time she realized its hinges were in the room with her. If she could remove the metal pins holding them together, she would be able to pull the door out of its frame, run to the nearest house, and ask to borrow the owner's phone since Graham informed her she would not find one here.

If Graham had wanted to properly contain a prisoner, he should have had the door installed the other direction so the hinges weren't accessible to those trapped inside the room. This oversight on his part made her wonder what else he hadn't thought of.

She walked up to the door, pinched the top of the pin in the bottommost hinge, and tugged upward, but it wouldn't budge. She paused, took a breath, and tried again. Her fingers kept slipping off the metal without getting a decent grip.

She let out a curse in Spanish. Her escape couldn't be thwarted like this. She would need to use something to pry the pin out of its place. Something like . . .

The lamp base.

Her heart began to flutter.

She picked up the lamp again and hooked the bottom edge of the metal around the head of the hinge pin. *This has to work. This has to work.* It became a mantra in her mind. Maybe if she believed it with all her heart, it really would work. Faith could move mountains and heal lepers. Surely it could open a door, too.

"I'm going to pull the pins out of the hinges," she said to the room. "I'm going to do it, and then I'm going to get out of here."

At first the metal lip at the bottom of the lamp kept slipping off the head of the pin, but finally it caught and she managed to slide the pin upward a few millimeters. She felt a sudden lightness about her. "I'm going to get out of here," she repeated, "and then I'm going to run."

There. The first pin was out.

In order to reach the top pin with her makeshift tool, she had to drag the bed over to the door and use it as a ladder. Soon that pin, too, was free.

She pulled the door out of its frame and dragged it aside, then rushed down the stairs. The front door sat mere yards away from the bottom step. It suddenly seemed too good to be true. She was walking into a trap. As soon as she put her hand on the knob, Graham would materialize in the entryway and shoot her.

She shook her head and stepped forward.

When she tried to turn the knob, it wouldn't budge. Panic welled up inside of her. Graham must have rigged the front door with a lock requiring those leaving the house to have a key.

Perhaps the location of the door hinges wasn't an oversight at all.

But maybe there was another exit not rigged like the front.

She raced through the kitchen to a mudroom at the back of the house that Graham had never showed her before. There—a rear door! But when she tried it, its knob wouldn't turn, either.

She'd been stupid to think it would work.

Not knowing what else to do, she ran back into the front room with the purple walls and the crucifix and parted the drapes so she could try to figure out exactly where she was.

Tall conifers lined the roadway on the other side of the street, which lay a slight distance away from her. Someone driving by would be able to see her standing in the window if they happened to divert their attention from the road to look at the house.

She remained transfixed by the sight of the outside world. Normal people lived out there. They didn't know she was here. They didn't know she existed. Which made her wonder: how many houses had she driven by in her life that contained someone like herself trapped behind its walls?

She put her hand on the glass. *Be free.*

But how could she be free? She would have to have tools . . .

That was it.

Tools. Which Graham kept in the basement.

She swiftly descended to the basement floor and held her hand over her nose. It didn't smell right down here. Graham had admitted to killing God knew how many people, so maybe everything in the dank room had become permeated with the smell of death over the years. Like blood and sweat and corruption all combined.

It wasn't something she wanted to think about, but she couldn't stop. There was the table where Mary had lain. Clean now, but not so clean. Dozens of people could have died in that very place over the years. Maybe even hundreds.

When had he found the time to do it?

As Lupe scanned the shelves for anything approximating a sledgehammer, a red spiral notebook lying on a workbench caught her eye.

An odd compulsion made her flip the cover open to see what Graham wrote in it.

The upper right-hand corner of the first page was dated October 5, 2000—almost fifteen years before. Then, in Graham's neat script, the following had been written:

Lindsey Montgomery. 36 years old. Religious background: Episcopalian. Thinks "diet Catholic" jokes are funny. Has one sister who lives in Idaho; doesn't often speak with her. Loves milkshakes and always dreamed of being a singer. Did some volunteer work at a soup kitchen in Eugene. Has cystic fibrosis. Not expected to live much longer. Says she can't wait to see God.

Halfway down the page, the ink switched from blue to black and the handwriting became slightly less legible.

She wouldn't stop screaming. It can't have been that bad. They say they want to see God but the second they realize they're dying they suddenly regain the will to live. Hypocrites! She's no different than the others. She kept saying her sister's name and then started calling for her parents. Wouldn't tell me what she saw. And to think of all I did for her!

Lupe glanced at the ceiling. No sound came from above. As much as she wanted to hurry up and find something to aid in her escape, the contents of the notebook had rooted her to the floor.

Hands shaking, she leafed to another page at random.

August 3, 2001.

James Arnett. 57 years old. Religious background: Catholic, but hasn't attended Mass for years. Says he believes in God but doesn't see the point of going to church and sitting in a pew for an hour each week. Worked as a mechanic for 35 years; had to quit because of health. He isn't sure he wants to meet God because God allowed his wife to leave him for another man.

In his final moments James said he saw light. I hope he was telling the truth and wasn't merely trying to appease me.

It scared Lupe to see into Graham's most personal thoughts like this.

It scared her even more when she realized she'd just wasted valuable minutes doing so.

She slipped the notebook inside her sweatshirt so she could study it more later on. Cursing herself for becoming distracted, she eyed a hammer hanging from a pair of nails protruding from a large piece of plywood leaning against the wall.

Perfect.

She lifted it from the nails and carried it upstairs. Breaking out the front picture window might draw the attention of a motorist, but it would also instantly alert Graham to the fact that she had escaped once he returned to the house. Breaking out the back might buy her a little time because Graham might not immediately realize she'd gone and might even still be there when the police arrived to take him into custody.

That is, if he didn't go upstairs and notice the bedroom door was no longer in its frame.

She returned to the back mudroom. The south-facing window seemed to beckon her. *Be free.*

"I'm going to escape," she said. "And everything is going to be okay."

She drew back the hammer.

27

BOBBY FELT an odd case of the giggles well up in his chest when he backed his Nissan into the driveway of a vacant house across the street and about a hundred feet down the road from Randy's home.

It was probably nerves. Nothing about their situation should have elicited laughter.

Bobby forced back his inappropriate mirth to better focus on the situation. They hadn't seen the gray car on the route back to Randy's house, and none of them had any desire to sneak up the lane and report back on whether or not the car still occupied the driveway.

"How long are we going to sit here?" Bobby asked, keeping his eyes fixed on the driveway entrance. Trees completely hid Randy's house and garage. Living that far back from the road might have made Randy more comfortable, but right now not seeing what was going on back there created a huge inconvenience for them.

"As long as it takes," said Randy.

Phil leaned forward so his head was between the two front seats. "He might not even be here anymore. We could be wasting our time."

"But we don't know that. If you have a better idea, please let us know. I'm all ears."

"You know my idea," Phil said. "Call the police and let them handle this. But you won't listen to me, so I don't know why you bother asking my opinion."

"Maybe we should all be quiet and pay attention," Bobby suggested. He glanced over his shoulder and saw a dark look pass between Randy and Phil, and thankfully neither felt the need to reply.

Minutes ticked by in silence. The sun passed in and out of clouds, and Bobby had to roll down the windows when heat began to build inside the car.

Phil slouched back in the rear seat with his gun resting in his lap, but in front of him Randy remained leaning forward in rapt attention.

More minutes passed. Bobby wondered how members of law enforcement stayed alert during stakeouts because his own consciousness was starting to ebb like Phil's.

"He could be waiting for you to come home," Phil said at last. A fly had entered the car through one of the open windows and he waved a hand to shoo it away.

Randy shrugged. "True."

"We could be waiting here for hours."

"Somebody's got to cave eventually."

"You think Graham's going to be the one to do it? For all we know he's planning on camping out until you show up."

"Fine," Randy said. "If he doesn't show within the next fifteen minutes, you can march yourself right up the driveway and take a peek at what he's doing."

Bobby pinched the bridge of his nose. "If you want someone to go take a look, I can do it. If I cut through the woods he probably won't see me." Not that he had any real desire to get out of the car.

Phil began to interject. "I don't really think that's—"

A gray vehicle became visible through the trees across the street and paused at the entrance of Randy's driveway with its right blinker on.

Bobby's heart nearly leapt into his throat. He started the engine and eased out onto the road the same instant the other car pulled out and headed for town.

"Keep back a little bit," Randy said in a low voice as if he feared Graham would hear him at that distance. "Try not to make it look like we're following him."

Bobby nodded. He wasn't stupid.

A bead of sweat rolled down his neck and into his shirt as Randy's driveway and the surrounding woods disappeared into the distance. He strained to see the person in the vehicle in front of him but all he could see was the back of a dark-haired head.

He tailed the car back into Autumn Ridge, allowing a car to merge between them to help avoid suspicion. They traveled a few blocks into the denser part of town and turned. Traveled a few more blocks. Let another car merge between them. Turned again. Traveled a few more blocks. Turned again.

Just as Bobby realized he'd passed the same Starbucks twice, Phil let out a mild oath. "He's taking us in circles!"

Bobby tried not to let despair take hold of him. "Maybe he just does this normally to make sure nobody's following him."

"Or he's smart enough to realize that a particular silver Nissan has been behind him this whole time."

Randy remained silent. Bobby sent him a mental thank-you. He wouldn't have been able to pay attention to their quarry if they started arguing again.

Bobby began to pride himself in keeping them on Graham's tail, thinking that following the man who wasn't named Paul last night had been God's way of giving him some practice in the art of vehicular stalking.

No sooner had he thought this when his pride received a hearty slap in the face. Bobby got stuck at a traffic light, and Graham didn't.

The three of them watched helplessly as the gray car receded into the distance and disappeared as it turned onto another street several blocks away.

"Nice," Randy said. "Did anyone get a look at his plate?"

Bobby felt his pride take another blow. In the heat of excitement at following the car, he'd forgotten to look. "I think there were some letters in it."

Phil began massaging his temples.

When the light changed to green a minute later, Bobby was at a loss about what to do. Even if he happened to guess the correct side street that Graham had taken, the old man would be long gone.

"Any ideas?" he asked as he brought the car up to speed.

Beside him, Randy cleared his throat. "Do you want to show us that house you found?"

"What house?"

"The one you followed that guy to last night."

Bobby tore his gaze away from the busy street to glance over at his passenger. "Why do you want to go there?"

"Just an idea I had all the sudden. That's all."

"Any objections?" Bobby asked, lifting his eyes to the rear-view mirror.

"At this point I don't care anymore," Phil said, looking resigned. "Just do whatever Randy says."

THEY ARRIVED at "Paul's" house several minutes later only to discover that, like earlier that morning, nobody was home.

They sat in the driveway in silence. Bobby drummed his fingers on the steering wheel and glanced at the road behind him. Beyond it lay an abandoned auto parts store of some sort. Too bad they couldn't go over there and ask about who lived in the house.

"Now what?" Phil asked. "Surely you don't think whoever Bobby saw at church last night was Graham."

"I don't think that at all," Randy said. "Bobby, you said Paul needed to speak with me. Right?"

"That's what he said. But I guess he could have been sent there to kill you and invented the whole needing-to-meet-somebody thing when he found out I wasn't you."

"Or he really intended to meet someone there, and he really wanted to talk to me." Randy unbuckled his seatbelt and opened the door. "You coming?"

Bobby pointed at the empty place where a vehicle should have been parked in front of the small garage. "Nobody's here."

"That's what you think."

Bobby glanced to Phil, who merely shrugged and put his gun away once more.

They got out and followed Randy to the porch. Randy immediately began rapping on the door.

Bobby opened his mouth. "I said—"

Randy waved his hand in dismissal. "You assume too much." He knocked again to no avail, then stepped back and eyed the door as if contemplating sending a kick through it.

Phil folded his arms. "Randy, I strongly suggest—"

Randy cupped his hands around his mouth and started to bellow. "Hey, Paul! Are you home? There's some people out here who want to see you."

Bobby felt his cheeks turn pink. It was starting to look like Randy's mind had finally cracked under pressure like an egg.

Phil ran a hand over his face. "God, help me."

To Bobby's surprise, a man of average build appeared at the corner of the house wearing gardening gloves and rubber boots. Though Bobby hadn't been able to see his eyes last night due to the sunglasses obscuring the upper part of his face, Bobby could tell right away this was the man who had called himself Paul.

Both Paul and Randy seemed equally surprised to see each other.

"Mr. Bellison?" The man dragged his arm across his pale forehead to wipe away a bead of sweat. The knees of his jeans were stained with dirt and bits of grass. "What are you doing here?" His gaze flicked to Bobby, and before Randy could answer, the man said, "Wait. I talked to you at the church last night." Bobby was grateful when he failed to mention that their meeting occurred while he cowered in the janitor's closet.

"That's right," Bobby said, glancing at Phil, whose eyes had grown round behind the lenses of his glasses. Just who was this Paul? Maybe if he introduced himself, Paul would do the same. "I'm Bobby Roland."

He held out his hand, and the man shook it in a weak grip after pulling off his soiled gloves. "Nice to meet you again, Mr. Roland. I apologize for not getting around to a more proper introduction last night, but what's done is done." He shoved his gloves into a back pocket and glanced apprehensively toward the abandoned shop on the other side of the road. "The sky itself has eyes. Let's talk inside."

Bobby and the others obeyed. Paul led them into a small living room that had a hardwood floor and simple furniture and instructed them to sit down on the couch.

"Did you look me up in the parish directory?" the man asked once the door closed. He sat down in a forest-green armchair and folded his hands together. "I don't prefer to advertise my place of residence."

"Actually," Randy said, "Bobby says he tailed you home last night. It turns out he's suspicious of black-clad men who turn up in churches late at night."

Spots of scarlet appeared on the man's cheeks. "You *followed* me? What in the world for?"

Bobby tried to hide his embarrassment by straightening his shoulders and looking purposeful. "You hinted that someone was after you. Someone who might hurt *me* in order to find you. If I was going to get thrown into something dangerous, I at least had the right to know where I might be able to find you again." He paused. "Who are you, anyway? Seeing as nobody's bothered to introduce you to me."

A faint smile played about the man's lips. "I'm Father Laubisch, the assistant priest at St. Paul's. And if you'll remember, you didn't see me there. You saw a man named Paul."

Bobby tried not to roll his eyes. This was stupid.

Father Laubisch went on. "And today you dropped by so Mr. Bellison can properly introduce us to each other—nothing more than that. Mr. Mason came along out of courtesy. I pray you'll stick to that story if anyone ever asks."

Bobby felt a small measure of relief when he saw that both Randy and Phil seemed to be just as clueless about what was going on. "I don't understand all the secrecy," Bobby said. "If you're the assistant priest, why did you need to disguise yourself last night? And who were you supposed to meet?"

"I'll get to that." Fear lined his face, and he threw a nervous glance at the front door. "Mr. Bellison, I should have told you months ago, but certain things have kept me from doing so. My apologies."

"Please just call me Randy. We're all friends here." He paused. "I think."

"I hope so." The priest looked so on edge that Bobby suspected he'd fly through the roof if anyone so much as sneezed. "Can you promise whatever is said in here doesn't leave this room?"

"I'll make that promise after I hear whatever you've got to say. I have no idea what this is about."

Father Laubisch closed his eyes. "God forgive me," he said in a quiet voice, then went on. "Several months ago I was hearing confessions while Father Preston was away at a retreat. I was there for about an hour and thought I'd seen the last of them for the evening, and just when I got up to leave the confessional I heard someone come in and kneel down on the other side of the screen, so I sat back down and greeted him."

Randy looked as enraptured as a child listening to a fairy tale.

Father Laubisch paused for several long seconds. "He stayed there for a minute without saying anything, but then he spoke up and told me he'd murdered sixty-three people. And he was flippant about it! I had no idea how to respond to him."

"Geez," Randy murmured, his eyes wide.

Father Laubisch continued. "He told me he wasn't sorry because his victims were already dying. The only healthy person he'd tried to kill had gotten away. I asked him why he was telling me this since I could phone an anonymous tip to the police, and he laughed and said it would be a violation of my vows no matter how anonymous I was about it.

"Then he stepped around the screen so we could see each other face to face. He was of slender build and had black hair, but I immediately recognized his gait." Father Laubisch closed his eyes again as if to block out the image of the man. "It was Graham Willard. And he had a gun."

The room grew more silent than a mausoleum. Bobby discovered he was clenching his fists so tightly that his fingernails cut into his palms, and he forced himself to relax them.

Go home, the voice whispered in his mind. *You'll be safer there.*

He brushed the thought away as if it were a speck of dust, though the temptation to heed its advice still remained.

"Sixty-three people," Randy said at last, his face bleached of color. He turned Bobby's Reds cap over and over in his hands. "I *lived* with the man. For years! How could he have gotten by with that without me noticing?"

"Maybe he was lying," Bobby said, finding the idea of murdering a single person bad enough as it was.

"I'm not so sure about that," Phil said. "Any time he left the house, he could have been . . . Dear God. What could have brought this on in him? He was a Servant!"

"He told me why," Father Laubisch said softly. "He said his first killing was an accident. A car accident, to be exact. He was thirty years old when it happened. It's my understanding that he began his new hobby soon after."

"Dear God," Phil repeated. "That was forty-five years ago."

"How does that turn somebody into a serial killer?" Bobby asked. The whole notion was ridiculous, and if he guessed correctly, Graham had probably made it up as a sort of lame excuse for his actions. "Lots of people are killed in accidents. That doesn't make the survivors decide to kill more people."

Father Laubisch stared at him with dark eyes that made him uncomfortable. "That's because most people aren't Graham Willard. He admitted that he'd become addicted to the act, just like someone might become addicted to alcohol or pornography, though he didn't show any remorse for it. He didn't seem to think he was doing anything wrong."

"Then why did he show up at the confessional?" Randy asked. "Do you think he's got a bit of guilt hidden deep inside that he's trying to acknowledge?"

"No, that isn't why he came." Father Laubisch glanced to Randy with a pleading look in his eyes. "Please forgive me. He didn't give me any other choice."

Randy's expression darkened. "Any other choice about what?"

The priest swallowed. "He held the gun against my head and made me swear to help him out in his scheme against you. He wouldn't explain why he'd tried to kill you or why he wanted to cause you any kind of harm. He just said I would need to report to him several times a week on what you were up to. He also said he would need my help in other matters whenever the need arose. I agreed."

Randy's lip began to curl, and Bobby could tell he was making a strong effort not to whip out his knife and test its sharpness on the man's neck. "Why would you do that to me? When you found out about us, you swore you'd protect me if I was ever in danger, just like Father Preston did."

The pinkish tinge returned to Father Laubisch's cheeks. "Because something inside me said I was better off saving my own skin at your expense, but rest assured that if he ever told me to cause you harm I wouldn't have gone through with it."

"Gee, isn't that reassuring?"

He let Randy's remark pass without comment. "I've been keeping an eye on you as often as I can, though this past week I had some personal matters to attend to, which is why I was unaware you'd chosen to quit your job. Which admittedly makes my job somewhat harder. I even had copies of your keys made one day when you'd left them lying on the office desk. Graham would need them, he said. Or someone he worked with did. Because there are others he's enlisted to help him. One of them is—"

"Lupe," Randy said. His face looked like it was made of stone. "I'm aware of that."

The priest let out a sigh of relief. "I'm glad you know, but I'm surprised she told you. If Graham threatened her the same way he threatened me . . . Graham said he would always have someone watching me. Someone who had no fear of carrying out his requests. If he caught me defying him, I would be 'taken care of,' to use his words." He fell silent for several seconds. "I know it doesn't sound like it, but I've done my best to keep you safe. Yesterday I created a diversion to make sure that Graham and his helper would be temporarily preoccupied. Then I took the opportunity to slip a note under the wiper blade on Miss Sanchez's car instructing her to meet me in the church parking lot. I've played along with Graham so well that he seems to believe I've been converted, but I know I'm still being watched. That's why I couldn't stay at the church any longer than necessary. Graham's assistant could find me and demand me to tell him why I was there so late in the evening since it's outside my normal routine."

"What were you and Lupe going to do?" Randy asked.

"I was going to ask her to go to the police with me. Our story would be more convincing with two of us to tell it. If we'd hurried, we could have contacted the police before Graham's assistant finished his task."

"Would you consider telling us what this task is?" Phil asked.

Father Laubisch shook his head. "Not yet. I don't want any of you to accidentally let word of it slip in front of the wrong ears. And since I don't know how many other people Graham has hired, we don't know which ears those are. But as Mr. Roland here knows, Miss Sanchez never showed up last night. I'm concerned something may have happened to her."

"It did." Randy briefly recounted the morning's events, including the news that Graham had gone to Randy's house, most likely intending to kill him. "And we lost him in the center of town. Do you know where we can find him?"

"Yes. We've met at a house northeast of—" A loud knock on the front door came so suddenly that everyone jumped. Father Laubisch rose and crossed the room. When he held his eye to the peephole in the door, he stiffened.

"Who is it?" Randy said, dropping the volume of his voice.

"A—a young man. Younger than you."

Randy got up to join the priest at the door, and Bobby followed. Father Laubisch stepped aside to allow each of them to look in turn. "I'm picking up a bad aura," Randy said once he'd taken a good look at the guy, "but I don't know him. What about you, Bobby?"

"Let me think." Bobby squinted. The unknown visitor had dark blond hair and was no older than twenty-one or twenty-two. He wore khaki pants and a white shirt, had shoulders that slouched a bit, and was neither fat nor thin: the kind of guy who could blend into any crowd without notice.

The sight of him triggered something in Bobby's memory. He had seen this guy before. A passing face in the streets, maybe. Or perhaps one of the customers at the restaurant from which he had so recently been fired.

Something inside of him said that Caleb would know him, too.

Randy tapped on his shoulder. "Earth to Bobby. Do you know him?"

"No, but I've seen him before. Somewhere around town, I think." The guy just waited, gazing out toward the road in a nonchalant manner as if he had all the time in the world.

He didn't look like a threat. But when he faced the door again to knock, the dark look in his eyes sent a surge of terror through Bobby's veins.

"Don't open the door," he said, his voice suddenly small.

Nobody moved.

He gave Randy a pleading look. "We should get out."

"How?" Phil asked. "He's probably got us blocked in."

"I didn't see another car out there. He must have walked."

"Do you see any weapons on him?"

Bobby eyed the visitor's clothing, looking for a bulge indicative of a poorly-concealed holster. "No. But he might have hidden them." He patted his pocket, where the kitchen knife was still nestled inside the towel. "Does this house have a back door?"

Father Laubisch cleared his throat. "Yes. But if you circle back around to the driveway, won't he see you?"

The visitor knocked again. His blue eyes narrowed to slits, and he jiggled the knob.

To Bobby's dismay, the door swung open. Father Laubisch had failed to lock it upon their entry into the house.

"Run!" Bobby bellowed before the visitor could step all the way into the room. He bolted down a hallway leading out of the front room, the others on his heels.

His feet ground to a halt when raised voices issued from behind him.

Phil grabbed Bobby's arm and dragged him onward toward the rear of the small house. They let themselves out the back door as quietly as they could—which wasn't that quiet at all, Bobby thought—and stood there on a wooden deck, indecisive.

Bobby made a quick sweep of the yard. There weren't many places to hide in the immediate vicinity. A grill and picnic table sat on the deck. A square shed guarded the back edge of the property, and behind that were woods.

Bobby suddenly felt they'd made a terrible mistake. "We can't just leave him in there," he whispered. "That guy must be the one Graham has spying on him. He'll kill him!"

Randy shook his head. "We don't know that. Come on, let's hurry to the car while he's still distracted."

Just as they started around the side of the house to where Bobby's car sat in front of the detached garage, the muffled sound of a gunshot issued through the walls.

Though the day was warm, the temperature of Bobby's insides grew colder than the Arctic tundra.

"Crap. No. *Move.*" Randy, whiter than a sheet, shoved Bobby hard in the side, urging him to continue to the car.

Bobby wasn't about to argue, though it seemed his feet had sprouted roots anchoring him to the ground. A man was dying in there. Or he was already dead, in which case there wasn't a thing any of them could do. *God, help us.*

He forced himself to keep moving, casting one nervous glance back at the house while he went.

When he stopped before his beloved Nissan, his heart sank into the approximate region of his stomach.

It appeared that his car sat upon four black deflated balloons. "My tires," he said dumbly. "He slashed them."

Phil scowled again only this time Bobby could see fear in his eyes.

Bobby suddenly had the overwhelming compulsion to run toward the woods at the back of the property. The trees there appeared to extend for several acres, perhaps even more than that. If he could conceal himself well enough among them, he would have time to call the authorities.

Yes, he would do that. It was the safest option he had.

28

BOBBY MADE an abrupt about-face as he made a beeline toward the line of trees, and the gray darkness of dizziness threatened to cloud his vision. *Please don't let me faint. Not when there's a guy with a gun coming after me.*

He wasn't sure if Randy and Phil had decided to follow him. There had been no time to explain.

The ground beneath his feet soon became covered in brown needles shed from the evergreens reaching for the sky above him. He caught glimpses of houses on other streets in places where the trees briefly thinned, but he didn't bother to run to any of them for help. If the gunman followed him into the home of an innocent party and killed them, too, he would never be able to forgive himself.

The land dipped into a small, damp gully and he jumped down into it, pressing his back against the wall of earth to minimize exposure. He couldn't hear the sound of pursuing footsteps. Had Randy and Phil been hurt? He hadn't heard any additional gunfire, but then again, he hadn't been listening.

With a shaking hand he withdrew his cell phone from his pocket. Dialing the emergency number filled his head with unpleasant flashbacks from six years before, and he shoved them away before they could upset him.

A male voice spoke in his ear. "This is 911. What is your emergency?"

"I . . . uh . . ." The words died in his mind. A priest had just been shot back there. What was he going to say? He swallowed and began again. "Someone's been shot at 2128 Maple Road. I mean, I didn't see it, but I could hear it through the walls. And I saw the guy who did it. He was about twenty-one, white, had sort of dark blond hair, and was wearing white and tan clothes."

The operator sounded dubious. "If you didn't see the shooting, how do you know what the suspect looked like?"

"Because I saw him on the porch just before I heard the shot. I just assumed—"

"Are you currently in a safe position?"

"Yes. I mean, I think so."

"Emergency crews should be there shortly. Whatever you do, do not try to confront him."

"I wasn't planning on it. And thanks." He ended the call—probably before he was supposed to—and shoved the phone back into his pocket.

As he sat there waiting for some other horrible thing to happen, he kept running the gunman's face through his catalog of memories. Where in the world had he seen him before?

It suddenly occurred to him that the gunman might have been the man smoking in his car in the parking lot at Lupe Sanchez's apartment complex the other night. Not that he'd seen the guy then (it had been too dark), but his gut told him that his guess was right.

Another minute passed. Some birds were twittering up in a branch. The sound of a lawnmower echoed through the trees somewhere to his left.

Then, somewhere, a stick snapped.

"Bobby."

The whispered voice nearly made his heart stop.

He jerked his head up to see Randy squatting on his haunches at the top of the gully; the ball cap jammed crookedly on his head. He glanced over his shoulder for a moment before climbing down beside Bobby and sitting Indian-style in the dirt.

Randy ran his hands over his face. Bobby noticed he had the shakes.

"Where's Phil?" Bobby whispered. "I thought he'd be with you."

"I don't know." Randy's mouth formed a straight line and he made a visible effort to compose himself. "When I saw you take off all I thought about was following you."

Bobby risked sticking his head over the edge of the gully for a few moments. A couple of squirrels raced their way up a tree trunk chattering at each other, but other than that, the forest was still.

He ducked back down. "I called 911."

"How intelligent of you."

The sarcasm in Randy's voice hit a raw nerve inside of him. "Look. What's it going to hurt if the police get involved in this?"

"For all I know, one of Graham's hired hands is a cop. He had some buddies on the force years ago, so it wouldn't surprise me. At this point, not much will."

"But you don't *know* he's still got friends who are cops."

Randy rubbed at the stubble on his chin. "I don't trust the police. They're no different from anyone else, and if you think otherwise, you've got a lot to learn."

"But they can hunt people down and arrest them. I'm pretty sure we can't do that."

"We might not be able to arrest anyone, but nobody's going to stop me from hunting Graham down."

Bobby shivered a little. "You're a Servant. Doesn't that mean you should love one another, or something? You make it sound like you're going to find Graham and get revenge on him."

"Not revenge."

"Then what?"

"I don't know. I do know I'll need to meet with him face to face. It's the only way to bring this to an end."

Bobby swiped a marauding ant off of his pants leg. "He'll kill you, though. And you said if you die without a replacement, evil will have free reign or something like that."

Randy closed his eyes for a moment. "It almost does now."

"Oh, I get it." Bobby didn't bother masking his irritation. "There's a lot of evil now, so what's the problem if there's a little more?"

"That's not what I meant."

"That's what it sounded like. 'Oh, I'll just let myself be killed because I'm too stubborn to call the cops, and never mind if demons take over the whole planet when I'm gone.'"

Randy's face turned the color of a beet. "Shut up."

But Bobby couldn't shut up. "If you're really that concerned about keeping evil in check, why don't you call the police about Graham and then hole up somewhere safe in the meantime? That's what I'd do."

Randy didn't say anything.

"How do you keep evil in check, anyway? You're only one guy compared to what, seven billion people?"

Randy seemed to count off several seconds in his head before speaking. "Even the tiniest flame can create light. Freeing people from the clutches of evil spirits may not seem like much in the grand scheme of things, but for those people, it means the whole world. It weakens Satan's power when people are freed, just as prayer weakens it. But here's something you need to remember— Satan only has power when we let him. It's just an illusion. Because God is infinitely more powerful than he is."

"Then why is it bad if you die without a replacement?"

Randy shrugged. "Who aside from a few clergymen is going to drive out spirits? It might take months for them to drive a spirit out of a victim. Generally I don't need any more than a week. And Jesus and his disciples could do it in a matter of seconds. They're my fore-fathers, you know. He gave them authority over spirits—almost the same authority that I have. When there's no one else on earth with that authority . . ." He shrugged again.

"How many people have you freed?"

"About a hundred and twenty-five. That's just over twenty a year."

"And they're all in Autumn Ridge?"

"No. Some live here, but other times I'm encouraged to leave in search of others who need me. I've been to California, Washington, Idaho, Nevada—even all the way to New York, as a matter of fact. Once I gain their trust, we make arrangements to come back here for the cleansing. Then they're sent to the safe house, and once they've recovered and healed from their ordeal, we send them home. I call on all of them from time to time just to check up on how they're doing." His expression faltered. "Some of them reverted. Maybe only four or five. The rest have turned their lives around, and a lot of them are paying it forward by helping other people with their problems."

"Are there other Servants anywhere else? Like in other countries?"

"I don't know. We don't have written records. It's possible there were other lineages of Servants that died out. For all I know, I'm the only one left."

When Randy fell into brooding silence, Bobby said, "If you die, could one of the former Servants take your place until a new one is found?"

"That's not how it works. A person can only hold that honor once. And what an honor it is to be chosen."

"I can imagine," Bobby said, even though he didn't. He stuck his head over the edge of the gully again. Still no sign of Phil. Bobby felt a growing concern for the man's safety. He had led them this way. If Phil had gotten hurt out here, it would have been Bobby's fault.

"What's the real reason you don't trust the police?" Bobby asked when he'd crouched back down again.

"You don't give up, do you?"

"Not if I can help it."

Randy became silent once more and nodded to himself a few times. "Let me tell you a little story," he said at last. "There was this kid I used to know. His daddy was a cop, and his mother was a pathetic waif who waited on her husband hand and foot even though he drank too much and liked to knock her around. Daddy got it into his head that it might be fun to do certain things to his son that he did to his wife—yes, those things—and when his son worked up the courage to tell his mother about it, she laughed and told him to stop making up stories. So the boy told the other police instead, and they didn't believe him either because the boy's daddy was a good cop and an upstanding member of the community and would never do anything like that to a child.

"It went on for years. And when the boy was finally nine years old, a neighbor caught sight of something he wasn't supposed to see through a back window and reported the boy's daddy to the authorities. The man went to prison and the boy got taken away from his mother because she'd failed to protect him from the creep even though they all lived under the same roof. If the cops had believed the boy the first time, he'd have been spared years of needless suffering."

Bobby hardly knew what to say. If he knew someone who had gone through that, he might not hold much faith in law enforcement, either. "Then what happened to him?"

"To the boy? He grew up."

"Was it you?"

Randy didn't answer. His eyes took on a faraway look, and Bobby knew then to drop the issue.

29

THE HAMMER struck the window so hard that Lupe's arm throbbed in protest, yet the glass remained undamaged. *"¡Me voy de aquí!"* she exclaimed, reverting to her native tongue. *"¡Me voy de—"*

A car door slammed outside.

She whirled around, holding the hammer behind her back in an instinctive effort to hide it. From her current position she couldn't see the front window or what lay beyond it, but she knew without a doubt that the owner of the vehicle was by no means here to save her.

Tears threatened to spill from her eyes not for the first time that day. Graham's return could mean only one thing.

Randy was dead.

Because of her.

The memory of the day Randy proposed to her popped into her head unbidden. They had gone to picnic at the beach at Roads End State Park, which was several hours north just off the Oregon Coast Highway. After they finished eating their sandwiches and chips and packed the basket back into the car, they walked barefoot down the beach hand in hand as the gulls swooped overhead and some children played beach volleyball a short distance down the strand.

Even though she and Randy had both been twenty-four, she'd felt as giddy as a teenager on her first date. The brightness of the day enabled her to forget the woes of everyday life, and she knew that as long as she stayed with Randy, she would be safe not only from the past but from herself as well.

At last Randy let go of her hand and pointed out at the water. "Hey, see that?" he said.

She'd squinted, unable to detect anything out of the ordinary on the lapping waves. "No."

"Look a little closer."

She did. But try as she might, she couldn't see anything that would have caught Randy's attention.

It occurred to her then that something was on her left ring finger that had not been there previously. Startled, she looked down and blinked at a bright sparkling thing set in a band of white gold.

She let out an involuntary gasp and held it closer to her face. Randy had slipped it onto her finger while she was distracted by their conversation. "Oh, Randy, it's beautiful!"

"Now you see it," he said with a wink.

"I . . . does this mean . . . ?"

He took her hand again, brought it to his lips, and gave her fingers a delicate kiss. "Lupe, will you marry me?"

She'd been praying for months that he would finally ask her. They had been together for about three years at that point, and while they'd tried to remain as chaste with each other as possible, they had difficulty remaining that way.

Their marriage would finally make everything complete.

"Of course I will!" she exclaimed, knowing that for the first time in her life all would be well.

They had embraced each other in full view of all the houses along the beach, and some other beachgoers who had been watching them began to cheer.

That day had been the best of Lupe's life. July 13, 2013. She would never forget it.

But now the day that had brought her such great joy would only be a bittersweet memory. Lupe choked back a moan. She couldn't think about it. *Wouldn't* think about it. Knowing that she and Randy would someday be one was one of the few things that had kept her going in her darkest moments.

And now she didn't even have that.

She straightened her shoulders and emerged into the kitchen. She laid the hammer on the table and took a seat in one of the chairs.

The front door swung open, admitting a flustered Graham Willard. Mud covered his shoes, his dyed hair was ruffled like he'd been running his hands through it, and one corner of his shirt's collar poked upward at an odd angle.

That, combined with the fevered glint in his eyes, made him look like a madman.

Madman or not, she decided she had never hated another human being as much as he.

Graham froze when he saw her, and his eyes grew round when he spotted the hammer lying on the table in front of her. She realized they were blue again. He hadn't put in the brown contacts today.

"I tried to escape," she said before he could speak, even though that would have been obvious judging from the fact he had left her locked in the upstairs bedroom. "But I realize it isn't meant to be. Please kill me now so I won't have to suffer anymore."

The old man blinked.

"I'm not trying to fool you," she said. "You've already killed Randy. I don't want to live anymore now that he's gone."

He worked the muscles in his jaw. The manic glint shined in his eyes again. "You think you know everything, don't you?"

"I'm not stupid. You left to kill Randy. Now you're back to set me free if you've kept your end of the promise. Well, I don't want you to keep it. Shoot me. I pray you've perfected your aim."

Color rose in his cheeks for a moment but they quickly returned to their normal pallid state. "I don't know why I bother listening to you. You're worse than my daughter Kimberly when it comes to making unnecessary noise."

She didn't let the insult faze her. "I found your notebook down-stairs when I was looking for a hammer," she said, having nothing better to say while she waited for Graham to fulfill her request.

This seemed to surprise him. "You looked in it?"

She didn't feel like telling him that the notebook was cur-rently tucked inside her shirt. "Some. I thought it was interest-ing how you wrote down all those little details about the people you've . . . you've killed. I just wondered if Randy and I would get a page toward the end of it."

He snorted. "The end of it."

"What?"

"You think this is the end? I'm not going to stop doing what I do just because you and Randy are gone. With Randy out of the way, I'll be a free man. I can never be free if he's still out there trying to find me." He grimaced. "And trying to change me."

Lupe tried not to let her fear show. He'd practically just admit-ted that he'd intended to kill her all along.

Instead of shooting her, Graham strode past her and grabbed a bottle of Smirnoff vodka, Worcestershire sauce, lemon juice, and a stick of celery out of the refrigerator and tomato juice and hot sauce out of a cabinet. He set about mixing the ingredients together in one of the tall glasses he kept lined up on one of the counters.

"What are you doing?" she asked. It was very much in charac-ter for him to not do as she requested, unless he planned on doing her in with a drink.

"You've got eyes. What does it look like?"

Lupe just stared at him, unbelieving. The man was making himself a Bloody Mary.

"Would you like one, too?" he asked, accidentally knocking the hot sauce onto its side and splashing it onto the counter.

He didn't bother cleaning it up, and the smell of it made her eyes water. "No thank you."

He gave a nonchalant shrug and continued working. When he finished mixing his drink, he put the bottles away and stabbed the stalk of celery into the red liquid, then took a seat opposite her at the table. He slid a box of Pall Malls out of a pocket, stuck a cigarette between his lips, and lit it up.

If he had been agitated upon his arrival, he was now calm and collected. He took sporadic sips between puffs on the cigarette, and his wrinkled expression softened into a dreamy grin of contentment.

"Why don't you just do it now and get it over with?" she asked, not bothering to mask the hard edge that had entered her voice. Graham's leisurely actions unnerved her more than anything he'd done to date. Was this his way of celebrating Randy's demise?

He breathed out a cloud of smoke that caught in her throat and made her cough. "I'm not ready yet. Preparations are currently being made, and in the meantime the two of us will sit here and wait."

"I don't understand."

"Do you need me to write it out for you in crayon so your little-girl brain can understand it better?" He leaned forward. A droplet of the Bloody Mary glistened on his chin. "If I were to go fishing, what would I need to ensure that I caught something?"

Lupe narrowed her eyes. "A worm?"

"Try again."

Oh. She knew what he meant now. What was the English word? "Bait," she said, remembering a second later.

"Not just any bait. Live bait."

The words and their implication nearly made her heart stop. A faint spark of hope glimmered inside her. "I thought you'd already killed him!"

"Not quite. My grandson has a little bit of work to do first."

"Your grandson?" Surely Kimberly's sons wouldn't have anything to do with him. She'd only met them a few times, but overall they seemed to be upstanding members of society who would gladly turn their grandfather over to the law if they knew where he was.

"Yes. Jack. He's got a good head on his shoulders. If you're lucky, you'll be meeting him soon."

She had never heard him mention a Jack before. "He's coming here?"

"No. We're going there. You didn't think this was my only property, did you?" He paused to down more of his Bloody Mary and made a show of smacking his lips, which made more of it get on his chin. "Lisa and I owned many properties over the years, if you'll recall. After she died I purchased other properties under a different name."

That made sense. Graham would have wanted to hide his sick hobby from everyone he knew, and the only way he would have been able to do that was if he could do it in a location that none of his acquaintances knew about. Plus, using a different name would have been smart. Undoubtedly all of the properties in his own name had been searched once he became a wanted man. In order to hide from those searching for him, all he would have needed to do was move into one of the other houses he had already prepared.

But how many were there? Two, at least. The man had to have been making money somehow during the past year, and rental income would have been one way to do it.

"You don't need to know how many there are," he said, reading her thoughts.

He was right. If she was to be killed before the day's end, it wouldn't make a difference if he owned two properties or a hundred.

Her newfound hope began to falter like a broken-winged moth. She couldn't let that hope give out. But she couldn't see what she could do to save either Randy or herself. As much as she hated to admit after her escape from the bedroom, she was more helpless than a newborn child, completely at the mercy of the one who had imprisoned her.

In contrast to Lupe's anguish, Graham kept puffing on his cigarette like the most carefree man in the world. And why shouldn't he be? Everything was going according to his plans.

While she waited for him to finish, she decided she had two options left.

One: She could pray for a swift and painless death for both her and Randy.

Two: She could pray for a miracle.

30

A CRACKING twig gave Bobby a jolt. He whipped his head to the right and saw a white-faced Phil Mason standing yards away with his gun drawn out in front of him. Pine needles clung to the Muse shirt Bobby had lent him as if he'd been crawling through the underbrush at some point since their escape into the woods.

Phil lowered the gun without saying anything, glanced from side to side, and joined the pair huddled in the gully. "Something's wrong," he said in a low voice.

Randy eyed the gun with revulsion. "You don't say."

"No. I don't mean this. Bobby, are you the one who called the police?"

Bobby cleared his throat before speaking, still shaken by Randy's tale. "I called 911 and told them somebody had been shot. Why?"

Phil's forehead furrowed with creases. "When you two went bolting away like a couple of bats out of hell, I thought I should stick around to see what was going to happen. Half of Autumn Ridge's finest showed up, guns out and all. Some took an interest in your slashed tires." He shook his head. "They were there for about fifteen minutes. Looked like they were talking to somebody out front. I think some of them went into the house. Then they all just up and left. Nobody got loaded into the ambulance or any of the cruisers. I heard one of the cops laughing like it had all been some misunderstanding."

"But I heard a gunshot!" Bobby said, suddenly wondering if his fear had made him misinterpret the situation. He'd been so certain the sound had been a gun—what else could it have been?

"You'd have been deaf to have missed it," Phil said. "But when they all left, I started thinking. What exactly did we hear before running out of there?"

"Father Laubisch and that man were shouting at each other," Bobby said. "And then when we made it outside someone fired a gun."

Phil pretended to examine his own gun. "Suppose I shot you. What would you do?"

Bobby shivered at the sight of the weapon. "I'd probably pass out if I didn't die first."

Before he could stop the man, Phil marched right up to him and punched him so hard in the arm that Bobby let out a strangled cry. Tears sprang into his eyes. "What was that for?"

"What did you just do?" Phil pressed, his eyes gleaming.

"I . . . screamed?"

"Exactly."

The man was nuts.

"Wait a minute," Randy said. "Being shot doesn't exactly tickle. Father Laubisch should have been making some kind of noise."

"Not if it was a really good shot," Bobby said as he massaged his arm. Phil had probably wanted to punch him all along and finally found a decent excuse to do so.

"But if it had been a good shot," Phil said, "the coroner would have been called and the emergency crews would still be there. If it had been a bad shot, they would have loaded Father Laubisch into the ambulance and rushed him to the hospital."

"So you're saying he didn't get shot at all?"

"That, or he pulled an Obi-Wan Kenobi and vanished the second he died."

They all fell silent.

Something clicked in Bobby's head. "They faked it." The man with the gun must have fired it into the ceiling or the floor and told the cops it had been an accident.

And Father Laubisch would have been there to corroborate it all. His apparent argument with the gunman had only been an act.

Randy must have been thinking the same thing because his expression morphed from shock into anger. "We need to get out of here."

"But we can't," Bobby said. "Remember my tires?"

"I can call a taxi once we get out of these woods," Phil said.

"Where are we going after that?"

A cell phone began to ring, sparing Phil from providing an answer. Randy glanced at his pocket, slid out his phone, and frowned. "It says Unknown Caller."

Phil snatched it out of his hand and accepted the call before Randy could object. "Hello?"

An astounding transformation came over the man's face. It had been pale to begin with, but the second the caller began to speak, it became whiter than a winter sky.

He drew the phone away from his ear and hit some buttons. "It's for you," he whispered, and passed it back to Randy. "I set it to speaker."

"Hello, Randy," said a garbled male voice.

"Where did you take Lupe?" Randy demanded.

"She's safe right now," said the voice that could only belong to Graham. Like the face of the fake gunman who had stood on Father Laubisch's porch, something familiar about it troubled Bobby deeply.

"I said, where is she?"

"I'll get to that. But you have to come alone. Of course you knew that already. If you drag those two peons with you they'll meet the same fate you do."

Bobby turned in a full circle as his eyes scanned the surrounding woods. How did Graham know he and Phil were with Randy? Was he hiding behind a tree watching them?

Phil must have been thinking along those same lines because he regained a shooter's stance and made a complete turn as he swept the woods with his gaze.

Bobby pulled the kitchen knife out of his pocket for lack of anything better to do. It wouldn't save him in a gunfight, but at least it gave him a few extra ounces of confidence.

"Where do you need me to go?" Randy asked.

"Get your friends out of there, and I'll tell you."

Randy gestured for Bobby and Phil to step away. Phil drew back several paces and continued to give the area a visual sweep, and Bobby made a show of scraping his feet in the detritus on the forest floor so it would sound like he was retreating.

"Okay," Randy said. "They're gone."

"I don't believe you. What a nice shirt Phil is wearing. Muse, perhaps? And Randy, I've never known you to be a Reds fan."

Bobby's stomach did a flip, and he gripped the handle of the knife even tighter. Graham *was* watching them. Or someone else was watching them and relaying the information back to him.

"How are you ever going to believe me?" Randy asked. "You can't see they've left me alone. I could be standing here all day waiting for you because you're too stubborn to accept it."

"You really think I can't see you?"

Bobby, seeing no old men or cameras in the vicinity, decided to test Graham's claim. He lifted the knife into the air and swung it around in sweeping arcs as if he were some kind of shaman about to perform a sacrifice.

If that couldn't get Graham's attention, the old man was either blind or lying.

Phil stopped to gape at him. Bobby held a finger to his lips and proceeded to stab at the air in front of him to fend off an invisible foe.

Graham made no comment about his unusual behavior.

Realization dawned on Phil's face. He beckoned to Bobby.

"He must have seen us up at the house," Bobby whispered when he reached Phil's side. Behind them, Randy resumed his discussion with Graham. "Or his buddy told him what you guys were wearing so he could pretend he could see us."

"You'll note he didn't say anything about what you're wearing."

"That's because he doesn't know me. He wants to mess with you two because you're the bigger threats to him."

Phil seemed to ponder this. "Makes sense."

"But he has to be wondering who I am."

"Probably, but you're not much of a concern for him right now. The Servants have friends. You could just be one of them."

While not intended to be hurtful, Phil's words stung. "I thought I already was."

"That remains to be seen."

It occurred to Bobby that Randy's voice had become fainter. He turned and saw that the man had walked down the gully in the opposite direction from where they stood, holding the phone to his ear again.

He'd turned off the speaker?

Phil strode off in that direction, taking light steps, and Bobby followed suit.

"—understand. Yes, Graham." Randy lifted a hand when he saw them approaching. "I give you my word."

He ended the call.

Phil's eyes grew livid. "Just what's going on here? Why did you turn the speaker off?"

Randy looked as grim as an undertaker. "Because I promised I wouldn't let anyone overhear."

"Why?"

The Servant's eyes gleamed with tears. "It's the only way he'll let me see Lupe. What kind of person would I be to leave her alone with him?"

Phil shoved his gun into its holster. The armpits of his borrowed shirt were damp with sweat. "Sometimes I wonder if you've gone funny in the head. You'll honestly risk everything to go get

286 | J.S. BAILEY

her? Look what happened the last time a Servant died without a replacement!"

"I don't plan on letting myself be killed."

"What are you going to do, then? Kill Graham? Where did he tell you to go?"

Randy just shook his head.

"You promised him you wouldn't tell, didn't you?"

"That's right."

Bobby couldn't believe Randy was acting like this, either. "If you go alone, we can't help you."

"You can help me plenty. Start praying."

Phil looked ready to throttle him. "Lord, Randy, you don't even have a replacement if something should go wrong!"

"I can't help that. *Yea, though I walk through the valley of the shadow of death, I shall fear no evil.* Have faith, Phil. God saved me from him once. I trust him to save me again."

"Shouldn't we at least know where to find you?" Bobby asked as anxiety made his heart race. "At least give us a hint. That won't count as breaking your promise."

Randy closed his eyes and was quiet for a long time. "It's far," he said, "but not too far. Back in the mountains a ways. And Phil, when was I born?"

Phil's eyebrows rose. "April Fool's Day. It's starting to seem fitting."

"In what year?"

"Nineteen eighty-nine. How does this help us?"

"You'll have to figure it out on your own."

"Why can't you just break your promise to him?" Bobby asked. "I'm sure he won't keep any promises he makes to you."

"That doesn't make it acceptable for me to lie."

"You lied to Father Preston," Phil said.

"And I regret that."

"Dude," Bobby said. "Lupe's life is at stake. Don't you think it's okay to lie to save her?"

A look of indecision entered Randy's eyes. Then he shook his head. "If I die today and meet my Maker, what would he say to me if I had sinned in order to save Lupe?"

"He'd say good job for doing your best."

Randy's head continued to shake. "I will not be like Graham. And I fully intend to keep it that way."

<hr>

THEY MADE it out of the woods onto another residential street, where Phil phoned a taxi to deliver them back to Bobby's house on Fir Street. None of them spoke along the way so they wouldn't receive unwanted attention from the sour-faced driver, but the tension between the three of them was so palpable that Bobby could feel its weight pressing down on them all.

The driver dropped them off at the end of Bobby's driveway and tore off with a squeal of tires after they paid him for the trip.

Stay here, said the voice in Bobby's head. *It's much safer if you do.*

Yes, it would be safer.

Which was why he climbed into the back seat of Phil's car and rode with them to Randy's place.

"You're sure you won't tell us where you're going," Phil said.

Randy gave them a barely perceptible nod. He marched toward the garage with his head held high. Phil threw Bobby an agitated glance, and they followed him.

Bobby reviewed Randy's hint from various angles. He had no idea what the year of the man's birth had to do with anything. Was 1989 the house number where Graham had imprisoned Lupe? There might be dozens of homes in the area with that number. There wouldn't be enough time to narrow them down to one.

It had to mean something different, but Bobby couldn't guess what else it might be.

Randy rolled up the door of the garage, exposing his newly-repaired Ford. He looked back at the two of them. "The valley comes in from the west and stops at the year of my birth," he said. "You follow?"

"Which valley?" Phil asked.

Randy shook his head.

"For the love of God, Randy, it's okay to tell me where he told you to go!"

"I'm not going to argue with you about that anymore. Wish me luck."

Phil looked like he was about to burst into tears. "I don't hold any stock in luck."

Randy gave him an iron stare. "What if it was Allison and Ashley instead of Lupe? Would you do the same?"

The muscles in Phil's jaw clenched, and his Adam's apple bobbed up and down. "I would do whatever had to be done to save them, including telling my friends where they are. I honestly think you're making a mistake."

"We'll find out, won't we?" Randy opened the car door and climbed inside.

The engine turned over in the Ford and Randy backed it out of the garage. He gave the two of them a solemn salute and set off down the lane between the trees, soon vanishing from their sight.

Bobby looked over at Phil's car. If they acted now, they could follow Randy to whatever rendezvous point Graham had indicated on the telephone, but something in his gut told him they needed to hold back. Graham would expect Randy to arrive with backup, and he could have hired more gunmen to watch out for any extra vehicles that showed up in Randy's wake.

The gunman's face from the priest's house rippled in the forefront of his mind. *If you could remember who I am*, it seemed to say, *then you just might be able to find me.*

But Bobby was at a loss. Linking together faces and names and the places where he had encountered them was a skill he had not fully mastered, and he cursed himself for it.

He and Phil stood there helplessly as the sound of the Ford's engine died away.

"So what are we going to do now?" Bobby asked.

Phil's eyes went out of focus as if he'd suddenly become lost in thought. Then he closed them. "Let's go inside," he said. "I can hardly think standing out here. Maybe sitting down will help clear my head."

31

AFTER SPENDING long minutes on the telephone in a different room, Graham blindfolded Lupe, bound her hands behind her, and forced her into the car; though "forced" wasn't the proper word since she permitted herself to be led willingly. She would be with Randy soon. Even if they were only together for a minute or two before they died, that would be okay.

In the front seat, Graham started coughing so hard that Lupe thought he might hack up a lung. He cleared his throat and coughed a few more times, and he became silent once more.

She hoped those disgusting cigarettes in which he indulged were finally causing him permanent damage. The sooner the old man ended up in the grave, the better.

An unknown length of time passed as she felt the car speed up and slow down and speed up again. When at last they turned off the road and parked, Graham led her out of the vehicle.

He walked her across an expanse of grass, and finally she heard the squeaking of door hinges as he guided her into a building that smelled of wood and damp earth. An old barn, probably. But more likely a storage shed since she couldn't smell any animals.

"You'll be staying in here until Randy arrives," Graham said.

"How long will that be?"

"You'll find out, won't you?"

And with that, he slammed the door, leaving her bound, blindfolded, and utterly alone.

———◆———

BOBBY TRIED the knob on Randy's front door, and to his surprise, it opened.

"He left that unlocked?" Phil asked, blond eyebrows arched.

"Looks like it." Bobby stepped over the threshold and turned on the light. Phil gently closed the door behind them.

They faced each other. Most of the antagonism he'd sensed in Phil seemed to have been replaced with intense concern.

"Have you thought of anything yet?" Bobby asked.

"No." Phil sat down on one of the IKEA couches and put his head in his hands. "Lord, *why* didn't we follow him?"

Bobby lowered himself onto the other couch. "Because Graham expects us to do that."

"You're probably right."

"You know I'm right. If he could get Father Laubisch and that guy to stage a shooting just to freak us out, then he's got to have more up his sleeve."

"You make it sound like you know him."

"But I don't. I mean . . ." He broke off. "His voice. On the phone. Is that how he sounds in real life?"

Phil gave him the faintest of smiles, but it looked more like a grimace. "Did you think he was distorting his voice? The man's smoked since before I was born. It's a wonder it hasn't done him in yet."

"It's just I swear I've heard him before. Only I don't know where, because I don't know anybody named Graham."

"You said you recognized the man who showed up on Father Laubisch's porch, too."

"Right, but I don't know where I could know him from, either."

"Do you think you saw him and Graham together somewhere?"

Bobby shrugged. "It's possible. We got a lot of customers at the restaurant I worked at. Some were regulars and others were just people passing through." He paused. "Do you know if Graham ever ate at Arnie's Stop-N-Eat?"

"I'm not going to pretend I knew what the man was up to at all hours of the day. Obviously, I didn't." His forehead furrowed in thought. "Hang on. I have an idea."

Phil rose from the couch and approached a bookshelf leaning against one wall. After squinting at the spines for a moment or two, he withdrew a large brown photo album and propped it open on the coffee table. "Randy isn't much of one for taking pictures," he said as he flipped through the pages, "but Lupe, Carly, and my wife like to give him snapshots to save. Come on, I know it's in here . . . there." He turned the album so Bobby could see an enlarged photograph of a group of people posing in rows on a beach, some dressed in swimsuits, some in shorts and t-shirts. "This was taken during a party we had on the coast a few years ago. You could say it's our whole little family. Let me know if you recognize anyone."

Bobby picked up the album and held it closer to his face. On the bottom row at the left, Randy and Lupe leaned against each other smiling as they sat barefoot in the sand. To their right sat Carly Jovingo (dressed in a somewhat revealing orange bikini, Bobby noted), a couple of women Bobby didn't recognize, Phil, and a blond, pigtailed toddler who was probably his daughter. In the back row stood some men and a few teenagers. A shriveled man with frizzy gray hair and stooped shoulders sat in a beach chair off to one side with arthritic hands folded together in his lap.

Bobby pointed. "That isn't Graham, is it?"

"Strike one. That's Frank Jovingo, and he just turned a hundred and one years old last month. This man here beside him is also Frank Jovingo, but we call him Frankie to avoid further confusion. He's Frank's grandson and Carly's father. Are you sure you don't recognize anyone?"

Bobby scrutinized the men in the back row. One of them looked like the middle-aged guy he'd passed in Randy's driveway that morning, but he couldn't be certain. A gray-haired man with a slight paunch around his middle standing next to him looked a decade or two older. "I'm not sure."

Phil picked up the album and turned it to another page. "Try again."

Bobby found himself staring at a bunch of four-by-six prints from that same beach party. In one shot, the women were all playing a game of sand volleyball, and in another, the gray-haired man with the paunch sat in a lawn chair sipping at a blood-red drink that had a stalk of celery poking out of it like a straw. Bobby could see his features more clearly in this image. He had laugh lines around his eyes, which were a pale shade of blue. He wore gray shorts and a brown, short-sleeved button-up shirt with a pack of red Pall Malls poking out the top of the breast pocket.

"This is Graham," he said. "Isn't it?"

"Good call."

"And you said he's seventy-five years old?" The man in the picture looked a decade younger than that.

"He was only seventy-two when this was taken, but yes. He liked to joke that his Bloody Marys helped keep him looking young, but you should see him when he walks. Shuffles around like the most decrepit person who ever lived. Based on what I know now, it had to be an act." Phil looked at Bobby with a questioning gleam in his eyes. "Do you know where you've seen him?"

"Give me a minute." Something about the lines in Graham Willard's face reminded him of someone—but who? He squinted. He moved the album away from him and turned it at an angle. He pictured the man sitting in a booth at the Stop-N-Eat sipping a Bloody Mary, but they didn't serve alcohol there, so the image didn't help him.

Then he remembered that the woman Randy questioned at Lupe's apartment complex said that a dark-haired man entered Lupe's unit.

In his mind, he pasted black hair onto Graham's head. He replayed the gravelly voice that came out of Randy's cell phone.

294 | J.S. BAILEY

"Nice to meet you, son," the old man said, though those weren't the words he used to address Randy. "Come on, I'll give you a tour of the place." In his mind's eye, Bobby saw the man inserting a key into a lock and pushing open a door. "I'm afraid it's not that big, but if it's just two of you in here, that should be okay, right?"

Bobby's eyes widened, and he clapped a hand over his mouth.

"Where have you seen him?" Phil pressed, his expression intense.

Part of Bobby's mind went numb with the realization that not only had he met Graham before but also wrote him a check every month to pay for his and Caleb's occupancy in the bungalow on Fir Street. "I don't believe it," he said. "It's Dave."

32

"WHO'S DAVE?"

Bobby's pulse thumped like the hooves of an out of control horse. "Dave Upton. He's my landlord. He drops by about once a month to make sure everything is okay with the house."

"Graham's daughter Kimberly's last name is Upton." Phil placed a hand on his chin, brooding. "You're sure he and Graham are the same person?"

Bobby looked at the photograph again and nodded. "I'm about a million percent sure."

"Then you'll find it interesting that the Graham Willard I knew owned quite a few rental houses over the years—just not one on the street where you live."

"You said he ran a drug store."

"He did that, too. But he must have other houses under this Dave name. That's how he's avoided the police. After he tried to kill Randy, he ceased being Graham Willard and became this other person instead."

296 | J.S. BAILEY

"Wouldn't his other renters know he changed his appearance? They should have suspected something was up. I met him at the end of June last year. When did he try to kill Randy?"

"On June fifteenth, so he would have already been evading law enforcement when you met him. And I agree that someone should have suspected something, unless you happened to be his only current renter."

Phantom fingers crawled across Bobby's skin and down his spine as he remembered something that Dave—no, Graham—had told him while he and Caleb read through the rental agreement. "He said the woman who lived there before us had become too sick to live by herself so she moved into a group home." He swallowed. "You don't think he—"

"I don't know what to think." Phil was already moving over to a dormant PC sitting on a side table. "But I've got an idea. Please pray it works."

———————◆———————

RANDY FINALLY found the place Graham indicated on the phone. A steep hill rose up from the south side of the road, and the north side consisted of a seemingly unbroken expanse of forest except for the place where a narrow gravel drive met the road.

He eyed the number on the battered mailbox and turned.

A metal gate that had been left open guarded the lane. Brambles grew close on each side, and if he hadn't known any better, he would have thought he was returning to his own home.

The structure at the end was most definitely not his house. It had two stories, yes, though the similarity ended there. Cheerful yellow siding made the house stand out like a highlighter, and the wide front porch housed a wooden swing covered in a flowery cushion and some pots spilling wave petunias over their edges.

Graham would have wanted people to look at this house and feel welcome. Come on buddy, pull up a chair and we'll be great friends.

The thought disgusted him.

An old barn, weathered and unpainted, loomed behind the house. The sight of it made uneasiness stir in Randy's gut.

Be calm, the Spirit said to him.

"I'm trying."

He got out of the car and slammed the door. The sound of it echoed off the sides of the house and barn and seemed to whisper through the trees before dissolving into silence.

He closed his eyes and listened.

Randy hadn't had the time to tell Bobby everything about his gift of Tongues. While it was true he could comprehend any human speaker and speak with him or her in turn, he also had a vague understanding of the languages of animals. It wasn't anything defined like human speech—more like vague ideas voiced by whatever sound the animal could produce—and it didn't always make sense to him because the brains of humans and animals were so vastly different from one another.

Animals did have the tendency to express their awareness of a human presence, which Randy could pick up from them easily enough.

Some birds perched in a nearby tree chattered about something they had seen. He strained to hear better. People. They had seen people, but now they didn't know where they were.

A lot of help that would do him.

Several minutes passed. "I'm here, Graham," he called. "Just like you wanted. So where is Lupe?" He took a step forward. "I know you're in there. Are you going to come outside with her, or am I supposed to come to you?"

Nothing.

He prayed that Bobby and Phil would decipher his hastily-concocted clues, and soon. It had been so tempting to break the promise he had made to Graham, but in order to be the Servant, one had to be as sinless as possible. Christ would not lie to save a soul. Randy wouldn't, either.

Lupe, please be okay. The woman he had chosen to be his bride had gone through more hell in her twenty-six years than most people could imagine. For most of her life, people had used her for their own gain, and now was no different. Like the johns and pimp who had used Lupe like a piece of meat in Nogales, Graham was using her to draw Randy in.

Which was why he would have to do his best to outsmart his former mentor. He would whisk Lupe away, call the police on Graham even though he had little faith in them, find a replacement, and then wed his beloved. With Graham behind bars, Randy would finally refurbish the outside of his house so he and Lupe would have a nice place to raise the children they hoped to have. Parenthood would be a whole new adventure unto itself since neither he nor Lupe had grown up in traditional homes. But they would love their children and nurture them, and life would be good.

But first things first.

He set off toward the house, wondering if Graham watched him while hidden just out of sight. He rapped on the door and stepped back. When nobody answered, he knocked again, and when a third knock didn't bring anyone to the door, Randy gave the knob an experimental turn and swung the door inward. Beyond it lay a dim room full of the amorphous outlines of covered furniture.

He glanced behind him to make sure he wasn't about to be ambushed. Then, maintaining utmost caution, he stepped inside.

———◆———

FATHER PRESTON sat at his kitchen table mulling over the explanation Tony gave him yesterday. *It's not what you think,* he'd said. Yes, that was all very good. It wasn't what Father Preston had thought. Surprise, surprise. Tony had only performed the actions he'd thought were right at the time.

But after praying about it the rest of that day and all morning so far, Father Preston decided he didn't quite like the things Tony had told him. He had tried to place himself in Tony's shoes. What would he, Father Preston, have done in that situation?

He would have notified the family first and foremost, even it had taken him all day to track them down and bring them the news.

Scratch that. He would have refused to become involved in the first place, even if that meant he would be killed for it. Tony claimed to be an unwilling participant who feared for his life. Father Preston had suggested calling the police right then, but Tony had balked at that. *No*, he'd said with palpable fear in his eyes. *I have to talk to the girl first. Then we can go to the police.*

Father Preston suggested that he should hurry up and do it, then.

The more he prayed about Tony's situation, the more God revealed to him that something about this whole ordeal was horribly wrong.

He prayed *he* was wrong.

Father Preston picked up the telephone and dialed up Ratchet Brothers Funeral Home. Perhaps his suspicions were unwarranted. But perhaps not.

A soft female voice answered. "Thank you for calling Ratchet Brothers. How may I help you?"

"Pattie? This is Father Preston." Many parishioners let Ratchet Brothers handle their loved ones' memorial services, so he was well acquainted with those who worked there. "I wondered if you could help me out with something for a minute or two."

"Sure thing, Father. What is it you need?"

He prayed that God would forgive him for the white lies he was about to tell. "I heard a rumor that one of our parishioners, a Patricia Gunson, had passed away, but nobody in her family notified me of the death. I wondered if they had contacted you about it."

"The name doesn't ring a bell. Let me check." He heard some tapping and clicking in the background as Pattie pulled up the information on a computer. "No, she's not here that I can see."

"Were you at work yesterday? Maybe whoever was there forgot to record the information about the arrangements."

"I was here all day, Father. Either the family chose a different funeral home, or you overheard a very unkind rumor."

Father Preston's stomach felt like it was full of knots. "I suppose I'll find out. I do have one more question, though."

"Yes?"

"Have you seen Father Laubisch? I thought he told me he dropped by there yesterday afternoon, but now I'm not so sure he did."

"You mean Father Anthony?" Pattie sounded confused. "No, he wasn't here yesterday at all. Why?"

Father Preston had always found it amusing how people insisted on referring to the younger priest by his first name when he preferred being addressed in the old-fashioned way, but today he found no humor in it. "Never mind. It's nothing. And thank you for your help."

"Not a problem. You have a good day, Father."

"You too."

They disconnected, and Father Preston set the phone down.

Tony, as he called the priest in private, had lied to him.

He began to see red. The younger man had done much more than fail to tell the truth.

There was only one thing left for him to do. Father Preston called the police.

33

RANDY CALLED out again once he had closed the door behind him. "Graham?"

The floor creaked beneath his feet as he stepped further into the room. All the curtains had been drawn. A sliver of sunlight fell onto the floor through a narrow gap in the fabric, illuminating thousands of dust motes dancing lazily through the air.

He found a light switch and flipped it on. Other than a coffee table, an armchair, and a couch covered in a dingy white sheet, the front room was empty. The floor consisted of imitation hardwood laminate. Footprints in the dust showed where someone had recently passed through from the front door to the kitchen. Judging from the shoe size, it had been a man.

He listened for any sign of movement but could hear none. Where was Lupe?

As a precaution, he withdrew his knife and held it at his side.

Randy glided from room to room, noting that in no way could this be Graham's primary residence. The only thing in the bathroom indicating that someone ever used it was a roll of toilet paper perched on the edge of the bathtub, and after a brief inspection of the kitchen cabinets to sate his increasing curiosity revealed a couple boxes of out-of-date crackers and not much else, he began to wonder just what it was that Graham used this house for.

A search of the second floor and the basement revealed neither answers nor the man himself.

Randy returned to the first floor and stared out one of the rear windows at the barn. A crooked weathervane in the shape of a rooster sat at the pinnacle of its roof, creaking back and forth in a light breeze. The windows appeared dark. They reminded him of eyes.

The barn. That was it.

Lupe was in the barn.

Goosebumps spread across his flesh, but they were quickly dispelled by a reassuring warmth that rose up within him.

Be brave, my child.

Randy nodded and swallowed a knot of fear. He couldn't lose his head now.

Lupe's life depended on it.

———————◆———————

RANDY LEFT the house through the front door and took slow steps around the side toward the barn. An old hand pump sat to the left of the barn next to some wooden pallets overgrown with weeds. None of this looked like a place Graham Willard would call home. He'd probably gotten the property for cheap and left it as it was, nice porch swing, junk, and all.

The ground had been disturbed behind the hand pump and pallets. The rectangular areas of overturned earth did not make Randy think that Graham had been planning on starting a vegetable garden. He caught sight of a newly-dug pit that had earth piled next to it and quickly averted his gaze.

He wondered if he had just seen his own grave.

His feet stopped in front of the barn door and refused to continue onward.

Father, give me strength.

He pictured Lupe as she was on the day he proposed to her. She had been as radiant as an angel. He didn't know what would happen to her if he didn't survive this. Phil and Allison might take care of her. They were good people. And it wasn't as though his and Lupe's parting would last an eternity. They would be united again in heaven—not as husband and wife, but as children of God.

The part of him that was pure instinct told him he needed to run away before he ended up with a bullet in his head. The part of him that wanted to protect Lupe from harm made him step forward.

After all, there was no guarantee he would die today.

The barn door hung on sliders. A rusty green sign emblazoned with the John Deere logo hung crookedly in the center of it from a single bolt.

He counted to ten before dragging it open.

The barn breathed the smells of dust, mold, and old straw at him.

He stepped inside.

In the spill of light entering the large, open space from half a dozen windows, he could see a figure at the far end of the barn bound to one of three central posts supporting the second-floor loft.

His heart nearly sprang into his throat. The slender figure had been wrapped in some kind of cowl so he couldn't see her face. Her back faced him; her head slumped to one side like she'd fallen asleep sitting up.

Bile rose from his stomach. Graham had done something horrible to Lupe—conked her on the head, injected her with a tranquilizer, what did he know?—and now she sat bound and seemingly as lifeless as a corpse.

It was so silent that Randy could hear his pulse's pounding rhythm in his ears. "Hey," he whispered.

Lupe gave no indication she had heard him.

He wanted to rush up and untie her but sensed he should wait since Graham had not yet chosen to show his face. "I'm here now, Graham," he said. "Are you going to come out?"

He thought about his options. He could try to negotiate his and Lupe's freedom or, if Graham became violent, Randy could try

304 | J.S. BAILEY

to injure Graham so that Randy and Lupe could escape with their lives intact. After all, harming another in self-defense did not constitute murder.

For a second he thought he heard something creaking up in the loft, but no reply came. Rats, he decided. The place might be full of them.

Without warning, the barn door rolled shut with a loud thump.

He whirled around to see who had joined him, but the unexpected change in lighting hadn't given his eyes a chance to adjust. Someone stood by the door just a few yards away from him. "Stay right there," he said.

Randy obeyed, and the man approached him with maddening slowness. His features came into view as he passed through the light coming in through one of the windows. Randy recognized him as the gunman from Father Laubisch's house.

He wondered if Father Laubisch was here, too. The priest could have been one of the rats up in the loft.

"Who are you?" Randy asked.

"First things first," the gunman said, flashing him an arrogant grin. He dropped the cigarette he'd been holding and ground it into the dirt with his foot. "Put your hands behind your back."

Randy's grip tightened around the knife's handle. "No."

"No? I see you're not familiar with my rules. If you don't set your knife on the floor and do as I ask, the girl dies. And don't even think of rushing me. If you think killing me is going to guarantee her safety, you're sorely wrong."

Randy bit his lip. He could easily overtake the gunman and pin him to the ground, but because he didn't know how many people Graham may have enlisted as backup, he refrained from doing so for Lupe's sake.

"Very well," he said, and prayed for additional strength as he gently set the knife in the dirt.

Randy turned so his back faced the man and immediately regretted his decision when metal cuffs fastened around his wrists with an ominous click.

"Excellent," the gunman said. "The old man seems to have been right about you. Now come over here and lean your back against this post."

Before Randy could disable the gunman with an unexpected kick, the man grabbed his arm and jerked him toward the supporting post closest to the door. Randy sat and allowed himself to be tied to the pole with a length of rope just like Lupe on the other side of the barn.

She still hadn't moved. *Wake up,* he prayed. *Please wake up.*

When the younger man finished securing the rope so tightly that Randy could feel the fibers cutting into his arms, he took a few steps back and placed his hands on his hips, assessing him as one would a specimen in a zoo. "And to think I didn't believe him when he said you probably wouldn't put up a fight if your girl got involved. I guess you're a holier man than I thought."

"Who are you?" Randy repeated. The same cloud-like aura he'd picked up in his mind at the priest's house had returned, indicating that the gunman was not possessed by evil spirits but lived in friendly accord with them.

Such a person could not be cleansed by a Servant or any clergyman skilled with the ability to drive out spirits, which was perhaps one of the greatest tragedies of all.

"My name is John," the gunman said, "but everybody calls me Jack."

Knowing his name didn't quite answer Randy's question. "How did you get involved in all of this? What am I to you?"

Jack smiled. "A project."

"How do you know Graham?"

"Ah. About that." Jack paused as if collecting his thoughts. Then his eyes made an involuntary glance toward the loft. "You see, the old man had a daughter named Stephanie. I see you've heard of her. When she was eighteen her ever-understanding mother caught her in bed with a nice young man from church and threw her out of the house. She's been living in California ever since. She's got a couple of kids now but never bothered to marry either of their fathers. I'm her oldest.

"All my life I knew something was missing. No father, no family other than Mom and my sister. She told me all about the argument she'd had with her mother. She said that one thing she longed to do was see her daddy again since she didn't get the chance to tell him goodbye. When I heard his name in the news a year ago, I knew it was time to go find him. I wanted to meet him before he got too old and dropped dead."

"I still don't understand why you've gotten involved in all of *this*."

The young man shrugged. "Because I wanted to."

A cold voice whispered in Randy's ear. *Mind your own business,* Servant. *He's ours, not yours.*

Jack grinned at him as if he'd heard the voice too, and Randy had the sudden impression that the guy's mouth was full of fangs.

Randy cleared his throat. "Where's Graham now?"

"Oh, somewhere," Jack said evasively. "He had to run out and grab a few things before he got started. I think he's beginning to slip a little in his old age." He winked. "I like talking to you, Randy. I've been spying on you and your girlfriend now for months, and it's nice to finally meet you face to face. It's funny, though. You don't look like someone who could be a servant of God."

"Are we supposed to look a certain way?" Now Randy's hands were going to sleep. He flexed them to keep his circulation going.

Jack cocked his head to one side. "I don't know. A little less rough around the edges, maybe. You look like someone who could do well in a fight. Has anyone ever punched you in the face?"

Before Randy could reply that yes, he had indeed been punched and preferred not to relive the experience, Jack's fist slammed into Randy's jaw so hard that the bone made a sickening pop. His stomach gave a lurch and tears welled up in his eyes, though he refused to let any fall.

"What?" Jack asked in a tone of false innocence. "Aren't you going to defend yourself? You must not really be tough at all."

Randy closed his eyes and leaned his head back against the pole. He had already learned the answers he'd sought the most, so it was no use continuing to speak.

But Jack wasn't finished. A sharp kick in the shin sent Randy's eyes flying open. "No time for that, sleepyhead," Jack taunted. "We've got to keep you awake for the fun."

Yes. Because tying innocent people to poles and torturing them was just a barrel of laughs.

"What?" Jack asked again. "You mean you aren't having a good time? I'm surprised you haven't asked me anything about *her* yet." Jack jerked his head toward Lupe. "She's just sleeping, you know. Nothing the old girl can't handle."

Randy began to strain against the rope in the hope it would break, but he might as well have been bound with steel cable.

"What did you do to her?" he asked in a low voice, fearing that if he spoke any louder his emotions might betray him.

"I could ask you the same thing." Jack's eyes glimmered, and Randy didn't like it. Never in his life had he felt so mocked, so *used*; except for all the times when . . .

No. He wouldn't even think of it.

He said, "I'm not the one who hurt her."

"Sure you are. Graham told me all about the two of you. You made her feel like a sinner with your false piety. Poor girl's come close to suicide more times than you could count, and it's all your fault."

Randy felt his blood come close to boiling. "*False* piety?"

Jack began to pace leisurely back and forth across Randy's field of vision. "I know what happened to you when you were a little boy. Graham said that's why you grew up in foster care. I for one think you enjoyed it. Maybe you're even the one who brought it all on. You just tattled so you could get attention and everyone could know what you'd done. And now you try to act like you're some holy man. I know better, though. Inside you're as full of sick desires as your good old daddy."

Randy's vision narrowed to the point where all he could see was Jack's gloating face, and he could feel the rope fibers cutting into his arms as he tugged against his bindings. His face burned with both shame and rage, and he knew that if he really was able to untie himself, he would beat Jack with his bare hands until he killed him.

Jack paused, still wearing that little smile. "I can see I'm getting to you. Mother always said I had a way with words. As I was saying, you made the woman you were supposed to love feel like killing herself because you convinced her that the things she did as a teenager were evil, when really all she was doing was following her female instincts."

Lies. They were all lies. Lupe had already been full of remorse when they met, and it was Randy who had reassured her that she would be forgiven if she gave her heart and soul over to God.

He closed his eyes and let out a long breath. Jack was undoubtedly part of Graham's plan. He knew his daughter's child was as warped as he was—maybe even more so, considering his demonic partnership—and had decided to use Jack to try to break his spirit before Graham came along to break his body.

"Where is Graham, really?" he asked. "I'd like to talk to him."

Jack took one step in reverse and crossed his arms. "Don't you like this little chat we're having? I think it's quite fun. I've learned more about you since you walked through that door than I ever could have learned by following you around." He placed a finger on his chin and pretended to study him. "You're a very angry man, did you know that? You hate me because you think I'm the polar opposite of everything you could ever have hoped to be."

Yes, Randy was angry right now, but the righteous anger he felt toward this impossible human being was far from being a sin.

It was what he might do with that anger that could potentially condemn him.

"You didn't answer my question," he said, struggling to keep his tone even.

Jack laughed. "I already told you he isn't here yet. He'll arrive when he arrives."

The soft creak he'd heard earlier sounded again from the loft. Randy narrowed his eyes. "I think he's here already."

The Spirit murmured an affirmation inside of him. Randy was right. Graham Willard, his surrogate grandfather and former friend, was hiding up on the second floor of the barn because he was too afraid of Randy to confront him.

Choosing to ignore Jack for the moment, Randy turned his head in the direction of the sound and called out. "Graham, get down here. You need to come look me in the eye yourself."

A cough issued through the boards that were his ceiling and Graham's floor.

Jack's grin broadened. Randy wondered what other lies he'd been spouting for the last few minutes. Maybe nothing he'd said was true at all.

The movement upstairs ceased.

"Come on, Graham. Be a man."

Still, nothing. Jack let out a snicker.

"At least tell me why all of this had to happen."

At first Randy thought that Graham would continue to ignore him, but then, ever so softly, the sound of shoes scuffing against floorboards issued from above at a sound barely above a whisper. Randy's eyes were drawn to a set of rickety wooden stairs in the back corner of the barn. A stooping figure appeared on them moments later.

Graham paused on the bottom step as if waiting for some signal to continue his approach. Could Graham really be that afraid of him? What exactly did he fear?

Jack turned toward the new arrival. "Aren't you going to do what the man says, *Grandpa*? He wants to talk to you."

Graham took one more step. Now he was standing on the barn's dirt floor. He held something in one hand but Randy couldn't see what it was. A weapon of some sort, he supposed. But with Graham acting so skittish, Randy began to suspect that Jack would be the one to ultimately kill him if things came to that.

Father, protect us.

"Graham," Randy said, "earlier today somebody told me you've killed at least sixty-three people. He might have been lying, for all I know, but I just wondered why you chose that path. I know you used to have a pure heart. If you didn't, God never would have chosen you as one of his Servants."

He fell silent to see if Graham would object to anything he'd just said. Graham's silence seemed to indicate that the things Father Laubisch told him were at least somewhat true.

Randy continued. "The person who told me about your murders said the first person you killed died in an accident. He said you became addicted to killing people. I just wondered how you progressed from one to the other, because as much as I think about it, I still can't understand why anyone would do that."

Graham took a couple of steps closer and stuffed whatever he was holding into one of his back pockets. The shuffle that Randy always associated with his walk had vanished. "I don't know that you could."

This was more progress than Randy had expected to make. "Do *you* understand?"

Another few beats of silence. "Yes."

"How did it happen? Who did you kill the second time?"

Now Jack himself appeared intrigued. Looked like good old Grandpa hadn't given him his full life story, either.

Graham cleared his throat. His eyes darted between the two of them, uncertain. "It was my grandmother. She was dying of cancer. I wanted to bring her comfort. I wanted to know what she'd see as she was dying. I was afraid that death wouldn't be as glorifying as I'd hoped."

To Randy's surprise, Jack's face paled a shade or two. "You killed your *grandmother*?"

"Yes, Jack, my grandmother." A biting edge filled Graham's voice. "If you'd seen her, you wouldn't have wanted her to suffer anymore, either. Most of my family couldn't even stand to look at her at that point, much less help her. And don't keep looking at me like that. I helped her overdose on pain pills. She was all too willing, and when the family found out what happened they assumed she'd done it herself. I'd wanted to smother her with a pillow but realized I wouldn't have been able to ask her about anything she might be seeing."

Jack wrinkled his nose. Funny how the murder of a distant grandmother of his could have this reaction in him. "And just what did she see?"

"I don't know. She started seizing, and all I heard was the word 'shadows.' Not very helpful, I'm afraid. But I was able to find peace within myself knowing she was no longer in pain."

"Can you find peace knowing you've murdered so many others?" Randy asked as he forced bile back down his throat. He had lived in Graham's house for years. The man had opened his doors for him and welcomed him in like a member of his own family since Randy had none of his own. They'd had parties together and worshiped together and had many long conversations sitting on the back patio in the evenings talking about theology and philosophy while Graham drank his Bloody Marys and Randy sipped on red wine, yet at the same time Graham had harbored this secret monster within him.

Maybe Graham didn't think he had done anything wrong.

Graham was slow to respond. "I was always at peace, Randy. Until I met you."

"What are you talking about?"

The old man's legs carried him away from the bottom of the stairs, past the unconscious Lupe, and finally halted about six feet away from Randy.

Randy's heart nearly stopped when he looked at his old friend's face.

Tears filled the old man's eyes. Graham Willard, the man who wanted to murder him, was crying.

34

BOBBY WATCHED as Phil pulled up an Oregon property search webpage and typed "upton david" into the search bar. Bobby crossed his fingers and held his breath.

A list of six properties came up on the screen when Phil hit enter. One was owned by a "David P. Upton" and another David had the middle initial F, but the rest of the houses, which were all in or not far from Autumn Ridge, had owners with no middle initial at all.

"I'm going to ignore these," Phil said, pointing out the first two.

Of the remaining four properties owned by men with that name, one was a certain bungalow on a certain Fir Street. "That's me," Bobby said, feeling queasy. If Graham had a penchant for killing people, why had Bobby and Caleb been spared? Had Graham just not gotten around to doing them in yet?

But wait a minute. Caleb had disappeared. Could Graham have forced him to write the note left on the refrigerator door so Bobby would think he was still alive?

It still didn't explain why Caleb's place of employment claimed he had never worked there, or how there had been no furniture indentations in Caleb's bedroom carpet.

Unless Caleb and Graham were working together. Graham might have sent the college student off on some mission that had required him to move.

But Bobby refused to allow himself to believe that. Caleb may have been aloof at times, but he would never willingly assist a murderer.

"Look here," Phil said, his attention focused on the screen. "One of them is on a Hidden Valley Road. I think I know where that is." He opened a new tab and pulled up Google Maps. He copied the Hidden Valley address and pasted it into the directions search. A green pin appeared on the map, and Phil zoomed in with a few clicks of the mouse. "And that road meets up with Route 89. This has to be where Graham told Randy to go."

Bobby stared at the thin threads of roads squiggling across the satellite image. Something didn't sit right with him. "Go back to the property page," he said as the brief glance he'd taken of the address list swam in his mind's eye. "I thought I saw something."

Phil did as he requested and muttered a soft curse when the four potential addresses appeared on the screen a second time.

One of Graham's other properties was listed as being on Route 89 itself. Phil copied and pasted that address into the directions search. The green pin jumped to a higher point on the screen. "It's just a few miles northeast of the other one."

"Which one do you think it is?"

"I don't know. We could check them out one at a time."

Bobby feared that if they chose to go to one specific house, it would be the wrong one and they would barge in on innocent renters who would then call the cops, preventing them from reaching the other house in time.

Phil fell silent. Then, "Is that intuition of yours telling you anything?"

"Only that we're all kind of in a bit of trouble."

"I don't think anyone would need your ability to figure that out."

"Sorry."

"If we had your car, we could have split up. I take a peek at one house while you do the other."

The very thought of investigating one of the houses by himself made Bobby's chest constrict with fear. Even though he had longed to become Rescue Man during his prepubescent days, in truth he was no hero. If he barged his way into the place where Lupe was imprisoned, he would end up dead, too.

"Bobby?"

He jerked his gaze up to discover that Phil was analyzing him with his stony gaze again. Heat washed over Bobby's face, and he said, "I wish I could help, but I don't think there's anything I can do. I can't control my premonitions any more than I can control the wind."

"It might be that way now, but it doesn't have to stay that way."

"What do you mean?"

A smirk tugged at the corner of Phil's mouth. "Even the most gifted person has to work to refine whatever it is he or she's been given. Try to focus and clear your head, because we're running out of time."

Bobby forced himself to count to ten before speaking. Phil was the only ally he had right now. He couldn't afford to say something that would widen the rift between them again. "I know we are, but I honestly don't have a clue which house they're at."

A pleading look entered Phil's eyes, and his jaw tightened. "Bobby, please listen. When I was a kid I had a knack for patching up people's cuts and scrapes and helping relieve their pain by touching and praying over them. I couldn't always control it. But I practiced as much as I could, and by the time I became the Servant my ability had been honed so well that I could even bring back some from the brink of death."

"Why can't you do it anymore?"

"That's something we can discuss another day." Phil placed his hands on Bobby's shoulders. "Look at me."

Bobby didn't want to, but he did anyway.

Phil gave him a piercing stare, and for some reason Bobby had the sudden impression that Phil's antagonism had not been a manifestation of dislike at all, but one of intense and constant worry buried deep inside the former Servant's psyche. "I need for you to relax. Can you do that?"

The amount of adrenaline coursing through Bobby's veins would have had him doing cartwheels if he knew how to execute them. He shook his head.

"Then close your eyes."

Bobby did as he was told and took in a ragged breath. "Sometimes when I try to relax I pretend I'm on a beach."

"Then do that."

"Now?"

He heard Phil let out an irritated breath. "If you don't think you can do it, I'll help. The waves are rolling in. The sun is out, warming you through and through. You're lying in a beach chair. A pretty woman is sitting next to you laughing at something you've just said."

His mind immediately conjured an image of him and Carly lying in the chair together.

Bobby reached up and gave the collar of his shirt a nervous tug.

"The gulls are flying overhead. The waves are still rolling in, lapping against the sand. You're becoming more relaxed and you're sure you're about to fall asleep right there with that pretty woman at your side. There's nothing wrong in the world. Everything is going to be okay. You and everyone you love are safe."

Even though Bobby found Phil's version of the mental exercise to be somewhat silly, he felt some of the tension leave his muscles. He cracked a grin. "Sounds nice."

"That's because it is. Now keep your eyes closed. I'm walking you over to the couch, and you're going to lie down."

Bobby allowed himself to be led to the couch. He sat down on its edge and eased himself onto his back, settling into the cushions as comfortably as he could.

"You've never been at peace like this," Phil continued, his voice becoming as gentle as the waves Bobby imagined lapping on the shore of this imaginary beach. "You feel as though you're floating on a cloud. You're at peace. And if you listen very closely, you can hear the voice of God himself saying he loves you and everything will be fine as long as you keep listening and trust in him."

Bobby hadn't thought it possible, but he could actually see himself on the beach as if he were there that very moment. He wasn't even sure if he heard Phil's voice anymore—it seemed to have melded with the sounds of the cawing birds, the salty breeze, and the rolling surf. But no matter. He was at peace, dream or not, and everything would be okay.

"Bobby?"

He looked up out of the beach chair. The sky overhead was a deeper blue than any he could ever remember. Carly had vanished. A heavyset man stood over him now, but since the sun hung in the sky behind him, he appeared as a featureless silhouette. "What?"

"I need you to listen to me." The voice held a hint of familiarity, but unlike the gravelly voice of Graham Willard, this one brought him an inexplicable comfort.

He squinted to try and see better. "I'm listening."

"You've got to have faith."

For a moment Bobby felt bewildered. "What are you talking about?"

"You may have faith in God, but you've got to have faith in yourself and your abilities, too. You were a mess when I died. You couldn't stand the thought of harm coming to anyone you knew again."

Bobby felt tears roll down his cheeks as he realized the identity of the speaker. "Dad? Is this heaven? I don't understand how—"

Ken Roland cut him off. "Your pain let you develop a gift you can use to help people. You've got to have faith that your gift will save others when you need it to the most."

"But I don't—"

"Promise me!" His voice became pleading—a tone Bobby had never heard the man use in life.

His father's seriousness unnerved him. "Promise you what?"

"That you'll do exactly what Phil Mason tells you. He knows what he's talking about. Right now Randy and Lupe need for you to trust in him."

His father was asking him to do the impossible. "But I don't know how to do it. What am I supposed to do?"

"Have faith, Bobby. That's all we ask."

Bobby's anxiety returned for an unwanted encore. He just had to believe he could use his ability to find Randy and Lupe, and he would be able to locate them?

"Promise," his father repeated. He took a step forward, and his facial features came into view. His eyes were two deep pools of wisdom, and he was smiling.

Bobby felt a slight boost of confidence. "I—I promise."

And with that, the beach and Ken Roland vanished, and Bobby found himself staring at the white ceiling of Randy Bellison's living room.

Phil had taken a seat in a chair across from Bobby, still watching him with utmost curiosity.

Bobby willed his body to return to that peaceful state. Randy hadn't broken his promise to Graham, and likewise he felt it would be wrong to break his promise to his father, even if the man had only been a figment of his imagination brought on by Phil's hypnotic words.

He imagined his limbs were turning into jelly. He slowed his breathing.

All he had to do was believe. How hard could it be?

Harder than not believing, that was for sure.

I'm going to find them.

His mind tried to rebel against him. The clock was winding down to zero. Even if they left for the right house this very moment, it might already be too late. The houses were both miles and miles from here. They could get pulled over for speeding. They could suffer an accident along the way and be killed, injured, or severely delayed in reaching their destination.

No. I'm going to find them.

318 | J.S. BAILEY

He pictured both Randy and Lupe in turn, even though he'd barely been acquainted with the latter. They would die unless Bobby jumped in and saved them like a skinny-armed Rescue Man who had a kitchen knife as a weapon and no cape.

All at once, a strange revelation blossomed in his mind.

"Well?" Phil asked.

"I don't understand," Bobby said, trying to decipher the information he had been given by the unseen power that had aided him so many times before. "They're at both houses."

"I find it hard to believe that both Randy and Lupe have developed the ability to be in two places at the same time. Try again."

"No, no, I don't mean that. I mean one of them is at one house, and the other is at the other house. But I can't tell who's where."

Blood drained from Phil's face like watercolors bleeding out of a wet canvas.

Then Bobby understood.

Graham had no intention of reuniting Randy and Lupe.

He had led Randy into a trap.

———◆———

LUPE HAD been shut away for centuries.

At least that's what it felt like. Graham had bound her wrists with zip ties, and they dug into her skin. Fortunately he hadn't tied her to anything, so she was free to walk around in the space as she pleased. Granted, she couldn't reach out and catch herself if she should stumble over something, so she took baby steps. Might as well measure the place while she waited for Randy to arrive.

The wall in which the door had been set measured roughly fifteen feet across. She leaned her full weight into the door to test the strength of the latch holding it closed, but it only gave a fraction of an inch. She would need to be the size of a bodybuilder to break it.

She tried to count her steps as she traveled along the next wall, but she tripped over an item that had been leaning against it and fell. Something clattered to the floor. A tool, perhaps? Maybe a shovel.

SERVANT | 319

She blanched. If it was a shovel, Graham might have used it to bury some of his victims.

Lupe completed her circuit of the building, encountering several other tools and even some crates along the way. Her initial thoughts had proved correct. This building was much too small to be a barn. Graham only used it to store equipment and prisoners.

Suddenly a memory flashed in her mind. When she tried to break the window in the mudroom, she had noticed a shed sitting a distance away from the house, but that information had borne no significance to her at that moment so she had forgotten about it.

It probably didn't mean anything. Lots of people had sheds at their houses. You had to have some place to stick your mower and four-wheeler and murder weapons, right? And for all she knew, Graham might have sheds at all of his houses.

She sat down on the floor and rubbed her head against the wall to try to get the blindfold off. It bothered her that Graham had made her leave it on. After all, what did he have to hide?

"COME ON. Let's go." Bobby rushed to the door, Phil close behind him.

"Are you going to remember where those houses are?" Phil already had his key out and passed Bobby as he dashed to the parked Taurus.

Bobby had taken mental snapshots of the satellite-view map and committed the addresses to memory, so he was good to go. "Yeah. You?"

"I think so."

They clambered into the car and fumbled with seatbelts for a second before Phil jammed the key into the ignition. They tore off down the long driveway so fast that gravel sprayed out from under the tires.

"We're stopping at my place so you can use my other car," Phil said. "I'll take the house on Route 89. You can take Hidden Valley. And try not to do anything stupid."

Bobby nodded. The fact they were going at all might have been seen as stupid by some. Who were they to come to the rescue? Despite the fact that Phil obviously had a concealed carry permit, Bobby had the feeling that the man was no more qualified to locate and free the couple than he himself was.

The registered nurse and the rookie janitor. A superhero team certain to strike crippling fear into the hearts of evil men.

Bobby didn't want for him and Phil to split up, but they had no other choice.

He shivered.

Bobby's heart had taken up occupancy in his throat when Phil whipped the car into the driveway of a well-kept ranch style house that was by Bobby's estimation only about a mile from the rental bungalow he'd already decided to move out of as soon as this ordeal concluded.

It made him sick to think he'd been funding Graham's twisted lifestyle for the past year. It seemed as if fate had latched onto Bobby's life with twisted fingers and turned it into a macabre joke. *Here you go, kid—a nice little house that has everything a guy like you could have asked for. Too bad you'll be helping a serial killer pay for his groceries.*

Phil left the engine running and went into the house, returning moments later with a different key. Bobby got out and took it from him. "Where's the car?"

"Hang on." He leaned back inside the Taurus and punched the garage door opener clipped to the sun visor.

An archaic Buick Century with flaking blue paint sat inside the garage waiting to be used. Bobby climbed inside, hoped it wouldn't die on him, gave Phil a solemn nod, and backed out.

As he pulled onto the street, the garage door closed and Phil followed him.

Bobby displayed the zoomed-in Oregon map inside his head and pictured the ancient Buick as a tiny blue dot marking his position. He was traveling northeast out of Autumn Ridge when Phil got stopped at a light somewhere behind him.

He couldn't worry about Phil. The man could take care of himself.

The town limits soon gave way to forest, and the homes he saw grew further and further apart. *Isolation*, whispered a voice. *The place where no one will hear your screams.*

He'd gone four miles into the evergreen forest when the tapping began.

It started as a single pebble that pinged against the windshield. Bobby assumed it had been kicked up by the vehicle in front of him so he gave it no more than a passing thought.

Half a minute later, it happened again—but the other vehicle had pulled so far ahead of him that he didn't see how it was possible for the second pebble to have been flung from beneath its tires.

Fear nearly loosened his bladder when he realized just what it was he heard.

Though part of him longed to shove the pedal to the floor to get to the house as fast as he could, he eased off of it a bit and allowed the other car to disappear around an upcoming bend.

Tap. Tap-tap.

"You can't scare me!" he said through clenched teeth as he struggled to focus on the road.

He began to understand why the unseen entities might be trying to frighten him. Something evil must have been watching him with hidden, baleful eyes; maybe even for years as they'd done with Joanna. When he went to Randy for the job interview, the spirit or spirits had not liked it. They tried to scare Bobby away from the man, and it had very nearly worked.

The fact that they didn't want the two to meet up seemed to imply that his and Randy's paths had been destined to cross for the greater good, whatever that might turn out to be. The spirits had tried to scare Bobby away a second time by flinging rocks and cans at the bungalow, but their plan backfired when Bobby chose to confront Randy about the "poltergeists" by showing up unannounced at the guy's house.

And then Caleb vanished, making Bobby go to Randy again since he had nowhere else to turn. Strangely, Bobby had heard no sign of the evil spirits from the moment he'd discovered Caleb's absence. It was almost as if his roommate had taken the spirits with him.

Until now. Now they were trying to stop him from reaching the house where either Randy or Lupe was prisoner.

Some larger pebbles sprayed against the windshield. Bobby did his best to ignore them. Keep his eyes on the road, that's what he needed to do. If he maintained his current speed, he could be at the house in twenty minutes.

What could it all mean? Why would the evil spirits—the demons—want him to stay away from Randy? Did they not want an outsider to find out about the Servants? Randy's job was to free people from demonic possession, and Bobby supposed that no evil spirits would take kindly to that.

But what did any of that have to do with *him*?

As he steered the Buick through another bend in the road, a strange revelation hit him.

If evil spirits had taken it upon themselves to cause him harm and distress, then conversely there would be good spirits in the world whose job was to protect him.

His missing roommate's face flashed briefly in his mind.

Bobby was so startled he almost lost control of the wheel. *No.* Caleb was a human being. He didn't talk much and kept to himself and liked to read about quantum mechanics. If . . . if an *angel* had been living in his house for the past year, wouldn't there have been more Bibles and fewer textbooks lying around?

Yet Caleb arrived in his life just when Bobby needed him to. He had been there to offer unbiased words of support. He kept his distance, but he was always there.

Heck, he had even gotten Bobby his new job.

And then he disappeared. And then the evil spirits had seemingly taken a vacation, too. Could Caleb have been working to fend them off for the past few days? If so, where was he now?

The barrage of pebbles ceased, but now something knocked around like a hammer under the hood. It didn't mean a demon was trying to ruin the car. The Buick had to have been at least twenty-five years old. This might have just been its time to break down.

The temperature gauge showed a slowly overheating engine. Maybe the car was leaking coolant all over the road. He looked in the rearview mirror, but the dwindling lanes behind him looked bare of telltale drips indicating a leak.

He wished he'd paid more attention when his father tried to teach him how to take care of a car.

He lifted his foot off the gas and allowed the car to coast a short distance, but it didn't stop the engine's temperature from rising. Going at this rate, he wouldn't last another mile before the thing went kaput.

He decided it was probably a good time to start praying.

"You've got to give me a hand here," he said as he pulled the car off the side of the road onto the gravel shoulder. Better to make a brief stop than to keep going and fry Phil's car. "I know I've ended up in this situation for a reason, even though you don't seem to want me to know what it is. But I can't help Randy and Lupe if I don't have a way to get to them. So please make the engine cool off so I can keep going."

He suddenly perceived that words were not necessary for his prayer. He killed the engine (was that the right thing to do?) and bowed his head, sending out a wordless plea that seemed to leak from every pore of his being.

At Randy's house, he'd had to believe he could determine where Randy and Lupe were. Now he had to believe that God would heed his request.

At once, a cold thought intruded upon his own. *Go home. Get out of here. We don't want you.*

Though it terrified him to do so, Bobby forced himself to pray harder. He prayed for protection from those attempting to unnerve him. He prayed for Caleb (if his wild assumptions about his room-mate were indeed correct) to stand guard over not only him but Lupe and Randy as well.

A horn blared outside the window. He jerked his head up in time to see Phil fly by in his Taurus.

Bobby silently thanked Phil for not stopping to help. That's what the demons would want. Any attempt to delay both of them would only be for the demons' gain.

His eyes filled with tears. "Please help me!" he cried as he felt something icy claw at his mind like the bloody talons of a beast.

He thought of his father, who seemed to have been with him for real on the imaginary beach Phil conjured in his mind. "Dad, help me! Pray that they'll leave me alone!"

His hands clenched into fists around the steering wheel. He couldn't let despair overtake him. Randy had freed dozens of people from the clutches of evil. Surely God himself could free Bobby without Randy's intervention.

The knocking under the hood continued for several minutes before ceasing, but that might have just been because the engine was no longer running.

No. He had to *believe*. Worry and doubt were two negative forces that worked together like partners in crime to ensure that belief failed.

"The car's going to be fine," he whispered.

He cracked open an eyelid.

The needle on the temperature gauge crept its way back into the normal range.

Relief made his chest lighten.

He waited sixty seconds before turning the key in the ignition again.

The engine turned over with ease. He let it run for another minute to see what would happen, grateful when the knocking did not resume and the needle stayed put.

It may have been his imagination, but the air in the car suddenly felt lighter, as if a thick blanket had been flung off of him.

"God," he said, "if you get Randy and Lupe out of this alive, I'll do whatever you want me to do with my life. I'll become a missionary. I'll work at a soup kitchen. Anything. Just let them be okay."

He was rambling like a nutcase. He was too pleased with his fortune to care.

Bobby checked for oncoming traffic and pulled back onto the winding road.

Everything would be okay.

Hc believed it.

35

PHIL MASON was a man of many flaws. He knew this. His ever-understanding wife, Allison, knew this. Randy and the rest of their "family" knew this.

And right now he despised himself for it more than anything in the world.

As a child, he had known that God would call him to do something special with the gift he had been given, but now it seemed that God was finished with him. Some Servants kept their ability once the mantle was passed on to another and some had it fade over the years like color bleaching out of an old snapshot.

Phil's ability had faded practically into oblivion. The only things he could heal these days were paper cuts, and that was only on occasion.

Sometimes he wondered if he had unknowingly done something that made God take back the ability to heal wounds—perhaps it was punishment for Phil's long spells of doubt following his predecessor Martin's death. Allison assured him that God still had a plan for him, but in the darkness of night Phil would lie in bed wondering if God was nothing more than an overgrown, omnipotent child who liked to set his own toys on fire just to see what interesting things they might do as they burned.

So yes, Phil had some problems, but so did everyone to some extent. Apparently he'd been wrong to doubt the Roland kid who'd crashed into their lives like a meteor falling out of the sky. He'd been wrong plenty of times before, and this certainly wouldn't be the last.

He prayed that Bobby wasn't wrong about where Randy and Lupe might be found.

Route 89 was a winding road lined with the ubiquitous evergreens that populated the forests of the Pacific Northwest. When he rounded one particular curve, he saw that Bobby had pulled the Buick onto the shoulder and sat as still as a stone behind the wheel with his head down.

His heart nearly stopped. What was the kid doing? Had he run out of gas?

He wanted—no, he *needed*—to know why Bobby pulled off the road. But he couldn't. There just wasn't enough time.

To distract his thoughts from Bobby, he repeated the address of the rental house to himself. It was coming up soon—he could tell from the numbers on the mailboxes on the sparse houses he passed.

Hidden Valley Road, the place where Bobby was supposed to be headed, appeared on his left. He prayed Bobby would hurry up and get a move on so he could get there in time.

Minutes later, Phil spotted a mailbox emblazoned with the number of "David Upton's" Route 89 address.

He turned into the driveway. The house sat back a short distance from the road. It had two floors and judging from the modern architecture looked like it had been built sometime within the past twenty years. There wasn't a garage, but a shed shaped like a miniature brown barn with white trim sat in the back yard. The lawn had recently been cut. A few tall trees stood in the yard like sentinels keeping watch over the property. Behind the house, the southern Cascades rose up toward the sky.

It didn't look like anyone was here. But he had to trust Bobby's intuition. Somewhere on this property, either in the house or out, was one of Phil's two closest friends.

His hand automatically reached for his gun. He would only use it to kill if absolutely necessary. Perhaps that was a personal flaw as well.

He climbed out of the car and approached the house with caution, wishing he hadn't left his tote bag in Bobby's car at Father Laubisch's house. Knowing that harm could befall anyone at practically any given moment, he found comfort in having a full medical kit on hand in case some minor emergency arose.

Then he realized he had no real plan. His initial goal was to ascertain whether or not Randy or Lupe was really being kept prisoner here and then call the police so they could take care of the rest, but he could only do that if he went inside and scoped the place out.

He'd never been in law enforcement. His specialty was aiding patients, not sneaking into hostage situations like the biggest dunderhead on the planet. Even his little gun wouldn't likely save his life if he suddenly came under fire.

This stank.

He started praying.

———◆———

LUPE GAVE a start when she heard the crunch of gravel and the slam of a car door somewhere beyond the shed. She had gotten the blindfold off a few minutes before by repeatedly rubbing her head against the wall, but the shed had no windows, so she couldn't see who'd just arrived.

Her heart fluttered like a songbird trapped in a cage. "Randy?" she whispered. Then, "Randy! Help me! I'm in here!" Graham and his minion were probably there with him, but she didn't care. "Randy!"

———◆———

PHIL HAD been trying to peer into one of the first-floor windows when a muffled shout somewhere close by made the hairs lift up on the back of his neck. He couldn't tell if it had come from within the house or not, so he held his breath and kept listening.

There. It came again. The voice was female, and it issued from somewhere to his left.

Relief flooded his veins. *Lupe.* He turned toward the sound of her voice and laid his gaze upon the wooden shed.

He broke into a run and arrived in front of the shed in less than ten seconds. "Lupe, it's me," he said, throwing a glance over his shoulder to make sure nobody was sneaking up behind him. "I'm going to get you out of here."

Lupe spewed out a string of Spanish words that Phil didn't understand. "Phil, you've got to watch out for Graham! Randy's supposed to come here, and Graham is going to kill him!"

"I think it's just the two of us right now," he said, figuring now wasn't the time to tell her that Randy wouldn't be coming here at all. He saw that the shed door had been padlocked shut. "All right. I need you to go to the far right corner of this shed, as far away from the door as you can."

"Why? What are you doing?"

"I'm going to shoot around the lock and get you out."

A pause. "Your right or my right?"

"My right." Then, just to be sure she didn't misunderstand him in her traumatized state, he walked around the side of the small building and banged on the wall outside of where he wanted her to go. "Right here. You got that?"

He thought he heard her sniffling, and the sound of it stabbed him in the heart. If it were Allison in there instead of Lupe, he didn't think he would have been able to keep his head long enough to do what was necessary to free her. "Yes," she said, her voice now inches away from him.

"Good. Now stay put until I've got the door open."

He returned to the front and fired one shot into the door and another into a shed wall on either side of the lock in order to weaken the integrity of the wood. Ears ringing, he gave the lock a swift kick and felt the wood start to splinter. Five more kicks, and the wood where the metal latch had been screwed into the door gave way.

Thank you, God.

He pulled the door open.

Lupe leapt up from where she'd crouched in the corner and barreled at him, looking as jubilant as a convict newly freed from a wrongful imprisonment. "My hands!" she said. "Can you untie them for me?"

She turned, and he saw that Graham had fastened her wrists together with two linked orange zip ties. "I've got scissors in one of the first-aid kits in my back seat," he said. "Come on." He started back toward the car but halted when he realized she wasn't following. "Lupe?"

She was staring at the shed, her face lined with concern. "He tricked me," she said in a soft voice. "He drove me out of here and took me right back so I'd think he was taking me to Randy."

"Can we discuss this in the car? We're running out of time."

Wordlessly, Lupe turned from the shed and followed him to the Taurus. Phil threw open the back passenger side door, tossed aside the blanket still lying on the floor, and popped open the first kit he saw. He rummaged through rolls of gauze and withdrew the tiny medical scissors in triumph. "Here you go. Lupe?"

Lupe had stepped away from the car and was gazing uncertainly at the end of the driveway.

A car had turned off the road and was coming toward them. As it pulled up and stopped beside Phil's Taurus, he saw that Father Laubisch sat behind the wheel.

A mixture of anger and fear coursed through him when the rogue priest climbed out and cast his gaze their way. Phil stepped in front of Lupe to protect her, tucked the scissors into his pocket, and raised his gun.

"Stop right where you are," he said.

Father Laubisch raised his hands. He had exchanged his gardening clothes for his black priest's garb. "Mr. Mason, please. Hear me out."

"I don't have time for this. I ought to shoot you right where you stand for your part in all this. Don't look so shocked. We *know*."

The priest appeared stricken. "I—I'm not collaborating with him. Far from it. The man on the porch . . . he was watching the house from the old shop across the street. He does that to make certain I don't try to pull anything. He wanted you to know he means business."

"Means business?" Phil gave a hollow laugh. "So he pretended to kill you so we'd be afraid of him. Makes perfect sense."

"He's a very bad man," Father Laubisch said somewhat lamely. "He was going to kill me if I didn't go along with what he wanted me to do."

"And what about now? Did he tell you to come here and check on Lupe?"

The priest's face darkened. "As a matter of fact, it was my full intention to let her out while the others are distracted and take her to the police station. I wasn't aware you would be here, too."

Phil smelled a rat. "I don't believe a word you've just told me." He kept his gun trained on the man and used his other hand to fish his cell phone out of his pocket.

"Phil," Lupe whispered. "Aren't you going to cut the ties off of me?"

She wasn't going to give up, not even when a sociopathic priest stood just feet away from them. He put his phone in his pocket, gestured for Lupe to step closer, and snipped both zip ties.

She brought her hands in front of her and began rubbing one of her wrists.

Phil continued. "I'm going to call the police. I'm fairly certain I know where Graham is right now. But what I don't know is what to do about you."

"I'm going to hand myself over. God knows I deserve it," Father Laubisch said in a soft tone, and left it at that.

"Good," Phil said.

He called 911. Fortunately Randy wasn't there to stop him.

36

RANDY OPENED his eyes and blinked a few times. His head felt groggy, and it was difficult to get a handle on his thoughts. Had he fallen asleep? He couldn't remember feeling tired. Strange. The last thing he could remember was . . .

"He's awake," a voice said at his shoulder.

His heart skipped a beat. Randy looked down at himself and discovered that his shirt had been removed, and that somebody had strapped him to a piece of plywood canted at a forty-five degree angle with his feet near the floor. His wrists were still tied and his arms were pinned beneath him, cramping from the unnatural position.

Directly across from him sat Lupe's motionless form.

This was not part of the plan.

Graham stood next to him holding a knife that looked as sharp as a surgical blade. The tears had vanished from his eyes.

Randy took that as a bad sign.

"I had to drug you," Graham explained. "I didn't think you would let Jack tie you down like this without a fight. Even a man of God like yourself will come to blows when his life is in danger."

Randy swallowed. His tongue felt like someone coated it in sand. "How long?"

"You've been out for no more than ten minutes."

It seemed longer, but such was the way of slumber.

"Now I understand that you love Lupe Sanchez very much," the old man continued. "Am I right?"

Randy couldn't remove his gaze from his fiancée, who was still wrapped in the cowl so tightly he couldn't even see a glimpse of her hair or skin. He was starting to wonder if Graham had killed her already.

He nodded.

"I'm going to give you the opportunity to live. Think about that. It's always been believed that if the Servant should die without a successor, evil will reign free in the world for the next eighteen years. Think of all the lives you'll save if you survive. Souls will be freed. Good deeds will be done." He paused. "Only one of you can live. You or Lupe. Lupe or you. Is saving one woman's life worth letting Satan win?"

Randy's blood ran cold. Graham was giving him an ultimatum too terrible for him to contemplate. Could he really let Graham kill Lupe if it meant he could go free? "Satan will never win."

Graham rolled his eyes. "I was a fool when I was a younger man. I thought we would be able to help people, but take one look at the world today and tell me what you see. Murders left and right. Rape. Abortions. Shootings. War. What you do is useless. Or is it?" He smiled. "That's for you to decide. Maybe you really are making a difference. Maybe we'll all go to hell in a hand basket the moment you croak. I don't know."

Amazingly, tears sprang to the old man's eyes again. "I loved you, Randy. You were the son I never had. Did you know? Some of my favorite times in these last few years were when we'd just sit down and talk about anything we wanted, and nobody was there to bother us. I miss that. I really do."

Randy gaped at him. Graham was truly, literally, off his rocker.

Graham continued. "You were always so good, humoring me like you did even when I knew I was bugging you half the time. But you were *too* good. I . . . I don't know. You made me remember what it was like." He grabbed his head with one hand and took in a ragged breath. "You made me jealous."

"Nice story, Grandpa," Jack said from Randy's right, "but can we get a move on?"

Graham waved a hand at him. "Let me finish. He wanted to know why, so I'm telling him. Randy, I told you I was at peace up until I met you. That was a lie. I'd only thought I was at peace. I'd listen to you praying each night. So earnest, so sincere. I remembered how it was back then, long before you were born. Feeling God's presence as strongly as if he were a flesh-and-blood human standing there holding my hand. I wanted to die to be with him like that again. But I was afraid to die. What might happen to me now? I don't know. I really don't know."

All of the possessed whom Randy had encountered during his career had visible signs that a demon tormented them. He alone could see its writhing black aura inside his mind and could literally feel the evil pouring off of them.

Graham couldn't be possessed. He had no aura, shadowy or black.

"You were too good," Graham said. A slight slur entered his voice. "I loved you but I had to get rid of you. If I couldn't see you anymore, maybe it would have been easier to forget what it was like."

Jack let out a melodramatic yawn. "Any day now."

Graham snapped back to attention. "My mind wanders in my old age. Randy, I was going to tell you the rules of this game. I've always enjoyed games, you know."

Randy narrowed his eyes. "Rules?"

"Yes. If you choose to die at my hand and let Lupe live, I'm going to cut you. Not all at once, though. That would be too easy. If I cut you and you scream, your dearly beloved will be shot by Jack." He allowed a small smile.

Randy felt like he was going to throw up. "In the name of our lord Jesus Christ, leave him," he said in the sternest voice he could muster. A demon may not have been influencing Graham's behavior, but something certainly was.

A muscle twitched in Graham's face. "What was that?"

Randy locked his gaze upon the old man's. "Whatever you are, be gone from him."

There. For a split second, something black seemed to flutter in the centers of Graham's eyes. Randy had never seen anything like it before, and it was gone before he could get a better look.

Without warning, Graham's arm lashed out, and he dragged the blade horizontally across Randy's chest.

It wasn't a deep wound, but it bathed Randy's skin in fire and he let out an involuntary cry despite what would happen if he did.

"That was too bad," Graham said. "Jack?"

Randy blinked back tears as Jack strode over to Lupe and raised his gun to her head. "No. *No.* Don't hurt her."

Jack shrugged, changed course, and aimed the gun at Randy's leg.

The sound of the shot echoed throughout the room.

The pain was so great that the remains of Randy's last meal came up his throat.

I've failed you, Father.

The Spirit whispered a reply. *You have never failed me. You have done all that I hoped you would choose to do.*

Randy didn't understand. The ways of God were often strange to him, and this was no different.

He was crying now. Jack had returned to Lupe's side and lifted the gun again.

He shot her in the head through the top of the cowl.

Randy lost it then. He flailed against his bindings, willing them to pull apart, to break, to let him be free so he could be at her side one last time. To hold her close as they both died together.

He let out a feral cry when the bindings wouldn't budge. "Graham! This isn't you! Can't you hear me? Stop all of this!"

Graham's only answer was another swipe of the knife, this time starting at Randy's neck and traveling down to his navel. Randy's mind went numb. Graham had carved a cross into his flesh, a crude mockery of all he'd once stood for.

His breath came out in ragged bursts. He couldn't endure the pain for much longer. *Father, please don't let me die.*

He started losing his vision, and now his eyes played tricks on him. He'd always thought he would see angels or the spirits of loved ones as he died, but there, in the corner by the steps to the loft, stood Bobby Roland.

Both Graham and Jack were too focused on Randy to notice that a visitor stood behind them. Unfortunately, Randy would have to bring Bobby's presence to their attention in order to accomplish what he hoped to do next.

Randy opened his mouth and said something to the kid, hoping his voice was strong enough for Bobby to hear him.

BOBBY FOUND the house on Hidden Valley Road (or, rather, the driveway for it) and felt it would be prudent to leave the car parked along the shoulder so as not to alert his demented landlord to the fact he'd arrived.

He trudged through the trees, hoping to circle around to the house and come up from behind since Graham might have hired some eyes to watch out the front.

He gripped the knife. Terror had sent every droplet of moisture in his body straight to his bladder, and he knew that if anything startled him now, he would wet his pants.

The heroes in the stories he had loved as a child never had to go to the bathroom. They were too focused on saving lives to worry about anything as trivial as that. But it got so bad as he drew closer to the house that he could barely concentrate on his mission.

He gritted his teeth and relieved himself on a tree trunk. Some hero he was turning out to be.

He continued through the trees until he could see the rear of the house. Nothing about the structure indicated that Randy might be a prisoner somewhere inside. He couldn't call the cops just yet because for all he knew, Randy might be here alone.

A loud crack came from the two-story barn. He could hear a man screaming in agony, and the sound made his blood run cold. *Randy.*

Two startled robins took off from where they'd been pecking for worms in the dirt and flapped out of sight.

He was glad he'd chosen to empty his bladder. It would not have been comfortable walking around with wet undergarments clinging to his skin.

He yanked out his phone and dialed 911; his mission of determining if Randy was here and in danger now complete. "There's a hostage situation in the barn at 9632 Hidden Valley Road!" he blurted before the operator had the chance to ask what the emergency was. "I heard gunfire! You've got to hurry!"

The female operator squawked something in his ear, but he didn't take the time to listen. Common sense told him he should stay put and wait for the cavalry to arrive, but something compelled him to move forward.

He shoved his phone into his pocket and ran toward the barn door. But no. He couldn't go in that way. He had to be stealthier than that if he were to make it out alive.

The sound of a second gunshot nearly sent him into cardiac arrest. He shook off his brief paralysis and hurried onward.

He came up behind the barn, where two cars—a gray Nissan and a Chevy Cruze—had been parked beside a man-sized door fastened with a latch that slid over a metal loop, but no lock was hooked over it at the moment. Carefully, quietly, he swung the latch outward and cracked the door open, Randy's screams growing louder as a result.

The sight Bobby saw upon entering the shadowy corner of the barn rendered him immobile. Randy was tied down to a piece of plywood propped at an angle against a table. Graham and the gunman from the priest's house stood beside him, and a person wrapped up in a white hooded robe was tied to a wooden post that supported the ceiling.

The shape of a cross had been carved into Randy's chest, and blood ran down it in rivulets. Randy caught sight of Bobby and stared, confused, as if he wasn't sure that Bobby was truly there.

338 | J.S. BAILEY

The things Randy had told him over the past few days whirled through his mind like debris in a tornado. Randy was the Servant. If the Servant died without a replacement, evil would reign unchecked because there wouldn't be anyone with sufficient abilities alive to counteract it.

Randy had no replacement. The man hadn't had enough time to find one.

Bobby gnashed his teeth together. Nothing that he could do would save Randy's life at this point.

Randy had been sobbing, but now he grew strangely still. His eyes became filled with understanding. Very faintly he said, "Bobby, do you accept this mantle of Servitude and everything that is associated with it?"

Bobby felt faint. Was Randy mad? Of course he didn't want to accept it. Accepting it would be akin to insanity.

But Bobby couldn't let the man die knowing he had failed a task of such magnitude.

"Yes," he said, certain he was about to vomit. "I'll do it."

Randy smiled, and his eyes closed.

Two heads swiveled in his direction. The gunman lifted his weapon, and the man Bobby had known as Dave Upton wore one of the most stunned expressions Bobby had ever seen. "Bobby *Roland*? What are you—"

The sounds all seemed to fade away. Something was changing. The gunman started toward him, but slowly, as if time itself had grown tired and was winding down to rest.

A light blossomed in Bobby's mind. Something was in there. Inside of him. Reading him like an open book. It trickled into his veins and spread throughout his body with such a warmth that he felt as though he'd be able to set fire to objects with his very touch.

Suddenly a terror so great struck him that he knew he had to run. The presence—whatever it was—was looking into every corner of his being. It could see every negative thought that had ever passed through his mind. It brought forth memories of every fight, every transgression, every unkind word he'd spewed forth from his lips.

He felt like he was standing naked on a stage with every eye in the world watching him. He couldn't do this. He was a horrible person. A sinner. He couldn't let the presence glimpse who he really was inside.

He bolted out the door and into the woods. Maybe he could outrun it. But no. It was inside him. He couldn't outrun the presence any more than he could outrun the blood flowing through his veins.

Tears streamed like two rivers from his eyes. He had made a terrible mistake. He had become possessed, not with something evil, but something so holy and pure that he felt like a worm in comparison.

When he judged that he was far enough away from the barn, he sank to the ground beside a massive, moss-covered tree and hugged his arms to his chest. "I'm sorry!" he whispered. "I'm so, so sorry. I'm not worthy of any of this. Please forgive me. Please."

You are forgiven.

Bobby blinked as the memory of his past failings faded from his consciousness. He felt a new lightness in his chest, and his fear ebbed enough that he was able to think more clearly.

He glanced around the forest as if seeing it for the very first time. Wind rustled the branches overhead. Rays of sunlight fell through gaps between them, illuminating the brown bed of needles that lay upon the forest floor.

More tears came to his eyes. Bobby no longer felt alone. God was with him now—but God had always been with him. He just had the senses to feel it.

He stood up on wobbly legs as sirens wailed in the distance. He couldn't just stay here. He had to move. Do something. Anything.

The approaching sirens grew louder and then ceased. Flickering blue and red light danced over the trees. As happy as he was that Graham Willard would finally be apprehended, it still grieved him knowing Randy was gone.

A twig snapped behind him. Bobby whirled.

The gunman stood no more than fifteen feet away, grinning like the Cheshire Cat. "Hi, Bobby," he said. "Remember me?"

340 | J.S. BAILEY

He nodded. The fellow before him had come to the bungalow to help Graham with some repairs a couple of months ago. He'd said he was Dave's grandson, John.

A shadowy aura like a gray storm cloud pulsed inside Bobby's head, and Bobby knew it held some significance that he could ponder at another time.

"I was going to ask you how in the world you became involved in this," the man continued, "but I decided I don't really care."

Bobby knew the man would point the gun at him before he even lifted his hand. He dropped the knife and barreled at him, letting out an animal yell that might alert the authorities to their position.

The gunman lost his grip on the weapon the moment Bobby collided with him. They fell to the ground in a tangle of limbs, and even though the other guy was somewhat meatier than Bobby, he seemed to be sufficiently pinned for the time being.

Bobby kneed him in the crotch just to be on the safe side, but suddenly the gunman wrenched one of his arms out of Bobby's grasp and a fist collided with the side of his head so hard that an entire galaxy of stars danced in his vision.

"Hold it right there!" a stern voice called to them.

Bobby wanted to say that he was doing his best to hold it, he really was, but the stars faded into grayness and the grayness turned to black, and he remembered nothing more.

37

GRAHAM WILLARD was more confused than he'd ever been in his life. First Randy seemed to think that Graham had a demon in him (which was preposterous), and then the boy who rented the bungalow in Autumn Ridge appeared in the barn like a ghost. He didn't understand. Bobby wasn't one of them. Graham would have known if he was.

But no matter. Jack had gone after him like a good boy, Randy was dead, and now he needed to leave and finish off the Sanchez woman so he could kick back and relax for the rest of the day.

It had been his original intention to reunite Randy and Lupe at the very end, but then that coward of a priest had given him a better idea. *Split them up,* Father Laubisch said. *That way you'll torment Mr. Bellison by thinking you're killing his girl in front of his face, and you'll be tormenting Miss Sanchez just as much when she realizes she'll never see him alive again.*

At first Graham hesitated. The joke with Trish Gunson had already played out—what better way to give Randy a complex than to have a girl with a heart disorder willingly allow herself to become

342 | J.S. BAILEY
possessed? A demon invited in like that would be incredibly difficult to drive out, and the strain on the young woman's body would
undoubtedly be too much for her failing heart to handle.

She had agreed to do it, though, and for that Graham harbored no guilt. But when Father Laubisch suggested they could use
Trish's frozen corpse as a stand-in for Lupe Sanchez and explained
the rationale behind it, he decided to agree.

Graham laid his knife down on the table and wiped his hands
on his slacks before coming around to stare at the Servant's face.
Randy's eyes were closed in quiet repose, and the blood on his
chest had begun to scab over.

Graham started crying again, and for a moment he wondered
why he had chosen to do this. Randy had never done him wrong.
He was a friend. *His* friend. And what was it he had told Randy
before killing him? He couldn't remember. Words had just started
pouring from his mouth in a torrent, and he had been unable to
control them.

He glanced at Randy's body again but cast his gaze away, gripping his head suddenly with both hands. Something was wrong
with him. Something horrible. Lord, he needed a cigarette, but
he'd left the pack out in his car and didn't want to walk that far to
get them. He just wanted to curl up and cease to exist, because if he
did he might find peace at last.

When the police barged their way into the barn minutes later,
they found an old man sobbing on the floor. He didn't even put up
a fight when they hauled him away.

<hr/>

BOBBY WAVERED in and out of consciousness, catching
disconnected fragments of images. He seemed to be in a moving
vehicle accompanied by a pair of young men. He started to ask
them what had happened, but then he was out again.

Next he lay in a room with walls that matched the color of the
sky. Someone spoke to him but it seemed to be in a foreign language for all the sense it made.

Ordinarily he would have been scared, but God was there with him, and everything would be fine.

Finally his eyelids fluttered open and stayed that way. He remained in the blue room, only this time he was alone.

He glanced down at himself and felt the heat rise in his face when he saw he wore only a white hospital gown, since that meant somebody had removed his clothing for him. A clear IV line snaked along his arm and ended at the crook of his elbow, where it had been taped into place.

He quickly diverted his gaze to a pair of vacant chairs pushed along one wall so he wouldn't be sick.

What was he doing here, anyway? The last thing he could remember was seeing Randy bleeding like a slaughtered sheep.

A sob rose in his chest. *No.* Not Randy. He couldn't die. He was the Servant.

Bobby felt cold as more memories rushed back to him.

No, Randy wasn't the Servant anymore.

Bobby was.

Or had he imagined it?

No. All that was very real.

Goosebumps spread down his arms and across his neck.

Don't be afraid, Bobby, for I am with you.

"I know," is all he managed to say before emotion constricted his vocal cords.

A fist rapped on the doorframe across from him, and he lifted his head to see a squat, middle-aged doctor standing in the entrance wearing her dark hair back in a ponytail. "Robert!" she said, stepping up to him with a smile. "It's so good to see you're awake."

He didn't bother telling her that nobody had ever called him by the formal name printed on his birth certificate. "What . . ." He licked his lips, which were as dry as his tongue. "Happened?"

She glided over to his bedside. Her warm demeanor made him relax. Her name tag said Dr. Tammy Nguyen. "First off, you can call me Doctor N. Are you feeling okay right now?"

He started to nod but then shook his head instead. "Thirsty."

344 | J.S. BAILEY

"I'll have a nurse bring you some water. But what about your head? Is your vision blurry?"

His head did hurt some, come to think of it, but the pain wasn't anything he couldn't handle. "I've got a headache," he said. "And I can see just fine."

Dr. N. proceeded to shine a light in both of his eyes and listened to his heart through a stethoscope. "All seems to be in order here. Do you hurt anywhere else?"

"Just my hand and elbow. I tried to break a window with them the other day."

The doctor raised her eyebrows. "You're going to have to take it easy for the next few days, okay? No sports, no fights, and definitely no breaking windows."

"I'll do my best. How long have I been here?"

"You were admitted about six hours ago," she said. "You were in shock and have a mild concussion, so we couldn't give you any sedatives. You fell asleep after we ran some tests and have been out ever since."

The news surprised him. "I was in shock? What was I doing?"

Dr. N. took a few moments to respond. "When you were brought here, you wouldn't respond to any questions and kept calling for someone named Charlotte. Is she a friend of yours?"

"My stepmother," he said, marveling at the fact that he had been unaware of all of this. The combined stress of seeing Randy bleeding to death, being possessed by the Holy Spirit or what have you, and getting the daylights punched out of him must have been too much for him to handle all at once, but thankfully it was all coming back to him now.

"Would you like to contact your family to let them know you're okay?"

"I can wait," he said. Ohio was three hours ahead of Oregon, and he didn't want to needlessly disturb anyone's slumber. He could call Charlotte in the morning and give her an abridged version of what had happened then. "How long am I going to be here?"

"You can leave as soon as we're sure you're in the clear," she said. "But first the police would like to ask you a few things."

Great. He'd already had his share of being interrogated by law enforcement this week. "Uh, ma'am? Before you send them in, is there anyone here to see me?"

"As a matter of fact, yes. I'll tell them you're awake." She rose and disappeared through the door.

Bobby closed his eyes. He was so exhausted that he wished he could postpone talking to the police until morning, too.

The sound of approaching footsteps made his eyes flutter open. In walked Phil—still wearing Bobby's Muse shirt, he noted with grim amusement—followed by none other than a red-eyed Carly Jovingo.

"What are *you* doing here?" he blurted.

Carly's cheeks turned pink. "Because I'm a decent human being. You should try it sometime."

Ouch.

Phil sat down in an empty chair and started rubbing his eyes. Carly remained standing, her arms folded tightly across her chest as if in defiance of something Bobby was unaware of.

Neither of them spoke, so Bobby broke the silence by saying, "Lupe?"

Phil gave a thin-lipped smile. "She's going to be okay. Graham locked her in a shed and apparently planned to take care of her after . . ." He shook his head, and tears welled up in his eyes. "Sorry. But you'll find this interesting. Father Laubisch showed up just as I was about to leave with Lupe, and he said he planned on rescuing her himself. I called the cops on him because I didn't trust him any more than I could throw him, and while we were waiting for them to show up, he said he'd convinced Graham to split Lupe and Randy up so he could save her. Father Laubisch, that is. He told me he was the one who took Trish's body as a stand-in for Lupe."

Bobby wrinkled his nose. "Wouldn't she have smelled?"

"She would have if Father Laubisch hadn't put her in a freezer. Somehow Graham was behind Trish's death, too. It's confusing. But it had been Graham's initial plan to—to reunite them and kill them together. If not for Father Laubisch, that very well could have happened."

"That's crazy."

"I know."

Bobby turned to Carly. "Where's Joanna?"

"She's still at the safe house. Roger's wife offered to stay with her so I could come here and be with you guys. But Phil kind of had to give away the safe house location because there wasn't enough time for him to pick her up and drive her there himself."

"Desperate times," Phil said with a sigh.

A young nurse came in with a cup of cold water. Bobby took it gratefully and downed it in a single gulp.

When she left, Phil's face grew longer. "I don't know what we're going to do."

Phil didn't know Bobby had chosen to step up and replace Randy in a last-second effort to be a hero. "I did it," he said.

The pair stared at him, uncomprehending.

It looked like he would have to do some explaining. "I replaced him. Right when he was dying."

He'd thought Phil and Carly would be relieved by the news, but their stares turned into gapes. "I—I didn't know what else to do," he said, his words now coming out in a rush. "I saw him there in the barn, bleeding, and then he looked at me and asked if I'd take his place."

"Are you sure you're the Servant now?" Phil asked in a low voice.

Bobby nodded. "All the sudden it was like something was inside me, looking at everything I'd ever said and done, and I got scared and ran because I didn't really know what was going on." The sensation of being analyzed had not returned upon his awakening here in the hospital bed, but he could still feel that another entity was there with him. Was there *within* him.

The sensation unnerved him, but he no longer felt frightened.

Phil shook his head in disbelief. "Do you even realize what you've done?"

"No, not really." *Don't be afraid.* "But it's what Randy wanted."

"Randy isn't dead," Carly said.

Now it was Bobby's turn to gape. "But I saw him!"

"He just came out of surgery awhile ago," Phil said. "He had to have a blood transfusion and about a million stitches and got a bullet picked out of his leg. He's asleep in his own room right now." He paused. "Lupe is beside herself. She's afraid he isn't going to wake up. The doctors are cautiously optimistic, though."

Bobby sat upright. "I want to see him."

"Now? They probably won't let you in. They almost wouldn't let Lupe in, but she threatened bodily harm to anyone who stood in her way."

"I don't care." Bobby swung his skinny legs over the side of the bed. He was barefoot and felt like he was wearing a handkerchief for all the good the hospital gown covered him, but he didn't care. "Here. Help me drag this thing," he said, indicating the IV stand to which he was still tethered.

"Bobby, he's on a different floor."

He gripped the stand and rolled it toward the door. "Then we'll take the elevator. If anyone asks, I'm looking for the bathroom."

"Uh, Bobby?"

He turned. Carly was blushing. "What?"

"You might want to put something else on first. You know, like clothes."

It was then he realized the hospital gown allowed anyone standing behind him to get a decent view of his back side. He yanked the sides of cloth together and said, "I think maybe you're right."

IN ORDER to spare his dignity, Bobby had Dr. N. called back into the room so he could be discharged. When an officer who had been waiting a short distance down the corridor came in to speak to him, Bobby promised he would answer all questions once he had seen his friend.

Now back in the sweaty, dirty clothing that the hospital staff had thankfully not sliced off of him; he, Phil, and Carly made the journey up to the next floor together in silence.

Lupe Sanchez leapt up from a chair in a small waiting area when they stepped out of the elevator, taking Bobby completely by surprise by giving him a bear hug that nearly crushed his ribs. "Thank you, thank you, thank you," she sobbed into his shoulder. "If it weren't for you, I . . . he . . ." She pulled back from him and wiped her eyes. "Phil told me what you did."

"I don't think he told you *everything* I did," Bobby said quietly, praying his face wasn't as red as it felt.

She gave him a questioning look but didn't press the issue.

Some other men and women he recognized from the beach photos shared the waiting area with Lupe. All stared at him with round eyes.

"Can I go see him?" he asked when nobody made a move to lead him to Randy's side.

Lupe gave a wordless nod. "Just for a minute. He's . . . in bad shape. Come with me."

Bobby was aware of multiple sets of eyes following him as she led him down a hallway and into Randy's room. He was grateful nobody tried to stop them.

Bobby felt all the blood drain from his face when he saw the figure lying in the hospital bed. Randy, too, had an IV. A monitor on a stand beside the bed showed the man's heart rate and a bunch of other statistics Bobby didn't know the meanings of.

Randy's chest rose and fell with silent regularity. It was the only outward sign that he lived.

"I told you it was bad," Lupe whispered, reading Bobby's thoughts.

He took her hand without hesitation and gave it a squeeze. "He's going to be okay," he said. "He'll wake up soon and be his normal self."

"If not for you, it could have been worse. You were the answer to my prayers."

He didn't doubt that, but it still made him feel uncomfortable. All his life he'd dreamed of being lauded a hero, and now that the moment for that had finally come, he wanted to receive no recognition for it whatsoever. God was the real hero. Bobby had just been in a convenient position to do what God had expected of him.

Bobby couldn't look away from the man he had known for just a few short days. "Randy," he said in a low voice, "I don't know if you can hear me or not, but I did it. I said I would replace you, and I did."

Lupe's eyes grew as round as goose eggs. "You did *what*?"

"I did what I had to do." And God knew he had been crazy to do it. But when faced with the alternative, there had been no real choice in the matter, had there?

Lupe's expression broke into the first real smile Bobby had ever seen on it. "He would be proud of you."

They went back out to the waiting area and Phil motioned him aside.

"So what happens to me now?" Bobby asked.

Phil gave a light cough. "In ordinary circumstances, you would be trained by your predecessor until you're ready to perform your duties."

"Trained?"

"You'll see." Phil's expression broadened into what looked to Bobby like a sinister smile. "Don't you worry. All of us are going to be here for you, no matter what might happen. You might say we're in this together."

And Bobby knew he had to believe him.

38

LATE THAT night, after answering the police's questions as best as he could (he'd feigned amnesia whenever they pressed certain points involving premonitions and such), Bobby went home with Phil. He'd considered making a brief stop at the bungalow to pick up some fresh clothes and his toothbrush but couldn't bring himself to set foot in there while the world remained dark.

Phil turned on a light as soon as they came through the door. "If you'd like, sleep here on the couch tonight. I talked to Allison before you woke up. She and Ashley plan on coming home tomorrow morning. Would you like a beer?"

Bobby took his shoes off by the couch and rubbed his eyes. "I'm only twenty."

Phil allowed a tiny smirk. "Since when has that ever stopped anyone? But suit yourself. I just might have some Sprite in the fridge, too."

Bobby couldn't object to that. He followed Phil into the kitchen-slash-dining area and sank into one of the chairs, feeling as though he had aged a decade since he crawled out of bed that morning.

Phil opened the refrigerator and got out a can of Sprite and a bottle of India Pale Ale for himself. "So. What am I going to do with you now?"

Bobby shrugged. "You'll have to start liking me a little more."

To his immense surprise, Phil threw his head back and laughed. "Blindly trusting every hooligan who shows up on your doorstep can get you stabbed in the back when you least expect it."

"I'll do my best not to stab anyone, then."

"After seeing what you did today, I have to believe that."

They fell silent as they nursed their drinks. The digital clock on the microwave read 12:01 am. Even though Bobby's body longed to succumb to exhaustion, his mind remained wide awake. "There's something I've been wondering," he said.

Phil raised his eyebrows.

"When that guy with the gun confronted me in the woods, it seemed like there was a grayish sort of thing inside my head. Did I just imagine that, or was it really there?"

Phil took his time answering. "As the Servant, you'll start noticing many things you never thought you'd see."

"What causes it?"

"I'm getting to that. Now say I'm your average criminal. I like to steal because I don't want to work for what I earn. I'm probably not going to have an aura of any kind." Phil paused to relish another sip of his beer. "Now say I'm a twisted man. I want to have dealings with Satan himself because he seems so much kinder than God. God just has so many *rules*, you know? Any smart person would know that turning away from God would set you free. Maybe I pray to Satan. Maybe I want to do his bidding on Earth."

Bobby knew that Phil only played the devil's advocate for the sake of example, but his words still gave him a chill. "And that's the kind of person who would have that aura."

"Exactly."

"Do you think Graham has that aura?"

Phil shook his head. "He didn't have it when I was the Servant, and Randy never saw it either. Those who are possessed have a darker aura, which you'll see soon enough."

Bobby scratched at his head in the sore place where the gunman had hit it. The police had been unable to catch him since he'd bolted away so fast, and a manhunt was currently underway for him. It was suspected that he had thumbed a ride from a passing motorist.

"You said something earlier about Graham being behind Trish's death," he said.

"Not just behind her death. He was behind her entire involvement with Randy. Father Laubisch has been on the inside, scared out of his wits as you can imagine. He was too afraid to come forward or stand up for himself. He said that Trish was supposedly a 'friend' of Jack Willard, though I'd hardly call what they had 'friendship.' Trish had a heart defect and wasn't expected to live for long, anyway. Graham got it into his head that it would be fun to send her to Randy and have her die under his care. She willingly had herself possessed. I can only pray she'll be forgiven for her ignorance. Graham probably sweet-talked her into it. But what's done is done." Phil dragged a hand across his forehead. "Bobby, I have to thank you for doing what you did, and please forgive me if I've seemed cold. God saw great potential in you, and if I can't trust his judgment, then I can't trust anybody."

As Bobby finished his Sprite, he couldn't help but agree.

RANDY FLOATED in a dream world. Shapes and colors whirled all around him. He saw clouds, he saw trees, he saw a lovely dark-haired lady dressed in violet walking toward him on the sand.

He felt at peace, but something was missing. The tangible presence of God had gone.

At first this realization sent a spike of fear through his heart. What had happened? Had he failed his Maker?

The images in his head shifted, and he saw himself strapped to a piece of wood that reminded him all too much of a cutting board, he being the slab of meat that was to be chopped into pieces.

Graham and that other man were there, and Bobby, too.

That was it. The reason Randy could no longer sense the Spirit was because Randy had passed the mantle on to Bobby so Randy could die in peace.

Only Randy had survived. He didn't know where he was or how long it had been since the altercation in the barn, but the steady thudding of his heart was a strong indication that he had yet to kick the bucket.

He allowed himself a smile. Bobby, the Servant? The kid had so much to learn, but he would learn it all in time.

Randy was flying now, high above the ground. It was winter. It was summer. It was all times rolled into one. He caught sight of Bobby working out in a gym doing push-ups and sit-ups and lifting weights, and then Bobby was with Phil drinking a Sprite, and then . . .

Randy's insides froze with the onslaught of terror.

"Bobby!" he shouted, though Bobby could not hear him. "Something's after you! Get out of there! Now!"

Bobby and Phil remained in Phil's house. The pair kept on talking as if nothing in the world were amiss, and nothing bad happened to them for as long as Randy watched.

Where was the danger? Was it here and now, or there and someday?

Randy knew one thing only.

It was coming.

Bobby's story continues in
SACRIFICE

ACKNOWLEDGMENTS

No author writes a novel alone, and the one you hold in your hands is no different.

For providing the main inspiration for this novel, I thank my husband Nathan Bailey. This story would not exist if not for you.

For helping me spot errors I was too blind to see, I thank Nathan Bailey, editor Robin Harnist, Katie Cross, and Gregg Hart.

For answering some of my medical-related questions, I thank Katie Cross and Todd Rosenhoffer. If the hospital procedures that appear in this story are incorrect, blame me, not them.

For being my friends for all these years and (sort of?) understanding my borderline-insane author brain, I thank Laura Custodio and Jennifer Habetz. I still remember the days of passing stories around in a notebook with great fondness!

For having my back and being my unofficial support group, I thank the wonderful writers at Read Write Muse, especially LaDonna Cole, Donna Kilgore, Laura Custodio, and Katie Cross, who have each slogged through my work at various points in time to help make it beautiful. (Seriously, I think at this point I owe Katie my life.)

I thank my parents, whose encouragement and support brought me to where I am today.

And I thank the Most High God, who designed me to write.

ABOUT THE AUTHOR

As a child, J.S. Bailey escaped to fantastic worlds through the magic of books and began to write as soon as she could pick up a pen. She dabbled in writing science fiction until she discovered supernatural suspense novels and decided to write her own. Today, her stories focus on unassuming characters who are thrown into terrifying situations, which may or may not involve ghosts, demons, and evil old men. She believes that good should always triumph in the end. She lives with her husband in Cincinnati, Ohio.

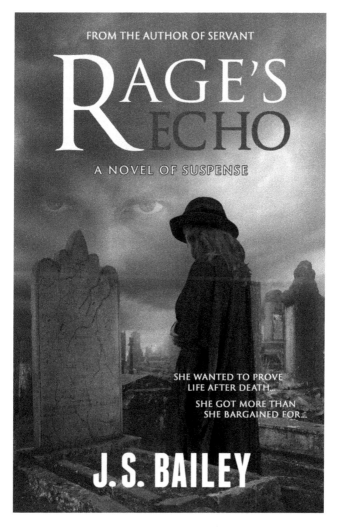

CPSIA information can be obtained
at www.ICGtesting.com
Printed in the USA
FFHW022225220419
51928537-57347FF